PRAISE FOR THE PREVIOUS BOOKS

"Arthur Conan Doyle would never have thought his iconic character may battle the undead. *Gaslight Grotesque: Nightmare Tales of Sherlock Holmes* blends horror and mystery as the legendary sleuth finds himself faced off against the supernatural through the pens of countless established and budding authors. The rational Holmes against an irrational world makes *Gaslight Grotesque* a very riveting collection." —Midwest Book Review

"...these are dashing tales worthy of the new vision of Holmes and fans will adore them even though this select anthology is by some deans of horror and science fiction." —Margaret Cannon, Globe and Mail

"*Gaslight Grimoire* is a welcome addition to the Holmes "fanon," joining the relatively recent collections of supernatural Holmes stories by other publishers..." —Dru Pagliassotti, The Harrow

"I would recommend this book to any fan of the men found most often at 221B Baker St., as well as fans of the horror genre." — Bitten By Books

"These ten stories plus three others, ably demonstrate that Doyle's legacy is in safe hands, with writers who, while they may revere and stay true to the source material, are capable of taking the legend of Sherlock Holmes into new and uncharted territory." —Peter Tennant, Black Static Magazine

---

ABOUT THE ILLUSTRATORS

Dave Elsey has demonstrated an extraordinary ability to create memorable characters using make up: from the fantastical creatures in the television series *Farscape* to his planet-wrangling skills in *The Little Shop of Horrors*. Dave is the cover artist for the Australian comic book *The Dark Detective: Sherlock Holmes*, and he recently won an Oscar for his special FX work for the movie *The Wolfman*.
You can learn more about him and his work at: **http://igorstudios.com**

Mike Mignola is an American comic book artist and writer, famous for creating the comic book series *Hellboy* for Dark Horse Comics. He has also worked for animation projects such as *Atlantis: The Lost Empire* and the adaptation of his one shot comic book, *The Amazing Screw-On Head*.
You can learn more about him and his work at: **www.artofmikemignola.com**

Luke Eidenschink is a 2009 winner of the International Illustrators of the Future Award. His work includes book and magazine illustration, custom design, fine art, and most recently graphic novel illustration.
You can learn more about him and his work at: **www.legendsedgeart.com**

Illustration by Mike Mignola

GASLIGHT

ARCANUM

Uncanny Tales of Sherlock Holmes

Edited by J. R. Campbell
and Charles Prepolec

EDGE SCIENCE FICTION AND FANTASY PUBLISHING
AN IMPRINT OF HADES PUBLICATIONS, INC.

CALGARY

EDGE

Edge Science Fiction and Fantasy Publishing
An Imprint of Hades Publications Inc.
P.O. Box 1714, Calgary, Alberta, T2P 2L7, Canada

Edited by J.R. Campbell and Charles Prepolec
Interior design by Janice Blaine
Cover Illustration by Dave Elsey
Front Interior Illustration by Mike Mignola
Interior Illustrations by Luke Eidenschink
ISBN: 978-1-894063-60-9

EDGE Science Fiction and Fantasy Publishing and Hades Publications, Inc. ac-
knowledges the ongoing support of the Alberta Foundation for the Arts and the
Canada Council for the Arts for our publishing programme.

Library and Archives Canada Cataloguing in Publication

CIP Data on file with the National Library of Canada

ISBN 978-1-894063-60-9
(e-Book ISBN: 978-1-894817-95-0)

FIRST EDITION
(J-20110710)
Printed in Canada
www.edgewebsite.com

TABLE OF CONTENTS

I HEAR OF SHERLOCK EVERYWHERE...

by Charles Prepolec

Welcome to *Gaslight Arcanum: Uncanny Tales of Sherlock Holmes*, the third in our series of anthologies to pitch Sherlock Holmes into weird and supernatural stories. Yes, that's right; third. The book you now hold in your hands follows *Gaslight Grimoire: Fantastic Tales of Sherlock Holmes* (2008 EDGE Science Fiction and Fantasy Publishing) and *Gaslight Grotesque: Nightmare Tales of Sherlock Holmes* (2009 EDGE Science Fiction and Fantasy Publishing). Let me tell you a little story about how we got to this point....

It was twenty years ago today, Sgt. Pepper taught the band to play... okay, maybe not, but time flies when you're having fun, and I've definitely been having fun with Sherlock Holmes over the last few years. It was 2006 when my co-editor Jeff Campbell and I first set out to plunge that most rational of detectives, Sherlock Holmes, into the murky realms of supernatural, or weird fiction. At that point it had been three years since we had edited our small press anthologies of traditional Sherlock Holmes pastiche — *Curious Incidents: Volumes 1 & 2* — and we were looking to do something else, something new, something different, maybe something a bit 'out there' with the character. Most of all we wanted to do something that would be fun — fun for us to put together, but more importantly, fun for our readers. It set me to thinking about exactly which Sherlock Holmes stories, by authors other than Arthur Conan Doyle, had given me the most pleasure over the years. Which were the most memorable or had left some strong impression on me? Which ones made me smile when I first read them? Given my lifelong enthusiasm for horror fiction, comic books and pulp tales, it should come as no surprise that my list was populated with books and stories that referenced these interests.

Fred Saberhagen's *The Holmes-Dracula File* and *Séance For A Vampire*, Loren D. Estleman's *Dr. Jekyll and Mr. Holmes*, Manly Wade Wellman and Wade Wellman's *Sherlock Holmes's War of the Worlds*, Martin Powell's *Scarlet in Gaslight*, Phil Farmer's *The Adventure of the Peerless Peer*, Cay Van Ash's *Ten Years Beyond Baker Street*, Michael Dibdin's *The Last Sherlock Holmes Story*, P. H. Cannon's *Pulptime*, Mark Frost's *The List of Seven* and *The Six Messiahs*, Ralph Vaughan's *Sherlock Holmes in the Adventure of the Ancient Gods*, Sam Siciliano's *The Angel of the Opera*, Kim Newman's *Anno Dracula* and *Diogenes Club* stories, Reaves and Pelan's *Shadows Over Baker Street*, etc. ... are the books, comics and journals that have left a lasting impression on me and colored my view of what I enjoy the most in Sherlock Holmes stories. Some are mash-ups with other characters, some are pulpy adventure, some are science fictional, and some are just outright horror stories, but all of them take Holmes beyond the confines of straight mystery stories, or slavish pastiche, and have some fun with the character.

Of course there were also various other factors that influenced our decision to take Holmes down the supernatural road. There seemed to be something in the air at the time, maybe a premonition, maybe an educated guess that the time for Holmes and horror was at hand. Magic and the supernatural seemed to be on the upswing in popular culture with the likes of J. K. Rowling's Harry Potter and Mike Mignola's Hellboy making it to the silver screen. Speaking of Mike Mignola, I'd be remiss if I didn't mention that a Batman story written by Mike, for DC's Elseworlds line in 2000 — *Batman: The Hell That Came to Gotham* — was a direct influence, to say nothing of the *Hellboy: Odd Jobs* prose anthologies edited by Christopher Golden. The former showed me that you could pitch an established detective character into a supernatural world without missing a beat and the latter practically served as a template for the sort of book we set out to produce in terms of both style and approach. We wanted to bring in writers who could work effectively with Conan Doyle's creation in much the same way Christopher Golden had successfully brought in writers to work with Mike Mignola's Hellboy. In short, we wanted folks who were fans of Sherlock Holmes who would take the character beyond the realm of simple pastiche. After a bit of thought Jeff and I put together a list of writers we thought would fit and deliver the sort of stories we were after. Some we'd worked with on *Curious Incidents*, others we'd admired for some time, and others still were friends and acquaintances within either the Sherlockian or fantastic fiction communities. In any event we were thrilled with the response and were delighted to have stories from Barbara Hambly, Kim Newman, Martin Powell, Barbara Roden, Chris Roberson and all the other talented writers we pulled together for our first Holmes/horror anthology. Rounding out the text was a fine foreword from noted Sherlockian, writer and my former editor at *Sherlock* magazine, David Stuart Davies. For the icing on the cake we commissioned an atmospheric cover by artist Timothy Lantz and interior illustrations from the amazing Australian Sherlockian Phil Cornell. We had our first book!

The question then became who would publish it? Happily, by the time we pitched the concept to Calgary-based publisher Brian Hades, of EDGE Science Fiction and Fantasy Publishing in 2007, a few other factors had come into play that would add to our project's appeal. First off, a Sherlock Holmes film was announced as being in-development by Warner Bros, which would bring Sherlock Holmes back into the pop culture limelight, a place from which he'd largely been absent since the Sherlock Holmes boom of the late 1980s. Secondly, Calgary had won the bid to host the 2008 World Fantasy Convention. The theme for the convention was "Mystery in Fantasy and Horror" with one of our writers, Barbara Hambly, as guest of honour. The logo for the convention featured a dragon wearing a deerstalker hat. If you want to talk about a perfect fit, it doesn't get much better than that! Serendipity is a wonderful thing. So we had a concept, writers, a publisher, a target date for publication and a great venue for a release. Finally, in October of 2008, *Gaslight Grimoire: Fantastic Tales of Sherlock Holmes* hit bookstores around the globe ... selling out its initial printing in under seven weeks. The book went on to garner some fine reviews, was short-listed for an Aurora Award and released in an Italian translation (*Il Grimorio di Baker Street*) by Gargoyle Books in 2010. Two of the stories — Barbara Roden's *The Things That Shall Come Upon Them* and Chris Roberson's *Merridew of Abominable Memory* — were picked up for John Joseph Adams' reprint anthology *The Improbable Adventures of Sherlock Holmes* alongside stories by Stephen King and Neil Gaiman. Not too bad for our first effort!

Needless to say we immediately began work on a follow-up, practically commissioning stories on the spot, over pints of Guinness, from writers Stephen Volk, Mark Morris, Lawrence C. Connolly, Barbara Roden and Simon K. Unsworth, at the launch during WFC 2008. Within a few months we also added stories from William Meikle, Neil Jackson, Leigh Blackmore, James A. Moore, Hayden Trenholm, William Patrick Maynard and of course my co-editor Jeff Campbell. Add in another cover from Timothy Lantz, a beautiful Hammer Horror-inspired frontispiece by comic book artist Neil Vokes, a foreword from Leslie Klinger and at WFC San Diego in October 2009 we unleashed *Gaslight Grotesque: Nightmare Tales of Sherlock Holmes* into the world.

All of which brings us more or less up to date and leads directly to the genesis of *Gaslight Arcanum: Uncanny Tales of Sherlock Holmes*.

If you've ever wondered what might have set Sherlock Holmes on the path to becoming a detective, then you're going to love our opening story from BAFTA winning screenwriter Stephen Volk. *The Comfort of the Seine* is a haunting tale of sorrow, wherein a young Sherlock Holmes takes a trip to Paris and finds an all too brief and unexpected romance that leads not only to poetic heartbreak, but also places him in the path of a mysterious and career-defining mentor.

In *The Adventure of Lucifer's Footprints* Bryant and May author Christopher Fowler weaves a tight tale of military betrayal where the galloping ghosts of the wrongful dead come thundering out of a storm to seek their vengeance.

A ghastly grimoire, written in the blood of a madman, is stolen from the monks who have guarded its secrets for centuries. To stop a string of terrible and inexplicable murders they turn to Sherlock Holmes, but can even the Great Detective withstand the pull of these cursed pages? Find out in *The Deadly Sin of Sherlock Holmes* by Tom English.

The influence of H. P. Lovecraft rears its head and the odd tentacle in William Meikle's *The Color That Came to Chiswick* — a pulpy tale of cosmic angst, alien invasion and beer. I can assure you that you'll never look at a St. Paddy's day pint in quite the same way after reading this one.

World Fantasy Award nominated writer Simon K. Unsworth returns to our pages with a classic country house mystery that is anything but cosy and traditional. There is terror afoot when we learn the secrets of the aged beekeeper in *A Country Death*.

The late Fred Saberhagen was, as mentioned earlier, one of the writers whose work influenced the direction of our Gaslight series, but due to his illness we never had the opportunity to commission a story from him for *Gaslight Grimoire*. He passed away in 2007. While we make a point of only publishing original pieces, as a tribute to Fred Saberhagen we're very pleased to be able to reprint a short story of his, *From the Tree of Time*, wherein a certain Transylvanian Count comes to the aide of Sherlock Holmes.

One of the great perks of editing this series is that I get to work with authors whose books and short stories I've read and admired for many years. Yes, no question, I'm an overgrown fanboy and I'm not above abusing my position to squeeze more stories from some of my favorite writers. *Gaslight Grimoire* allowed me to work with Kim Newman, Barbara Hambly and Martin Powell. In *Gaslight Grotesque* I was able to work on stories by Stephen Volk, Mark Morris and James A. Moore. For this present volume I had the great pleasure of working with another of my heroes, Simon Clark. A ghostly voice, from a man long dead, rises along a telephone wire from the ocean floor in *Sherlock Holmes and the Diving Bell*.

I'm pleased to bring back the multi-talented (you should hear him play guitar and sing) Lawrence C. Connolly for another go-round with Sherlock Holmes. In *The Executioner* we finally learn the truth of how Sherlock Holmes managed to rise from his apparent death at the Reichenbach Falls.

Calgary writer Kevin Cockle's *Sherlock Holmes and the Great Game* gives us a Sherlock Holmes who is not at all what one might expect from Watson's reports. At times reminiscent of Hammer Films' *The Lost Continent* the story is a rollicking and mystical adventure of Aztecs in the Arctic.

Paul Kane pits Sherlock Holmes against the most implacable foe ever faced by man and forces him to unravel *The Greatest Mystery*. Eliminating the impossible is definitely not an option in this story.

Vegas, baby, yeah! Tony Richards takes us to that Mecca of lost souls in this 21st century tale of the immortal Sherlock Holmes. Bodies drained of blood turn up in the desert and Holmes must venture into *The House of Blood* to find out why.

Our final entry has Kim Newman returning to the Gaslight series with another fine and fun novella in his ongoing series of Moriarty and Moran stories. The rascally Moran learns firsthand the price of obsession in *The Adventure of the Six Maledictions* when the Professor assembles a collection of not-so-desirable trinkets ... and their owners come calling.

There you go, dear reader, twelve uncanny tales drawn around Sherlock Holmes and his weird world. I had a hell of a lot of fun bringing together these stories and hope you have as much enjoyment in reading them.

While the notion of combining Holmes and the supernatural seemed a might bit odd back in 2006, it appears to have caught on, as I write this in 2010. The big-screen film *Sherlock Holmes* (2009) had Holmes investigating an occult conspiracy, a cash-in film from The Asylum had him facing robotic dinosaurs and a villainous steampunk Iron Man, Wildstorm comics had Holmes saving London from a zombie apocalypse, and the follow-up series pits him against Dracula. A television series placing Holmes in modern-day London has been released, to great acclaim, by the BBC, and various other 'fantastic' projects keep coming. The wheel turns and Sherlock Holmes is once more enjoying a boom. Enjoy it folks, but remember who sent you!

Cheers,
Charles Prepolec

THE COMFORT OF THE SEINE

by Stephen Volk

My Dear Lestrade,

It is not a huge deductive leap to know you are at this moment wondering why, upon my recent death, this document is presented into your hands, and not those of my friend and chronicler Dr. Watson. The truth is, I cannot bear the thought that he might construe my privacy on these matters for so many years as something of a betrayal.

After you have read it, please place the enclosed securely in the files of the Black Museum at Scotland Yard. The reason for my not wanting this "adventure" to come to public attention in my lifetime will become clear in the reading of it.

But now, as the evening light is fading, I feel a heavy debt not to depart carrying an unwritten chapter of history to my grave, and if my arthritic hand will hold this pen long enough, I shall put the record to right.

Read on, detective. For what could be of more peculiar interest than the solution to a mystery where it seemed no mystery existed?

—Holmes

Youth is a country visited fleetingly, at the time with the only intention of reaching another destination, but in which we later wish we had lingered longer, whilst our energy was boundless and our eyesight good, and the colors of the world less grey and circumscribed. One ventures near cliff edges. One climbs branches, unable to conceive that they can snap. And one leaves one's home country on a whim, feeling no more than a sleeve tugged urgently by an eager and fresh-faced friend. Thus, at the age of twenty, I found myself abandoning my studies in chemistry, zoology and botany at Sydney Sussex, Cambridge, to accompany the Scales brothers to Paris.

A fellow science student with whom I shared digs, Peter Scales, had coerced me to tag along with him and his sibling, Olaf, a young painter. They were twins, but beyond the superficial similarities — *identicalities* — the lads could not have been more *dissimilar* in terms of personality. Olaf wore an overcoat like a Prussian cavalry officer, tartan waistcoats and extravagant facial hair. Peter on the other hand was quite happy to be the wallpaper in a room. But it was fun to see the pranks they played, teasing the passengers on the cross-channel steamer, being seemingly in two places at once, doffing their hats first inside the cabin, then on deck, as if a single person had been transported by magic from the first location to the second. We laughed. Yes, I laughed not infrequently in those days.

Our journey had been prompted when Olaf heard that Renoir, Monet and Degas were exhibiting in the studio of the photographer Nadar. This was the very birth of the era of "Impressionism", you understand — when the word was first used by the critic Louis Leroy to ridicule Monet's *Impression, Sunrise*, thereby accidentally naming a movement. "Come on Yorkie!" cried Olaf (I still had quite a pronounced accent from the land of my forebears in those days). "It'll be tremendous! The colors. You have no idea. These painters will be world-famous one day, mark my word. They'll be hanging in museums!" I was by no means certain of that, and had little or no interest in art, but his enthusiasm was infectious. How could I refuse? England had become a bore. Disraeli was Prime Minister at the age of seventy. And we were young.

The other ulterior motive was, frankly: I spoke French. Not well, but enough. I'd learned it at my great-uncle's knee, and though I had hardly any memory of him, the old *je suis* ran in my blood. Peter even quipped I had a nose like a Frenchman.

So, whilst the brothers sought out paintings that captured the fall of light, I was content to observe the fall of light itself on the architecture of the great city around me, and the atmosphere of *boulevards* once trodden by revolutionary feet, walls that still echoed with the Communards' bullets and the cries of shop-keepers taken to arms, shockingly, within all-too recent memory. It was hard to believe: the streets I saw before me were regimented, grand, beautiful, populated by civilised and polite citizens of the modern day, yet behind that beauty lurked a spirit quick to anger and pitiless in its violence.

Having explored the Conciergerie, the grisly staging-post before the guillotine, I found myself walking along the Quai de la Corse with the intention of crossing the Pont Notre Dame to delve into Les Halles, the so-called "belly of Paris", when I heard a female voice behind me:

"Monsieur!"

Instinctively I turned, and to my surprise the unmistakable scent of lilies hit my nostrils. Indeed, a lily itself was being thrust towards me. Equally instinctively, I pushed it aside, glimpsing the vagabond creature in rags and bonnet trying to force it upon me.

"Non! Monsieur. Monsieur..." she insisted, following me, in fact blocking my path as I turned away.

"Elle mourra," she said.

I was taken aback. A strange phrase which I instantly translated:

It will die.

For some reason this gave me pause. *She* gave me pause. What would die? What was she telling me — or warning me of — and why? I felt a prickling sensation of unease across my shoulders, a vestigial memory awakened of the supernatural talents of gypsies....

The beggar girl thrust the flower at me again, her arm outstretched. *"Elle mourra,"* she repeated.

It will die.

What a fool! She meant that if she did not sell the flowers in her basket by the end of the day they would have to be thrown away and wasted. Laughing at my own stupidity, I took the lily and urgently dug into my pocket for change, but by the time I looked up from my palm she was disappearing into the Place Louis-Lépine. She glanced back from under the trees, the sunlight catching the corners of her eyes like the dabs of a paint brush. Then she was gone. Her act — the simple gift of a flower to a complete stranger — done.

That night the boys and I went to the Café Dauphine, not far from our lodgings in the Rue Quincampoix, and sank several "nightcaps". They lost themselves happily in their cups, but, intoxicated in quite another way, I could not concentrate on a word they said.

The next morning, after dressing, I suggested we walk through the Marché aux Fleurs, the flower market on the Place Louis-Lépine. The twins humoured me, with no idea my stomach was churning at the prospect that I might not see the girl again. But there she was, standing at her stall, in sturdy workman's boots, cardigan tied sloppily round her waist, woollen balaclava under her second-hand bonnet, ruddy cheeks and pink knuckles, full lips spare of the gaud of make-up, nattering in a Parisian dialect incomprehensible even to my ear, giving the uncouth males around her a run for their money.

"All right," said Olaf. "Hi-ho. Go and speak to her, then."

"I have no idea what the deuce you mean."

"Do you not?" He laughed, sticking his hand in his waistcoat and making a mime of a beating heart. "I thought he was interested in the botany here," he said, nudging his brother. "But obviously it's the biology he's got his eyes on."

"Rot."

"Own up, Yorkie, old boy. It's not a crime, for Heaven's sake…"

I turned on my heel, not wanting to show them my cheeks were flushed.

We spent the rest of the day touring the Louvre, but I was beginning to grow sick of their company. Nothing to account for this, other than the fact that their jocular presence prevented me openly seeking the flower seller for fear of incurring their puerile taunts. Yet it was a preoccupation that refused to leave my mind. I was simply unable to banish it.

"My gosh. He really is sickening for something, this lad," said Olaf later, sipping strong black coffee of the kind only palatable in France. "I think Cupid's arrow has really struck its target this time…"

I was tempted to punch him on the chin. As it was, I grabbed my coat and returned to the Marché aux Fleurs, buying her a silly gift along the way in reciprocation for the flower she had given me.

It was late afternoon by now and the working day almost at an end. She did not see me at first. I loitered like a felon, content to observe the way she folded the brown paper to make bouquets and made gay little ribbons of rope or twine. Her grace was an attribute that captivated me. *She* captivated me. The hand upon her hip, the sway of her shoulders, the toss of her head. The ragged edges of her skirts skimming the cobbles. The wisps of reddish hair curling from the soft cleft at the back of her neck.

In the end I could not disguise that I was staring at her — and finally our eyes met. I thought suddenly she might find me foolish, but as soon as she laughed and made a little curtsey I felt at ease. I handed her my gift. She looked at it with astonishment bordering on awe, the expression on her face utterly delightful.

"*Je m'appelle Sherlock,*" I stammered, like a schoolboy.

"*Sheeur-loque,*" she attempted, waiting for me to continue the conversation, but I could not. My courage punctured by the stray guffaws of some hefty-looking laborers, I lowered my head with embarrassment. In defiance of their ridicule she kissed my cheek. I can remember the warmth of her lips even now, as if a Lucifer had been struck inside me. I felt all at once weak at the knees and as powerful as a steam train. And, even as I fled stupidly, thought: if my next breath were to be my last, I shouldn't care.

Over breakfast Olaf said there was nothing like someone else's tragedy to raise his spirits. Peter asked if love was a tragedy, then? His brother told him in a pitying tone that he'd led a sheltered life. Refusing to enter into their *badinage*, I combed my hair fastidiously in the mirror and sped to the flower market without a word, determined that this time my shyness would not get the better of me.

Now, those who have followed my exploits later in life will know I have been confronted on occasion by scenes of unutterable horror — at the risk of disappointing you, this was not one of them. In fact the sight of her stall bolted up when all the others were open gave me at first only a mild sense of disappointment. She was not there — today — perhaps for good reason. I had no cause, *at first*, to believe anything untoward had happened. No reason at all. And yet … my heart told me otherwise.

The longer I conversed with the stall-holders, showering them with inquiries, the more the grip of foreboding took hold. My only response was a series of immensely irritating Gallic shrugs. Nobody knew where she was. Nobody even knew her name. How on earth could that be?

The questions multiplied. By the time I returned to the apartment I was beside myself, fretting visibly, but received no real sympathy from the twins. Yes, Peter could see I was upset, but in his naivety wondered why. Olaf on the other hand could only belittle my concerns.

"Isn't it obvious? She shut up shop to go off with a man. Brazen hussy."

"She wouldn't do that."

"Why not? How do you know? How could you possibly know? You've only just met her."

"She's not a hussy, I know that much."

"Rich men. Tourists. Poverty-stricken women on their own have to make a living in all sorts of ways." He saw me glaring at him, and held up his hands. "I'm just telling you the possibilities."

"I'd really appreciate it if you didn't," I said through tight lips.

The following day I returned to the market, hoping against hope that a different scene would greet me. It did not. The padlock on the sorry-looking flower-stall was firm. A fat knife-sharpener scraped at his stone. The laborers unloading carts joked and whispered, rolling up their sleeves to show off their biceps to giggling waifs. What were they concealing? What did they know? I was determined to return, and return until I saw her — or know the answer why.

Two more days passed before I sat the brothers down and told them my absolute fear that some terrible calamity had befallen her. And that, in order to prove or disprove my conviction, I had resolved to visit the Paris morgue.

Now it comes.... Dear Lord, how I have postponed many times describing this, the most painful part of my narrative. Not that the details are vague — far from it. The images in my mind are pin-sharp and all too hideously indelible. I venture, should all my memories slip away tumbling like rubble down a slope as my life grows interminably longer and more brittle, this scene alone will remain. I even pull my dressing gown around my shoulders now, as I feel the icy chill of those walls upon my body...

Imagine a gentleman's convenience with the dimensions of a palace. The same white tiles on every surface. The same overwhelming sibilance. The same residual smell of toxic substances masked by acrid disinfectant. We passed under pebbled-glass gratings through which could be seen the feet of Parisians going about their daily work, oblivious to the macabre and poignant scenes below.

Mentally, I urged the line to move faster. A woman up ahead was dabbing her eyes with a handkerchief, her backdrop a haze created by several hoses dousing the bodies. The cadaver of a large, hairy man with half his head missing silenced some dandies come for whatever perverse thrill they sought from the experience. If I was not sickened by that, I was sickened by what I saw next. For, amongst the dead, arranged with uniform indignity upon marble slabs, lay the flower girl's corpse.

It knocked the air out of me and Peter caught my elbow. What was most shocking was the exhibition of every inch of her pale, untarnished skin. Skin I had never touched, yet presented here for the entire public to see. Had she been touched? Had they touched her? Rage clouded my vision. But when the callous spout passed over her, spraying water and giving the illusion of movement across her flesh, I could bear it no longer. I dashed forward, plucking the strand of hair thrown into disarray over her face by the hose.

"For pity's sake, Sherlock..."

I shook my head vigorously. Lifted her ice-cold hand to my lips.

A moronic attendant shoved me back towards the line, barking that it was forbidden to touch the corpse. *"Ne touchez pas le cadavre! Écartez-vous du cadavre!"*

I felt another harsh prod against my chest and launched at him and would have killed him, had not Olaf's tall frame stood separating us. The man backed away from my fiercely blazing eyes and spat in a drain.

"It's time to go," said Peter softly. "You need to sleep and you need to get out of this damned awful place."

My eyes were red raw and I had no idea how much time — minutes or hours — had passed and what had occupied them but my devastation. I was sitting on the floor near the foot of the slab with the rain from the hoses dripping down the walls.

"My dear fellow," I heard his brother's voice. "Peter's right. There's nothing you can do."

"Go. Go, if you want. Both of you. I'm going to stay."

The next full hour I spent alone with my — how can I use the word? But I shall — *beloved*.

Presently the gas dipped lower and I heard footsteps and the rattle of keys. It became apparent I was the last visitor in the place, and was compelled to tear myself in agony from her side. I walked, leaden, to the stairs, but once there the terrible urge for one final glance overcame me.

There was no doubt — but at first there had been *only* doubt, so unerringly, absolutely *strange* was the picture before me. A man — *was* it a man? —stood over the bier: an elderly man with snow-white hair covering his ears, a pair of tinted *pince-nez* perched on the bridge of his nose, a black cape covering his entire frame, bent over the corpse, owlish head hovering but inches above her, as if smelling the bouquet of a fine wine. Toad-like, barrel-chested and with spindly legs, he made no sound — there *was* no sound but from the water of the hoses. His hands moved in alacritous gestures, almost those of a mesmerist. As I watched, dumbstruck, he went about his odious theatrics as if I were invisible. Was I invisible, and this a vile construction of my harried mind? If so — what did it *mean*? Why had I not seen him before, or heard his footfall?

Immediately I hurried to the nearest morgue attendant — the one who had manhandled me. But no sooner had I caught his arm and turned to look back than I saw, open-mouthed, that the apparition was gone.

"*Excusez-moi. L'homme aux cheveux blonds,*" I gabbled. "*L'homme qui etait là-bas, habillé en noir. Cest qui?*"

The morgue attendant looked entirely baffled. "*L'homme, monsieur?*"

"*Oui. L'homme. Le vieux avec les lunettes.*"

The attendant looked over a second time then shook his head, opening the iron gate for us both to exit. "*Je n'ai vu personne,*" he said.

I have seen nobody.

The twins tried to placate my anxiety with stiff alcohol and poor explanations, suggesting it was a visiting doctor or anato-mist, but nothing they came up with accounted for the *manner* of the figure's intense interest, or the *diligence* being applied to the macabre task. I could see now from their faces their answer was that I had seen something whilst the balance of my mind was unhinged. I laughed bitterly. Olaf said that I must know as a biologist that, when a person suffers a shock, their powers of observation become temporarily unreliable.

"Not mine," I said. "I assure you. Not mine."

Come the morning, Peter reminded me our tickets on the ferry were for noon. He said he and his brother fully intended to return to England at the prescribed time. I said very well, but I was afraid I could not join them. My studies were of scant impor-tance to me now, and my trickle of inheritance would be enough to sustain me. In any case, I wasn't worried if it didn't. The point was, I could not live with the mystery. The mystery of the girl about whom no-one cared or grieved but me. The mystery of the girl over whose corpse a vile old man bent in sensual enquiry. The mystery of the girl who, out of nowhere, said to me:

Elle mourra.

It will die. The flower will die.... But also — my God, why had I not thought it before? My stomach knotted as I watched the ferry depart—

She will die.

I returned to the morgue, where the flower girl's corpse still lay naked, nameless and unclaimed, convinced more than ever that this flesh-and-blood ghoul was somehow implicated in her death.

The same odious morgue attendant recognized me from the night before, and seemed keen to avoid me. Minutes later I saw a few coins placed into his hand by one of the bereaved and he tugged his cap, which told me this rogue's silence could be bought cheaply — and had. I gravitated to the other, slightly more savory employee at the wooden booth next to the stairs and described the man in *pince-nez*, whilst pointedly pressing coins into his palm. After which he whispered, yes, he *had* seen him, too. Several times.

"Comment s'appelle-t-il?" I asked.

The man's eyes darted shiftily right and left. He coughed into his hand, turned the register towards me and ran a grime-encrusted finger down the line of signatures forming a column on the left.

"Dupin," I read aloud.

It meant nothing to me. The only "Dupin" I knew was a mere fictional character, the brilliant detective in Edgar Allan Poe's story *The Murders in the Rue Morgue,* a supremely far-fetched fantasy in which a devotee of the so-called science of "ratiocination" works out that the culprit in the gruesome murder of a mother and her daughter (whose throats were cut and bodies mutilated) is in fact, amazingly, the pet Orangutan of a sailor, trained to shave its owner with a straight-razor. I recalled the tale only vaguely and dismissed the connection as quickly as it occurred to me.

"Do you know anything about him?" I asked in French. "His profession?"

"Détective," came the terse reply.

I smiled and gave him a few more centimes for his trouble. The old man of the morgue was disguising himself, clearly. Or he *was* a detective named Dupin, the factual basis of Poe's story;

or, again, a detective who *took* the name from Poe. All were possibilities, and all unedifying. The words came back to me:

Elle mourra.

In what dreadful capacity could the girl have known that she would die? And if it was her expectation, how could it feasibly be any kind of accident? Did the white-haired man know? Indeed, did he execute the deed? Was this man the murderer? What was his connection to her if not? And why did he visit this place of the dead with such incessant regularity ... for now I saw *Dupin* in the ledger on page after page, back, long before she met her death, long before I even met her...

I was only aware of the footsteps on the stairs when they abruptly stopped. I spun round and saw a shadow cast by gaslight upon the stone wall, hesitating, frozen before descending. I recognized the fall of the cape, the cut of its upturned collar, the spill of the cravat. The very frame was unmistakable, albeit faceless. It ran.

I was up, after it in an instant, but the bats'-wings of the cape flew upwards to the light with supernatural speed for a man of his advanced years. By the time I emerged into the street, breathless and blinking into the sun, I saw only the door of a carriage slamming after him. I hailed another, almost getting myself trampled by hooves as the reins were pulled taut. We gave pursuit, my head in a whirl, my heart pounding as I urged my driver at all costs not to lose our quarry.

After ten or fifteen minutes, to my relief I pinpointed the distinctive St-Médard church on my right and that gave me my bearings. Leaving behind the medieval-looking streets of Mouffetard, we eventually turned from the rue Geoffroy Saint-Hilaire into the rue Cuvier, which I knew to border the famous Jardin des Plantes. My transportation pulled to a halt and I climbed out, paying swiftly in order not to lose sight of the man I pursued.

To my astonishment, at a leisurely pace he entered the Ménagerie, France's largest and oldest public zoo, created during the Revolution for the unhappy survivors of the one at Versailles — those not devoured by the hungry mob — and a new population of animals rounded up by the armies of the Republic from far-flung lands abroad. He walked on an unerring path, seemingly impervious to the hooting calls of jungle birds and the pacing of lions. I followed until he came to a halt, his back to me, looking through the bars of a cage.

I approached him from behind, careful not to surprise him unduly until I was directly upon him, then yanked him round to face me.

The countenance of a negro grinned at me, his smile radiant in a sea of ebony. His curly hair had been covered by the hat and scarf, his age — which explained his athleticism — not much more than my own.

"My name is Adolphe Le Bon," he said in immaculate English, with a pitch as *basso profundo* as I have heard in my life. "At your service, *monsieur*." He touched the brim of his top hat. "A gentleman said to give you this." He handed me an envelope from his inside pocket. *"Bonjour.* Or should I say; *Au 'voir?"*

Whereupon he strolled away, in no particular hurry, and I found myself considering the contents of the letter unwrapped in my fingers — a jumble of proof-readers' symbols and numbers amounting to nonsense — whilst gazing through the bars at the rubbery, wizened visage of an aged and enfeebled Orangutan.

What game was this? A game I was compelled to play, obviously. Downing coffee at a street café, I stared at the hieroglyphs on the sheet of paper, cursing that if only I had Dupin's deductive power to decipher them — or those of his creator. Then I remembered — of course! —in another of Poe's tales, *The Gold Bug*, a code showing the whereabouts of buried treasure is broken by elucidating which character predominates, and relating it to the order of frequency of letters generally in the English language. Even so, how did I know this was in English? I was in Paris. What was the order of frequency of letters of the alphabet in *French?* Then the notion came to me that this was not a code *similar* to that in *The Gold Bug*: it was the *exact same* code as in *The Gold Bug.*

I sped to an English book shop I knew in Saint-Germain, purchased their only copy of *Tales of Mystery and Imagination* and secluded myself in a corner. *"As our predominant character is 8, we will commence by assuming it as the e of the natural alphabet..."* Within minutes I had translated the cryptograph. What I held now in my hands was an address. But that was not all I had discovered.

In thumbing through the pages, I had naturally alighted upon *The Murders in the Rue Morgue.* And by chance my eyes had fallen upon a certain name: that of "Alphonse Le Bon", who was arrested for the extraordinary crime— *"a ferocity brutal, a butchery without motive, a grotesquerie in horror absolutely alien from humanity"* —before the real culprit was incarcerated: a large, tawny Orangutan of the Burmese species.

By fading light I walked to the Pont Neuf, crossing the river to the Île de la Cité, where I sensed the man in the rue de la Femme-sans-Tête confidently awaited me.

I struck a flint to read the name-plates of the apartments. All were blank. I saw a handle which I pulled, presuming that it sounded a bell somewhere within the belly of the old building, though I heard nothing. Laughter came from a lighted window opposite and I wondered if this was a district of ill-repute. It was the kind of shriek which could be interpreted either as extreme pain or extreme pleasure and I preferred to think the latter.

"He expected you an hour ago." The door had been opened by Alphonse Le Bon, now wearing a tail coat and bow tie.

I stepped inside. A matronly woman in a cloth cap stood half-way up the stairs.

"Madame L'Espanaye will show you up."

Madame L'Espanaye? Then I remembered…

"EXTRAORDINARY MURDERS. —This morning, about three o'clock, the inhabitants of the Quartier Saint-Roch were aroused from sleep by a succession of terrific shrieks issuing, apparently, from the fourth storey of a house in the rue Morgue, known to be in the sole occupancy of one Madame L'Espanaye…"

Another character stepped from the pages of fiction… Or fact?

I followed her, trailing my hand through the thick dust on the banister rail, dreading with every step that I was entering some kind of house of insanity, a realm where the imagined and the real were interchangeable. Where the fabrications of *grotesquerie* took the place of the norm. Where actors — if they were actors — took the place of the killers and the killed. I looked over the parapet of the mezzanine to see Le Bon far below, staring up at me.

Madame L'Espanaye curtseyed and drifted backwards into ash-colored shadows. I was left alone in front of a door.

I pushed it open to find myself in a Louis XIV room so packed with all manner of artefacts (once my eyes had accustomed themselves to the gloom) it had all the semblance of a fusty and abandoned museum. A museum of clocks was my first impression: pendulums from the Black Forest; cuckoo clocks from Switzerland; automated clocks from America, all blending into a whispering, clacking, clicking chorus of ticks and tocks. But there were other denizens in the shadows. Vast collections of pinned butterflies hung like oils. Not one human skeleton, but several. Stuffed birds of extravagant plumage. I reached out to touch a macaw — quickly to realize as its beak nipped my finger it was not stuffed at all. To my greater astonishment, it spoke.

Who is it?

"Mr. Holmes," I replied, announcing myself to my unseen host.

Who is it?

"Sherlock."

Who is it?

I hesitated, fumbling for words. "An Englishman. A student..."

A laugh came from the darkness as a man poked a fire in the small grate. "There lies the way to madness, *monsieur*. Or enlightenment." In spite of the glow of revivified coals, I could not yet discern his features.

"I disturbed it," I said. "I didn't know it was real."

"Quite possibly the feeling was mutual."

As he held a candle to the flames and set it in a brass holder beside his high-backed leather chair, I saw illuminated the old man who had been arched over the flower girl's corpse. Now, by contrast, settling back, crossing his thin legs, he looked professorial, almost statesmanlike, and I found it hard to envisage him as the insane criminal I had imagined, with his high forehead and weak mouth. But common sense also told me the most devious and successful criminals were those who passed for ordinary men and women. And intellect did not preclude a person from committing abominable acts; merely added strength to the possibility of them evading capture.

"You laid a trail for me to follow. Why?"

Dupin shrugged. "I do so admire — detection."

"You may not like what I have detected."

He took his time to light a cigar, puffed on it and used it to indicate an empty armchair facing him. I sat down and found his open case of Hoyo de Monterreys offered to me, then shortly afterwards a tray of various cut-glass decanters. I abstained. There were secrets to unveil and I would unveil them.

"I know who you are," I said. "But not why you are here."

"If you applied the science of ratiocination, Mr. Holmes, you would."

"The brain is a curious organ and often it needs relaxation but sometimes it needs to be spurred by fear or anxiety for the pieces of the puzzle to fall into place."

Dupin hazarded a thin smile. "Illuminate me."

"Pieces, shall we say, such as the bust of Pallas semi-hidden in the darkness over in that corner. Such as the talking bird I encountered upon entering. Such as the cipher I was given. Such as the appropriation of certain names from certain tales. The ape..."

"Circumstantial."

"Perhaps. As is no doubt the way you wrote the date in the register at the morgue, which I thought barely notable at the time. The French, like we English write it for brevity, day, month, year. Alongside the name *Dupin* however, the date reads month, day, year, in that order — much in the manner of an American."

Dupin sat in silence and allowed me to continue.

"You see, *monsieur*, it was not until I left the bookshop with this volume under my arm that the very obvious conclusion occurred to me." I produced *Tales of Mystery and Imagination.* "For, as in *The Purloined Letter,* it had been in plain sight all along. Yet it was not until I thought of my good friends — the two brothers who so uncannily resemble each other that, to a stranger, they cannot be told apart — that the picture was complete."

"Indeed?"

"Indeed, *monsieur.*"

"And will you share with me that — conclusion?"

I took another, smaller volume from my pocket.

"The prefatory items in the *Tales* were instructive but inadequate. I returned to the bookshop and luckily found upon the shelves a copy of Thomas Holley Chivers' *Life of Poe*, published by Dutton in 1852." I looked into Dupin's eyes but they held no expression — not even, particularly, of interest. "Edgar Poe died on the 7th October 1849, the theory being that he had been the victim of a so-called cooping gang. The congressional elections were in full swing in Baltimore and, because there was no register of voters, bully boys were being employed by candidates to round up derelicts and get them drunk enough to register false votes a number of times in succession." I referred to my notes and underlinings in the Chivers.

"He was found by Joseph Walker, a compositor at the Baltimore Sun, lying in the street outside Cooth and Sergeant's Tavern on East Lombard Street, which served as a polling station.

"Dr. Snodgrass received a letter from Walker about a gentleman rather the worse for wear at Ryan's 4th ward polls, and found the writer without his customary moustache; haggard, bloated and unkempt. His clothing, I quote: 'a sack-coat of thin and sleazy black alpaca, ripped at intervals, faded and soiled, pants of steel-mixed pattern of cassinett, badly-fitting, *if they could be said to fit at all...*"

I put particular emphasis on this last phrase, but it had no effect on the listener.

"Poe was taken to Washington hospital," I continued, "where he experienced exceeding tremors of the limbs, and active delirium. When questioned in reference to his family, his answers were incoherent. When asked where he lived, he could not say. Towards the end, in his stupor and torment, he called out for 'Reynolds! Reynolds!' — which onlookers took to refer to the navigator of the South Seas, an inspiration for *The Narrative for Gordon Pym* — until his poor soul was finally at rest." I looked up. "But he is not at rest, *monsieur* — is he?"

Dupin had sunk back in his seat, the wings of which served to conceal his face in shadow. He placed his fingertips together in a steeple.

"Yes, a man was found drunk in a gutter," I said. "But he called out 'Reynolds' in his delirium because that was his own name. And nobody would listen. He was identified by the Malacca cane borrowed by Poe from Dr. John Carter simply because the object had been placed in his hands by another. On the evidence of witnesses themselves this substitute was more 'haggard' yet more 'bloated' than Poe (perhaps the word 'fatter' would be more accurate) except Dr. Snodgrass recognized his friend's clothes, albeit that they *hardly fitted* the occupant. Of course they didn't. Because the man was not Poe. Poe was alive. *Is* alive."

Who is it? squawked the parrot.

"And the mystery of the missing moustache is self-evident," I said. "For one can dress a double to look like one's self, but one cannot force him to grow facial hair he does not have. And so you shaved off your own."

"Bravo!" Dupin laughed and clapped his hands. We had been conversing in French but he spoke English now for the first time, with the musical lilt of a Southern gentleman. "Many have tried but none has got so far! Le Bon, the cognac! This is a cause for celebration! Chevalier Auguste Dupin has met his match!" The dapper negro emerged from the gloom and poured me an ample glassful. "I do not partake myself."

"The stuff can be the death of you."

"I fear water will be the death of me now." Poe grinned, holding up a glass into which he had poured clear liquid from a jug.

"A 'way to watery death' is not quite the poetic thing, is it? I quite resist banality, in death as in life."

"And the death of the flower girl?" I made it quite clear in my tone that I had not forgotten the purpose of my visit. "What is the poetry in that, sir?"

He avoided my question.

"Let me first tell you of the last weeks on this earth of Edgar Allan Poe." Whilst he spoke the manservant Le Bon circled the room lighting candles. "It had been a year of wild dullness.... I was drumming up support for a five-dollar magazine and trying to convert my Philistine countrymen to literature — an impossible task. I came to the conclusion I could only raise money by lecturing again: with tickets at 50¢ I could clear $100 — if sober. So, with the ferocious spirit of the true dipsomaniac I took the oath of abstinence, prostrated myself at the Sons of Temperance: a solid challenge to my cravings — but, alas, unattainable.... The word 'teetotal' had hardly wettened my tongue before — I fell, spectacularly.... My lecture was stolen. I descended further into debt: but these are excuses. The true drinker repels the very idea of his own happiness. We deem the prospect of solace intolerable.

"I had to leave Richmond on business, but the real reason was a desperation to escape. Escape my own shabby dreams, and, ringing like a foul tintinnabulation, the doctor's warning after Philadelphia that one more drop of the hard stuff would see me to the bone yard. Truth was, my life had become all pose and no prose. Fancy-mongering was wearisome now. I was a performing dog wandering the miasmic stars of Eureka. So I propped up the steamer's bar, wishing most the while a maelstrom would suck it down, and me with it.

"As you said, the streets of Baltimore were *en fête* with election fever. I went unnoticed in streets teeming with drunks filthier drunk than me. I was on a spree. Maybe my last. I was determined to put and end to this life, little knowing I would start a new one.

"Outside a tavern a man pestered me for a game of cards. He wanted to win back money he had lost, because he was sailing for Europe the next day and didn't want to arrive penniless. The man was drunk, drunker than me — so drunk he was not even aware that, a little thinner in the girth and thicker in the cheeks, he was my double. I did not even remark upon it and I drank with him until he passed out in an alley. I thought he was dead. I felt his pulse.

"Then, with a thundering heart, I saw an extraordinary opportunity to reinvent my life, if I had the audacity to carry it through. He, being dead, had nothing to lose, and I everything — *everything* to gain. I took a ticket from his inside pocket, made out in the name of 'Reynolds': his passage across the Atlantic. I changed clothes, taking all his identifying belongings and giving him mine, finally leaning the Malacca cane I had borrowed from Dr. Carter against his knee: the final piece of evidence that this dishevelled inebriate was Poe.

"I took the ocean crossing, shaving off my moustache and cutting my hair lest someone identify me. No-one did. On arrival I read of my own demise, of poor Reynolds calling out his name again and again: my *doppelganger*, my *William Wilson* calling for his own identity to be restored, in life, in death — but, alas, it never was.

"He was interred at the Presbyterian cemetery on Lafayette and Green Street. My premature burial. I read the despicable death notices penned by Griswold, twisting the facts, emphasizing my bad points and down-playing my good, but I could hardly react to any attack on my former identity without exposing my new one. As it was, I feared someone might uncover my ploy, the police or the Reynolds family, and come looking for me, so I changed my name again on arrival."

"To *Dupin?*" I said. "Your most famous character?"

Poe shook his head. "Not at first. To begin with I stayed with my friend Charles Baudelaire, the poet. He had read many of my works before I died. For that reason, and my innate Francophilia, I gravitated to Paris. He'd translated my piece on Mesmeric Revelation in *La Liberté de Penser*. He saw me as a mystic and visionary and the inventor of skillfully engineered tales, and had written to tell me as much, so it was fitting I turned to him in my hour of need. He kept me under lock and key in rooms at the Hôtel Pimodon, always in penury over the years, partly because he kept me afloat too.

"We had certain similarities. His stepfather General Aupick he despised, as I despised mine. He endured a life of money troubles, as had I. He was afflicted by bouts of pessimism, as was I. Arrogant, as was I…. But his *vie libre* was also a *vie libertine*, centred on the taverns of the Latin Quarter. He hated solitude. I welcomed it. To begin with I ventured outside rarely, if at all. I helped him with his satirical contributions to the *Corsaire-Satan*, and later with *Les Fleurs du Mal*. He in turn brought me the world, by way of the Café Tabourey or the *Théâtre de l'Odéon*.

"After a while he introduced me to his Bohemian cronies as 'Dupin' — his little joke. The name wasn't known in France because in the first translation of *Rue Morgue* the detective was re-named 'Bernier' for some reason unknown to either of us. And 'duping', you see — the pun was deliciously appealing.

"Baudelaire's French versions of my tales appeared in *Le Pays*, and *Adventures d'Arthur Gordon Pym* in *Moniteur universel*. I helped him out with some details about compass bearings and such, and acted as his lexicon of the Southern states. But his abominable life style took its toll. As a former imbiber of substances — I had not touched a drop since my resurrection — I saw all the signs of a hopeless addict. He collapsed with a cerebral disorder on the flagstones of l'Église Saint-Loup in Namur, upset by a poem he'd read about happiness." Poe attempted to smile. "They sent a confessor in his last hours, but by then all he was saying was *Bonjour*, like a child."

"I'm sorry."

He waved the sentiment away.

"No more... Nevermore...." He gazed into his glass of water. "Every day is an act of will. Which is something. To have a toe at the very edge of doom and resist the urge to plummet."

I found myself saying out loud: "I too have dark valleys."

He sipped and placed the glass on the table beside his chair.

"Then you and I have similarities too."

"But why use the name 'Dupin' if you didn't want to be found?"

"Who said I didn't want to be found?" He rose, wrapping a woollen shawl round his shoulders. "Perhaps I was waiting for the right person to find me." He walked to the macaw and stroked the back of its neck with a curled forefinger.

"Whilst he was alive Baudelaire kept me reasonably secluded, but to keep me from going mad with inactivity of the mind he would bring me puzzles in the form of stories in the newspapers. Robberies. Murders. Abnormal events. Inexplicable mysteries. I would study them and, if I could, write to the newspapers with solutions. As I had done with *Marie Rogêt*. Always under the inevitable *nom-de-plume* — 'Dupin'. From the moment I set foot on French soil, with that poor sot in my coffin, I found I had no more stomach for writing fiction. Death, madness, my trademark — I'd had enough of that. The raven had croaked itself hoarse. It is one thing to write a detective story. You know the solution and simply confound the reader. But to deduce by the powers of logic in *real life*...? That is *true* art. And I felt it stimulating to accumulate skills to that end. Pretty soon the police got to know the name and would come to me for help. It was no more than a game at first. But a game that kept me alive."

"As the re-naming of your servants is also a game," I interjected. "Le Bon, Madame L'Espanaye ... in the manner of a charade. Surrounding yourself with characters of your own creation to keep the real world at bay. To feel safe."

"But I am safe. Immensely safe, *now*." As he walked to the mantel shelf his eyes gleamed in the sallow light of the candles. "For I am no longer, you see, under the glamour of my pernicious gift: my imagination. Anyone who has ever studied my stories properly knows they are all about one thing: the awful toll of madness, the horror of lost reason.... *Rue Morgue* says it all, for anyone with eyes to see. That even the absurdest, most abominable crime can be solved by rationalism. Well, rationalism was my driftwood in the storm. It was my salvation, Mr. Holmes — as it can be yours."

I was startled. "Mine?"

He stared at me, dark eyes unblinking with intensity. "We human beings can be the ape — the basest instinct, dumb force of nature — or we can excel, we can elevate ourselves." He tapped his expanse of forehead. "By civilization. By enlightenment. By perception. By the tireless efforts of eye and brain...."

He spoke with the utter conviction of a zealot, or lunatic. A chill prickled the hairs on the back of my neck. I asked myself if the "awful toll of madness" had indeed been left behind him, or was I in the presence of a maniac who had committed one crime by his own admission and could easily commit another to cover his tracks?

I rose to my feet, frightened now.

"Why am I here? Why did you bring me?"

By way of reply there resounded four brisk knocks at the double-doors to an adjoining chamber — so sudden that it made my heart gallop. Poe had turned away and was adjusting his string tie in the mirror, as if he hadn't even heard my voice, or simply chose to ignore it.

"*Entrez*." He moved only to deposit the stub of his cigar into the flames.

The double doors yawned open and in silence four men emerged from the dark as if from another realm. They marched in slow formation with their backs erect, the reason for which became hideously clear — they carried a coffin on their shoulders. My chest tightened. I found I could not move, powerless but to watch as they laid it down in the firelight in the centre of the room, resting on two straight-backed chairs arranged by Madame L'Espanaye.

The pallbearers straightened. One I recognized as the morgue attendant who had lied to me, now shuffling back into the shadows whence he came. Another, the elegant Le Bon in his spotless shirt, had procured a screwdriver from somewhere and was proceeding to unscrew the lid of the casket as a continuation of the same odd, balletic ritual.

I looked at Poe. He was idly, at arm's-length, leafing through the pages of the *Life of Poe* I had placed on the side-table, then shut it disinterestedly and tugged at his cuffs. It made my blood run cold to realize that, far from being alarmed by this extraordinary intrusion, he had *designed* it.

Each screw emerged, conveyed by Le Bon, like a bullet in the palm of his kid-gloved hand to a kidney-shaped dish. As he circled the coffin to the next, and then extracted it with the lazy precision of a priest performing Eucharist, I was filled with a growing presentiment of what I was about to behold: what I *had* *to* behold, to make sense of this, if it made any sense at all. After the lid was prised off the loyal negro blended into the darkness of the adjacent chamber, closing the doors as he did so.

I stifled a sob at the inevitable sight of the flower girl's body inside, the bluish-purple shades of *livor mortis* bringing a cruel blush to her ears and nose.

"Dear God. This is obscene..."

"No," said Poe. "*Death* is obscene. But death, when all else is removed, is no more than a mystery to be solved."

"Sir—" I could hardly spit out the words, so full was I of repulsion. "You have — abandoned all that is human, and decent and... and *good* with your *delusion...*"

He remained unutterably calm as he gazed into the casket. "If you truly believed that — sir — you would have walked away long ago."

"What makes you think I cannot walk away this second?"

"Because, sir, you cannot walk away from the mystery. That is your curse."

"You are mad."

Poe smiled and quoted from a familiar source: "True, nervous — very, very dreadfully nervous I have been and am; but why will you say that I am mad?" Then his eyes hardened. "You know I am not."

He fetched a candlestick and set it down closer to the corpse, the better to illuminate the indecent marbling of her once flawless skin.

"Though your powers of deduction are elementary, by now you will have realized the purpose of my clandestine visits to the morgue. The meticulous observation. I was of course undertaking exercises in ratiocination. The building offers me subjects in the purest possible sense. On every slab, every day, a code, a cipher to be unlocked. The application of logic telling the very tale the dead themselves cannot. What better place to perfect my craft?" He chuckled softly.

"This hobby amuses you?"

"Of course. What is there in life, my dear Holmes, if not to be amused?"

"Damn you!" I pushed him away from the coffin.

"You see? Emotion rules you completely. It surges when you should keep it at bay. To what end? If you wish to discover why she died ... If you want to know the truth of what happened to her, there is only one course open to you: the cold and relentless application of rationality."

"I loved her!" I roared, turning away.

After a few seconds he whispered behind me: "*I also loved one who died.*" His voice was disembodied, sepulchral and totally, alarmingly devoid of self-pity. I felt guilty at my outburst and listened in earnest to the terrible words he uttered: "Her gradual decline ... From imp to skeletal invalid. Not the loss of love over days, over a glimpse, an idea, but over years. From childhood to womanhood, in a laugh. Over the lengthening of her bones and the plumping of her hips, then to watch it snuffed out by the red death running in her blood. Listening to time, whose hands creep towards midnight. Thinking, what right did I have to sob, to weep, to wish for it to happen, *yes* — to will the chimes and choking to come, when all suffering will cease for all but the living?"

I turned back to him, wiping away tears with the heel of my hand.

He had none.

He said: "I can think of no higher endeavour than to banish hurt and pain from people's lives by the application of logic. I understand your grief, sir. God knows, no man stands my equal in that subject. But one must look upon death and see only that — *Death*. One must stop being victim to the petty frailties of our own conjecture. Instinct. Guessing. Terror. Love. Such fripperies are the sludge which gums up our nerves and dampens our intellect. And self-perpetuates, like a virulent disease. The very king of pests. Like alcohol, emotional supposition is toxic to our system, but our system rebels against being deprived of it. It must be abandoned, and dependence on it shed, lest it rule our lives completely."

Seeing the torture of unanswered questions in my eyes, Poe picked up the candelabrum and circled the coffin, looking down at what lay inside, the tiny, jewel-image of her face glimmering on his black irises.

"I shall proceed as I always do, with general observations, moving on to the nature of the crime. Your friend was raised by devout Catholics, in the city of Nîmes, from which she absconded and became a scullery maid…"

I was choked with disbelief. "You can't possibly…"

"I assure you, everything I say is arrived at by the painstaking application of my methods. At the morgue I procured her clothing, which had not yet been incinerated, and her petticoats were imprinted with a faded workhouse stamp of Ste-Ursule of Nîmes. The flesh on her back, sad to say, betrayed healed scars which indicated the application of a scourge used specifically by Catholic nuns. And the condition of her hands, ingrained with blacking invisible to the naked eye, presented ample proof of her time in service. But what concerns us here primarily is the manner of her death…"

He bent over the corpse, finger tips on the rim of the coffin, exactly as he had done in the morgue, and sniffed, taking the air into his dilating nostrils in short gasps, eyes closed as if savoring its bouquet like a connoisseur of fine wine.

"The scent of putrefaction is repulsive to most individuals, quite naturally: as human beings we have bred ourselves over millennia to abhor decay. Which is a great shame, because its study I've found to be invaluable. Just as a tea-taster can discern subtleties in a blend that the uneducated could not possibly discern, I have trained myself over the years to be able to assess the olfactory distinctions between stages of decay. This, when combined with other observations — visual, tactile — enables me, most often, I would say *invariably*, to be able to pinpoint to the day, sometimes to the *hour*, the time of death. These are not extraordinary talents, my dear Holmes, but ones that most people could apply, given the inclination and training. Foremost, I noticed immediately the corpse had not decomposed as swiftly as it might — always a good indication of immersion in the intense cold of water. This was confirmed by finding none of the customary bruising caused by the effect of gravity on an inert mass on land — *ergo,* she either drowned or was committed to the Seine very soon after dying. Since there were no *pre-mortem* signs of violence on the epidermis, my conclusion was therefore the former.

"The wind that night was unseasonably harsh," he continued. "Coming as it did from a south by southwest direction. The covers of the stalls were flapping and she was the last of the stall holders to leave. She was in high spirits. Perhaps she even contemplated that she might have been in love."

"Do not tease me," I snapped.

"On the contrary. I am delivering the facts, however shocking or unpalatable they may be. Now, do you wish me to carry on?"

I had no alternative but to nod.

"Alone now, she feels a few dots of rain in the air and opens her parasol. A new parasol from her young admirer. In a flash it is caught by a sudden gust of wind, plucked from her hands. She grasps after it, but in vain." This he acted out in spasmodic motions. "She chases it, but it bounces away across the Quai de la Corse, taking flight, this way, that, cart-wheeling down the boatman's steps and landing in the mud ten, fifteen yards beyond.

"And so she ventures out — but the mud is not as firm as it looks. It acts like glue. It is up to her ankles before she knows it. Frightened, she tries to extract herself, but only sinks deeper. Almost certainly she cries out for help, but nobody hears. The river level rises. Water fills her mouth, her lungs. Soon she is submerged completely."

"This is outrageous…" I breathed.

He ignored me. "In time, buoyancy lifts her and carries her away in the predetermined arc of the current to the jetty near the Pont Ste-Beuve. The activity of the morning boats dislodges the submerged corpse once again and it travels, aided by the wash of tourist vessels and commercial traffic, lodging temporarily against the supports of the Pont Cavaignac on her way to her final port of call, the Pont Olivier Knost, where the body is spotted by passers-by and conveyed by the authorities — *requiescat in pace* — to its resting place, the City Morgue."

I shook my head, struggling hard to assimilate all he had told me. Struggling to believe that such deductions were possible. Wanting to reject them as fabulous, as fictional — as another of his fanciful *tales…*

My doubt all too visible in my features, he explained: "Upon minute examination, I found slivers of timber in the knots in her hair. Under the microscope these fragments showed algae matching those upon the vertical struts of the jetty near Pont Ste-Beuve. I also found fragments of paint and rusted metal in a *post-mortem* gash on her skull, the shade of blue matching that of the Pont Cavaignac.

"After my first examination of the body in the morgue, I sent Le Bon out on a mission with three questions. One, what was the prevailing wind that night? Two, what was the color of the paint used on the Pont Cavaignac? And three: is there a factory near the Pont Notre Dame, working through the night, producing sufficient noise to cover a drowning girl's cries for help? There was. A printer's shop, hard at work producing the next day's news. Upon whose pages, alas, come the morrow, the mystery of a missing flower girl did not merit so much as a single line."

A bitter sadness rose in my throat. I was numb with astonishment, dazzled, uncomprehending, light-headed, on the brink of alarm. The feeling was not unlike love: I wanted to be seduced, I wanted to believe, to succumb — yet everything told me to protect myself from harm, to dismiss that which drew me so compulsively to it.

Poe placed a hand on my shoulder.

"There was no murder, no murderer, no rhyme nor reason, no conspiracy, no plan, no suicide..." he said. "Just the wind, the water, the mud, the current.... Sometimes Nature itself is the most devious criminal of all."

I turned away from him and looked into the crumbling coals of the fire. The heat from it dried and prickled my eyes but I continued to stare without blinking. A coke had fallen out below me and he lifted it back into place with long-handled tongs. He was silent for a while and I was grateful for that. I heard him refill my glass of cognac and place it on the table beside my chair. The other chair opposite creaked as Poe once again occupied it and crossed his spidery legs. I had a sense of a snowy halo in my peripheral vision. The black loops of a string tie. A weak mouth. A massive brow shadowing the eyes of a nocturnal Caesar.

"Your logic is faultless except for one thing," I said, controlling the quaver in my voice. "The parasol. It strikes me as something of a conjecture."

"Not at all. I might *conjecture* that what took her out onto the mud must have been something of meaning to her, something of sentimental value, which is why she felt compelled to retrieve it. I might *conjecture* that, given there has been a parasol seller on the corner of the rue de Lutece for twenty years, that is what I would have given her as a gift, had I been in love. But my business is not conjecture." He picked a small red parrot feather from his sleeve and examined it between his fingers. "I know she was the last to leave the market simply because, upon enquiry, nobody remembered seeing her leave. I spoke to the knife sharpener and he told me the only unusual thing that day was she had a parasol — one he had never seen before — and an object altogether too *bourgeois* for someone of her status in society. It stuck in his mind, he said, because she walked up and down like a queen, her smile radiant. He said, in fact, he'd never seen her so happy."

Happy. The last word had a devastating effect on me. It immediately drained me of everything but remorse. The feelings I had patently kept submerged for days welled up and overwhelmed me. I could do nothing to stop them. They broke the banks and I wept like a child.

"Now. Look at her."

Poe took my hand and wrapped my fingers round a candlestick. It lit my way to the coffin, where the prone, lifeless husk that had once been so vibrant shimmered in its amber glow.

"Géricault, when he was painting his *Raft of the Medusa*, locked himself away with no company but dead bodies and even shaved his hair off to eliminate completely his need for contact with the outside world. All so that he could concentrate completely on the work at hand."

I wondered why he was unrolling a cloth bag of surgical equipment — scalpel, forceps, scissors — but my query was soon answered.

"We are going to stay here, like Géricault, for however many hours it takes until your tears run dry. Then we will be done." He lifted the cloth cover from a microscope on a desk. "You shall grow to know her as only God knows her. And then your wisdom will have outgrown your pain, and you will be free." He walked over to me and placed an object in my hand.

It was a magnifying glass.

Dawn light began to outline the shutters as the screws were secured once more round the rim of the coffin lid. Poe rolled down his sleeves, buttoned his cuffs, and sent Le Bon with a message for the unscrupulous attendants from the morgue to come and remove the body.

"We shall say no prayers for her," he said. "She goes to the ground and becomes dirt, as we all shall."

He opened the windows.

The air became fresh and clean. Slowly the noises of ordinary life and work permeated from the cobbled bustle of the street. A gentle bathing of the everyday was welcome after a long and suffocating night of cigar fog and candle wax. By sunlight, the apartment in the rue de la Femme-sans-Tete was no longer a prison, no more a threat, a labyrinth with some Minotaur, part god, part monster, at its centre.

"I am not, nor have I ever been, *healthy*." He pinched my nostrils and drew the razor carefully down the cleft between my nose and mouth. A gobbet of soap hit the water in the bowl. "For my sins, a sedentary existence and the habitual use of alcohol and opiates is now written upon every organ in my body. At sixty-five I am heavy and weary, rheumatic and vulnerable to colds. My stomach is a harsh critic. I take quinine, digitalis and belladonna: one loses track of what produces the symptoms and what treats them. Truth is, I cannot know how many summers I shall endure..." He did not look into my eyes, focusing only on brushing more soap into my bristles. "Having no biological offspring, I have long harboured the desire to pass on what I have learnt of the science of ratiocination to someone else in this world before I take to dust. I have sought a pupil. A young adept of sorts. Foolish perhaps. Vanity, certainly..."

"That was the purpose of your test."

"You found me, Holmes, and in so doing, I found you. Even though the clues were abundant, you were the first to show the propensity to solve such puzzles. Perhaps it is arrogance — that has always been my fatal flaw — but I do believe there may be some merit in my methods. I know the young despise the old, quite rightly and *vive la revolution!* —but..."

I was stricken with incredulity as I gathered the nature of his proposition.

"*You* would teach *me*?"

"There is a price, of course." He wiped the straight razor in a cloth, both sides. "The price is your heart. Your *tell tale* heart.... The tale it tells is always a lie, and always leads to pain." His sad eyes turned to mine. "Is it a cost you are prepared to pay, Sherlock?"

I took the cloth from his hands and wiped the residue of soap off my face as he waited for my answer.

We played four hundred games of chess, and a thousand games of cards. He taught me every intricacy of luck and chance, and every statistic that disproves every superstition. He dissected every belief like a pinned-out frog, occasionally making it kick for demonstration purposes, then revealing how the effect was achieved. He knew the machineries of life and mind and held them in his head like railway timetables. He revealed to me the foolishness of crowds and the absurdities of love, the fallacies of poor thinking, and the whirring cogs of the criminal mind. My old education was over and my real education begun: my training to be the outsider, observing life but not being in its thrall.

We argued over Hegel's *Logik*, observed by the beady eye of a parrot named Griswold. We pored over Giovanni Battista Morgagni, and Taylor's seminal work on pathology and toxicology, the first in the English language.

We read by lamp light. We slept on the floor or in our chairs but more often talked through the night.

When we were busy, and the doors bolted so we would not be disturbed, food and drink was lowered on a rope through a trap door from upstairs by the loyal servant Le Bon.

I was made to memorize a hundred imprints of soles of shoes. And a hundred types of house brick. Coins. Coral. Types of dentition. Birds' eggs. Navigational equipment. Moths.

Blindfolded, I learned how to identify cigarette brands by smell alone.

The nature of breeds of dog — not to mention their owners.

He would show me a hundred Daguerrotypes and direct me to deduce the maladies from the patients' photographs alone. And more. *More, more,* he taunted me. *What more do you see?*

Hour after hour, day after day, the room became clearer, as if a veil were lifted. As if my eyes had been put through a pencil sharpener. As if the world, muddy and intangible, were slowly being made clean and whole.

Habitually we would visit the aforementioned Ménagerie, and always pay a special pilgrimage to the old Orangutan named — I remember it clearly — Bobo.

Sometimes, after supper, as we walked beside the Seine, Poe took my arm. He liked a stroll, but sometimes his vanity meant he left his walking cane at home. He would tell me not to nag him when I reminded him of the fact. Often we sat on a certain bench and gazed at the Moon reflected on the water.

Watson spoke in derogatory fashion of my lack of knowledge in the field of astronomy. The truth is, I know not too little, but too much.

Poe taught me to listen to the music of the spheres.

Giordano Bruno said there is no absolute up or down, as Aristotle taught; no absolute position in space; but the position of a body is relative to that of other bodies. Everywhere there is incessant relative change in position throughout the universe, and the observer is always at the centre of things.

The observer. The detective.

I spent three years with Poe before he died and he taught me — not "all I know" (such a claim would be absurd) — but *how* to know. He was no less than a father to me, and the only thing he ever asked in return is that I keep his secret from the world.

We were sometimes seen around Paris: C. Auguste Dupin, with his white hair, black cape and yellow sunglasses, and his young English assistant.

Some mysteries were solved.

The affair of the so-called "phantom" of the Paris Opera. The case of the *horla* and its tragically afflicted seer. The "crying spider" of Odilon Redon.

We applied arithmetic to decadence and catacombs.

I never resumed my studies at Cambridge. My university was that of Poe: of detection, and of life.

As he became frail I cared for him in that and another apartment, smaller, but with a view of the Bois du Boulogne.

He observed life from the window. We tested each other in deducing the characteristics of walkers on a Sunday afternoon. He'd bemoan my pipe tobacco. I'd in return call him a pious ex-drunk.

When his eyesight went, I read to him aloud. I remember all too well his reaction to *Notre Dame de Paris* by Victor Hugo. The tragic fate of Quasimodo made him grimace with emotion. I thought he had been moved by the fates of the hunchback and Esmeralda, but he quickly retorted it would have been better in verse … and *shorter*. Though he muttered that it was obviously influenced by his own *Hop Frog* — and most inferior to it.

He was cantankerous and conceited, vain as a poodle and unmelodious to the ear. But I have never known a more intelligent or *electric* individual, which almost always excused his inveterate rudeness and dire fluctuations of mood.

Most of all, I owe him my vocation. Sherlock Holmes — *detective*. What would I have become, else?

It will be a surprise to no one that my friend had a fear of being buried alive, and therefore stipulated in his will that the examining doctor open a vein in his neck to ensure no such ghastly mistake could be made. In the event the medic was all thumbs I had to perform his final wish myself.

Thinking of the grave in far-off Baltimore and its false incumbent, I watched the smoke rise from the Paris crematorium in a black plume.

The bird of death was silent at last, the black fading to white, the book of grotesquerie and wonder closed, the coffin breath exhaled, the great, unfathomable mind becalmed and untormented at last. He exists now only on every bookshelf in England, and in my final thoughts.

As I now lie close to death myself, I know more clearly than ever what my master — *the* master — knew: that Nature is chaos. Chaos is truth. Death is the final mystery. And our only defence is knowledge.

Infinite knowledge. Infinite, and futile, knowledge.

STEPHEN VOLK was recently nominated for both the Shirley Jackson and British Fantasy Award for his novella *Vardoger*. His writing has appeared in *Year's Best Fantasy and Horror, Best British Mysteries, Best New Horror* and *Gaslight Grotesque*. Stephen is the creator/writer of the series *Afterlife* and *Ghostwatch* as well as many other film and television projects. The Society of Fantastic Films awarded him their International Award for contributions to the genre.

THE ADVENTURE OF LUCIFER'S FOOTPRINTS

by Christopher Fowler

I must say from the outset that the shocking business of Lucifer's footprints is something I cannot fully explain. And although there was a solution of sorts, it caused a rift between myself and my old friend that may never be fully healed. To this day, it chills me to the marrow to think of our foray into the dark netherworld that lies beyond the reach of rational science.

I have written elsewhere that although I recall the events laid out herein, I cannot place an exact date upon them, for I was not long married when I came to call upon Holmes once more.

I do remember the gutters of Baker Street running with melted ice and snow, the sky a sickly winter yellow above the chimney pots, which tempts me to place my visit on a Saturday in the late February of 1888. Should I venture to the vaults of the bank of Cox & Co., Charing Cross, and unearth my battered tin dispatch box, I would find among the many papers some notes which might be constructed into an account of what happened during our time in Devon. But I can still barely bring myself to believe what happened. And indeed, there is no logical explanation — I can only set down the facts as they occurred.

It began, as these things so often did, with a visitor to Holmes' rooms.

"This is really most inconvenient," said my friend when he heard the doorbell and peered down from his front window.

"You don't know there is a caller for you," I ventured, for it is true that my friend's suppositions sometimes seemed to me a little glib.

"Mrs. Hudson does not take calls at this time," he replied briskly. "The butcher's boy is not due this morning, and the lady standing on the step is dressed in a style of finery that was at its height in London two years ago, which suggests she is up from the country — not a social call, for she would visit her milliner first, but a matter of urgent business."

Moments later the door opened and Mrs. Hudson requested to speak with Holmes. "Sir, there is a lady for you who will not be put off," she said. "I have asked her to wait—"

"Mr. Holmes, you are a consulting detective, are you not, and as such I should be able to call upon you as I would a doctor?" said the lady, coming into the room and removing her gloves.

"I have said as much myself, Miss—"

"Woodham, Lucy Woodham," said the lady, as forthright as she was pretty.

"Please Madam, take a seat and pray tell me what I can do for you. This is Dr. Watson, a trusted friend and confidant. You may speak freely in front of him."

I have travelled up from Devon today to see you because you came highly recommended to me by Miss A---, for whom you handled a most delicate matter," she began. "My father is Major General Sir Henry Woodham."

"A most valorous gentleman, Miss Woodham," said Holmes, impressed. "A favorite of Her Majesty's, I believe."

"Indeed, sir, although you might not credit it to see him now, for he is a broken man."

"Why so?"

"It began three months ago, when the footprints first appeared. And it has recently culminated in death and madness."

I saw the sparkle in Holmes' eyes and felt his excitement like electricity in the room. He knew the game was afoot. "Please be seated and tell me more, starting at the beginning," he said.

"My father retired from the military world, but found life hard to adapt to at Belstowe Grange," Miss Woodham explained. "He inherited the property from his grandfather, and upon his retirement we moved from Worcestershire to Devon, hoping to restore the house to its former glory. It wasn't long before we heard the stories."

"What stories?"

"You must understand that Belstowe Down is a close community, Mr. Holmes. It centres around the rows of villagers' cottages, the parish church and the grange. It is quite ancient. There was supposed to have been a Roman encampment at the site. Storms often wash away the roads, keeping the village isolated and its residents prone to superstition. There is a legend that says when a terrible crime has been committed, the Devil sends his legions of the lost to take ghastly revenge upon the perpetrator."

"And your villagers have recently had reason to believe this has once more come about." Holmes tamped his pipe and sent aromatic blue clouds into the room. "Please describe the circumstances."

"On Sunday afternoon the head groom and his stable boy had been returning the horses from exercise when a sudden storm arose. The sky blackened and the wind howled, bringing squalls of rain that hammered at the house and flooded the grounds. I and my father watched from inside the grange. When the tempest finally passed, the stable boy was discovered in a state of shock from which he has not recovered, and the groom was found lying in the middle of the lawn with his throat cut deep from ear to ear." Miss Woodham paused, quite overcome with emotion, but gathered her wits and continued. "But that was not the worst of it."

"What more could have happened?" I cried, feeling sorry for this fetching young lady who was clearly so distraught.

"I think we had better come directly to the grange with you to see for ourselves," said Holmes.

A quick consultation of Bradshaw confirmed a train leaving within the hour. I suggested staying in the village inn, but Holmes felt it was wiser not to alert the local populace of our presence, and so took up Miss Woodham's offer of rooms on her father's estate.

The main body of the building at Belstowe Grange was Jacobean, wood-panelled, high-ceilinged and flagstone-floored, impossible to adequately heat and gloomy with shadows near the rafters. I imagined that Major General Sir Henry Woodham would be 'the Very Model' as Mr. Gilbert might say, ramrod-backed and stern of countenance. His illustrious military career spoke volumes, and yet the gentleman who greeted us was but a shade of his former self. His sallow skin hung loose upon his stooped bones, his eyes were dark with approaching shadows and he started at the slightest noise.

"I'm glad you could attend us, Mr. Holmes," he said, shaking our hands with relief. "This is the most confounded business, and I am deuced if I know what the answer might be. I can only think that the villagers are right, and the Devil himself has cursed this place."

"There is no time to be lost. Perhaps we should start by seeing your stable boy," Holmes suggested. "Where is he now?"

"He is attended by a nurse upstairs," said Miss Woodham, "but I fear you will discover little from him. The lad has not uttered a single word since witnessing the death of his master."

Jacob, the stable boy, lay pinned by hard white linens in a small room at the back of the house. His pale face stared straight up, his eyes unmoving, his lips dry. Holmes sat beside him while I shone a light in the lad's eyes to measure the contraction of his pupils. "He is in shock," I told the nurse. "He must be regularly fed beef tea and kept warm. In time he will make a full recovery."

Holmes was talking to the lad, speaking so quickly and softly that none of us could hear what he was saying. After a few minutes, the boy's mouth suddenly opened and he began to whisper the same thing over and over, something that sounded like 'Phantoms of the dead.'

"I fear we will get no more from him today," said Holmes, rising sharply. He seemed hardly concerned for the boy's health, and only wanted more information. "Come, Watson, we need to see the body of the groom. Perhaps Dr. Watson might be allowed to examine him?"

"He is lying upstairs in the Barley Mow, awaiting the verdict of the coroner," Miss Woodham explained. "Mr. Charlton can take you to him in the brougham."

A short, barrel-chested man with luxuriant grey mutton chop whiskers and the sun-darkened face of an outdoorsman appeared beside the Major General.

"Mr. Charlton can be trusted with anything you might have to say," said Sir Henry. "Like myself, he was a cavalry officer at the Crimean Peninsula. I have known him for well over thirty years. Many in our village fought for their country, but few were actively engaged with the enemy like Charles and myself."

We made our way through scowling drinkers and climbed the worn stairs in the local alehouse, where we found the body of Elias Peason, the head groom, covered with a winding sheet that had grown dark with his blood. I removed the cloth and studied the wound at his throat. "This cut was not made with a razor," I exclaimed, "but with a sword. It is too wide and deep, and was performed in a single sweep."

"Bravo, Watson," Holmes exclaimed. "I knew I could rely upon your medical knowledge to help us out. But regard the look of sheer horror on his face. What did he see in the moment of his death?" He turned his attention to Mr. Charlton. "Were the pair of them together throughout the course of the storm?"

"I am given to understand so. They were seen from the road by a passing ostler who insists that the boy ran off at the height of the storm, leaving his master alone."

"He saw the groom die?"

"He says the man uttered an unearthly scream and fell to the ground, and that he was entirely alone."

"You know this witness? He is reliable?"

"He is known to partake of strong drink upon occasion."

"Do you have any reason to suspect the lad?"

"Not at all. He had the greatest respect for his master. You will see for yourself, sir. There is fear in his face, but no cruelty in his heart. During my time in the army I have seen men kill and be killed in turn, and I would swear the boy is innocent."

"Then whom do you suspect?"

"I think you had better see the rest of it, sir," said Mr. Charlton, bringing us to the lawn where the body was found.

The half-acre of green behind the grange was still flooded from the storm. Around us the tops of tall beeches shook and whispered as if telling secrets. As we approached the spot where the groom had been killed, Holmes strode forward with a look of excitement on his face. Almost at once I saw what he saw, but could not make sense of it. "What is that?" I asked.

There appeared to be hundreds of indentations surrounding the space where the body had fallen. The earth was as churned and broken as if a flight of stallions had been driven across it.

"Did the groom release your horses before he was attacked?" asked Holmes.

"No sir, these prints were not here before," said Mr. Charlton. "The horses were affrighted in the storm, but were still stabled behind locked doors."

"The prints appear to start at the edge of the lawn and lift away on the far side," called Holmes. "There are no other marks beyond them. It's almost as if they came down from the sky to attack the groom."

"Whatever could have left so many hoof prints?" I asked, but no answer came.

"We have found them here before, sir, regularly for the last three months, sometimes numbering in their hundreds, cutting across the fields in a single flight."

"There are no herds of wild horses in the area?"

"Not to my knowledge, sir, not since the grazing lands were fenced."

"When was the last time the prints appeared?" asked Holmes.

"Two weeks ago to the day, sir."

"And before that?"

"The Saturday previous, just after dark."

"That is suggestive," Holmes replied, but I could not see how. Later that evening we joined Sir Henry and his daughter in the candlelit retiring room after dinner. Usually by this stage Holmes had a rough idea of what he was up against, but this time he remained uncharacteristically silent on the cause.

"Did your groom have any enemies?" he asked, stroking his thin nose thoughtfully. It was the kind of elementary question he usually had no need of raising.

"None at all," said Sir Henry, pouring brandies. "He was also a Crimean veteran. Military men form allegiances that last a lifetime."

"Men without enemies are rarely found with their throats cut," muttered Holmes, sinking into his armchair. "I think I should hear more about this local legend of yours."

"Then you should speak to Reverend Horniman," said Sir Henry. "I understand he is something of an expert on the subject."

As we retired for bed, Miss Woodham stopped Holmes on the landing, anxious to speak to him beyond the hearing of Sir Henry.

"Mr. Holmes, I do believe the Devil is at work here," she whispered. "My father is in fear of his life, and even Mr. Charlton — usually the most stoic of gentlemen — seems to have taken fright. Something terrible is haunting this house, and you are our last hope."

"I will do what I can, Miss Woodham, I promise you that." Holmes laid a reassuring hand on her arm, but would say no more.

The next morning dawned bare and bitter, but dry at least. We walked to the parish church, planning to have a word with the reverend after his first service.

"We are honoured to have encouraged the attention of London's famous consulting detective," said Rev. Horniman, welcoming us into the now emptied church, "but this is a terrible business."

"I was hoping you could enlighten us about your village's strange superstition," said Holmes.

"I can show you something that has lately come to light concerning the legend, if that would help," the Reverend offered. He returned from the sacristy bearing a parcel of oilskin cloth and carefully unwrapped it. "This was found buried in the parish grounds. Our gravedigger was turning sod in preparation for a new grave when his spade struck something hard."

Inside the cloth was a glistening medal with an ornate clasp, being in the form of an oak leaf with an acorn at each extremity.

"But why would anyone bury such a thing?" I asked, looking up at Holmes. My companion seemed thunderstruck, and with barely another word set off in the direction of the village. It was all I could do to keep up with him.

"Really, Holmes," I exclaimed, "I think you might have been a little more civil to the Reverend, he was only trying to help."

"Civility has no importance when lives are at stake," came the reply. "Come, my friend, we must head back to the Barley Mow."

"Are we to view the corpse once more?" I ventured.

"No," said Holmes, "we must speak with the farmers who drink there."

We found a surly group of red-faced men in dirty smocks seated around the bar. Holmes had realized that the best way to win them over was to stand a round of drinks, and soon had them talking. I had assumed he would want to prise gossip from them about the stable boy or the head groom, or perhaps about Sir Henry and his treatment of his tenants, but instead Holmes wanted to know about the patterns of the weather.

"This land is dipped between three hills," said one of the farmers. "The rain clouds come a-sweeping over the trees and the air gets trapped, see, so we get more'an our fair share of storms — they start by swirling around in the vale and can't break back out."

Holmes turned to nudge me. "It is as I suspected," he said. "And can you stout fellows recall the most recent sequence of storms?"

We came away with a full record of recent bad weather attested to by the farmers. I could not see the relevance of this information, and as Holmes hurried us away in the direction of the grange I asked him what he hoped to find.

"I have a part of the puzzle but no more than that," he admitted. "To reach the true solution I begin to wonder if I must think the unthinkable. Let us catch up with Sir Henry, for I fear there is another storm coming in that could place him in great danger."

"A storm?" I cried. "I realize we are in the countryside where there is a greater risk in such meteorological events, but surely the Major General has nothing to fear from bad weather."

"It is not the storm Sir Henry has to fear," replied Holmes, "but what hides inside it. Tell me, Watson, do you believe Our Majesty when she says that God has chosen the English people to lead the world?"

"Well, I believe she was elected by God to lead our nation, and as she is the head of the most powerful empire on Earth I imagine that gives us great strength."

"Yes, but is it truly divine right? What if our belief is wrong?"

"It is something I cannot think about, save for the fact that, as a doctor, I believe that all peoples of the earth are created equal, and are just in different stages of development."

"Hm. Wise words, my friend, but there are some who would find your opinions heresy. Come, we must find Sir Henry before another crime is enacted."

"Surely you cannot think he is the culprit!" I interrupted.

"No, Watson, but I think the ghosts of his past are unleashing an unstoppable evil upon this estate."

We reached the hall just as a fresh storm broke overhead. Divesting ourselves of our wet topcoats, we went to find the Major General, but were halted by Miss Woodham.

"There you are," she said. "My father was quite unseated by the rising storm and has gone out to await your arrival — did you not pass him? He was going to the top of the drive."

Holmes uttered an epithet not suited for female ears and turned on his heel. I followed, running to keep pace. We crossed the torn-up lawn and searched right and left. Sir Henry was standing between the lines of darkening beeches, but it was hard for me to keep sight of him. The rising gale was tearing leaves and even branches across our path.

"Can you hear that?" called Holmes. "It sounds like voices."

Indeed, I fancied I heard in the blast of wind that caught my ear the sound of crying voices, in great pain, terror and yes — anger. The sky was bruised in roiling shades of black and brown. "We must get Sir Henry to safety!" I shouted. "The stables are at our back."

With a few long strides, Holmes had seized the old military man and pulled him away, but even as he did so I saw the hoof prints begin to appear. They were puckering the soil directly ahead of Sir Henry, thundering toward him. "This is madness!" I cried. "It's as if the very gates of Hell are opening!"

The ground spat and tore all around us, clods of earth flying in every direction as the unseen hooves smashed and crushed the turf underfoot. There was a terrible slashing in the air, and Sir Henry flinched as if struck.

Reaching the stables, we tore open the doors and thrust Sir Henry inside. He offered no resistance, and collapsed on the hay bales as we battened down the entrance once more. It was then I saw that he had been cut — not deeply, as Holmes had been able to pull him back from harm, but enough to cause a fast flow of surface blood from his arm. I tore a horse blanket into strips and quickly staunched the bleeding.

As the wind and rain hammered the walls and clattered across the tin roof, thunder smashed so loudly that we could not hear each other speak. And so we remained for half an hour, until the worst of the tempest had passed and escaped to the hills once more.

"What devilry is this?" gasped Sir Henry. "Please, Mr. Holmes, go and make sure that my daughter is safe."

Holmes went ahead, and I brought the Major General back to the house, but he was much depleted in energy. Upon arrival, I took the liberty of pouring him a brandy, and had one myself. Then I set about properly cleaning and dressing his wound.

Feeling that we were safer in assembly, the five of us, Holmes, myself, Miss Woodham, Sir Henry and Charles Charlton gathered in the great room and waited for the clouds to clear, but by now night had fallen. Upstairs, the nurse sat with the mute stable-boy, whose dark eyes continued to stare at the ceiling as if seeing beyond into the blackest reaches of space.

A servant passed through with tapers and lit the room, dispelling some of our fears. We gathered around the fireplace, feeling stronger but no less disturbed.

"Some thirty years ago we all fought the Russians," said Sir Henry. "I believe the souls of our dead enemies have returned, to continue their war against us from beyond the grave."

"I think not," Holmes replied. "I can explain in part what is happening, but there is one more piece of the puzzle still to place."

"Please, Mr. Holmes," entreated Miss Woodham, "shed any light you can on these terrible visitations." As she spoke, we heard the wind begin to rise once more, and a fresh squall of rain hit the leadlight windows.

"The storm has circled and is coming back once more," said Mr. Charlton as the candles closest to the window guttered and blew out.

Holmes ignored the noise of the tempest and continued. "It is said that the forces of nature have the power to open rifts between our world and the next. Each time the Devil's hoof prints have appeared, it has been during a time of natural disruption. This, after all, is the season of storms. As the possessor of one of the finest rational minds in the country, I cannot condone such thinking, you understand, but I appreciate how such beliefs arise. And then there was the matter of the little curate, Reverend Horniman, who set me thinking further." Holmes dug into his jacket pocket and held up the gold medal. "Three months ago, at the very time these attacks first started, the Reverend's grave-digger unearthed this medallion in his churchyard. In itself it is a rare enough piece, being awarded to those who fought in the Crimean theatre of war. But this particular one, with the ornate oak leaves on the cross-bar, is given only to those who had direct engagement with the enemy."

"I have one in my possession," said Sir Henry. "My head groom was also in my regiment, and possessed another."

"Indeed, sir. I took the imposition of checking. You may be aware that there are several other men from your regiment living in this village."

"After the war, many of the men who had fought together chose to resettle in their old villages, and many recruits came from Devon."

"But I believe there is another medal like this, with the oak leaf cross bar, held by someone in this very house." Holmes looked at Mr. Charlton.

"The one you found in the churchyard is mine," said Mr. Charlton in shame.

"But why, man?" cried Sir Henry. "Why would you bury such an honour?"

"Because I could not bear to look at it," said Mr. Charlton. "For what it represents, and the way it makes me feel. I hoped never to see it again. I determined to bury it soon after receiving it." He turned to Holmes. "The other old soldiers in the village don't know, sir. They are not a part of this."

"A part of what?" coaxed Holmes.

"It was a secret held by only the three of us; and I am the most to blame for I carried out the order."

"I think you had better tell us the truth now, Mr. Charlton," said Holmes, with urgency in his voice as the storm continued to rise.

"It sounds as if the wind is trying to tear off the roof," said Miss Woodham, glancing to the ceiling with apprehension.

"You must understand the difficulties we faced, sir," continued Mr. Charlton, as more candles were snuffed out, and only the fluttering flames in the fireplace lit his face. "The British army was poorly prepared to fight the Russians, and even more ill-equipped for the attack on the Crimean Peninsular. From the shore where we arrived to the battlefield was a lengthy and difficult journey by mule. Lord Cardigan and Lord Lucan were fools too busy baiting one another to take proper care of their troops. Food supplies were dropped at the dock and left to rot because we had no way of getting them to our men.

"It was I who made the decision to requisition the horses for the cavalry officers. I thought I could take them for our comrades, and the food supplies would be delivered by mule through the mountains. I did not know that most of the mules had died, and that without them there was no way of the food getting through."

"I knew our comrades needlessly died of starvation when they should have lived to fight the enemy," said Sir Henry, shocked. "But I did not know of the part you played, Charles."

"I'm sorry, sir. Believe me; had I known the results of my actions, I would not have acted thus."

"Then these are not the spirits of avenging Russians, but of our own men!"

"Are there others in the village who are privy to this knowledge?" asked Holmes. "It is vital that I am in full possession of the facts."

"No sir," said Mr. Charlton, "for I made sure that the requisition copies were destroyed. The secret resides solely with me, and now the deed is being punished. The dead do, indeed, return. And the lives of all those who survived in place of their fallen comrades are at risk."

"Pish," said Holmes. "I do not believe in ghosts. You think the spirits of the fallen have been enticed by the Devil to take revenge against you? That they ride from Hades to take your lives?"

"Sir, I know this to be the case, and you have seen the hoof prints yourself, not made by horses but by the cloven-footed devils upon whom the soldiers of the dead must ride, for you see — *they had no horses of their own.*"

"It is madness to consider such superstitious nonsense," said Holmes, but even as he spoke the wind howled down the chimney, blasting a great inferno of cinders out into the room, extinguishing the few remaining candles. Miss Woodham and myself stamped out the burning embers, but now the far window had blown in, as if the Devil himself was leaning against the walls. The full fury of the storm was attempting to enter the house.

"I must go out there and offer myself," said Mr. Charlton wildly. "It was I who exposed my guilt before God by burying the medal, and now I must save Sir Henry while there is still time."

"Listen to me, Mr. Charlton," said Holmes, "I honestly believe you blame yourself for angering the dead, but it is a storm that caused the churning of the ground, and lightning that slashed the throat of your groom, nothing more."

"That is not true, Holmes, and you know it!" I cried. "I saw the wound for myself."

"You are a man of science, Watson, you cannot believe this too!"

Mr. Charlton ran to the door and flung it wide. We started after him, to pull him back into the safety of the room, but we were too late. He ran out onto the lawn and shouted at the sky, where a funnel of thick black cloud was spinning down towards the earth.

We felt the ground shake beneath us as great brown clods of mud were torn in a channel that roared toward Mr. Charlton like a platoon stampeding through a valley. The 'Phantoms of the Dead', as the stable boy had called them, had returned. We watched in horror as Mr. Charlton's body was slowly lifted in the air, punched and twisted this way and that, as if unseen creatures were pushing at him. Blood flew about his face and neck, then his chest and arms, and finally his limbs were torn and stretched until they broke. We could hear each crack and cry from below, where we stood. When he was eventually released and fell, we saw the slashes across his stout form that had parted clothing and flesh all the way to the bone, cutting him to ribbons. Mr. Charlton was dead even before he had hit the ground.

A spectacular flash of lightning illuminated the scene. For a brief second I saw — or fancied I saw — the fiery horned devils who bore the dead on their backs, armed with unsheathed cavalry swords. And then they were gone, thundering back into the rolling clouds, born away by the tempestuous night.

"No more!" Holmes slammed the doors shut at his back, leaving the fallen man outside.

"No, Mr. Holmes, now there is only me, and I am an old man whose time has come," said Sir Henry, as his daughter ran to his side.

"Father, the Devil has had his due," exclaimed Miss Woodham. "Mr. Charlton has made right his terrible mistake."

"Perhaps that is so," said Sir Henry, "for there is no greater crime than when an officer has made his own men suffer."

"You are wrong, sir," said Holmes with some passion. "The greater crime is to engage the enemy in the sure belief that God is on your side." He turned to me. "Come, Watson, I feel we should return to London tonight. There is nothing more to be done here."

I had never seen my friend in a mood like this. He was angry. Not detached and analytical, but furious that he was being forced to face the impossible and consider it real. I felt sure that back in London he would bury his doubts once more in work and the syringe.

My last view of Sir Henry was as a sickly old man being comforted by his daughter, slumped in his armchair before the dying fire, disturbed by doubts that he might have spent his life believing in things that were not true.

Holmes and I returned to London, but during the long train journey home we did not speak of the case again, for fear that it might have awoken a chasm between us that no amount of reason could ever fill.

CHRISTOPHER FOWLER is the multi-award winning author of over thirty novels including the recently released *Bryant and May Off the Rails*, the eighth novel to feature Bryant and May. In addition to writing novels and short stories Christopher has written comedy and drama for BBC Radio One (including the Sherlock Holmes story *The Lady Upstairs*), has written articles and columns for a variety of publications and recently completed *Celebrity* for the stage.

THE DEADLY SIN
OF SHERLOCK HOLMES

by Tom English

Hundreds of years ago, around the time of Magna Carta, while England endured the growing pains of an empire in its infancy, and kings and kingdoms waged endless wars across Europe; and long before Prince Wilhelm von Ormstein's dalliance with the woman Irene Adler, the aftermath of which, were it not for the intervention of Sherlock Holmes, might have ended in a royal scandal in Bohemia, yet another chapter of history was being written in a Benedictine monastery in an obscure Bohemian village. Its consequences would span centuries, and dreadful would be its effects.

The architect of this singular item sat hunched behind a tiny, splintered table in a bare cell illuminated only by a thin shaft of moonlight from a high, narrow window. He was dying. His arms, legs and face were lacerated with hundreds of self-inflicted cuts, his clothing scarlet with blood. When three robed men appeared at his door, he looked up weakly from his bloodstained fingers and smiled.

"Where is it, Brother?" asked one of the men.

"Of what do you speak, Abbot?"

"Brother Josef, Brother Ehren, bring the candles," the abbot said to the two monks behind him. "Search his cell — quickly!" He turned back to the man seated before him. "We know of the hellish instrument you have forged this night. God has revealed it to me in a dream."

"More a nightmare, I should think. For the power of the thing shall be hideous, its ministry implacable."

"How dare you use consecrated paper!" said Brother Josef.

"Where is it?" the abbot asked again.

"Gone out into the world," said the dying man, clinging to the edge of his blood-smeared desk.

"You have corrupted an instrument of God," cried Brother Josef. "Where is it?"

"As I have said, Josef, it is gone. Spirited away by the Prince of the Air."

"Satan!" Brother Ehren said with disgust.

"Certainly not your weakling god," he replied.

"You stand at death's door," said the abbot. "Have you no fear? Tell us now where the thing is hidden."

"Hidden?" laughed the man behind the table. "In this tiny room?" He coughed hard and struggled to regain his breath. "Nay," he said hoarsely, "though you search for it, you shall not find it. For I have sent it out into the world. To baptize all men into a new age of darkness."

On a bone-chilling night in early May of 1891, a hooded figure crouched over the dead body of a young woman on Clements Lane in the district of Westminster, London. An icy rain spattered against the grey cobbles and ran away in grimy rivulets towards the Thames. From the south the faint peal of Big Ben marked the midnight hour. While two other men watched from nearby, the veiled figure knelt before the corpse, a Bull's-eye lantern in one hand. His free hand moved quickly and expertly over the woman's body as he probed the bloodstained clothing. After several moments, he heard a voice above him ask, "Well?"

The man looked up from the corpse. "Well *what*, Lestrade?" he asked irritably. "This infernal rain has scrubbed the street clean. Despite what the good doctor may have written about my abilities, I cannot work without clues."

"She was obviously another drab who got more than she asked for," said Inspector Lestrade, pulling up the collar of his coat. "But her face, Mr. Holmes! Look at her face! Why would anyone do such a thing?"

"This was no streetwalker, Lestrade. Observe the clothing. It appears to be new and of the highest quality. This woman was dressed for an evening out. What brought her *here*, so far from the beaten path?"

Holmes tossed back the hood of his Ulster. The rain had died away to a fine mist that shone as a halo around the street lamp at the end of the lane. "This rain started a little after 3 p.m., but this woman is not dressed for inclement weather. As you can see, she has no cloak at all." He motioned to the man in black coat and derby standing next to Lestrade. "Watson, notice the blood about the eyes and mouth — how thickly coagulated it is."

Watson knelt and winced at the mutilated features.

"Yet the body is face up," said Holmes. "The heavy rain would have washed away most of this blood — had it not been so thickly clotted. Now, since you put the time of death at only a couple hours ago, and it has been raining since three..."

"Then the wounds were inflicted somewhere else," Watson said. "Some place dry enough to allow the blood to congeal."

"Come," said Holmes, "we can learn nothing more here. The scent has grown cold, and so have we. What will Mrs. Watson have to say, should I detain you any longer?" He turned to Lestrade, who quickly gestured to two uniformed policemen to remove the dead body. "If I can be of any further assistance..."

Lestrade watched the two men walk down the lane toward the Strand and disappear into the shadows. A few minutes later he heard two shrill blasts from a cab whistle — telling him that Holmes had hailed a hansom.

That same night, several streets away, a man sat alone in a dimly lit room and wept bitterly. He held something in his arms, something heavy and cool, which he gently caressed. He laid the object on his lap, wiped the tears from his eyes, and then opened it with a trembling hand.

"It's gone!" he cried. "Gone!"

When Watson called on Holmes at his Baker Street lodgings the next morning, he found the detective sitting before the fire, absently scraping away at the violin that rested across his knees. Each screeching note from the Stradivarius sent a chill up the doctor's spine, making him cringe and grit his teeth. "Holmes! If you please!" he cried, tossing the morning newspaper on the table.

Holmes glanced at the headlines. "Miss Anne Skipton. Certainly not a streetwalker, and yet *The Times* is alluding to the Whitechapel murders of two and a half years ago."

"You must admit," said Watson, taking the other chair by the fire, "there has been no murder this gruesome since the days of Jack the Harlot killer."

"And already *The Times* is capitalizing on it."

Holmes set aside the Stradivarius and was about to say something when he was interrupted by a knock at the door. Mrs. Hudson entered, followed by an elderly man wearing a battered black hat and faded cassock. A dull metal cross hung from a chain about the man's neck.

"Ah! A client," said Holmes. "Thank you, Mrs. Hudson."

The man removed his hat and bowed, revealing a thick, tangle of gray hair. "I am Brother Eduardo. I have come on behalf of … well, you will not have heard of our order. It is a little-known off-shoot of the Benedictines, whose mission is to safeguard certain antiquities."

Watson smiled. "A secret society?"

"Excuse me," Holmes interrupted, "this gentleman is my good friend and colleague, Dr. Watson, and I am Sherlock Holmes."

The old man nodded. "Not secret, Dr. Watson. The Church is well aware of our presence. Perhaps, though, our day-to-day activities may be somewhat obscure."

Holmes motioned for the man to be seated.

"I was referred to you by a Mr. Lestrade. He feels my problem is not a matter for Scotland Yard."

"And what is your problem?"

"My brothers and I have hopes that you will be able to locate a missing book."

Holmes turned to Watson. "Our friend Lestrade has a habit of sending us his … more interesting cases."

"He told me of both your amazing abilities and your genuine goodness," the monk said anxiously. "And I pray you will be able to discern my deep sincerity when I say that this matter is of the utmost importance. I would not have come to you were it not so."

"I discern that you are indeed a man without guile," said Holmes reassuringly. "Surely you are also a humble man, to be so long in the service of your order as to attain a position of authority and yet choose to remain a novice."

At the surprise on Brother Eduardo's face, Watson used a finger to trace a circle about the crown of his own head: "The lack of a tonsure, quite elementary."

Holmes sighed heavily.

"In many ways, Mr. Holmes," said the monk, "we are all novices. Not one of us is ever fully capable of solving the great mysteries of this world."

"Really!" said Holmes. "You quite obviously have not come here to flatter me, Friar. So please, tell me about this missing book."

"It is a bound manuscript known as the Codex Exsecrabilis."

"*Cursed Book*," remarked Watson, taking notes.

"Watson," said Holmes, "be a good fellow and fetch my copy of *Librorum Prohibitorum*."

"You will not find it listed on the Church's index of banned books," said Brother Eduardo. "It is a singular work ... composed in the early thirteenth century by an apostate monk in Podlažice, Bohemia. The manuscript pages mysteriously disappeared the night they were written, and were not recovered until 1477. By then the pages had been bound."

"Describe the physical appearance of the book," Holmes interrupted.

"It consists of vellum sheets gathered in wooden boards. The boards are covered in leather and ornamented with a metallic cross — an inverted cross. It is rather large and weighs over 32 pounds. The codex remained in Benedictine possession for over a hundred years ... at a monastery in Broumov, until it was forcibly taken to Prague to become part of the collection of Rudolf II."

"Bohemian Kings," muttered Holmes, "I am besieged with the consequences of their mischief."

"Rudolf was a student of the occult," said the monk.

"An avocation that did nothing to help him prevent the Thirty Years' War."

"And when the Swedish army plundered the region, his entire collection was stolen and removed to Stockholm. A few years later the Swedish Royal Library allowed us to purchase the codex. Since then — except for three or four brief periods — the book has been in our safekeeping. Until three days ago. We are extremely anxious to locate it!"

"No doubt. Such a valuable and coveted book as…"

"Our desire to recover the codex does not stem from cupidity. The book has the power to corrupt the souls of decent men!"

"Your desire to protect us from this book is a noble one, Friar, but I believe each of us should be free to read and decide for ourselves what is moral and praiseworthy."

"But Mr. Holmes, the Codex has been linked to numerous crimes! In fact, it is directly responsible for several ghastly murders."

"Is this book so poorly written," Holmes asked drily, "as to incite the reader to violence? Then why not simply fling the offending volume into the fireplace?"

The old monk nervously fingered the tiny cross hanging over his heart and stared mutely into the detective's piercing eyes.

"Friar, if I am to help you, I must have all the facts, and I must have them now."

"The facts will sound like fancy, I fear," the monk said at last.

"Allow me to be the judge of that."

"The codex is a compendium of evil acts, Mr. Holmes — all of them hideous, hellish. When anyone reads a passage from the book — and I stress, *anyone* — that person is compelled to enact what has been read, no matter how monstrous the deed. Later, after the evil has been enacted, the passage literally fades from the page, leaving absolutely no trace of the words."

"That is indeed a fanciful tale," said Holmes. "One worthy of Oscar Wilde, I might add."

"The book must be found," Brother Eduardo pleaded, "before it falls into the hands of another poor soul who will be powerless to resist its call."

"But, Friar," Holmes said soothingly, "a book composed by a thirteenth-century Benedictine scholar is undoubtedly written in Latin. How many people tramping the streets of London would be able to read such a book?"

"To be precise, the codex was written in the Vulgate. But that has never prevented anyone from reading it, regardless of a knowledge of Latin."

"And how do you explain this?"

"It is difficult to explain the unexplainable," the old man said slowly. "The author of the codex had been confined to his cell for breaking monastic vows. His abbot had ordered him to do penance by transcribing several sacred documents. The manuscript *should* have been a common prayer book, but Brother Moriarty had long been under the sway of the Prince of Darkness."

"*Moriarty*," said Watson. "That does not sound Germanic."

"It is ancient Gaelic for 'greatly exalted.' In a perverse way, he lived up to his name: power accompanies exaltation — and his manuscript has become a source of relentless power. According to legend, he called upon Satan to anoint his writing, then repeatedly cut himself to supply the blood with which the codex was written. When finished, he was more dead than alive and the manuscript had mysteriously vanished."

Holmes withdrew a pipe from his pocket and examined its charred contents distractedly.

"Throughout the ages there have been many blasphemous books," continued Brother Eduardo. "Were this simply another such volume, we would not concern ourselves with it, but the parchment upon which it was written had been consecrated for sacred documents. Moriarty poured into that parchment everything that is evil. Somehow, on the night of its satanic creation, the codex took on a life of its own. Now, it is trying to revert to its original holy state."

"Fascinating," said Holmes, yawning.

"You must believe me! When an evil passage is read from the codex the reader is forced to enact that evil — and the passage is then wiped clean from the book! I assure you, Sir, many of its pages are now blank!"

"I believe only in those things which can be proven. You claim the book has special properties, but you have given me no proof."

The old monk stood and bowed. "You were our last hope, Mr. Holmes. Please forgive me for taking so much of your time."

"A moment, Friar. I may not believe the legend tied to the codex, but I *will* help you to recover it. Tell me the circumstances surrounding its disappearance. You said it was three days ago. Where?"

"The library of All Hallows in Longbourn."

"I was not aware of a monastery in Longbourn."

"Our home is in Rome. We were in London on Church business and were extended hospitality by the priest at All Hallows."

"You brought the codex to London? Why?"

"It accompanies us wherever we go. I cannot give you the full reason for this — other than to say we are sworn to protect it."

"Very well," said Holmes. "We will accompany you to Longbourn."

Judged by its dour façade, the Church of All Hallows was particularly uninviting: a squat and decrepit edifice of crumbling brick and stained glass windows darkened by decades of soot. At one corner of the church, fronting the narrow street below, an imposing tower rose up against a gray sky; a much older structure, built of huge blocks of blackened stone, that stood out from the rest like a rook on the corner of a chess board, thought Watson, stepping from the four-wheeler.

"How long have you been staying here?" Holmes asked, following Brother Eduardo inside the tower.

"We arrived six days ago," said the monk. "We would have been on our way the next morning but Brother Paolo fell ill. Father Twitchell insisted we stay until he was well enough to travel. He said we would have the place to ourselves, for he was going up to Cambridge to attend to a Church matter and would be away for four days."

"When did he depart?"

"The morning after our arrival."

"And when was the last time you remember seeing the codex?"

Brother Eduardo opened a large oak door and waited for Holmes and Watson to enter. "It was certainly here in his library the night after he left. It was gone the next morning."

The priest's study was large but austere and, like the tower rising above it, clearly much older than the rest of the church. Heavy beams crisscrossed the ceiling and extended down the windowless walls. At one end of the room was a massive desk covered with curling documents and open books. Behind the desk a high shelf held numerous volumes recording births, burials, and other church history, their leather bindings dry and brittle with age. All this was illuminated by a single great log burning in the massive fireplace.

Holmes circled the room, making a quick inspection of the bare floor. "Other than yourself," he asked the monk, "who else might have had access to this room?"

"Only my brothers. The study was kept locked to safeguard the codex."

"How can you be certain of this?"

"Upon his departure Father Twitchell entrusted me with the keys to the Church, including this room."

"Then I wish to speak to your brothers — but to each individually. Please go and ask one of them to step in."

Holmes walked to the fireplace. It was wide and deep, and almost a foot taller than the detective. He extended his hands before the blazing log. "I daresay, Watson, I could fit my entire bed upon this hearth. No more chilly nights!" he said longingly.

The library door opened slowly and the first of two monks entered, a stout, balding man who went by the name of Brother Paolo. Holmes soon ascertained that the man had been seized with severe abdominal pains the night of his arrival and, until yesterday morning, had been far too ill to leave his bed. The detective thanked him and instructed the monk to show in his brother Eugenio.

When Eugenio entered, followed by Brother Eduardo, Holmes quickly realized the young man was a *true* novice, for he was hardly more than eighteen and demonstrated little of the qualities of meekness and humility that characterized the other monks. Holmes turned to the fireplace. "This is an inviting blaze. Certainly it is a temptation for someone in possession of an undesirable book. Tell me, Brother Eugenio, could the codex have found its way into the fire?"

"We do not burn books," the youth said petulantly.

"A book does not simply disappear from a locked room."

"We believe the codex has escaped," said Brother Eduardo, "just as it did the night of its creation."

"Escaped?" Holmes said peevishly. "Did it flap its pages and fly up the chimney? I should like to speak with the priest on his return."

"He is due back tomorrow, but surely you cannot suspect Father Twitchell of taking the book!"

"At present, I suspect no one," said Holmes, "But I must question everyone. I shall call upon him tomorrow afternoon."

In the carriage, on the way back to Baker Street, Watson turned to Holmes and asked, "The murder last night — could it somehow be related?"

"Possibly," said Holmes, lighting a cigarette.

"*Could* the codex have some occult power?"

"We have dealt with many mysteries which at first appeared to have their explanation in the supernatural — like the case of that wretched hound upon the moors. In the end, all of them proved to have a logical explanation. No, Watson, when it comes to the art of detection, I give no credence to tales of the supernatural. Like the hound, these bothersome little things nip at our heels and send us hurrying down the wrong path of investigation. How unfortunate that our history is riddled with myths, ghost stories, rumors of witches. On the stage of life, they have provided unintentional moments of 'misdirection': for as long as our focus is upon such things the real and important matters of human existence will always elude us.

"Nevertheless," he continued, "I am eager to pit my skills against the bibliomane who stole this book."

"But if the book has indeed fallen into the hands of some as yet unknown collector, it is hardly likely he will part with it. The book might be shelved in any one of a hundred private libraries."

"If this enigmatic gathering of paper and ink is indeed a nexus for crime, then its presence cannot remain a secret for very long. I assure you, it *will* come to light."

Hours later, in a boardinghouse in London's East End, a weary man slumped in the corner of a shabby room and opened the Codex Exsecrabilis. He ran his hand down the blank page and shook at the memory of what he had done to the retired seaman in the next room. He would have to be going soon, he thought, before the body was discovered; but then, that probably would not be until the next morning. He turned the page in the book and began to weep again. He wept at the prospect of killing once more, or perhaps doing far worse; and because he knew he would go on reading - until he had reached the final page of the codex.

Holmes was mildly surprised when Father Twitchell arrived at Baker Street the next morning. "I knew you wished to speak to me about the missing codex," said the priest. "I returned from Cambridge early this morning and decided to save you a trip by coming here straightaway."

"What can you tell me of this strange book?" asked Holmes.

"Only what I have read of it in Brother Eduardo's monograph. Were you aware of the pamphlet?"

"I would be interested in reading it. Do you know of any book collectors in your parish?"

Before Father Twitchell could answer, there was a knock at the door: Watson entered the room and quickly introduced himself to the priest, who shook the doctor's hand vigorously.

"I confess to being one of your avid readers," said the priest. "Such marvellous adventures — quite exhilarating."

"Excuse me, Father, are there any book collectors among your flock?" asked Holmes.

"Not that I am aware." The priest turned to the shelves above Holmes' desk. "You have some interesting volumes here. Are you a collector of books?"

"A book is not unlike a soup tureen. Though some may covet it for its shape and pattern, it is only the broth inside that interests me. No, I keep books only to have easy access to the information they record, but I did, however, notice a few rare volumes in your own library. Do *you* collect books?"

"Not unlike you; only for what they can tell me."

"Is there anyone in your parish in desperate need of money? Someone who might have chanced upon the codex, realized its rarity, and seized upon the opportunity to take it to a bookseller?"

"A few of my parishioners are indeed poor. But the codex was in my study, and my study is not open to the church. In fact, it is always kept locked."

"May I ask why?"

"Even priests need some small bit of privacy, Mr. Holmes. At any rate, I hope that you do not suspect anyone in my congregation."

"Not at present. But if I do not soon uncover a substantial lead in this investigation, I will need to start questioning the more needy members of your church."

"I am afraid I would not be able to assist you in such an endeavour. Most of what I know was told to me in the privacy of the confessional. I cannot break my vow to protect this confidentiality."

"That is admirable, Father, but how far should such a vow extend? Should one protect the identity of a thief?"

"No one in my congregation is guilty of stealing the codex, Mr. Holmes."

"The book did not simply vanish into thin air."

"You must not underestimate the supernatural power of this book."

"Now you are speaking nonsense, Father."

"Why is it so hard for you to believe in the supernatural? You have devoted your life and talents to the struggle between good and evil."

"The struggle between good and evil is your domain. I apply myself to the scientific study of crime and criminals."

"Then let us lay aside any theological bearing on the matter, and simply contemplate a metaphysical universe — a sphere beyond this existence."

"Can I see it, or touch it?" asked Holmes sardonically. "Where, pray tell, is this metaphysical world of yours?"

"It surrounds us. But as long as our focus remains fixed on the affairs of the physical world it remains invisible to our mortal eyes."

"Two worlds inhabiting the same space?"

"Even the materialist admits we simultaneously inhabit two plains of existence. We move about a three-dimensional world even as we are passing through a *fourth* dimension, that of time."

Holmes removed the watch from his vest pocket. "The passage of time I can measure. Show me your measurements of the so-called supernatural world, or do not waste my time."

The priest stood and took his hat. "The power of the codex is real, Mr. Holmes. I wish it were not." He strode to the door. "You would do well to read Brother Eduardo's monograph."

"Thank you, Father. And may I recommend Winwood Reade's *Martyrdom of Man* to you?"

When the priest was gone, Watson threw down his notebook and scowled. "You know, Holmes, at times you really are too much!"

Holmes spent the better part of the next day in the Reading Room of the British Museum. When Watson met him for lunch at Simpson's, Holmes laid a thick pamphlet on the doctor's charger.

Watson read the title aloud, *"A Most Uncommon Prayer Book, Being a History of the Codex Exsecrabilis and a Documentation of its Known Crimes.* It looks rather extensive."

"The sins of the book, Watson, documented by the friar in shocking detail. The man's willingness to believe in the absurd is unseemly, but his treatise bears all the hallmarks of serious scholarship."

"What a remarkable concept that one should commit a crime for no other reason than because one has read of it in a book."

"The idea has interest, for a crime committed in this manner would be without apparent motive, and therefore more difficult to solve."

Holmes lit his pipe. "Brother Eduardo links the codex to many of the most sensational crimes of the last several hundred years — all of them supposedly committed during those 'three or four brief periods' to which he alluded, when the codex was not in the brotherhood's possession." He blew out a tiny cloud of smoke. "Our humble friar attempts to cast a new light on the early eighteenth-century crimes of Jonathan Wild, and I must say, his monograph has me rethinking the poisonous career of Thomas Griffiths Wainwright."

"So what is our next move?"

"Lunch, dear fellow — we can do nothing until another crime is committed."

When Watson was awakened by his wife early the next morning, he learned that Holmes had sent a message urging the doctor to meet him at Scotland Yard. Although he had planned on devoting the day to his Kensington practice, Watson had long ago developed a craving for Holmes' little adventures and was soon in a cab racing toward Victoria Embankment. Upon his arrival, Holmes informed the doctor of an event he hoped would be the key to recovering the missing codex: sometime during the previous morning, a Longbourn bookseller had repeatedly stabbed his wife with a paper knife.

"Mr. Avery Felton," said Holmes as he and Watson entered the man's prison cell, "my name is Sherlock Holmes. I am a private consulting detective come to further investigate the circumstances that have brought you to this wretched place. Cooperate with me and I will do all I can to help you."

Felton stared at the floor. "I have read of you, Mr. Holmes, but you cannot help me. I killed my wife... stabbed her in the back... as she washed the breakfast dishes! I loved her!" he sobbed. "Why did I do it?"

"Have you come across a leather-bound manuscript, adorned with an upside-down cross?"

He shook his head.

"Are you certain — it is a heavy book, very old, some of its leaves may have been blank."

"I would remember such a book. What does it have to do with me?"

"Where did you go yesterday?"

"Nowhere, I stayed home."

"Then why *did* you kill your wife, Mr. Felton? Did you have an argument with her?"

"My head is spinning."

"Think, man!"

"We were having breakfast. Everything was perfect. She left to clean up. I was lounging at the table with the morning post."

"Was there anything unusual in the mail?"

"Just letters from other booksellers." Felton ran a hand across his face. "Except one which was absolute gibberish."

"In what way?"

"I am not a formally educated man, Mr. Holmes. I am well read, and I understand many things, but I do not speak any foreign languages."

"Where would this letter be now?"

He shrugged. "Still on the table, I suppose."

Holmes tossed several torn envelopes and creased sheets of paper upon the table of his sitting room. "These letters are unremarkable. As Felton said, they are simply correspondence from his associates about book-related nonsense."

"So we came up empty-handed," said Watson.

"Perhaps not."

Holmes pulled a magnifying lens from his desk drawer. "The only other scrap of paper in Felton's place was this blank piece I found upon his kitchen floor. That alone is significant." He briefly studied the item. "It is, as I first suspected, a very old piece of parchment... a fragment of a much larger leaf... torn off in some haste. The creases confirm that it was folded to fit inside an envelope. Also, there are several tiny water stains, which I believe are noteworthy. Beyond these salient points, it is nothing more than a thin sheet of sheep skin... soaked and stretched, then scraped smooth to remove the hair." He took a large beaker from the shelf. "Unless I can prove that it was torn from our missing codex."

Holmes raised the parchment to the light. "Behold, Watson," he said, "an invention as important to the dissemination of knowledge in *its* day as Gutenberg's first printing press was in the fifteenth century! Proving what Plato wrote about the impetus of need: 'Necessity, who is the mother of invention'!"

"How so?" laughed Watson.

"Parchment was invented in the ancient Greek city of Pergamum," said Holmes, "where — according to The Book of Revelation — Satan was enthroned." He crumpled the fragment and dropped it into the beaker. "In the second century B.C. Pergamum established a great library rivaling even that of Alexandria." He added just enough water to cover the parchment and began stirring the mixture briskly. "Up until then, the collected knowledge of civilization had been transcribed on papyrus, which was produced only along the Nile delta in Alexandria; and which had been over-harvested towards local extinction. Whether due to an inability to supply the material, or a desire to shut down its rival library, Alexandria ceased exporting papyrus."

Holmes decanted the water into a test tube. "So Pergamum invented a more than adequate substitute — one much cheaper and easier to produce than papyrus. It remains an excellent example of adaptation under changing circumstances."

"Holmes, you amaze me!"

He waved away the compliment. "I am preparing a monograph on paper and papermaking. It will be an invaluable resource in criminal investigation, and I daresay, had it been available at the time, the Bank Holiday Blackmail Case would have been brought to a far more satisfactory conclusion!"

Holmes withdrew a vial of white crystals and tossed a few into the test tube. "Parchment allowed the great Library at Pergamum to continue operating — until Mark Antony emptied its shelves and made Cleopatra a wedding present of its 200,000 volumes. *She* was a conniving woman, Watson." He removed the stopper from a reagent bottle of clear liquid and inserted a glass pipette.

"Now, let us see what this torn leaf has to tell us," said Holmes. "Brother Eduardo insists the codex was written in blood. If at some time there was blood on this scrap of parchment, a sufficient amount of it has been dissolved into this solution. This reagent will precipitate that blood as a brownish sediment." He added several drops and swirled the test tube.

"Nothing!" snarled Holmes. "Perfectly clean. So much for legends!"

"What if the legend is true," asked Watson, "and all trace of the evil writing has vanished?"

"Blood does not simply vanish. Some trace would remain, and my hemoglobin test is capable of detecting blood at concentrations of barely one part in a million." He smoothed out the parchment and blotted it dry. "Either there was no blood on this parchment to begin with, or..."

Holmes walked to the fireplace and filled his pipe. "How does one prove or disprove the supernatural?" he murmured, dropping into his chair. He took off his shoes and sat cross-legged, smoking his pipe.

Watson awoke at the call of his name. He had dropped off to sleep with *The Times* in his lap, while Holmes had been puffing at his pipe and, a while later, quietly puttering about his desk.

"Watson, would you mind taking care of something for me?" asked Holmes.

The doctor arose from his chair and stretched. "Run an errand? Yes, of course."

"I have written out some instructions for you," he said, extending a folded sheet. "Please read them and make certain everything is clear."

Watson unfolded the sheet, glanced at his friend's distinctive scrawl, and gasped. He looked down at Holmes sitting calmly at his desk. The detective's left hand was wrapped with a handkerchief, his jack-knife and a saucer of dark red liquid at his elbow. Upon the blotter lay a Latin dictionary and the doctor's service revolver.

Watson dropped the note. His body abruptly stiffened as the most abhorrent idea went racing through his mind. "No!" he cried in genuine terror. A cold sweat broke out over his face, which had gone as white as a sheet. Within seconds he began to shake involuntarily — except for his hands, which he kept tightly clenched by his sides.

Holmes realized the doctor was struggling hard to control himself: his mouth had become a pale trembling line, his eyes two coals burning with hatred. Holmes glanced at the revolver upon the desk, then quickly returned his gaze to the seething volcano of emotion standing before him. His hand moved toward the gun but Watson sprung upon it like a Bengal tiger, snatching the revolver from the desk.

Watson pressed the barrel to Holmes' forehead and gazed into the detective's widening eyes. "God help me," he said, squeezing the trigger.

When the hammer fell Holmes flinched at its sharp *click*.

Watson dropped the gun upon the desk and crumpled to the floor where he lay sobbing uncontrollably. Holmes lifted him into a chair and handed him a glass of whiskey.

"Holmes! How could you?" he cried.

"My dear friend," said Holmes, deep concern written upon his features, "please forgive me, but I could turn to no other for such a test. You have a heart that is genuinely good. Fair weather or foul, you are constant in your friendship, and so you have become for me a barometer by which I am able to gauge all that is noble in men."

"I wanted to kill you! And I would have, had—"

"Had the revolver been loaded, but I have far too much respect for your prowess with a gun to—"

"Did you stop to think I could have bashed in your bloody brains with the butt of it!"

"*That* idea," Holmes said resentfully, "was not written upon the parchment!" He took the empty glass from Watson's trembling hand and moved to refill it. "Nevertheless," he said softly, "you are right. It *was* a dangerous experiment... which might well have proved deadly." He extended another whiskey to the doctor. "And it was indeed a sin to pull it on my dearest friend."

Watson wiped his sweat-soaked face and took the glass. "You might have warned me."

"That would have ruined the whole experiment. Besides, you would have refused to read it."

Holmes picked up the note where Watson had dropped it. "Astonishing!" he cried. "It is blank again!" He hurried to the microscope to examine the fragment. After a minute he looked up from the eyepiece. "Not a trace of what I wrote — not even an impression made by the pen!"

Holmes walked to the fireplace, the parchment gripped tightly in his clenched fist. "Now that I know the power of the codex is genuine," he said angrily, "I want to know why the accursed thing was not destroyed centuries ago? All those despicable crimes could have been prevented!"

After several minutes, Holmes coolly remarked, "The apostate monk who created the thing... this Brother Moriarty... in many ways, he was a Napoleon of crime. Even now, hundreds of years after his death, he dispatches his orders on these parchment leaves."

Holmes gazed at the wrinkled page in his hand. "That miserable bookseller rotting away in jail is a pawn. Whoever mailed this page to him simply wanted to drag a red herring across the trail of my investigation. Whereas it was intended to lead me astray, it has only served to strengthen an earlier suspicion." He shoved the parchment into the drawer of his desk and locked it. "Watson, are you recovered enough to accompany me to Longbourn?"

"If the codex was *half* as dangerous as you claimed, you should have destroyed it when it first came into your possession," said Holmes.

"For hundreds of years we Benedictines have devoted ourselves to the preservation of books," said Brother Eduardo. "The codex is one of a kind. Destroying it would have been a crime."

"But by not destroying it," said Watson, "you and your brothers are indirectly responsible for far worse crimes."

"But we have worked hard to keep the book from being read."

"And yet it *has* been read," said Holmes.

"True, there have been two or three times when the codex was not in our possession."

"I believe there have been *many* times," said Holmes. "Your monograph was published over a decade ago. I believe it needs extensive updating. The Whitechapel murders, for instance. Who was reading your book in 1888?"

"The codex *did* escape that year... for several months," said the monk, unable to meet Holmes' gaze. "But we have tried so hard. We have cared for it for centuries."

"Cared for it?" asked Watson.

"The Brotherhood considers the codex to be a living thing," said Father Twitchell.

"At first," said Brother Eduardo, "our order saved the book from the fire because of its rarity. Years later, we made a startling discovery about the nature of the codex. It had developed a form of intelligence." He paused. "We believe it has a living soul."

"You are quite mad," said Holmes.

"It bore the sins which one man poured onto its pages. Now it seeks redemption from those sins."

"You may leave us now, Friar," said Holmes.

"Like any soul, it is deserving of redemption," said Brother Eduardo, walking to the door. "But unlike the man whose sins it now bears, the codex is not human... and therefore, not eligible for the same redemption offered to men."

"Astonishing," cried Watson, after the monk had left the room.

"That old man actually views the book as his brother," said Father Twitchell, "a member of his own order, in fact — which is why the codex accompanies the Brotherhood whenever they travel."

"This case has given me a headache," said Holmes, walking to the fireplace. "Father, may I trouble you for some water?"

"Allow me to make you a cup of tea."

"No, please, water is fine."

When the priest returned with a glass of water, Holmes thanked him and drained it of all but an inch of liquid. "I have been admiring your fireplace," he said. "I have never seen a hearth as large as this one. I imagine it is quite ancient."

"Like the rest of this tower," said Father Twitchell. "This hearth actually took up the better part of the wall. I had the opening made smaller by bricking up the front edges."

"And still it is a hearth of enormous dimensions," said Holmes. "But returning to more important matters, someone in your parish is responsible for mailing a page of the codex to Mr. Avery Felton."

Holmes crossed over to the priest's desk and set down the glass. When he withdrew his hand he managed to spill the remainder of the water. "How clumsy of me. I have made a mess of your desk."

"That is quite all right," said Father Twitchell, with thinly disguised irritation.

"When I received news that a bookseller had murdered his wife," said Holmes, "I naturally assumed the codex had come into his possession."

Father Twitchell nodded, eyeing the spilled water. The desktop, weathered and slightly warped from years of similar abuse, was far from being level, and already the tiny puddle had begun to migrate toward a battered leather volume he had been reading. He glanced about for something to mop up the liquid and, when nothing presented itself, grew visibly agitated. When the water had crept to within half an inch of the book the priest hurriedly snatched it up before it got wet. "What is your point?" he snapped, carefully examining the edges of the volume.

"Father Twitchell," asked Holmes, "do you have a burden for books as well as for souls?"

"I beg your pardon," he said, recovering his composure. "It has been a long and trying day. What else did you wish to ask me?"

"Could someone in your parish have wished to divert my investigation?"

"I am not sure."

"Of course, there is another possible motive: sending that page could have been a plea for help. Tell me, Father, how does one track down a book which, according to Brother Eduardo, does not wish to be found?"

"Where would you go, if you were overburdened by the sins of your past?"

"I might seek a priest," said Holmes. "One who would hear my confession, or — if my sins were on paper — one who would *read* them. For I have lately learned that no matter what the consequences, a priest would never divulge my secrets."

Holmes held out his hand. "It is over, Father. Where is the codex?"

Father Twitchell sprang from behind his desk and charged across the room, shoving Watson on his way.

"Holmes!" the doctor cried. "He's running into the fire!"

"Quick, Watson! Follow me!" said Holmes, running to the hearth. He leapt over the great blazing log and then whirled about. To his left was a narrow opening in the blocks, barely more than a foot wide, and perfectly hidden from view by the newer bricks.

"Hurry," cried Watson, now at his friend's side, "this heat is unbearable!"

Holmes quickly squeezed sideways through the opening, followed by the doctor. They found themselves in a narrow passageway, with the sound of footsteps echoing in the blackness ahead of them.

Watson groped for a match as he and Holmes felt their way down the passage. "The footsteps are fading — he is getting away!"

"I doubt that."

The two men stumbled upon a wider chamber. They could feel a strong current of cool air blowing past them in the darkness. Watson struck a match, illuminating a large circular room. There were other passageways leading off the chamber, and narrow stone steps that wound up the center of the tower into the shadows above. "Which way did he—?"

"Quiet," whispered Holmes.

From the gloom above their heads several bits of crumbling mortar suddenly rained down, cascading on the lowest steps. Holmes raced up the stairs with Watson close behind. When he reached the top of the tower, he found the priest standing at the edge of the parapet, clutching the codex and staring down at the street.

"Father Twitchell," Holmes called gently, "please come away from the edge."

The priest spun about to face him. "It is too late," he sobbed. "The things I have done.... I can never forgive myself!" He took a step backward, the codex held tightly to his breast, and plummeted into the darkness below.

The sidewalk and cobbles of Baker Street were littered with shattered glass. Watson could hear it crunching beneath his feet when he stepped down from the carriage. He looked up at the open windows of Holmes' sitting room, briefly wondering what new eccentricity awaited him, and then hurried up to see his old friend.

Watson immediately felt the breeze upon his face when he opened the door. He strode across the room, past Holmes who was gazing sullenly into the fire, and stood before the two windows overlooking the street. There was no glass or mullions left in the frames. The doctor sighed deeply. "There is a decided draft in this room, Holmes. What on earth have you been up to?"

Mrs. Hudson tapped at the door and then ushered in three monks.

"The thing you seek is upon the table," Holmes said without rising.

Brother Eduardo hugged the book. "We are greatly indebted to you, Mr. Holmes."

"What a pity," said Brother Paolo, "that in offering absolution to a damned soul, Father Twitchell should lose his own."

"What do you mean?" asked Holmes.

"He committed suicide," said Brother Eduardo, "for which there is no forgiveness."

"And why is that?"

"Only God has authority in matters of life and death," said Brother Eugenio. "In taking his own life, Father Twitchell usurped that authority. He will burn in hell."

"I believe you are wrong," said Holmes. "Your faith is founded upon the belief that in a supreme act of benevolence, God sent His only son to take upon His shoulders the sins of the world, but after His son died for those sins, He was received back to His father.

"Gentlemen," Holmes continued, "how can you believe anything less in the case of a priest who, led by love, took upon his shoulders the sins of the book, and ultimately died for those sins? Father Twitchell's suicide was an act of sacrifice. *If* there is a heaven, I believe you will find him there... waiting for you."

Holmes motioned to the door. "But these are theological matters, of which I am out of my depth."

"Perhaps not, Mr. Holmes," said Brother Eduardo, departing.

"Holmes, is it wise to leave so much power in their hands?" Watson asked after the men had left.

"Most of the pages in the codex were blank once again, the parchment having long ago reverted to its original state: clean and blameless. What does it say in Isaiah? 'Though your sins be as scarlet, they shall be as white as snow.' I assure you, those leaves were as white as snow. Except for one last section of manuscript, which I sliced out of the binding while slightly averting my eyes, lest I should inadvertently read some of that hellish text. The pages I removed contained the last remaining words of malediction. I took the liberty of burning them shortly before you arrived. It is doubtful the Brotherhood will hazard too close an inspection of that volume; but if they should, they will not notice its thickness diminished by a mere few leaves."

Holmes turned back to the fireplace. "And I cannot imagine the codex will mind. For it is better to lose a few pages than to lose one's soul."

Watson took the chair next to Holmes. "For a man who has just solved an extremely unusual case, you seem rather down. You must not hold yourself responsible for the death of the priest."

"When Father Twitchell hurled himself from the tower, I plunged with him... into the depths of despair."

"But why, Holmes?"

"You were planning to ask me how the windows were shattered. No," Holmes smirked, "it was not one of my little experiments taken flight. When I burned that remaining evil signature an astonishing phenomenon occurred." He closed the collar of his dressing gown and hugged himself. "A black plume billowed from the fireplace. It was not smoke, but rather something more solid, something slick and oily in appearance. It behaved like a giant snake. I now wonder if it was not similar to the material referred to among spiritualists as *ectoplasm*."

"That's incredible!"

"Yes, but I have had the misfortune of seeing it."

Holmes walked to one of the shattered windows. Below him, Baker Street clattered and hummed with the activities of London life; a confusion of men and women, carriages and horses, all bustling to and fro across the soot-grey cobbles. "The damned thing bifurcated before exiting through these *closed* windows."

"You've grown pale," said Watson.

"I have a strong constitution, but I admit the sight of it has unnerved me."

"You have clearly had a shocking experience. Come and sit down. I will ask Mrs. Hudson to bring up some breakfast."

"Not just yet. There is something I wish to say first."

Holmes went back to the fireplace and dropped into his armchair. "A significant part of me plunged with that accursed tome... and was dashed against the pavement below: a bit of my philosophy, perhaps; certainly my spirits. Remember the horrible depression through which I suffered in the Spring of '87?"

"We came through it."

"I feel there are even blacker depths waiting to engulf me now. Which is why I am going away."

"Going away, Holmes?"

"These last few days I have witnessed many strange things — otherworldly phenomena which I cannot explain." He shuddered. "I have come to realize there is a significant tear in my logic. I must set myself to mending this tear before the entire fabric of my reason is rent asunder. To accomplish this I need time to think. I need a change of scenery; as cozy and as safe as they are, I feel the need to temporarily escape the confines of these rooms."

"But where will you go?"

"The Continent," said Holmes, gazing at the mezzotint hanging above the mantel: a reproduction of the Reichenbach Falls in Switzerland. He seemed to lapse into deep thought.

"Perhaps Tibet," he said at length, "to visit the Dalai Lama."

"But what of your work?"

"I have always felt it my duty to use my unusual talents for the public good, and in all the years you have known me, and before then, I have never forsaken that responsibility. But now…" He shrugged. "I am in need of a very long holiday."

"And what of all the people who have come to rely upon you? What will I tell them when they come calling and learn that their champion has disappeared, leaving them with no one to whom they can turn? That you are on holiday? Sightseeing? They will never understand."

"Tell them whatever you wish." Holmes grunted. "Tell them I am dead, for all I care."

"I am not very good at fabricating lies!"

"Come now, Watson!" laughed Holmes. "You underestimate your abilities as a fabulist. You have yet to chronicle a single case of mine where you have not played fast and loose with the facts."

The following day, after leaving Victoria Station where he had seen Holmes off to the Continent, Watson returned to Baker Street to contemplate those empty rooms. Later, while a glazier set about repairing the shattered windows, Watson sat at his friend's desk and started writing what he felt might very well be the last story in which he would ever record the singular gifts that had distinguished the best and wisest man he had ever known.

Tom English is an environmental chemist for a US defense contractor. As therapy he runs Dead Letter Press and writes curious tales of the supernatural. His recent fiction can be found in the anthology *Dead Souls* (edited by Mark Deniz for Morrigan Books) and issues of *All Hallows* (The Journal of the Ghost Story Society). He also edited *Bound for Evil*, a 2008 Shirley Jackson Award finalist for Best Anthology, featuring stories about strange, often deadly books. Tom resides with his wife, Wilma, and their Sheltie, Misty, deep in the woods of New Kent, Virginia.

THE COLOR THAT CAME TO CHISWICK

by William Meikle

I hoped that my friend Sherlock Holmes would be more settled when I called on him that evening in May of '87. His recovery
from his travails in France, and the subsequent excitement in
Reigate, meant that a period of house rest was prescribed. As
ever, he paid little attention to my ministrations and pleadings,
and over the course of the previous fortnight had driven poor
Mrs. Hudson to despair with a series of petty requests.

On my last visit she had pleaded with me to do my best to
calm my *patient*. Indeed, she had worked herself into such a state
that I do believe had any longer time passed it would have been
her, and not Holmes, who would be coming under my ministrations.

It was Holmes himself who greeted me as I entered the house
in Baker Street.

"Come in Doctor Watson," he said in a near perfect impression of Mrs. Hudson's Scots brogue. "You'll be wanting some
tea?"

He laughed, and fair bounded up the stairs to his apartment.
I had not seen him in such good humour for several months.

I discovered why on entering his rooms ... he had a new
case. Several sheaves of paper lay scattered on his desk, his brass
microscope was in use off to one side, and a glass retort bubbled
and seethed above a paraffin burner. An acrid odor hung in the
air, thick, almost chewable. The whole place reeked of it, despite
the fact that the windows were all open to their fullest extent.

Holmes noticed my discomfort.

"It is nothing," he said.

"I doubt Mrs. Hudson will agree," I said.

"Do not worry Watson," Holmes said. "Our esteemed land-lady has gone to Earls Court with the widow Murray."

"The Wild West show? Yes, I have seen the posters around town. It is said it will be a great spectacle."

I had wished to inquire as to Holmes' opinion on the authenticity of Mr. Cody's show, but it was obvious that his mind was already elsewhere. He stood over the microscope, studying the slide contents intently.

"What have you got there Holmes?"

In answer he passed me a sheet of paper.

"This came in several hours ago."

It was a note on letter-headed paper, from the Fullers Brewery in Chiswick, and addressed to *Sherlock Holmes, Consulting Detective* at this Baker Street address. The note proved to be short and to the point.

"Dear Mr. Holmes," it began. "In the past three days we have encountered several problems with our brewing processes in our main Tuns. We suspect sabotage, but are unable to prove the cause, and our own chemists have drawn a blank. I have sent a sample from our latest fermentation, and would appreciate some of your time in its study. I shall be happy to discuss your remuneration by return of post."

It was signed, *Gerard Jones, Chief Brewer.*

"Examine the paper," Holmes said. "There is something peculiar on the left edge near the bottom."

I immediately saw what he meant. The edge seemed bevelled and on closer examination proved to have a greenish tinge.

"What is it Holmes? Some form of algal growth perhaps?"

"That is what I am trying to determine," Holmes replied. "But so far I am having little success."

He motioned me towards a jar that had been partially hidden behind the microscope.

"The sample mentioned within the letter is there. See what you make of it Watson."

As soon as I picked up the jar I knew I had never seen anything like it before.

The jar held a pint of fluid but it did not look like anything resembling any fermentation of ale I had ever seen. As I held it up towards my face the contents shifted and the acrid odor grew so strong that I almost gagged as it caught at the back of my throat. The fluid was thick, almost solid, and a deep emerald green. It flowed, as if the whole thing were a single organism.

"It seems to have some of the properties of a slime mould," Holmes said. "And it responds to external stimuli with a range of defensive adaptations."

Holmes took the jar from me and placed it close to the paraffin burner. The green substance surged, piling up against the glass wall of the container.

"And this is in the vats in the brewery?"

Holmes nodded.

"It would appear so. Our task is to prove whether it has been introduced deliberately, or whether it is an accident of nature... of some kind."

Holmes allowed me to study the sample he had mounted on the slide. There was no evidence of any cellular structure, or any differentiation in the material. Nothing existed to show that the thing was in any way alive. Yet it clearly moved. Even the small amount present on the slide pushed and surged against its confines with such violence that I stood back quickly in surprise. In doing so I knocked the bottom stage of the microscope, and swung the mirror away such that it no longer lit on the slide. I bent to rectify the problem but stopped as soon as I looked in the eyepiece.

Despite the lack of light I could still clearly see the sample. It glowed, giving forth a faint green luminescence. When I pointed this out to Holmes he at once drew the curtains and dimmed the lamps. It immediately became apparent that there was far more to our problem material than we realized.

The full expanse of Holmes' desk glowed a sickly green, the miasma hanging in the air a full two feet or more above the surface. Holmes showed me his hands ... they too shone dimly.

I frog-marched him downstairs and both of us scoured our hands with carbolic soap until no trace of green remained. When we went back upstairs the sight that met us made us pause in the doorway.

The curtains were still closed, however the darkness only accentuated the effect. The sample jar sat square in the middle of Holmes' desk and the air seemed to dance, an aurora of light hovering in an almost perfect globe around it.

Armed with vinegar and salt I set to cleaning and disinfecting as much as I could see. Holmes could scarcely take his eyes from the jar and merely stood, contemplating the sheer *strangeness* of it, as I worked.

I was nearly finished in my task when a knock came downstairs. Holmes requested that I answer, and I went down, opening the door to Inspector Lestrade. He too was given pause by the sight of the jar on the desk, and might have been standing there yet, had Holmes not pressed him about his business. Even then he did not take his eyes from the jar.

"I understand you are commissioned on following up on the sabotage at the Fullers Brewery?"

Holmes refused to either confirm or deny this fact, as Lestrade continued.

"The saboteur has upped the ante," he said. "We have a brewer in hospital and foul play is suspected... a poison as yet unidentified." He was still staring at the desk. "I presume this came from Chiswick?"

As ever Holmes stayed quiet, but he did request that I accompany Lestrade to the hospital to talk to the stricken man.

Holmes motioned towards the jar.

"The study of this requires more rigor than I can provide here," he said. "I shall remove this to the safety of a laboratory at the University and seek council from several Society Fellows. I shall meet you later in the Brewery."

Lestrade was unusually quiet in the carriage on the way to the hospital, and would not speak of the condition of the victim.

"I would rather not prejudice your opinion Doctor," was all he would say on the matter. I began to understand why when I was shown into a small room in the hospital. The corridor outside smelled strongly of carbolic soap, and I noted a strange reticence on the part of the staff to venture close to the doorway.

I walked inside to find a young man writhing on the bed, tearing at his throat.

I called for assistance and moved to his aid. A bloody dressing, a green smudge clearly visible, lay discarded on the bedcovers. The man's head turned to look at me. The whole bottom half of his face was a bubbling mess of green-tinged gore.

Lestrade came quickly to my side and pinned the man's arms, holding him down. Just the sight of us seemed to calm him somewhat, but he was obviously in great pain. His wounds seethed, the green slime seeming to feast on his flesh. I have seen many men die of disease and corruption in warmer climes, but nothing of this speed or destructive capability.

I had just bent to tend to the man when he screamed louder and his eye *popped*. Green-tinged fluid ran down his cheek and started to bubble at the join of neck and shoulder. The covers fell away from his chest and Lestrade moved aside, retching. Below the waist there was little left of the man, merely a rolling mess of green slime. The patient was past caring. He gripped my left hand tight and squeezed, just once, before the life went out of him completely.

I decided not to wait to see if the slime would continue progressing after the death of its host. I dragged a sickly-looking Lestrade from the room and called once more for assistance. This time it was forthcoming.

The poor man's remains were quickly removed, and both Lestrade and I went with them to the incinerator, standing there for long minutes to ensure that the job was done properly. I also ensured that all who had been in contact with the patient, Lestrade and myself included, washed thoroughly with soap and hot water. I checked us both for any hint of the slime. Lestrade continued to look pale and sickly, even after I gave us the all clear.

"What in God's name did that to the man?" he asked me. I'm afraid I did not have an answer for him. But I resolved there and then to find out. I would not stand to watch any more men die in such a fashion — not if I were able to do something about it.

I left Lestrade in the hospital to clear up the situation and headed for the brewery.

It was late evening by the time a cab deposited me outside the brewery. The sound of cheering and applause came faintly across the river from where Mrs. Hudson was no doubt enjoying the spectacle of gunplay and horsemanship. Standing there in the quiet dark I began to regret not bringing my own weapon on the trip.

There was no sign of Holmes, or indeed of anyone else. I knew that any large London brewery should be running an overnight operation, given the thirst of the population for their product. For the brewery to be sitting in darkness was an ominous sign. I considered waiting for Holmes, but all my thoughts were of that poor man's pitiful death in the hospital room. I had a feeling that, if I wanted to stop further deaths, I would need to move quickly. This contagion had a manner that suggested it would spread rapidly. It was not as Holmes' companion, but as a doctor, that I crossed the road to the brewery.

I was grateful for what little light came from the gas lamps around the walls, but their flame only accentuated the shadows in the tall empty hall. Four large copper vats dominated the large room. The air smelled almost sweet, with a hint of bitterness where fresh hops joined the tang of fermentation. Beneath these well-remembered odors I also sensed something new — a hint of the same acrid tang that had assaulted my nasal passages back in Holmes' room. Before I stepped further than the doorway I peered into all the corners, searching for any trace of the luminescence. I found none. Nevertheless it was with some trepidation that I stepped inside.

It was obvious to me that someone had deliberately introduced a poisonous material into the brewing vats. Their reason was as yet unclear to me, but the thought that this might have been going on for some time made my blood run cold. There might even, at this very moment, be drinkers quaffing tainted ales all across the capital. In my mind's eye I saw the slime *seethe* in the flagons, saw the terror in the drinkers' eyes as the contagion took them and started to feed. The fear of the consequences strengthened my resolve. I moved further inside.

A cloud moved. Suddenly moonlight washed through the hall from above. It made my search somewhat easier. I found nothing around the nearer of the two vats and almost relaxed. That all changed when I rounded the third vat and almost walked into a mist of green luminescence. As I moved closer I saw that it rose from a body on the floor — the remains of what had been a man, but was now a seething mass of green protoplasm. The slime seemed to notice my presence and began to slump and flow over the brewery floor, moving so quickly that I was forced to take several steps backwards.

My retreat was halted as the luminescence swelled and flared, engulfing me in a globe of dancing light. At once I felt calm, almost serene. Shadows flitted around me, wraiths made of little more than thin green fog. I felt no fear, no compulsion to run — merely the innocent curiosity of a child. I stepped forward towards the rolling carpet of green.

The arrival of my friend Sherlock Holmes saved my life. All he did was place a hand on my shoulder, but that was sufficient to break the spell under which I had been placed. I looked down to see the green slime merely inches from my brogues and getting closer.

Holmes stepped forward and threw a handful of white powder over the green carpet. It immediately retreated, black pustules bubbling and bursting across the surface. My eyes started to sting and water. Holmes turned and smiled grimly, showing me another handful of white powder.

"Caustic soda," he said. "It seems to be efficacious."

He wore a canvas satchel over his shoulder. It gaped wide, showing it to be crammed full with the powder. Before I could inquire further Holmes strode away from me, following the retreating slime.

"Come Watson," he called. "Let us beard Grendel in his lair."

I followed, keeping a safe distance from the scattering of lye. The slime dragged itself away before the powder. A high, fluting cacophony echoed and whistled around us, as if the bubbling pustules screamed in agony. Within seconds Holmes had the remains of the creature cornered under the copper vat in the leftmost rear of the brewery.

Holmes continued to throw handfuls of lye, at the same time calling out to me over his shoulder.

"Watson. I have need of your old pen-knife."

I moved forward, following Holmes' gaze. There was a large dent in the tun just above head height. Deep inside was a small lump of darker material, like a pebble embedded in the copper.

I took out my knife and started to work the lump free while Holmes kept the carpet of slime at bay. I was so intent on my task I did not notice the new arrivals on the brewery floor, only becoming aware of them when Holmes called out in despair.

"No. Not yet!"

I managed to free the pebble and dropped it into my waistcoat pocket. I turned to see three men clad in oilskins standing behind Holmes. They each carried long hoses and were spraying the floor all around. Suddenly the place smelled less like a brewery and more like a hospital as soap and bleach washed over our feet.

My brogues were ruined, as were Holmes' leather boots, but he had not yet noticed. His gaze was fixed on a drain in the center of the floor. It sat in a slight dip, so that all spillage would flow towards it. The pressure from the hoses washed across the slime and sent it sailing in bubbling foam.

"Stop!" Holmes called, but it was too late. The last hint of the green substance disappeared down to the sewers below.

We found Lestrade out in the street coordinating proceedings. The hosing down of the brewery went on for several hours while we stood outside, smoking and keeping an eye out for any return of either the slime or the luminescence. After a time

Lestrade announced himself satisfied and called off the clear up. Holmes proved harder to satisfy. He insisted on waiting until almost dawn, spending the intervening hours stalking the floor and peering in every corner of the brewery. Twice he asked to see the *pebble* I had dug from the vat. Both times he returned it to me with a grunt of displeasure. The sun was throwing an orange tinge across the sky before I was finally able to persuade him to leave.

He said nothing in the carriage on the journey to Baker Street, merely sat, elbows on his thighs and fingers steepled at his lips, deep in thought.

Mrs. Hudson ministered to our hunger, providing a hearty breakfast that I took to with gusto. Holmes scarcely ate a mouthful. He had already taken the pebble from me, and pored over it intently, subjecting it to a variety of assays and investigations. By the time I finished my breakfast he seemed to have come to some conclusions. He called me over and handed me a magnifying lens.

"I believe we have found our source," he said to me. I immediately saw what he meant. The *pebble* was a small rough stone. Holmes had managed to slice it in half and I looked down at the inner hemisphere. There was a small hollow almost dead center, hardly bigger than my little finger nail. It carried the barest tinge of green.

"The stone itself is mostly iron," Holmes said. "With a trace of nickel. I do believe you are holding your first visitor from beyond this world."

After that Holmes seemed to settle somewhat. We sat by the fire and lit our pipes. He repeatedly quizzed me on my *experience* inside the luminescence.

"It was dashed peculiar Holmes," I said. "I have experienced something similar before, while watching a Swami perform the rope trick in Delhi, but even there I felt in control. This time it felt like my very will had been drained from me. If you had not intervened, I do believe I would have given myself to it."

Holmes nodded, and went back to staring into the fire.

I left in the early morning to fulfill an obligation to a sick friend. When I returned Holmes was scarcely in any better spirits. I found him on the doorstep, delivering instructions to a group of urchins who were gathered around him as he distributed pennies.

As I entered I saw Mrs. Hudson packing cleaning materials back into the cupboard.

"Please Doctor. Can you not get him to settle? He'll be the death of me with all this commotion."

Holmes seemed oblivious to his landlady's protestations.

"We must be vigilant," he said, as we once more sat by the fire. "As a doctor you well know the dangers of contagion re-emerging after a period of dormancy."

I saw that a black mood had descended on my friend, one that only action might shift, but there was no news forthcoming. In the late afternoon I went to stoke the fire. I searched for the old pair of bellows I customarily used, but they were nowhere to be found, and Holmes merely smiled at my mention of them.

We sat in conversation as darkness started to fall once again, our discussions ranging wildly with much speculation as to the nature of the green organism. Despite our intellects, we were unable to come to any firm conclusions. And I disagreed vehemently with one proffered by Holmes.

"I suspect a rudimentary intelligence is at work," Holmes said. "That much was obvious in the way you yourself were lured into the trap."

I tried to argue the case for instinct, citing many examples in the animal world of trap setting, but by then Holmes was once again deep in thought. I contented myself with a fresh pipe of tobacco as I made some notes on the progress of the case so far.

Matters came to a head in the late evening.

"My eyes and ears are ready for anything out of the usual," Holmes had said.

The news brought by the urchin who came to the door certainly qualified as *out of the usual*. To my eyes he looked like any other grime-ingrained child of the streets, but Holmes immediately saw something I had not.

"It is on a boat?" he asked, even before the child had spoken.

The child smiled, showing more gaps than teeth.

"That it is Mr. Holmes sir. 'Tis down at Vauxhall Bridge. They say 'tis a *ghost ship*, for it is all quiet and green like. Ain't nobody going near 'till the coppers have had a look. That Inspector Lestrade has been sent for."

Holmes gave the lad a thrupenny bit and sent him on his way. I was dispatched to find a cab. Holmes himself went back inside and returned wearing a heavy coat. It seemed to bulge at the back, as if he carried something bulky underneath, but I knew from experience not to ask until he was ready for his revelation.

I only asked one question on the trip down to Vauxhall.

"How did you know about the boat Holmes?"

He smiled thinly.

"The boy had fresh pitch on his fingers. I smelled it even before I saw it. There is only one place you find tar of that sort — on the deck of a boat."

He said no more as we bounced through the city, rattling like peas inside the cab. Holmes had requested speed and offered extra payment. The driver did not disappoint and had us at Vauxhall in record time, if a little shaken.

A small crowd had gathered on the bridge, looking down at a moored boat. Despite the fact it was not quite yet full dark, the luminescence was immediately apparent, a dancing green light that ran up the masts and along the rigging of the schooner. The gathered watchers had the good sense to stay well back.

The same could not be said of the two policemen down on the dock itself. Holmes shouted a warning, but they took no heed, stepping onto the boat while we were as yet too far away to go to their aid. By the time Holmes and I descended the steps to the dock the policemen had already gone aboard and disappeared down into the hold.

Holmes was in no mood to wait. He ran down the steps and I was hard pressed to keep up with him as he jumped on board the boat. I joined him at the hatchway leading to the hold. I realized we were already inside the glow of the luminescence, but I felt none of the compulsion I had undergone earlier. Nevertheless my heart beat a little faster as we went down in to the bowels of the vessel.

Screams rose from beneath us. Holmes shed his overcoat. I stood behind him so was not able to see the full scope of the apparatus, but he carried two metal tanks on his back, secured at the shoulders with thick canvas straps. The tanks looked heavy, but did not slow Holmes as he descended the steep steps to the hold. Saying a silent prayer I followed close behind.

At first it seemed we stood in impenetrable darkness but as my eyes adjusted I began to make out shape and shadow around us. The screams we had followed had already faded, replaced by the sound of piteous weeping to our left. I could make out Holmes ahead of me as we moved towards the wails.

We were too late to do anything for the poor policemen. One lay dead, green foam at lips and ears. The other would be following him soon. Most of his chest was a bubbling ruin. He tried to speak but green fluid poured from his mouth and even as I bent to his aid he fell back, eyes wide, staring, unseeing.

I realized I could see Holmes' face, his pale features seemingly behind a green mask. I turned to see the source of this new light. The entire far end of the hold was an aurora, sickly green shot through with an oily sheen, which cast rainbows before it. Under other circumstances it might even be called beautiful.

Below the swirling lights lay a darker patch that seemed to *ripple*. I saw two ale casks, broken into splinters — the source of this recent outbreak.

Holmes walked forward towards it. I saw he held his fire-bellows in hand. A soft hose led to the tank on his back. He pushed the bellows together and sent a spray of liquid ahead of him. I smelled bleach. The shimmering light flared then faded and the dark green mass retreated.

Holmes kept walking, close enough to reach out towards the green luminescence.

"Careful, Holmes," I called.

"I must know," he said, almost a whisper. "Is it an invader, or a missionary?"

Before I could stop him he stepped inside the glow. I was about to step up beside him, but he raised a hand. I heard his voice as if from a great distance.

"Stay back Watson," he said. "This won't take but a minute."

The dancing light played around him and the green carpet at his feet seethed, but still Holmes stood perfectly still. I saw him reach forward with his free hand and play it through the light. A new rainbow followed his movements.

"Fascinating," I heard him say, then he went completely quiet. The slime at his feet started to creep again, moving towards Holmes. He showed no sign of trying to avoid or avert it. I moved to one side to look at his face. He had a glazed, far off look, lost in reverie.

He had fallen into its snare.

With a yell I leapt forward, just as the slime surged. As he had done for me, I placed a hand on his shoulder. At once the spell was broken … and just in time. The light flared so bright as to be almost blinding. At the same moment the slime surged, again a wave flowing over Holmes' feet and ankles. He pushed at the bellows, twice, spraying bleach around us. Once again I heard the high fluting screams, deafening in the confines of the hold, as pustules formed and burst all across the creeping carpet.

The slime retreated.

I pulled at Holmes' shoulder.

"Quick Holmes, let us beat a retreat before it returns."

"Not yet, Watson, there is something at the heart of this that bends its will against us. I would rather like to have a look at it."

He projected more bleach in the direction of the slime and it fell back.

It was darker now, the luminescence having shrunk and faded until it ran in a layer less than an inch thick over the surface of the rolling slime. We followed its retreat across the hold until we stood before the burst and broken barrels. The remains of the slime had retreated to the shelter of a curved section that seemed nearly intact.

Holmes motioned me forward and we peered into the gloom.

"Take a close look Watson," Holmes said. "We may never see its like again."

A darker patch of green sat there in the midst of the last small puddle of slime, an oval shape like a large dark egg. An oily green sheen ran over it and it pulsed rhythmically, almost as if it were breathing.

"Is this the source of the contagion?" I asked.

Holmes nodded.

"Although I am no longer sure of its intelligence. I detected nothing while under its influence to suggest it is anything other than what it seems."

I watched the thing pulse.

"And what do you suggest Holmes? We cannot allow this thing to escape into the general population."

Holmes was deep in thought.

"Indeed Watson. And while the scientists at the University would love to study this, there is a chance that the military would gain hold of it. I have heard of their experiments with Mustard gas. This thing would merely give them another excuse for developing weapons of terrible destruction."

I could see it in my mind. Whole battalions marching on a field of green, heads raised to the heavens in screams as they *melted* from the feet up.

My decision was simple.

"End it Holmes. End it here."

He nodded and squeezed the bellows. The slime surged, one last time, and then fell back, smoking. One final high whistle pierced the air then it was gone.

We stood there for a long time, watching, but all that remained of the terror from beyond was a patch of blackened material among the broken debris of the barrels.

WILLIAM MEIKLE is a Scottish writer with ten novels published in the genre press and over 200 short story credits in thirteen countries. He is the author of the ongoing Midnight Eye series among others, and his work appears in a number of professional anthologies. He lives in a remote corner of Newfoundland with icebergs, whales and bald eagles for company. In the winters he gets warm vicariously through the lives of others in cyberspace and drinks a lot of beer … some of it from Chiswick.

FROM THE TREE OF TIME

by Fred Saberhagen
(from an idea by Eric Saberhagen)

"Very well then," said Count Dracula. "If you wish a story of mystification, I can provide one."

It was a raw, rainy spring night, not long ago, and the two of us were standing on a street corner in a northern city. Folk far madder and perhaps less probable than either the Prince of Wallachia or myself walked those streets as well, but in the presence of my companion I scarcely gave them a thought.

"I will be delighted," I replied, naturally enough, "to hear whatever tale you may wish to tell."

Dracula halted at a curb, the wet cold wind stirring his black hair as he stared moodily across the street. He had doubtless paused only to gather his thoughts, but a quartet of youths swaggering along on the other side of the street interpreted our hesitation as timidity. They loitered in their own walk, and one of their number called some obscenity in our direction. My companion did not appear to notice.

"I am sure you are aware," he began his tale to me, "that with vampires, as with the greater mass of the breathing population, the vast majority are peaceable, law-abiding citizens. We seek no more, essentially, than breathers do: bodily nourishment (any animal blood will do for sustenance); the contemplation of beauty, and affection, as nourishment for the soul; an interesting occupation; a time and place in which to rest (some native soil being, in our case, very important for that purpose).

"It makes me laugh" —he laughed, and across the street four youths simultaneously remembered pressing

business elsewhere— "yes, laugh, to contemplate the preposterous attributes that have been bestowed upon my branch of
the human race by those breathing legendizers who have never
known even one of us at first hand. Of course I am not talking
about you, my friend. I mean those who have learned nothing
since the last century, when the arch-fool Van Helsing could
imagine that the symbols and the substance of religion are to
us automatically repellent or even deadly. As you know, that is
no more true of us than of — of some of the breathing gangsters
who once made this very city legend."

My friend paused, frowning, doubtless wishing that he had
chosen some other comparison. I hastened to assure him that
I would do all in my literary power to expunge from human
thought the kinds of misinformation that he found so distaste-
ful. He nodded abstractedly.

"Nevertheless," he went on, "in our society as in yours, the
rogue, the criminal, exists. I need not belabor the point that the
psychopath who happens also to be a vampire is infinitely more
dangerous than his mundane breathing counterpart. Even apart
from the fact that very few of your breathing people truly believe
that we exist, effective countermeasures against our criminal
element, while not impossible, appear to be uncommonly difficult for you to manage. The Cross, as I have said, is no deterrent
at all — except perhaps to vampires of such religious nature that
their consciences would be painfully affected by the sight: such
probably do not pose you a major problem in any event.

"Garlic? Even less efficacious than it would be against some
breathing ruffian — surely useful, if at all, only against the more
fastidious and less determined. Mirrors? Useful to detect and
identify us by our lack of any reflection; but with no application as weapons, except as they might be used to concentrate our
great bane, natural sunlight. The older and tougher among us
can bear some sun, you know, at least the cloudy, tempered sun
of the high latitudes.

"Fire? By daylight, through which period we are compelled
to retain whatever form we had at dawn — and moreover are
likely to be resting in lethargic trance — yes by daylight, fire can
be effective, whereas by night we easily avoid it.

"Ordinary bullets, blades of metal, clubs of stone, all can cause
us momentary pain and superficial injury, but do us virtually no
real damage at all. Any trifling harm inflicted soon disappears.
Silver bullets are only advocated by those who confuse us with
werewolves, or certain other creatures of the night.

"The best practical defence is doubtless to remain in your own house, admitting no one suspicious. No vampire may enter a true dwelling unless invited — but once invited, he or she may return at any time.

"And, if we consider the offensive means that ordinary breathing folk can hope to use successfully against us, almost the whole truth is contained in one short and simple word."

By now we were strolling again. My companion was of course impervious to the chilling effects of wind and rain, but I was shivering. Taking note of this, Dracula gestured as we were passing the door of a decent appearing tavern, and gratefully I preceded him in. We were seated in a dim, snug corner with mugs of Irish coffee before us — his of course remained untouched throughout our stay — before he spoke again.

"That one word," he said, "is wood. Ah, wood, that oh-so-nearly-magical stuff, that once was living and now is not. Ah, wood... and that leads me to the story that I wish to tell."

It was (Dracula continued) almost a century ago, and in another great city, one grimier and in some ways grander than this one, that I made acquaintance — never mind now exactly how — with a certain professional investigator, a consulting detective whose name was then even better known than my own. We were an oddly matched pair, yet on good terms; he understood my nature better than most breathing folk have ever been able to do. Still I was greatly surprised one day when I received a message from him saying that he wished my help in a professional consultation. Naturally my curiosity was much aroused, and I agreed.

My friend the detective and I traveled down by train from London to a certain country estate in Kent. The house was a great gloomy pile, built during Elizabethan times. Its owner, besides being a man of considerable wealth, was something of an antiquarian, and also much interested in what he still called natural philosophy. It was not he, however, who had invited us to the estate, but his only child. She was a grown woman, and married for a year. And it was she-whose real name I cannot tell you even now, for at the time I swore that it would never pass my lips — she who conducted us on our arrival, with urgent speed, into a closed room for a private consultation. The room was large, and mostly lined with books, with new electric lights in its far corners, and on the huge desk an old-fashioned oil lamp, whose rays fell on a collection of curious items evidently brought together from the ends of the earth. I saw a whale's tooth, a monkey's skull, along with other items I did not immediately recognize. A small table at some distance from the desk held a microscope and various specimens. Along with their burden of books, the room's many shelves held stuffed birds and animals.

"And now, your ladyship" began my friend the detective, "we are at your service. You may speak as freely before Dr. Corday here" —he glanced in my direction— "as before myself."

The lady, whose considerable beauty was obviously being worn away by some overwhelming fear or worry, now appeared on the verge of collapse. "Very well." She drew a deep, exhausted breath. "I must be brief, for my father and my husband will both soon return, and I must save them, if I can...

"The incident that haunts me, that has driven me to the brink of madness, occurred almost exactly a year ago, and in this very room. I must confess to you that before I was married, or even knew Richard well, I was acquainted with a man, named Hayden. I have outlined to you already, sir, how that came to be—"

"You have indeed, your ladyship." My companion gave an impatient nod. "Since our time is short, we had better concentrate on what happened between you and Hayden in this very room, as you say it was. That is the aspect of the case in which I most value Dr. Corday's consultation."

"You are right." Our hostess paused again to collect herself, then plunged on. "I had not seen Hayden for many months. I was beginning to manage to forget him, when almost on the very eve of my wedding, he appeared here unexpectedly. I was alone in the house except for a few servants, my father being engaged on some last-minute business in London having to do with the arrangements.

"Hayden, of course, knew that I was alone. And his purpose in coming was an evil one. He had brought with him some letters — they were foolish letters indeed — that I had written him in an earlier day. The letters contained... certain things that could have ruined me, had Hayden given them, as he threatened to do, to my prospective husband. I protested my innocence. He admitted it, but read from the letters certain phrases, words I had almost forgotten, that suggested otherwise. Hayden would destroy me, he swore, unless — unless 'Here and now in this very room' was how he put it — I should — should—"

For a moment the lady could not continue. My friend and I exchanged glances, of sympathy and determination, in a silent pledge that we would do everything possible to assist her. It must be hard for folk with experience only of the late twentieth century to grasp what a threat such letters could represent, to understand what impact the mere suggestion of a premarital affair could have had at that time and place, on one in her position. It would have been regarded by all her contemporaries as the literal ruin of the young lady's life.

"I was innocent," she repeated, when she was able to resume at last. "I swear to you both that I was. Yet that man had some devilish power, influence... I had broken free of it before, and as he faced me in this room I swore to myself that I would never allow it to gain the faintest hold on me again.

"'Sooner or later you will have me', the villain said, sneering at me. 'I have now been invited into your fine house, you see.' Those were his words, and I have puzzled over them; alas, a greater and more horrible puzzle was to come.

"I retreated to the desk — I stood here in front of it, like this. Hayden was just there, and he advanced upon me. I cried at him to stay away. My hand, behind me on the desk, closed on a piece of stone — much like this one." With that her ladyship raised what would now be called a geode from among the curios collected on the huge desk. "I raised it — like this — and warned him again to stop.

"Hayden only smiled at me — no, sneered — as if the idea that I might refuse him, even resist him, were a childish fantasy that only a childish creature like myself — a mere woman — could entertain. He sneered at me, I say! His handsome face was hideously transformed, and it seemed to me that even his teeth were... were... and he came on toward me, his hands reaching out."

The lovely narrator raised her chin. "I hit him, gentlemen. With the stone. With all my strength. And — God help me — I think it was as much because of the way in which he looked at me, so contemptuously, as it was because of anything I feared that he might do.

"I hit him, and he fell backward, with a broad smear of blood across his forehead. I have the impression that only one of his eyes was still open, and that it was looking at me with the most intense surprise. He fell backward, and rolled halfway over on the carpet, and was still.

"I was perfectly sure, looking down at his smashed face, that he was dead. Dead. And I swear to you that at that moment I felt nothing but relief... but for a moment only. Then the horror began. Not an intrinsic horror at what I had done — that came to me too, but later — but horror at the fact that what I had just done was certain to be discovered, and at other discoveries that must flow from that. Even though I might — I almost certainly would — be able to plead self defence and avoid any legal penalty, yet inevitably enough information must be made public to bring ruin down upon me — and disgrace upon Richard, whom I loved...

"I suppose that in that moment I was half mad with shock and grief. Not, you understand, grief for the one who, as I thought, lay dead—"

My friend interrupted. "As you thought?"

"As — let me finish, and in a moment you will understand."

"Then pray continue."

"My eye fell on the door of the lumber room — there." It was a plain, small, inconspicuous door, set in the wall between bookcases, some eight or ten feet from the desk. "I seized Hayden by the ankles — to take him by the hands would have meant touching his skin, and the thought of that was utterly abhorrent to me — and I dragged him into there."

"May I?"

"Of course."

Taking up the lamp from the desk, my friend moved to open the small door, which was unlocked. The lamplight shining in revealed a dusty storage closet. Its walls and floor were of stone, its ceiling of solid wood; there was no window, or any other door. The chamber was half-filled with a miscellany of boxes, crates, and bundles, none larger than a bushel, and all covered with a fine film of dust that might well have lain undisturbed for the past year.

Our client joined us looking in. She said: "The room was very much as you see it now. My father uses it chiefly for storage of things he has brought back from his various travels and then never finds time to catalogue, or else judges at second thought to be not worthy of display.

"I dragged Hayden — or his body — in there, and left him on the dusty floor.

"Understand that this was not part of any thought-out plan for concealing what I had done. It was only a shocked reaction, like that of a child trying to hide the pieces of a broken vase. Hardly aware of what I was doing, I came back here to the middle of the room, and picked up from the carpet the stone that had done the deed. I carried it into the lumber-room also, and threw it on top of that which lay on the floor already. I then came out of the lumber-room and closed its door, and locked it — though it is rarely if ever locked — with a key I knew was kept in the top drawer of my father's desk.

"Then, with my mind still whirling in terror, I looked around. The letters, where were they? Still in Hayden's pocket, for now I remembered distinctly seeing him replace them there. It might be wise to get them out, but for the moment I could not think of touching him again.

"And there was blood on the carpet. I had noted that already, in my frenzied panic. But now, as my mind made its first adjustment back toward sanity, I saw that the spots were only two or three in number, and so small against the dark pattern that no one entering the study casually would be in the least likely to notice them. Here, gentlemen, is where they were — over the past year they have faded almost to invisibility."

My companion had crouched down and whipped out a magnifying glass, with which he scrutinized closely the indicated section of the carpet. He stood up frowning. "Pray continue," he said again, his voice non-committal.

"I was still hovering near the desk, in a state of near-panic, not knowing what to do, when as in a nightmare I heard a brisk knock on the door to the hall, and the voice of my beloved Richard. A moment later, before I could say anything at all, the hall door opened and Richard came in. From the look on his face, I knew immediately that he was aware, at least, that something was gravely wrong.

"My fiancé evidently already knew much more about Hayden than I had ever suspected. Perhaps the duke, Richard's father, had employed investigators — to this day I do not know what had made my dear one suspicious of me. But he was full of suspicion on that day, and with cause — though not with as great cause as he feared.

"Richard confronted me. 'He was seen coming in here, the man Hayden. Do you tell me that he is not here now?'"

"I do not remember what I said in reply. I must, however, have looked the very picture of guilt.

"Richard looked quickly round the study, even peering behind pieces of furniture where a man might possibly have had room to lie concealed. It took him only a moment to do so; the furniture was then very much as it is now, and offered, as you can see, little in the way of hiding places.

"He tried the door of the lumber-room then, and I was sure for a moment that my heart had stopped.

"'This door is locked. Do you know, Louise, where the key is kept?'"

"I understood perfectly that he would force the door at once if no key were available. Silently I went to the desk, and got the key from the upper drawer, where, in my confusion I had just replaced it; I handed it to Richard, still without a word. At that moment I knew with certainty that final ruin was upon me, and I could not bear another instant the horror of waiting for the blow to fall. I thought that after Richard had seen what I had done, then, in that moment of his greatest shock, I might appeal to him. I could only hope that he loved me as truly and deeply as I did him.

"But his gaze was black and forbidding as he took the key from my hand and turned away. He was in the lumber-room for only a few moments, but I need not tell you what an eternity they seemed to me. When he reappeared, his face was altered; yet even as I gazed at him in despair, a sudden new hope was born within my breast. For his new expression was not so much one of horror or shock, as one expressing a great relief, even though mingled with shame and bewilderment.

"For a moment he could not speak. Then 'Darling', he said at last, and his voice cracked, even as mine had moments earlier. 'Can you ever forgive me for having doubted you?'"

"Without answering, I pushed past Richard to the door of the lumber-room.

Everything inside, with one great exception, was just as I had seen it a few minutes earlier before I had locked the door. There were the dusty crates and cartons untouched, certainly, by any human hand in the intervening time. There on the floor, in lighter dust and hardly noticeable, were the tracks left by my own feet on my first entrance, and by the horrible burden that I had dragged in with such difficulty. There was the stone with which I had struck the fateful blow — but the piece of stone lay now in the middle of the otherwise empty patch of bare floor. Of the body of the man I had struck down there was not the smallest trace."

My friend the detective emitted a faint sigh, expressing what, in the circumstances, seemed a rather inhuman degree of intellectual satisfaction. 'Most interesting indeed," he murmured soothingly. "And then?"

"There is very little more that I can tell you. I murmured something to Richard; he, assuming that my state of near-collapse was all his fault for behaving, as he said, brutally, made amends to the best of his ability. To make the story short, we were married as planned. Hayden's name has never since been mentioned between us. Our life together has been largely uneventful, and in all outward aspects happy. But I tell you, gentlemen — since that day I have lived in inward terror… either I am mad, and therefore doomed, and imagined the whole ghastly scene in which I murdered Hayden; or I did not imagine it. Then he was only stunned. He somehow extricated himself from that lumber-room. He is lying in wait for me. Somewhere, sometime… neither of you know him, what he can be like… he still has the letters, yet he has in mind some revenge that would be even more horrible… I tell you I can bear it no longer…" The lady sank into a chair, struggling to control herself.

The detective turned to me. "Dr. Corday, it is essential that we ascertain the — nature of this man Hayden." A meaningful glance assured me what sort of variations in nature he had in mind.

I nodded, and addressed myself to the lady, who had now somewhat recovered.

"At what time of day, madam, did these events occur? Can we be absolutely sure that they took place after dawn and before sunset?"

The lady looked for a moment as if she suspected that madness was my problem instead of hers. "In broad daylight, surely," she replied at last. "Though what possible difference…"

I signed to my friend that I must speak to him in confidence. After a hurried apology to our client we withdrew to a far corner of the study. "The man she knocked down", I informed the detective there, "could not possibly have been a vampire, because the force of the blow that felled him was borne in stone, to which we are immune. Nor could he, even supposing him to be a vampire, have shifted form in broad daylight, and escaped as a mist from that closet under the conditions we have heard described. Nor could he in daylight have taken on the form of a small animal and hidden himself somewhere among those crates and boxes."

"You are quite sure of all that?"

"Quite."

"Very good." My friend received my expert opinion with evident satisfaction, which surprised me.

For my own part, it seemed to me that we were getting nowhere. "My life has been very long," I added, "and active, if not always well spent. I have seen madness… much madness.

And I tell you that the lady here, if I am any judge, is neither mad nor subject to hallucinations."

"In that opinion I concur." Still my friend did not appear nearly as disconcerted as it seemed to me he should. There was, in fact, something almost like a twinkle in his eye.

"Then what are we to make of this?" I demanded.

"I deduce…"

"Yes?"

Again the twinkle. "That one of her father's trips abroad, before the wedding, took him to Arizona. But of course I must make sure." And with that; leaving me in a state that I confess approached speechlessness, my friend went back across the room.

He approached our client, who still sat wearily in her chair, and extended both his hands. When she took them, wonderingly, he raised her to her feet. "One more question," he urged her solemnly. "The stone with which you struck down Hayden — where is it now? Surely it is not one of those still on the desk?"

"No," the lady marveled. "I could not bear to leave it there." Going back to the door of the lumber-room, she reached inside, and from a shelf took down a pinkish stone of irregular, angular shape, a little larger than a man's fist. This she presented to my friend.

He turned it over once in his hands, and set it back upon the desk. A confident smile now transformed his face. "It is my happy duty to inform you," he said at once, "that the man you knew as Hayden will never bother you again; you may depend upon it."

Dracula paused here in his narration. "In a moment I was able to add my own assurances, for what they were worth, to those of the famed detective. That was after I had walked over to the desk and looked at the weapon for myself.

I knew then that the man struck down with it could indeed have been a vampire; nay, that he must have been. For when he died of the effects of the blow, there on the floor of the lumber-room, his body, as is commonly the case with us, had at once undergone a dissolution to dust, and less than dust. His clothing, including the letters in his pocket, had, as would be expected, disappeared as well. No humanly detectable trace was left when the fiancé opened the door a few moments later."

"A vampire?" I protested. "But, he was struck down with a stone…"

"I was looking," said Dracula softly, "at a choice Arizona specimen of petrified wood."

FRED SABERHAGEN is the author of many popular science fiction and fantasy books including the *Berserker* series, *Swords* trilogy and *Lost Swords* series. A special tip of the deerstalker for the classic novels *The Holmes-Dracula File* and *Séance for a Vampire*.

THE EXECUTIONER

by Lawrence C. Connolly

I awoke in an overstuffed bed, in a chamber larger than the whole of my London rooms. Coal burned in the fireplace, but the main source of light came from electric bulbs in two wall-mounted sconces, each trailing a wire that snaked along the wall before vanishing into a hole beside a curtained window.

A cabinet stood open near the fireplace. A tweed suit hung inside. Beside the cabinet, on a dressing table, lay an array of personal items: shirt, collar, tie, leather case. Of these, all but the case appeared to be mine. How they and I had come to be here, I had no idea. Nor did I know where *here* was.

There was a darkness in me, an emptiness that suggested I had slept far longer than a single night. Yet I recalled no dreams, only the distant memories of a cliff, water, and the body of a man broken on jagged rocks. I had tracked him across the continent, seven-hundred miles to a precipice in the Swiss mountains. The chase had ended there, with him lying dead at the base of a cataract, and I remember looking down at him, watching his body grow larger, expanding in my view as if his broken remains were rising toward me. But in truth it was I who was moving, hurtling downward, still pursuing him even as he lay smashed below the falls. And then, just as the speed of my plunge reduced his body to a blur, I hit the water.

After that, I remembered nothing.

I pushed back the covers and tried getting up. My body ached, the pain worsening as I swung my legs over the side of the bed, looking down at what should have been the floor. But in that instant, it was as if I were back on the cliff, losing my grip on a jagged ledge....

I blinked.

The memory receded. The floor returned. No body beneath me now, only a pair of slippers, fleece-lined, scuffed along the toes. I put them on, feeling their familiar indentations. Like the things in the cabinet and on the table, the slippers were mine.

I found a chamber pot beneath the bed. It was chipped but clean. I knelt beside it, still trying to make sense of where I was. Then I stood and crossed the room, shuffling like a man twice my age, coming at last to the window where I pushed back the curtains and looked out at a moon-lit night. Mountains cut the horizon, jagged peaks of rock and pine. Water roared, muted by distance. *Reichenbach*, I thought. *I'm still in Meiringen.* I pressed my face to the window, looking for the falls, seeing only a curl of mist rising from a chasm halfway between me and the distant peaks. And on the edge of the precipice....

I cupped my hands around my face, blocking the glare from the electric lights until I discerned a silhouetted man standing on a ledge. He wore a greatcoat, hem billowing in the wind. But other than that, and the long hair that whipped about his head, he stood so still that he might have been a statue.

The glass fogged. I wiped it with my sleeve, but when I looked again the figure was gone.

I turned from the window, this time noticing a dining cart and chair behind the dressing table. Had they been there before? A covered tray sat atop the cart, as did a pitcher, drinking glass, smoking kit, and a large sealed envelope. I left the window and raised the cover on the tray: bread, cheese, smoked meats. I covered them again, sat in the chair, and inspected the smoking kit. The case was mine, as were the contents. I took out the pipe, filled its bowl, and turned my attention to the envelope. Inside, I found a letter written on a single sheet of foolscap, folded twice. The handwriting was of a size comparable to the paper: large, elegant, and executed without a single blot or amendment.

It read:

> *Dear Mr. H:*
>
> *If you are awake and reading this, then my efforts to restore you have succeeded. You no doubt have many questions, as do I. To that end, I propose a test, one which may commence whenever you are ready.*
>
> *The procedure is simple.*

I would like you to dress as soon as you are able. Leave your room and descend the staircase at the end of the hall. From there, you will make your way to a lighted chamber on the ground-floor. One of my servants will be waiting. Do not let his appearance alarm you. He will give you no worry as long as you move directly to the chair that awaits you.

You are to sit in the chair and remain in it until the conclusion of our interview, which will commence shortly after you are seated. The chair will be partitioned from the rest of the room by a velvet rope. Under no circumstances are you to venture beyond the rope.

If these instructions seem eccentric, I apologize; but I assure you they are absolutely necessary. Perhaps, soon, you will understand my reasons for them. In any event, your cooperation is not requested, it is absolutely required.

You may be wondering about the personal items in your room. Many of them are indeed yours, sent here at my request by your brother Mycroft. One of the exceptions is a pharmaceutical case. Considering your condition, I thought it prudent to supply something for your pain.

The food is from my private stores, the water the purest in Switzerland.

There is no need to thank me for any of these things. Nor do I expect thanks for having pulled you from the Aare. Indeed, it is I who am indebted to you for an opportunity to test my procedures, and possibly to untangle a knot that I have been wrestling with since the night of your fall.

In light of such considerations, I remain…
your host, caregiver, and
most humble servant,—
M Adam

The clothes were indeed mine.

I dressed slowly, favouring my right leg, hip, and shoulder, which I realized, once I had removed my nightshirt, were badly bruised. I found a pocketbook in the jacket pocket. It was new, as were the banknotes inside. A heavy weight in another pocket proved to be a Webley revolver. I had begun carrying one like it in response to threats from the man who had become my obsession, the man I had last seen smashed on the rocks at the base of the falls.

I did not bother with the pharmaceutical case. My pain was severe, but anything strong enough to take away its edge would certainly do the same to my wits.

Leaving the case on the table, I left the room.

More electric fixtures burned in the hall, positioned to illuminate a line of paintings, large reproductions of familiar masterworks. I paused beside one, resting my leg, studying what appeared to be a watercolor of God creating the first man. In it, God hovered in the air, bending low to exhale the breath of life into his creation. I stepped closer, drawn by the expression on God's face. He looked terrified. An inscription in the painting's corner read:

"Elohim Creating Adam"
by M Adam, 1888
after W Blake 1795

The other paintings featured similar subjects. In each, the face of God was the same: slender, pale, apparently terrified.

I reached the stairs and gripped the banister, slowing my pace until I reached a long hall where the only light came from a doorway thirty feet on. I moved toward it and stepped inside.

A creature greeted me. It was of human size, except for its arms and head, which were disproportionately large. It resembled an orangutan. Yet it was hairless and dressed like a servant, and its fingers, when it raised them to indicate the waiting chair, were long and delicate.

The chair stood beneath an overhead light, the beam focused so precisely that the rest of the room remained in darkness. I looked again at the servant, recalled the assurance of M Adam's letter, and sat in the chair. The overhead light expanded as I settled back. More lights came on illuminating the room which turned out to be a small library lined with books and paintings. Across from me, perhaps fifteen feet distant, a second chair sat beside a closed door.

I leaned forward, peering across the velvet rope that stretched in front of me. A wave of vertigo ensued. The room shifted before me. I felt myself falling.

"No, sir!" The servant grabbed me. "You must not move, sir." It spoke with a disarmingly sweet voice, almost singing. "Master Adam told me to make sure you—"

A latch clicked from across the room.

I sat back. My vision cleared. Then, across the room, the far door swung wide.

A dark man entered, bowed slightly, and extended his hands. "Please," he said. "Don't get up." He spoke English, seasoned with the vowels of a man more accustomed to French. "Stay seated and save your strength."

I did as he said, watching as he took his seat across from me.

He was of average height, yet his form conveyed a sense of stature, immense size. He wore his hair long and straight, like the Indians of the American plains. His skin, too, was uncommonly tanned, though lighter than his lips, which were as black as his hair. But despite such features, there was something noble about him, almost beautiful, and somehow familiar.

"I'm relieved to see you looking so well," he said, his diction recalling the tone of his letter: clear, precise, confident. "How is your pain?"

"It lingers," I said, startled by the thinness of my voice. It seemed as atrophied as my limbs. "How long have I been here?"

"Since I pulled you from the flood."

"That was yesterday?"

"No."

"How long?"

His gaze narrowed, as if studying me from across a great distance. At last, he said: "Nearly four weeks."

I flinched.

"Not four weeks from your perspective," he added quickly. "Time is for the living, and you, Mr. Holmes, have spent nearly a month in the realm of the dead."

"I'm not sure I understand."

"I think you do, Mr. Holmes. My words are plain. You were dead. Your suicide was successful."

"My suicide?"

"Excuse me if I speak candidly, but there's no need for pretence. I found your suicide note."

"But I didn't—"

"Please. There's no need to argue. Perhaps if I start the story at the beginning, it will be easier to follow."

"Please." My voice, which had grown stronger through our brief exchange, now faltered again. "I'm listening."

He shifted in his seat, leaned back, and then proceeded in a tone more suited for oratory than conversation. "My home," he began, spreading his hands to indicate the space beyond the library. "This secluded estate in which you find yourself stands near the brink of the Reichenbach Falls, less than a quarter mile from the site of your death. It's a wild place, but the location suits my work. The river powers my generators, just as the hills and valleys power my mind. When I am wrestling with a problem, I wander the valleys, climb the cliffs, and contemplate the wonder of the *first* creator. I find answers in His works, but four weeks ago, while walking a path above the falls, I found a note resting on a boulder, held there by a cigarette case." He paused, inviting comment.

I gave it: "You found my letter to Watson?"

"Yes. That was the salutation: 'My Dear Watson'."

"But that letter contained instructions, not an admission of suicide."

He smiled, showing rows of straight, white teeth, so perfectly aligned they might have been carved from marble. "No? Perhaps not in so many words, but it did speak of a final act and the pain it would cause friends and family. And it gave the location of documents, instructions for the disposition of your estate."

I could have explained those points, but there was a more pressing concern. "The letter," I said. "Did you take it?"

"No. I left it on the boulder, with your cigarette case. I left your walking stick as well. It was clear you had left it to mark the location, to make it easier for your 'Dear Watson' to find your final testament. And there was no need for me to take the document. I have perfect recall. One look and I owned the form and content of the note: the names, details, tone, penmanship. That night, after pulling you from the flood, I drafted a letter in a hand and voice identical to yours. I sent it to your brother. It was a perfect forgery, though the minuteness of your hand required me to employ the use of a pantograph device. I tend to write large. Indeed, I do everything large. The sins of the father visited upon the child." He smiled again, more broadly than before; giving the impression that he had just revealed something about his origins. I might have asked for clarification, but the matter of his forgery was more pressing.

"So you wrote to my brother," I said, trying to get ahead of the story. "Instructing him to send supplies."

"And money," he added. "Some of which I used to purchase those few things your brother did not provide."

"So Mycroft knows I'm alive?"

"He does. But I have — that is to say, *you* have — sworn him to secrecy. The rest of the world believes you are dead." He sat back, studying me as if from a great distance. "It was suicide, to be sure. But a martyr's suicide. You trailed a criminal to the brink of the falls, threw him over the edge, then leaped after him."

"I did not leap. I lost balance."

"Yes, it often comes to that, a loss of balance. My father—" He turned away abruptly, cocking his head as if listening to a voice behind his chair. But there was no one there, only a wall of books and an empty doorway. He raised a hand, cupped it to his ear, listened a moment longer, and then turned again to face me. "I'm sorry," he said. "I must go." He stood, and once again I was struck by the impression of size. He was a man of average height with the poise of a dark god.

"Shall I wait here?" I asked.

"No." He started toward the door, but then he paused, gripping the back of his chair as if clinging to a cliff. He looked back at me. "This conversation is over. Indeed, I fear I've already explained too much."

"But I still have questions."

"Yes. I'm sure you do. I would expect no less. But this meeting is over. A carriage will take you into town. From there, you can arrange passage—"

"You mentioned a test."

"I did." Again, he started toward the door.

"So I assume it has begun," I said. "This meeting is part of it, as is my dismissal. You tell me I can leave, but it's really a challenge... a challenge for me to stay. Am I correct?"

He paused within the doorway. "I give you my leave, Mr. Holmes. You may take it as you wish." He bowed, deeper than before, then left me alone with the servant.

I pushed up from the chair. "One moment!" I advanced toward the ropes. "One last question!" The vertigo came again. I felt myself falling, and then....

"No, sir!" Giant hands grabbed my shoulder, turned me toward the door. "Not that way." The servant led me from the chair, directing me back the way I had come.

The ground floor hall was lighted now, with electric sconces illuminating the line of paintings that I had hurried past on my way to meet my mysterious saviour. Most of the art depicted scenes similar to those in the upstairs hall, but one was different, the portrait of a man with delicate features, rendered in the romantic style of the Regency Era. It depicted a young scholar seated amid old-world ruins: a crumbling arch, fallen walls, distant mountains. A journal lay open on his lap. He held a finger to his head, thinking as he peered from the painted canvas: wide brown eyes, straight nose, pensive lips, pale skin. I knew those features, having seen them before in the faces of God in the upstairs paintings. But there was something else....

I stepped closer, reading the inscription:

"Posthumous Portrait"
by M Adam 1872
after J. Severn 1845

The servant watched from the library arch, peering at me from around the doorframe. The lights were still on behind its massive head, but, as the opening stood at a right angle to the hall, I could not see the room, only the light spilling from the arch.

"Do you need anything?" the servant asked.

I pointed to the painting of the young scholar. "Who is this?" I asked.

"The master's father, sir."

So that was it. M Adam's paintings of God the creator had been modelled on the likeness of his own father. Yet I sensed there was more meaning here, a more poignant connection.

"What was the father's name?" I asked

"It was Victor, sir."

"Victor Adam?"

"No, sir," the servant said. "Adam is what the master calls himself. It is not a family name. The father was Victor Frankenstein."

Yes, that was it!

I looked at the face in the painting, recognizing the wan complexion of the audacious Genovese student whose autobiography had caused a sensation in the early part of the century.

I knew the story.

Victor Frankenstein had died on board an arctic vessel. He had been 27, widowed, childless, and obsessed with tracking down and destroying an artificial man of his own design.

I considered these things, wondering if it were possible that my host, the man who had restored my life, might be the artificial man described in the young scholar's book. But that artificial man — or creature, for surely such a thing could not be considered a man — had supposedly died in the arctic along with his creator. And even if the creature had survived, the events recounted in the scholar's book had taken place over a century ago. The creature, if it still lived, would hardly resemble the hearty, dark-skinned man I had just met in the library. And there was something else, the matter of size. One of the most striking details from the scholar's book had been the creature's stature — eight feet tall, according to the text.

The man I had just met was of average height. Or so he had seemed.

"Excuse me, sir." The servant sounded impatient. "May I help you to your room?"

"No." I turned from the painting. "But I should like to have another look in that library."

"Sorry, sir." The servant stepped into the hall, not blocking my way, but letting me see that he was prepared to do so if necessary. Even if my body were not battered and sore, I would be no match for those orangutan arms.

"Some questions, then," I said. "Will you answer some questions?"

"Sorry, sir. I believe my master wants you to find those on your own." And with that he stepped back through the arch and swung the door closed from the inside. The hall rang with the click of an engaging latch, leaving me alone with a clear sense of what I needed to do.

I turned and shuffled toward the stairs.

My bad leg was throbbing by the time I reached my room. I opened the pharmaceutical case, finding that it held a hypodermic syringe and six glass vials of morphine. I opened one of the vials, filled the syringe, and placed it back inside the holder. I did not secure the clasps, but instead simply folded the case closed before slipping it into the pocket of my coat. Next I checked the pistol, opening the gate to make sure it was satisfactorily armed. Then I closed it again, aligning the hammer with the empty chamber. Finally, I opened my smoking kit, removed my pipe tools, and left the room.

The lights in the upstairs hall were much dimmer than before. M Adam no longer needed me to see the paintings. I realized, as I hurried past them, that he had been playing many moves ahead of me the entire night. Now, descending the stairs, I resisted the urge to think that I had gained on him. Chances were he was still playing me, manoeuvring from a position of strength.

The door to the library was still closed. I looked through the keyhole. All the lights were still on.

Left on for me. He expects me to break in.

Using my pipe tools (the spoon to apply torque while the poker worked the pins) I picked the lock and opened the door. Then I entered. The chair and velvet rope stood as before, their careful arrangement pointing to the room's sole purpose — not as a library, but as something far more specialized.

I closed the door behind me and stepped forward, past the ropes and toward the centre of the room. With each step, the room changed. Shelves that had appeared parallel when viewed from the chair now appeared out of plumb. Likewise, framed paintings lost their squared corners, becoming trapezoids. And the floor, which had appeared level from the edge of the room, now sloped downward beneath a rising ceiling. These realities, which had previously been masked by both the precise positioning of the chair in which I had been sitting and the carefully controlled lighting of the room, were now plainly obvious.

M Adam's chair grew as I approached it, towering over me. I reached up to grasp its armrest, resting my leg as I looked at the door through which M Adam had entered the room. I now saw that the opening had indeed been designed to accommodate a man of gigantic stature, easily eight-foot tall, possibly more.

I was still contemplating the significance of it all when someone called from the short end of the room. The voice rang out, musical but nonetheless threatening. Looking around, I saw the servant standing near the hallway door. The same slanted lines that had reduced M Adam to normal proportions now expanded the servant to gigantic size. More than ever, he resembled one of those jungle orangutans, with a massive body dwarfed only by the size of its gigantic head and arms.

"You were told not to return here!" the servant said.

"Yes." I stepped away from the chair, steadying myself on both legs, trying not to look as wounded and vulnerable as I felt. "I was told that, but I was goaded to the contrary." I reached into my pocket and removed the pharmaceutical case, hiding it behind the chair while the servant started toward me, steadying itself on giant arms as the floor sloped downward. The monster seemed to shrink as it moved, but the loss of stature did nothing to allay the threat. By the time the beast man had reached the centre of the room, it was charging.

I gripped the syringe, waiting until the thing was almost on me. Then I swung the needle around, jabbed it deep, and squeezed the plunger. By then the huge hands had grabbed me, throwing me down, pinning me to the floor beside the doorway. For a moment I flashed to my last memory of Reichenbach Falls, being pinned against a high ledge with a madman straddling my chest. My training in the eastern arts had served me then. I had been able to use my opponents force against him. But here the opposing weight was too great. I was at the mercy of the beast man, helpless to resist as it grabbed me tight and lifted me from the floor. Then, as it prepared to throw me across its back and carry me from the room, its face went slack. In a blink, we were both falling: beast man crashing against the base of the chair, me landing atop him.

My hip spasmed. I rolled away, forced myself into a crouch, and tried standing. The pain intensified. I slumped back against the chair, bracing myself while the servant breathed noisily, lying on its back, eyes open but seeing nothing.

The syringe and case had fallen near the chair. I crawled toward them. Nothing was broken, but still I resisted taking an injection, using my will to ignore the pain as I stood, crossed to the gigantic doorway, and entered the space within.

The way veered left, opening into a lighted corridor. The walls were stone, older than the wood-panelled rooms and halls behind me. But here, as before, the lights were electrical, bolted to the walls and trailing wires that snaked toward a chamber about twenty feet back from the forced-perspective room.

I paused, slipped the pharmaceutical case back into my pocket, and drew the pistol. Then I pushed on, watching the chamber's interior come into view: tables strewn with strange instruments, walls affixed with snaking wires and twitching dials, air reverberating with the hum of unseen engines. And over all of it, becoming clearer as I passed through the doorway, a long shadow that could only belong to my host and saviour, the giant who called himself Adam.

"Impressive," he said, speaking to me even before I had completely entered the room. "You do justice to your reputation. I can only hope that you do not think the same of me."

I found him sitting with his back to the door. This time, I saw him as he was: a creature of astounding proportions, so large that I might have taken him for a statue. He kept his back to me, dabbing a bit of paint on an easel-mounted canvas. He was working on a reproduction of Pieter Brueghel's *Fall of Icarus*, which he seemed to be painting from memory. The canvas, like the artist himself, was enormous.

"You may put the pistol back in your pocket." He spoke without looking around. "I did not provide it to be used against me." He lowered his brush, turned slowly, and gave me the benefit of his magnificent face, a countenance more like that of a god than a monster, with a complexion so uniform that it might have been fashioned from silk. No blemishes or scars, and yet the face filled with wrinkles as he smiled, seeming almost to shrivel as he flashed rows of marble teeth. He seemed pleased to see me. "So you have your answers, Mr. Holmes? Have you deduced who I am? *What* I am?"

"Yes. I think so."

"Say it then. What am I? What is it they call me in the world I am hiding from? What is my name out there?"

"Frankenstein's monster," I said.

His smile broadened, wrinkles deepened. "Really? *His* monster? Not simply *Frankenstein*?"

"I've heard that, too," I said.

"And what about other things? How my father stitched me together from cadavers, gave me a criminal's brain?"

"Yes," I said. "I've heard that, though I don't recall your father's book mentioning such things."

"People make their own versions," he said. "Things become grander in the retelling; more sensational."

"It's much the same with stories about me," I said. "I'm hardly the master of deduction that people think I am."

"I wondered about that," the creature said. "It's why I decided to test you, gauge your resourcefulness, your commitment to solving a mystery. From what I can see, the reputation does you justice." The creature stood, towering over me. "I need to show you something." He turned, heading toward an antechamber and the sound of humming engines.

I followed.

"I understand that people don't believe my father's story," he said. "Probably because so few of them have actually read his book." He looked down at me. "But you have?"

"Yes," I said.

"Did you believe it?" he asked. "Before tonight, before meeting me face to face, did you believe such things were possible?"

"No." I said. "I took it for fiction."

"But you *did* read the book?" he said, pressing the point that seemed to matter a great deal to him. "And you recall how my father became a student of the human form, its growth and decay? How he studied the dead to create life? Not to reassemble pieces that had once lived, but to make a new kind of man — wiser, stronger, more beautiful than any that had ever been born of natural means."

"But by your father's own account, the creature was neither wise nor beautiful."

"Yes," Adam said. "But that was his madness talking. He disowned me, and I suffered as a result. And he did, too. I saw to that. Before it was over, we had lured and pursued each other to the brink of ruin. I survived, but only by virtue of his handiwork. He had endeavoured to make me immortal, and so he had. In that, at least, he had succeeded."

We crossed the threshold into the adjacent room, into the drone of compressors and electric current. Vats lined the walls, metal tanks that appeared to be fashioned from locomotive boilers, each fitted with portals too high for me to look through.

"Do you recall the part of my father's story that deals with size?" he asked.

"You mean about the difficulties of working in human scale?"

"Yes." He paused beside a portal. "I have the same problem." He bent down, bringing his face level with mine. "I'll show you." He extended his hands. Together, they encircled my torso. "Do you trust me?"

I looked him in the eye and discerned no trace of malevolence. "All right," I said.

He took hold, lifting me from the floor. I felt like Dante in the hands of Antaeus, putting my faith in a force that could crush me if it wished. But the grip was gentle, warm. I gave myself over to it as the giant man held me to a portal. Inside, I saw one of the orangutan creatures, like the servant I had left sedated in the library. It was naked but sexless. Indeed, the parts of its body that were human size lacked any detail at all. The arms and head, however, were fully realized.

"They are the best I've been able to do," he said. "Their internal organs are no larger than yours, yet they fail quickly. I would give them normal-sized arms and heads, but I need servants who can think, speak, and use their hands. Until I can maintain function at smaller scales, I need to compromise." He pulled me away from the portal, lowered me back to the floor. "I'm making progress," he said. "One day I'll be able to create servants who can travel freely through the world of ordinary men, go into town, procure supplies. Until then, I must make do with written correspondences and the trust of a few local business men."

"They come here?" I asked, realizing there was no way he himself could blend inconspicuously with the company of men.

"Yes," he said. "We meet in the library. It's better that way. Some of them know the ruse. A few don't. I trust, given the money they make on my investments, that none of them really care that I am a monster."

"You built the room yourself?"

He nodded. "It took years. The entire house took years. But I've had time. I don't sleep, never tire, don't age."

"And money? How did you come by that?"

"My father had a large estate," he said. "By forging his name, I was able to acquire his share. When his brother died, I got it all, liquidated the family assets, invested. It was a slow process, but I had more time than any man has ever had. My wealth has grown, but these things are not important. The thing I need to show you is in here." He paused beside another tank, leaned toward the portal, looked inside. "You spent nearly a month inside one of these tanks," he said. "The same fluid in which I grow my creations nurtured your wounded body. I do not cut and stitch dead flesh any more than my father did, but by studying his journal I have learned the art of creating, growing, and kindling the spark of life. It was lucky for you that you missed the rocks when you fell from the cliff." He looked toward me now, and in his expression I discerned a hint of the terrible thing that lay within the tank beside us. "I entered the whirlpool and hauled you from the flood," he said. "And then, seeing the remains of your rival dashed upon the rocks, I went back in."

"Professor Moriarty?" I whispered, speaking the name of the evil that had been my obsession.

"Yes," the creature said. "I read his name in the note you left for Watson, and although I knew that the battered carcass on the rocks was that of your enemy, I felt compelled to save him, too. There was a time when life meant nothing to me, when I killed indiscriminately to torment the one who tormented me, but that's behind me now. I understand that life is a gift that must be created at every opportunity, protected at all costs, and rekindled whenever possible. You healed because you were still in one piece. Your rival, however—" He glanced again at the portal, frowned, then bent toward me. "Come." He wrapped me in his hands. "I'll show you."

This time the transit from floor to portal seemed to take longer. My mind was racing, reverberating with dread for what I would see when I looked through that window, but I resisted the urge to turn away as the creature brought me level with the glass.

Inside, Moriarty's remains floated in a bath of milky fluid, drifting in the slow spiral of cycling nutrients. He had but one eye, lidless and swollen, peering out of a broken face. At least,

I assumed it was a face, though other than the eye there was little to identify it. The nose and lower jaw had both been ripped away, leaving wounds that would never close, hollows in which I saw the wet workings of throat and sinuses. The head itself was elongated, the sides evidently pushed out by a concussive blow to the rock. The impact should have killed him, and I suppose it had, but Adam had brought him back, revived him, returned the fires of life to the cracked and broken kindling of his flesh.

"I could not leave him," the creature said, his voice sounding distant even though he spoke close to my ear. "I did terrible things when I was young, but I have since sworn to become a force of life and healing. So I nursed him even as I nursed you, but I cannot keep him. He needs to face judgment, and that is your domain, not mine. When you leave, you must take him with you."

A truncated body bobbed beneath Moriarty's ruined head. I saw a pair of arms, one ending below the elbow, the other little more than a knotted stump beneath the shoulder. The torso was no more complete, scarred and tapering to a flesh-wrapped spine. No hips. No legs.

"Take him with me?" I asked. "Back to London?"

"To face judgment," he said.

"But how?"

"That's up to you."

"But can he be transported?"

"Yes. He has stabilized. Soon he can be removed from the tank, swaddled in gauze, carried like an infant, a little heavier, perhaps, but not much."

Moriarty stared. I sensed he recognized me, perhaps even heard what the creature and I were saying.

I pushed away from the glass, making it clear I'd had enough. He lowered me to the floor.

"I can't do it." I said.

He crouched before me, a father stooping before a child. "You would rather leave him here, in my care, knowing that I am bound by personal honour to keep him alive? Restore him if and when I can? Let him return to the world if and when he is able to walk into it on his own?"

"You would let that happen?"

"I would," he said. "I must. It is the way I've chosen." He leaned closer, confiding. "He needs to face a justice that I am incapable of providing. Perhaps, in your hands, he will find it."

The swaddled mass screamed as Adam wrapped it in gauze, and though a dose of morphine temporarily stilled the cries, they resumed before the carriage left the castle gate. I thought of what Adam had said about justice, realizing, as the deformity wailed and sputtered on the seat beside me, that there was no need for either Moriarty or me to return to London.

The road followed the river, and when I was certain we were far enough downstream from Adam's estate, I told the driver to stop. He was one of Adam's long-armed monstrosities, wrapped in a cloak to mask his shape. I suspected it was the same servant that had confronted me in the library, though it gave no indication of knowing me. Nor did it seem the least curious about my intentions when I carried the wailing parcel to a cliff overlooking a wide, rapid stretch of the Aare.

I knew now why Adam had supplied the loaded pistol: considering my pain, it would have been a shame to waste any more morphine on Professor Moriarty.

The gunshot echoed through the canyon.

The thing stopped screaming. I picked it up and hurled it over the cliff, its gauze unravelled as it fell, streaming out, whipping in the wind, collapsing when it struck a rock. It bounced once, then vanished into the current. It resurfaced briefly a few hundred feet downstream, smaller than before, then it vanished for good amid the churning waves.

I returned to the carriage.

"So it's done?" the servant said.

I offered no answer, but climbed back into the carriage and shut the door.

The carriage rocked, then continued down the road.

I would not return to London. My work there was finished. I would go elsewhere, write to my brother, have him send what I needed. Perhaps, in seclusion, I would find the same redemption that had eluded M Adam's creator. Perhaps, if I lived long enough, I would do justice to the gift of a second chance.

The **LAWRENCE C. CONNOLLY** novel *Veins* was a finalist for the Black Quill and Hoffer awards as well as inspiring the audio CD *Veins: The Soundtrack*. His new supernatural thriller *Vipers* was released in 2010. In addition he has two short story collections available, *Visions: Short Fantasy and SF* and *This Way to Egress*.

A COUNTRY DEATH

Simon Kurt Unsworth

The detective waited outside; he was, technically, a guest of the local force here and, although they had called for him, he would not enter without invitation. Whilst he waited, he looked around the place to which he had come. The building was set back from the road, both it and the gardens that embraced it small and neat. And what gardens! The edged beds full of flowers that blazed with colors, the smell of their perfume heavy, swollen. The lawns, green and dense, danced around both sides of the house, disappearing from sight in rich swathes that seemed to catch the light and feed upon it. The detective saw that his impression, gained on the journey here, was correct; this was a home designed for privacy. There were no other buildings nearby, and the roads that led to it were little more than tracks. Even the edgings of flowers gave the impression of a wall; beautiful, vibrant, but a wall nonetheless, a barrier between this place and the outside. Whoever lived here did not want intruders.

Whoever *had* lived here, of course. Although there were few details in the summoning telegram, the force was unlikely to have called upon him for anything less than an unexplained, unexplainable, death. The solving of these things was what had made his reputation, it was where his skills lay, and it was where his interests took him. It was what made him valuable.

"Sir?" The speaker was an old man, older even than the detective, probably brought out of retirement to act as constable. The war had depleted the manpower available to the force, despite its protected status, and as the conflict went on anyone with experience, no matter how minor or how long ago it was gained, was being called back to add substance to the ever-diminishing thin blue line. *It should be a matter of national thanks,* thought the detective sourly, *that the same calling that has removed the men who had up 'til that point defended the virtues of law and order has also removed most of those who strove hardest to attack them. Ah well, in all things balance.* Aloud, to business now, he said, "What's happened?"

"We don't know," replied the constable. "It's awful, like nothing we've seen, any of us. The others, they left me here to wait for you. We wouldn't have sent for you but we can't... we don't..." The man tailed off, and the detective saw that there were tears in his eyes. He was extremely old and his lined face had a sagging, waxen look. Taking another breath of the fine summer air, letting the sounds of bees and birds wash around him and clothe him in their freshness, the detective said simply, "Show me."

The inside of the cottage was as neat as the garden, although considerably more cluttered. Bookshelves, crammed with books and journals and papers, piled two or three high in places, lined the already narrow hallway. An occasional table groaned under a mass of post and newspapers. More books and papers sat on most of the stairs. Here were the first signs of disarray, the detective saw, with piles disrupted and tilted and some of the papers scattered down the steps. There was no telephone, he saw, and no pictures on what little there was of free wall space. The constable led him upwards, stepping carefully over the scattered papers.

"Was it like this when you got here?" the detective asked.

"Yes, sir," replied the constable. "I touched as little as possible and didn't move anything. I know that's important in this sort of thing. When there's been a... when someone's died." He stopped at the top of the stairs. "It's in the study," he said, gesturing to the farthest door. "I can't go back in, don't make me, please sir."

"The man doesn't have a live-in," said the constable, swallowing audibly as the detective pushed open the door. "He has a woman, Mrs. Roundhay, who comes daily. She came this morning, but he wasn't up like he normally is."

"When had she last seen him?"

"Yesterday, when she left. About four, she reckons. She came back this morning at about nine and couldn't find him. The back door was open so she came in and looked around but he didn't answer when she called. She checked all the downstairs rooms before she went upstairs and into the study and found him.

Found his body." There was another swallow, this one liquid and loose, and the detective called, "That's fine, Constable. Go downstairs and get yourself some water, I'll join you there soon. Many thanks."

The study was, if possible, more cluttered than the hallway or stairs, with all the available space seemingly taken up with books, papers, journals and ornaments. The body was on the floor in front of the desk, twisted in a heap of loose sheets and spilled tobacco, and something that had been spilled from an overturned tin and which looked like old, dried grass. A chair had been knocked back and lay against the nearest bookcase. The room smelled of vomit, although the detective could see none, and something else, something sweet, sickly and sharp. The remains hardly looked human.

Whoever the man was, he had clearly died in agony. His flesh, what the detective could see of it, was distended and yellowing; pockmarked with tiny dots of blood. The face was bloated to the point where the skin looked as though it might split. It looked somehow poisonous, the wattle of the neck ballooning over the collar in angry ridges. His hands were also swollen, the knuckles lost in the tide of grotesque, puffy flesh. His mouth was open and his tongue protruded, and even that was swollen, covered in the tiny dots, black pores against the rich and fetid purple. One eye had swelled entirely shut; the other had managed to retain an opening on the world, and in the tiny arc the detective saw, against a reddened sclera, the blackened pitch of a pupil grown vast in terror and pain and death. It was like nothing he had seen before.

After noting his initial impressions, the detective went downstairs and spoke with the constable again. "It's a strange one, to be sure," he said. The constable nodded; a look of gratitude on his face. *Strange or not,* that expression said, *it's someone else's responsibility now; not mine any more, but yours.*

"I'm sure that there's a rational explanation though," the detective continued. "We simply need to apply ourselves and find it. Logic will prevail." He paused, thinking, and then said, "It may take some time, though. Can you make arrangements for the coroner to collect the body, and tell him I'll talk to him when he has completed his investigations?"

"Yes, sir. I called him, he's on his way."

"Excellent. In the meantime, we have work to do here. We shall have to inspect the premises fully, and talk in more detail with the housekeeper. We shall need to build a picture of the victim, of his last days, of his life. Oh, incidentally, what do we know about him?"

"He came from London originally, sir, and retired here about ten years ago. He kept himself to himself mostly, didn't have many visitors but received lots of post. He almost never left this place."

"And the day of his death, the days earlier? How was he? As normal?"

"No, sir. Well, not on the day of his death, anyway. He was, well, distracted. Worried."

"Sterling work, constable, sterling work! I see you are going to be an asset to this investigation. I presume you got this from the housekeeper?"

"Yes, sir, I've been chatting with her over tea while you've been upstairs with the... with him."

"Good, good. So, to work! Perhaps we should start at the beginning, yes? Tell me, what was the victim's name?"

"Holmes, sir. Sherlock Holmes."

As Brabbins further questioned Swann, two morgue attendants arrived and took Holmes' body away in a silent ambulance, the red cross on its gleaming white side a vivid scar against the verdant fields.

"He was either outside and came in, or the attack started in the kitchen. From there, he went along the hallway," Brabbins said to Swann. "I'd imagine he was staggering by that point. Look, there are streaks of boot polish along the skirting where he's kicked it, and on at least one of the shelves, the books are in disarray. More disarray," he amended, looking at the masses of books that sat on each shelf. "See, these books here are damaged, knocked over, probably as he grasped at the shelf to keep himself upright. There are smears from his fingers here, and here, yes?"

"Yes," said Swann, doubtfully. "How do you know that those marks weren't there beforehand, sir?"

"Well, firstly the books themselves. There are many of them, to be sure, but they're stacked neatly and well kept except for these few. And consider, are there other marks, Constable Swann? The shelves, the surfaces not covered in books are clean, dust-free. I'd say our Mrs. Roundhay—" gesturing towards the kitchen where the housekeeper was still crying and drinking tea, "—keeps this place gleaming, wouldn't you? No other marks, and certainly not one so large. And look—" Brabbins put his hand onto the mark, letting Swann see how it matched the pattern of fingers slipping across the wood and into the damaged books.

"No, whatever happened to him, it happened quickly. There are no signs of disorder in the kitchen, no signs of a struggle of any kind. He fled his death along this hallway, but couldn't move fast enough." Brabbins went slowly down the hallway and onto the stairs.

"He went up the stairs, and he was careless, knocking over the piles of books and paper, but why? What was up here that he thought might help? Where was he going?"

"The study?"

"Yes, but *why*? Why there and not the bathroom or the bedroom? Why the study?" Their discussion had taken them to the room in question, and Brabbins stepped in, gesturing for Swann to follow. "Tell me what you see." Swann followed, clearly reluctant.

Although the body had been removed the man, Holmes, was still a presence in the room. These were his papers and books, his curios on the shelves in front of the books, his tobacco and his pipe on the desk. This was his space, and Brabbins knew that he and Swann were intruders here.

"It's a study," said Swann.

"Good," said Brabbins. "Tell me more. Tell me what you *see*."

"It's messy, like the hall. Lots of things. How a person could work here, I don't know. How could you tell where things were? There's piles of newspapers, the desk is covered in manuscript sheets with writing on, there are books open on the desk and magazines all over."

"Very good. Go on."

"There's a picture on the desk, the only one I've seen in the house, of a man with a moustache. He's got a doctor's bag at his feet and a revolver in his hand. There's a pipe on the desk and more papers on the floor. They're crumpled, as though he pulled them to the floor when he fell. Some of them are bound together. There are matches loose on the desk and tobacco on the floor."

"Did he decide to light a pipe for himself, one last smoke in his death throes, do you think?"

"No," said Swann, his voice defensive, and for a moment Brabbins wondered if he had gone too far. No matter. "The tobacco's fallen out of his pouch, or spilled when he went for the matches. There's none in the pipe or near it."

"Well done, Constable. Please, continue."

"I don't know what else to say," said Swann. "I can't see anything else, I don't know what you're looking for. There's pine needles on the floor with the papers and tobacco, and some old wood and burlap. It looks like he tried to fill his smoker but dropped it before he could."

"Smoker?" asked Brabbins, startled. "What's that?"

"The tin," said Swann in a tone that was somewhere between wary and disbelieving; it was either so obvious to him that he was worried he was wrong, or it was genuinely obvious and he couldn't understand why Brabbins couldn't see it. "It's smoker fuel. Look, the smoker's under the desk."

"Smoker?" said Brabbins again. "You mean his pipe?"

"No, that," said Swann, pointing to a thing that looked like a lantern with a kettle funnel welded to it, lying on its side under the desk. "It's a smoker. You put needles and wood and burlap in and burn it, and it makes smoke."

"Why?" asked Brabbins, mystified.

"You need the smoke," said Swann, "to calm bees."

The parlour was filled with piles of concertina files, three or four deep from the walls and to the height of perhaps five feet, tied with cord or ribbon, as though to stop them bursting. Some were old and some newer, the corners of the files less worn and the ribbons less dull. Experimentally, Brabbins opened one of them and withdrew sheets at random. The first one was a handwritten letter.

> *Dear Mr. Holmes*
> *My brother has been vanished these past six months and I suspect he may have come to a terrible end at the hands of his wife, a selfish and unpleasant woman. I know you don't do your investigations any more, but surely you can make an exception to help bring a vicious harridan to justice and give my family some peace?*
> *I pray that I will hear from you soon.*
>
> *Yours in God*
> *Bernadette Murray (Mrs.)*

There was a Cheam return address on the letter, and at the bottom in a different hand was written *No*. The other sheets

Brabbins withdrew were similar: requests to help find missing family members, to solve robberies, to discover the whereabouts of missing wills. One even asked Holmes help in finding a missing pet, *much loved and missed and Oh Mr. Holmes if you could see my child's face you would surely be unable to resist our request for your assistance.* The last one Brabbins looked at was typed, on paper headed with the insignia of the Manchester Constabulary. *Dear Mr. Holmes,* it read, *We have a most difficult series of violent attacks and would request your assistance in solving them.* Brabbins stared around the hundreds of files, thinking that if each contained the same as this file, then that was thousands upon thousands of requests, more and more arriving daily. What had Swann said? That he received a lot of post? And he read all of them; the repeated handwritten *No* told Brabbins that. *My God, he thought, if this is what each day brought him, no wonder he tried to seal himself away.*

Naked, Holmes' corpse lay on its back on the metal table in the morgue whilst Rivers, the coroner, talked and pointed. "It's not technically poison because he didn't ingest it," he said, "so it's venom, although I don't suppose it makes much difference to him now, does it? It was administered mostly to the flesh of the face and hands, which explains the amount of swelling and tissue damage in those areas."

Rivers was a GP, he had told Brabbins, called in to help in those rare incidents when there was a need for a medical opinion on a corpse. The morgue was tiny, little more than a cupboard, tiled a pale, sickly green that reflected the two men as they moved around the body, their images hovering like vapor at the corner of Brabbins' eye. It smelled of harsh soap and embalming fluid and the loose, wavering scent of flesh that was rotting despite the chill. There was another odor emanating from the body, the one that Brabbins had first come across in Holmes' study, bitter and cloying, yet oddly sweet.

Holmes must have been tall and imposing in life, thought Brabbins. Prostrate on the table, though, he was shrivelled and splayed, his belly a sliced and yawning cavity, his flesh sagging back from his bones like an ill-fitting suit. The swelling of his face and hands made him look clownish, a caricature of the aquiline man that he had been in life. The puffy flesh had deflated slightly, and in relaxing and dropping away, the skin had pulled back from both of the man's eyes, leaving their bloodshot gaze focussed on a point somewhere beyond the ceiling of the mortuary in rapt, cold attention.

"I haven't identified the poison yet," said Rivers. "I may not be able to. If you want a theory, it was smeared on something, or it was in something, and then his assailant attacked him, stabbing at him. At his face and hands, mainly, although there are some punctures on his neck and some on his lower arms." Rivers held up his hands, nodding at his cuffs as they pulled back from his wrists, and said, "Defensive wounds, I'd imagine. The weapon was thin and sharp, probably a needle. It may even have been a hypodermic, given the depth of some of the punctures in the flesh."

"Thank you," said Brabbins. He leaned in close to the corpse, looking at its stretched, sloughing skin. There were even wounds in the swept back, thinning hair, he saw, areas of scalp where the poison had caused the man's head to bulge and swell. His tongue had collapsed back into his mouth, lay curled and dry in the shadowed depths. Brabbins thought of the room full of pleading letters, of the person that this man must have been, and felt a wave of sadness wash over him. This had been a human being, a good one by all accounts, and someone had hated him enough to murder him, to *slaughter* him. Brabbins sniffed deeply, trying to lock the smell of the dead man and the sight of his bruised, distorted face deep in his mind; then he rose to go.

Swann was gone when Brabbins arrived back at Holmes' house. Evening was closing in, so Brabbins couldn't blame the man. He had gone to ... what? A Mrs. Swann? Some doughty housewife warming slippers and a meal in a tiny kitchen? Brabbins smiled at the image and wondered how the man would tell his wife of his day, of bodies and detectives and rooms full of papers and a study that was cluttered and claustrophobic and smelled like spoiled humanity. Perhaps the man was a widower, and would sit in a dark and lonely home, talking to no one but himself. Brabbins supposed he should have asked, had a conversation with the man, but had long ago realized that he wasn't inclined to that sort of thing. Those things were distractions, getting in the way and watering down his attention. The case was all; the dead man and the cause of his death.

Before leaving, though, Swann had made a start on the papers from the parlour. Piles of them were out of the folders and on the floor, and more were on the table in the kitchen. The man hadn't left a note, which Brabbins took to mean that he had found nothing of interest. Most of the piles in the parlour itself were more requests for help, from all over the world. Each had the word 'No' written at the bottom, solid and emphatic.

The pile in the kitchen looked to be more recent, invoices and household bills. Swann had weighted this pile down with an empty cup, Brabbins saw with distaste. It had left a tea ring on the uppermost paper, a pale circle blotted across the top of an invoice for *comb replacement pieces* from a company in Liverpool.

Actually, Brabbins saw, the paper on the kitchen table was in two piles, one face down and one face up. They gave the impression of a job half-done, something partway complete. The cup was almost like a bookmark, he thought, a place marker to ensure that the task could be taken up from the point at which it had been left. He leafed through the face up pile presumably the unchecked ones, finding them all handwritten sheets, covered in notes and drawings.

Was this the last thing that Swann had read? Had it sparked something in the man's brain, or had he simply reached that point and thought, *That's it, time to go home.* Somehow, Brabbins didn't think so. It was the half-finished look of the piled papers that did it, the sense of something partly complete, not abandoned but simply interrupted. Swann was old, yes, had struck him as inexperienced, yes, but lazy and inefficient? No.

So, if something had flared in the man's mind, what had he done next? And where was he now?

Brabbins stood and went walking, slowly pacing the length of the hallway, going into the parlour and the lounge and finally coming to the bottom of the stairs. Nothing had changed; at least, nothing that gave Brabbins pause. Upstairs? The papers on the steps had been placed back into their piles, he saw, but one had a sense of *ruffledness*, as though it had been sifted through and then placed down. Swann? Brabbins looked through the pile and found that it was mostly more correspondence. Why this pile above the others, he wondered. There was nothing in it of interest as far as he could see, nothing that would seem to tie into Holmes' death. It seemed to be a set of letters between Holmes and a London publishing house, mostly about royalties. The last letter mentioned a 'new project', Brabbins saw, and his policeman's instinct told him that this was the one that Swann had been interested in. It was more crumpled, placed more roughly back into the pile than the others, but why was it important? What had Swann been thinking?

The study door was open, and it had been shut when Brabbins left. He stepped inside and saw immediately that things had changed; some of the papers from the floor had gone and the others were in new piles, scattered differently. *Swann read something downstairs, in the papers on the table, and it ... what? Made him think? Caused some kind of realization? He came upstairs, stopped on the way and read more, read something else that confirmed his suspicions, or at least strengthened them into something more solid, and from there he came into the study and sorted through the papers on the floor.* And on the desk, Brabbins saw more had gone from there, as had the smoker from the floor and some of the smoker fuel. The matches were still on the desk, though. *He wanted some of the papers, others not, and then he left the study, left the house. But to where?*

The garden was a frayed mess of shadows and night. The light escaping from the doorway around Brabbins lost its strength as it stretched away, soaking the lawn from a rich green to a torpid, heavy grey. The plants and bushes that lined the lawns were little more than blacker streaks in a night that was lightless and warm. There was a smell in the garden, a mingled scent of exhaling plants and clean earth.

And something burning, or burned.

Brabbins walked cautiously down to the edge of the lawn and started across it. As he moved deeper into the shadows, the smell of burned things became stronger and he heard a noise, a somnolent hum. He raised his lantern, letting the pale light dance across the ground ahead of him. More lawn. He had the sense of it widening around him, opening out to become a field; the grass felt longer under his feet, the ground rougher, less cultured. The smell had changed as well, shifting from the sweet breath of flowers to the denser, richer aroma of roots and soil and wood.

Brabbins felt exposed here, as though he had swum further out from shore than he realized, to where the water suddenly went cold and the waves were made of stone rather than cotton. He turned, looking back towards the building and the pale squares of light falling from the kitchen windows and doorway as he walked. The distance between him and Holmes' house stretched, dark and sly, and then he realized that the sound had changed and that shapes were emerging from the gloom about him.

They were low and hard-edged, paler smears in the darkness revealed by his approach. The low sound had changed as well, had shifted and become less rested, more anticipatory, although anticipatory of what Brabbins could not tell. Whatever it was that was making the sound, he had the impression that it knew he was there, was watching him carefully, judging and gauging and waiting. It was a grating buzz, oddly metallic and sharp, and it scraped across his exposed skin like a toothache. He turned slowly back around, completing a full circle with the torchlight leaping ahead of him and about him like an inquisitive tongue. There were six of the shapes, solid white boxes on little legs, set at irregular intervals across a pasture of some kind. The noise came from all the shapes at once. He took a cautious step back, feeling his way with his heel because he suddenly, *definitely*, did not want to turn his back on the boxes.

They were hives. He was a city boy, true, but even he recognized the slatted shapes of beehives. There were no bees, at least none that he could see, but he assumed that it was the creatures making the sound inside the hives. He took another backwards step and the sound rose in pitch, cold and glitteringly alert. He had heard bees before, enjoyed their warm hum in the air around him in summer gardens, but this noise was something different. It was ferocious, a noise of warning and threat. Another step, and he was at the edge of the pasture, almost out from the hives. Their pallid shapes seemed to face him as he went, horridly observant and aware. Another step, another. Another and his questing heel bumped into something that rolled and gave under him, and his balance yawned wildly for a moment and then he fell. The torch bounced to the ground by his head, dancing and jittering before it settled and the beam came to rest on what he had fallen over, and Brabbins saw it and screamed.

It was Swann; or at least, it had *been* Swann.

The man's face, caught in the beam of light, leered in black and swollen misery at Brabbins, the flesh darkened and gross. His head was massive, like a scarecrow's made out of some misshapen, rotten vegetable; his eyes were bulged shut, the lids erupting and pressing together, and his mouth was open, but compressed to a dark, tiny O by lips that had blistered towards each other. The skin looked taught, ready to split, and it was covered in beads of blood, some of which had trickled and collected and slathered down the man's cheeks like aged, dank tears. The swelling made his chin a shapeless ridge above a neck that bulged and strained against his uniform collar, where his police number glittered, silver and pitiless. It was Swann made into a caricature of himself, drawn by a hand that was both mocking and humourless. The smoker was lying by him in the centre of a scorched circle of grass.

All of this Brabbins saw even as his scream was newborn, still rising into the air in a great, whooping arc. Under it, the sound of the bees leapt in pitch, climbing with the scream to a sharp, inhuman shiver. Brabbins clambered to his feet, rolling against Swann as he did so and feeling the man's flesh shift like water in a balloon. He grabbed, almost by instinct, the sheaf of partly charred papers that were still clutched in the dead man's hand (also bloated and black, he saw) and then he was running. As he did so, he had the impression of the hives boiling, of a ragged cloud gathering in the air above them and starting towards him and then he was concentrating on the house, on Holmes' house, on the faint yellow square of the doorway.

The bees were closer; he could hear them even over the pant of his own breathing. Their noise was constant, furious, mounting, itching in his ears and prickling his skin. He ran, moving swiftly from the meadow and onto the lawn, with its neat grass and sentinel plants, and as he went the bees were a cloud about him, almost invisible in the darkness, it was as though the night itself had come alive and had stretched out writhing arms to take hold of him. He ran, and the bees closed in.

Brabbins dashed through the doorway as the first bees started to land on him; one banged into his shoulder and span away, another flashed into his face and then was gone, more landed on his arms and dashed against his legs. Their buzz was a pitiless shriek that reminded him of drills and saws and factories full of sweat and dirt and poverty, and then he was into the house, slamming the door behind him. The swarm, for he could think of no other word for it, banged hard against the door behind him, a thousand or more tiny impacts making a noise like cloth being torn asunder, louder and louder as the tiny creatures battered themselves against the door. More struck the glass of the windows in a staccato beat, and then Brabbins' hand flamed with pain.

It was like nothing he had ever felt, a burning, roaring sensation that swept rapidly across the back of his hand and clutched at his knuckles and wrist. Looking down, Brabbins saw a fat bee crawling across his hand. He shook his hand, trying to dislodge it, but it clung on and stung him again, causing another wave of pain to coruscate in his palm and fingers. He used his other hand to knock the creature off, sending it to the floor, and then stepped on it before it could right itself and lift into the air. More crawled over his arms and legs, and he knocked them off with the papers, swatting at them and stepping on them until they were all dead. The bees outside seemed to redouble their efforts to gain entry, as though they knew of their fallen comrades.

Brabbins thrust his hand under the tap, letting the cold water play across his flaming skin. It was already swelling, he saw, rising around twin punctures. He scratched at them, half-remembering advice about getting out beestings, but all that emerged was his own blood, somehow paler and with a yellow tinge. *Is that poison? Is that what killed Swann? And Holmes?* he thought, and suspected that it was.

When his hand felt marginally better, although it remained reddened and swollen and painful to move, Brabbins picked up the papers from where he had dropped them, and then went through the house. The lounge and parlour had open fireplaces, piled with logs and kindling, so he shut the doors to both rooms, thankful that they fitted snug in their frames. He also shut the kitchen door, closing off the noise of the bees to a lesser degree. Already, tiny dark shapes were gathering on the outside of the small glass pane in the front door, their indistinct forms filling the available space. From behind both of the doors he had closed came the faint sound of something striking the wood, not hard but repeatedly. Brabbins went upstairs, checking all the windows as he went. None were open; the house was sealed.

Finally, Brabbins took the papers into the study, righting the chair and sitting down, noticing as he did so that he was shaking, nauseous. *The poison?* he wondered. *The fear?*

The Bees.

For a moment, he tried to put the bees out of his mind; they had him penned in the house, and he had no idea why they were acting so aggressively, but his policeman's instincts, honed by years of sifting through humanity's mud and detritus, of making sense from the senseless, told him the answers lay in the sheets of paper that Swann had been holding.

They were bound, he saw, neatly written and tied at the top and bottom left corners with loops of thick twine. He recognized the writing as Holmes' from the repeated 'No' on the letters, the words firm and decisive. The paper was thick and heavy,

expensive, and the writing was interrupted here and there with
illustrations and tables. *Is this what Swann died for?* Brabbins
thought as he looked at them. *Holmes? Two men, dead because of
this?*

Yes, he thought, and began to read.

> *It is my belief that British bees can be improved,*
> Brabbins read on the first page, *by the introduction of
> new queens from other breeds which possess the correct,
> desired, and beneficial traits. Having achieved some suc-
> cess in the breeding, and becoming familiar with the habits,
> strengths, and weaknesses of the more usual Western
> Honey Bee, in this paper I shall describe the initial attempts
> to improve upon this breed and outline any results that are
> obtained.*
>
> *Whilst the Western Honey Bee is currently the uni-
> versal breed hived in Britain, and is ideally suited to both
> the climate and the geography of this land, increasing
> industrialization and the spread of towns and concurrent
> population growth may require, in future, a bee that can
> travel further in search of pollen, or which has a longer
> breeding and production season and from which increased
> amounts of honey and wax can be harvested. Accordingly,
> looking overseas for hardier breeds to increase the value and
> usefulness of our stock is the only logical thing to do.*
>
> *Initially, of course, a suitable breed must be identi-
> fied and procured. Clearly, not all breeds will be suitable
> for husbandry because of differences in temperament or
> physiology. However, many come from the same root stock
> and so may prove to be viable partners. I shall endeavour
> to explain here why various breeds were dismissed and to
> show how the ultimate decision was made.*

Brabbins stopped reading and leafed through the next few
pages, seeing little of interest other than detailed descriptions
of breeds and their failings. Names such as *Buckfast Bee, Midnite
Bee, European Dark Bee*, and *Carnolian Bee* jostled alongside
phrases like *movable comb hives, Langstroth spaces* and *Dadant
design*. English, but still another language.

Eventually, Brabbins came to a new paragraph that read, *After
exhaustive study, it is clear that we must look further afield for the*

required breeding partner. Records of the earliest beekeepers, although scant, identify several species cultivated in more isolated regions, often by monks or other closed communities. These are the rarest of breeds and ones about whom little but the briefest of facts are known, except those which were written down by their original keepers. Of these, most can be dismissed immediately as variants on the breeds already discussed. However, one would seem to be an ideal candidate: the Northern Wild Bee, *occasionally called the* Volk's *or* Wolf Bee. *Almost unknown outside of a tiny area of Russia, this animal may be the perfect partner in this experiment.*

Below this were a series of diagrams, close up of bee parts that Brabbins only partly recognized; a segmented eye, a rounded body with measurement details alongside it, a wing. Further down were tables, each annotated with phrases like *queen breeding pattern* and *season lengths and gestation and hatching cycles.* Below each table was a short explanation of the way in which the Northern Wild Bee was an improvement on the Western Honey Bee. Finally, a longer paragraph ended the section: *The Northern Wild Bee has a larger body and can travel further in a day than Britain's indigenous bee population, giving the capacity for greater range and for greater honey and wax yield. It is physically stronger and has evolved to live in the harsher climes of northern Europe. It was transported to Germany in the early nineteenth century but proved a difficult creature to manage and did not last long, leaving only a few wild colonies scattered across the northern countries, their spread controlled by the depredations of the harshest of winter climates and the landscape. Despite problems sourcing the Northern Wild Bee as a result of the current world political situation, eggs were gathered from the remaining wild colonies and the experiment is now ready to begin. What follows is a record of its progress.*

Brabbins stopped reading and leafed through the remaining papers. They were written as diary entries, some with illustrations, each dated. The earliest contained repeating phrases like *breeding rates* and *cross-breed production* and, once, *reproduction characteristics and techniques* which made Brabbins rub his face in wonderment. What had this man, Holmes, done? Played with his bees while the letters piled up in his parlour, while the war raged in fields black with torn earth and death, and while tiny individual tragedies happened in back-alleys and homes across the country? For what? Wax and honey? And what had he *done?*

The next entry Brabbins read started with the word *Success!* and another picture, this one a delicately drawn picture of a bee. To Brabbins, it looked like any other bee; furred, with a bulbous body and head, and wings covered in the tracery of veins. Holmes had clearly seen differences to it, though. He had arrowed parts of the diagram, each arrow neatly labelled, *31% average increased mass, larger wingspan/distance for flying, slightly increased brain capacity.* There was more, but Brabbins stopped reading and flicked on to the next entries.

> *April 2nd: I have set up a single hive of the Northern Wild Bee crossbreed, alongside my existing Western Honey Bee hives; by doing so, I hope to show scientifically how much greater the productivity of the new strain is in comparison with our existing breeds. Already, the bees seem to be travelling farther and wider than the drones from the other hives. The pollen they collect is a different color, as though it includes content from plants that the other bees cannot reach or find. The first yields of honey have been promising in amount, although its flavour is slightly bitter and leaves a strange taste in the mouth after it is swallowed. The comb that contains it certainly seems sturdier, and the wax that can be harvested of a very high quality. One unexpected thing about the new breed is that its size gives it some increased ability to stave off the soporific effects of the smoker, requiring an increased level of caution from the keeper to avoid stings.*

Brabbins flicked back through the paper and found the picture of the bee, so neatly drawn and dissected upon the page. Even now, he could hear the bees battering themselves against the windows of the kitchen and front door and the wood of the two room doors, their angry buzz and the timpani of their impacts like the stuttering of some distant machine. *They haven't given up,* he thought, and turned back to the sheaf of paper.

> *April 23rd: The experiment goes tolerably well. The honey and comb yields are noticeably greater from the new hive than from my existing hives, leading me to believe that my original conjecture was correct — yields can be substantially increased by the application of scientific principle to bee-rearing. However, further unexpected elements have arisen that need consideration. The increased size of*

*the bees, and their wilder nature, has led to an increased
aggression and a greater preparedness to sting. The stings
themselves are extremely painful, far more so than those of
the Western Honey Bee or any of the other common breeds,
and cause high levels of swelling. The venom of the bee
would appear to be more powerful than that of its more
usual cousins, and longer acting. Unusually, the crossbreed
bee does itself no damage when it uses its sting, meaning it
can sting repeatedly without experiencing harm, and each
sting seems capable of delivering a venom load.*

Looking at his still aching hand, Brabbins smiled in humourless agreement. What had Holmes said the bee was sometimes
called? The Wolf Bee? That fitted; it was fast and vicious and
worked in a pack, overwhelming by sheer weight of numbers
and tenacity. Even now, the sound of them was filling the house,
bleeding in through glass that felt increasingly thin and fragile.
Although a heavy curtain covered the study's small casement
window, Brabbins could hear noises coming from behind it; the
solid impacts of things repeatedly banging against the glass,
and the fierce hum of the bees. Somehow, they had found this
window, knew he was behind it. Was it the light? No, there were
lights on in the other rooms. Could they hear him? Smell him?
He didn't know enough about bees to be sure. Perhaps it was just
a coincidence? No. No, the bees were targeting him, he didn't
know how he knew but he knew it, was sure of it. They were
chasing him.

Hunting him.

*May 1ˢᵗ: The breeding cycle is faster, and the queen
produces more eggs than the Western Honey Bee queen.
The hive is already full, leaving no space for new combs,
and the larvae are already larger than would be normal at
this stage of their development. The workers are bringing
in more nectar (by my estimation) than the bees of the other
hives. As a consequence, the social structure of the hive is
showing some unusual developments. Chief among these is
that, each morning, there are a number of bees and larvae
on the ground under the hive, some barely alive, but most
dead. Observations of the hive at night have shown that
the bees and larvae are placed there by other bees, pushed
out of the hive entrance in a constant stream through the
hours of darkness. I can only assume that some kind of cull*

is occurring each night, with those found to be imperfect or underdeveloped or underperforming in some way being removed to make way for new workers. There seems little other explanation, although what imperfections the dead creatures may have exhibited is hard to fathom. Certainly, investigations of the bodies have revealed no obvious flaws or deficiencies.

May 3rd: The hive is proving increasingly difficult to manage, even under optimal daytime conditions. The bees are extremely aggressive and defensive, and although they eventually calm under the influence of the smoker, their activity in the period before the soporific takes effect is somewhat unnerving. The bees begin, as would be expected, by trying to sting me, but seem to learn extremely rapidly that their primary weapon is of little use and cannot pierce my protective clothing. Then, they begin to cluster around the seams of the clothing, especially at the wrists and neck, and also across the facial netting of the helmet. It is almost as though the bees know to block my vision by gathering thickly across the material. Sometimes, the weight of the bees on the net is so great that it is forced close to my face and my vision is filled with naught but brown fur and stings and I have to shake the net clear of the creatures before I can carry on. In higher animals their clustering around the seams of my clothing might be taken to indicate an understanding of how it is designed and where its weak points exist, but in bees this is, of course, illogical. They almost certainly gather there simply because they are the areas that offer them the greatest purchase. Still; it is a strange coincidence.

Another strange thing: the hive seems ready to produce another swarm. There are definite signs that a second queen is being matured by one group of the drones, and she is already bigger than the larvae in the surrounding cells. This is, of course, extremely early for a second queen to be developing, and must indicate further evidence (if it were needed) that the Northern Wild Bee is ideal to introduce into the ecosystem of Britain. Such speed in new swarm development will allow for a greatly increased production of honey and wax, and shows that already this experiment is proving to be successful.

There followed several pages of diagrams showing the bees, or parts of them, from a variety of angles. One picture caught Brabbins' eye and he sat for a moment staring at it. In it, Holmes had carefully illustrated a dissected bee, using arrows to neatly label particular pieces of it. By one thing (which looked to Brabbins like a twisted balloon), Holmes had written, *Poison sacs.* Beneath this were a series of figures, the most noticeable of which was third in the list: *23% larger.* 23% more venom, the ability to sting repeatedly, increased aggressiveness; Christ, what had Holmes done here? thought Brabbins, and then, because he had no other option, he read on.

> *May 9th: It is not a second queen. Since hatching, it has remained in the hive and shows no inclination to either challenge the current queen or to form its own swarm and seek to establish its own colony. Rather, it seems to have removed some of the duties that were previously carried out by the existing queen, who seems to have been relegated to a simple breed production role. Whilst it is impossible to know how bees communicate within the hive, by observing the new social hierarchies developing it has been possible to ascertain that the new creature appears to be in control. It spends far longer than the queen engaged in complex inter-plays of movement and touch with the drones and warriors, whereas the old queen is rarely approached now apart from feeding rituals.*

> *May 11th: The new creature continues to grow, and although it is not as large as the queen, it is now consid-erably larger than the other inhabitants of the hive. The queen continues to be a presence and have a role in the hive, producing egg after egg, but she is clearly no longer the driving force behind the hive's activities. She is fed and her occasional needs are attended too, but that is all.*

> *May 14th: I have come to a startling conclusion: the new creature is not a queen, but a king. Long thought a myth, the Northern Wild Bee appears to allow the development of a king bee as well as a queen in its society. The king, slightly physically smaller than the queen, takes charge of the day to day running of the activities and of the work undertaken, controlling the actions of the workers and guards in a way*

that previously had been the responsibility of the queen. This will bear watching carefully, as it may indicate the advent of a new stage in the rearing and cultivating of bee societies.

May 19th: The bees have killed a dog. I would scarcely have believed it if I had been simply told, but I watched the incident occur, and I trust the judgement of my own eyes. The animal, a local farm dog, I believe, was in the field when I went to make my morning observations of the hives. As I checked my Western Honey Bee hives, it played around my feet, obviously hoping for reward. Upon my approach to the new hive, however, the bees started to gather in a black cloud in the air above us. At first, I thought this might be the emergence of a swarm, and that I had been wrong about the king; that it was simply a queen and that what I had observed was simply an unusual, more complex, process by which new queens are hatched and become independent. However, I was wrong.

The bees fell onto the dog with a noise like the shriek of a saw stuck in wet wood. One minute, it was at my feet, happy and panting and canine, and the next there was simply a mass of bees, so many that the shape of the dog was lost below. It howled, once, a terrible sound of pain and confusion that rose in pitch before it was cut off. The animal had its mouth open, its tongue covered in bees, all thrusting down with their stings, their abdomens clenched and pulsing. I used the smoker, to no avail; the bees seemed to have achieved some kind of blood lust, a rage that allowed them to shake off any effect from the smoke. When I tried to knock the bees off the dog, to give it a chance to run, they performed their usual activity of clustering in my visor, blocking my vision. They were so thick about my arms and head that, although I could not feel their stings through my clothing, the weight of them was obstructive, preventing me from moving my arms effectively, and causing in me a claustrophobia, as though I was under water with no hope of surfacing.

The bees, once the attack on the dog was over, left me. That the dog was dead was obvious when the bees rose, as though to one command, and flew back into the hive. The corpse they left behind was terrible. They had managed to

puncture the dog's eyes, blood and ocular fluid had spat-
tered down the sides of its snout, glistening and staining
its fur in dark streaks. Its tongue had swelled to the size
of a bull's so that the sides of its face were pushed out, and
pink flesh emerged from between its teeth. What I saw of
the gums showed that they had stung it there and, although
its fur may have offered it some protection, its flanks bulged
with poison. It had voided its bowels in the extremities of its
fear and pain and the smell of it was strong and foul. Over
that smell, however, was another, the olfactory equivalent
of the strange, bitter aftertaste of the honey produced by the
hive. When I went to move towards the hive, the cloud of
bees reappeared and although they did not attack, the threat
was clear. I left my field in a state, for the first time in my
life, of terror.

May 20ᵗʰ: Following the attack on the dog, I have found
myself carefully considering the facts of this most curious
of cases, and the fears that it has raised in me. The dog
posed no threat to the bees, yet they attacked anyway. The
assault was swift, unforgiving, unprovoked, and merciless,
and whilst it may have only been a stray farm dog that took
the brunt of the savagery on this occasion, I cannot guaran-
tee that this will always be the case. I am beset by images of
a child from the village, or a farmhand, or Mrs. Roundhay
one day straying too close to the hive and raising the bees'
ire. Without the benefit of protective clothing, they would
be killed as surely as the dog was, and I am tormented by
visions of a person, the bees clustered about them as he lies
in the field by the hives, his flesh swollen and blackened,
and the smell of venom hanging in the air around them.

The vision does not end there. Past the dead on the
ground, in the distant fields and in the woods and eaves
where bees make their homes, I saw new hives being con-
structed, some by man and some by the bees themselves,
their ordered waxen combs containing worker after worker,
each equipped with a savage and pitiless sting and with
venom that burned. I saw, somewhere deep in these hives,
the gestation and birth of new kings, each as violent and
aggressive as the other, and I heard an inhuman buzz fill
the air. It is not just the regrettable incident with the dog
that has caused these visions, however, but another thing.

*In my tending to the other hives over the past weeks, I have
noticed an increased aggressiveness in the bees and, this
morning, I found in two of them the larval stage of the king
bee.*

    *I have little choice now. I shall study the hives carefully
for the next day to ascertain when activity in them is at a
minimum and the risk at its least, and then I shall burn
them and all of their inhabitants. My experiment has been,
in the strangest way, too successful, and is at an end.*

Brabbins put the papers down. The last of them was dated
the day before Holmes' death, and he wondered how it had happened; had the man approached the hive without his protective
clothing? No, he was clearly not stupid. Had he underestimated
the bees? Brabbins thought that perhaps he had, and had paid
for that underestimation with his life. He had treated them as
something limited, mere insignificances to remove but not to
regard warily, neither intelligent nor able to plan. They had
known what was coming, somehow, and had attacked Holmes
pre-emptively. Had they swooped down out of the sky as he
took a last turn around his garden before bed? The night had
been warm, Brabbins remembered; maybe he was in the house
with the back door open and the bees had come in, a last, awful
visitor for the man who had helped so many others in his life. He
would never know, of course, but it nagged at him, leaving a hole
in the picture he had painted for himself of what had happened.

"Solved," he said quietly to himself, not liking the way his
voice trembled. "The dead man was killed by bees of his own
breeding because he trusted to the logic of the situation rather
than the reality of it. It is impossible for bees to plan, and so they
cannot have plans to act upon. They cannot predict or assume
or pre-empt, for they are bees. Only, these bees can, and they
did, and the impossible became possible." He stopped; his voice
sounded like it came from someone else's throat, distant and
scared. And Swann? Had he understood? No, he thought not.
He had known the bees were a part of it, but not how. How could
he? Wandering out there, blithely approaching his own death.
Brabbins swore, his fear giving way to anger. They were bees.

    Bees.

Brabbins hand throbbed, the fingers aching as he flexed
them into a tight fist. Standing, he drew back the curtain from
the window. Even if it had been daylight outside, he would not

have been able to see; the glass was covered, filling the small space with ever-moving brown shapes. They crawled over one another, lifting away and then battering back into the pane in waves, as though seeking some synchronisation in their attacks. The glass was smeared with pale fluid, he saw, dribbles of it coming from the stings that banged against the window with sharp little clicks. It gathered in little puddles against the bottom of the wooden frame. The window shook as the creatures banged into it. *How long before they manage to break through?* he thought. *How long before they find another way in, something that I've missed?*

Brabbins went down the stairs. He wondered briefly about trying to distract the bees somehow, getting them to gather against one part of the house whilst he ran from some other exit but dismissed the idea immediately. Holmes' house was miles from anywhere, and the bees would catch him before he got far. Fire? No. He would never stop the bees getting to him, and he could hardly burn them off the windows without burning the house down. He was trapped.

No, he suddenly realized, he was not. A search of the downstairs of the house turned up Holmes' beekeeping clothing in a cloakroom. Hurriedly, he shrugged it on; trousers and a white smock. Holmes had been taller and the legs and sleeves gathered in bunches around his ankles and wrists, but he tied the cuffs as tight as he could round his wrists and ankles. Before pulling on the gauntlets and net helmet, he put Holmes' papers on the kitchen table, weighting them with the mug that Swann had used for the same purpose earlier in the day, and next to them he scrawled a note that said simply: *These are genuine and their contents should be treated with the utmost seriousness. Look for my body and tell my wife I love her. Insp. W. M. Brabbins.* At least that way, if something did happen to him, there was some record of what had happened. His body, and Swann's in the garden, would add weight to the evidence. They'd have to believe it.

Brabbins pulled on the helmet and gloves, tying them as tightly as he could, trying to ensure that he left no gaps between them and the other garments. Had he put them on correctly? He had no idea. Only time would tell. Finally, he went to the front door. The bees against the other side of the small porthole window in the centre of the door, as if they sensed his intention, began to beat themselves against the glass even more furiously. *Perhaps they do know what I'm planning. I don't suppose it would surprise me if they did; nothing would at this point,* he thought. He readied himself but, before he could open the door, there was a *crack* from behind him.

Undecided, Brabbins paused, and there was another *crack*. It came from the kitchen, he realized, was audible even through the closed door. In spite of himself, he went down the hallway and opened the door slightly, peering cautiously inside the room. At first, he thought that what he saw was a shadow, or the way the netting draped across his face moved in front of his eyes, but then he realized that it was bees. One of the panes of glass had cracked and a piece of glass fallen away, and bees were crawling in through the tiny hole, tumbling over themselves in their desperation to get in. Once in, they rose into the air like burned paper drifting above a fire, circling in odd, elliptical patterns. Instead of coming towards the door, however, towards him, they flew to the centre of the room and clustered around the manuscript on the table, burying it in an undulating, shifting blanket. The mug weighing the paper down toppled over and rolled until it stopped, prevented by its handle from turning further. Its inside contained bees, he saw, so many of them that they filled it like viscid liquid. Under their hum, the bees were making another sound, a moist, mulching noise that made him think of tiny jaws chewing and tearing. Pieces of paper began to flutter out of the mass and then he realized what they were doing to the manuscript and he turned and ran.

As though his movement had caught their attention, the bees coming in through the window shifted, arrowing out of the kitchen and gathered around him as he ran, the first of them landing on him, crawling across his visor and interrupting his vision with dark shapes the color of fury. He crashed into the front door, his gloved fingers pulling clumsily at the latch as more bees swarmed in the air around his head and shoulders and their companions on the other side of the glass became even more agitated. He had no choice now. Yanking open the door, he started to run.

With a hum that was more like a shriek, the bees were about him in seconds.

SIMON KURT UNSWORTH story 'The Church on the Island' was nominated for a World Fantasy Award. His short story collection *Lost Places* was recently released by Ash Tree Press. Simon's work has also appeared in the anthologies *Shades of Darkness, Lovecraft Unbound, Exotic Gothic 3, At Ease with the Dead* and *Gaslight Grotesque: Nightmare Tales of Sherlock Holmes*.

SHERLOCK HOLMES
AND THE GREAT GAME

by Kevin Cockle

Where dogs had got at them, blood was caked into snow —
frozen like stained glass in grisly ruby pools.

"Ice picks," Holmes muttered, indicating trace evidence in
the shattered dome of the nearest igloo. "Here. And here, you
see." Watson did not see, though he had no doubt.

"People-killing arrows," Holmes continued, stooping to
examine one of the shafts used against the slain. "Not hunting
arrows. Deliberate and pre-meditated Watson, all of this. Very
much so."

Watson shuddered, repressing memories of similar atrocities
seen years ago and a world away. Afghan mountains meshed
with Canadian ice in his imagination: slaughter was slaughter whenever, wherever; the vividness could not be unseen.
He shifted the weight of the Lee Enfield .303 on his shoulder
and cast his gaze out into the bleak blue-white horizon. Here
and there, a body dotted the landscape. Dark piles of fur stark
against the white.

Holmes stood, his tall frame given impressive bulk by the
Caribou-skin parka and breeches supplied by the North West
Mounted Police. His aquiline nose protruded just past the edges
of the hood, betraying his lean lines. If not for that angular, fine-
boned face, Sherlock Holmes would have seemed a bear of a
man with the weight of kit upon him.

"Not for food, nor materials," Holmes said, boots grinding
on snow as he made his way through the hunting settlement.

Stopping at a smaller imploded igloo, he regarded the huddled occupants. "Raiding is a poor strategy in the north, Watson, one rarely sees it. Not slavers..." he paused in mid thought. "Hold on." He circled the igloo, eyeing the tracks all round.

"Here, Watson! Signs of a struggle... one of these unfortunates being led away. Yes! This was it — this was the prize they sought. Confident beggars — they've made no effort to conceal their tracks!"

"We follow, then?" Watson said, shivering at the thought.

"Definitely," Holmes smiled. "The game, dear Watson, is most assuredly afoot!"

Watson caught the look in Holmes' eye — that look so often described as a cocaine-induced glaze in the written accounts, but which in truth was of a far different nature altogether.

"Holmes," Watson said, lowering his voice, "do you really see these clues in the snow, or have you divined them? Are you certain a captive was taken?"

Holmes grinned. "One way or the other, I have seen it, and it is true. Come!"

With urgent energy, Holmes marched back to the dog sled. Two junior constables stood waiting, faces white as the snow they stood upon, anxious eyes peering out from fur-lined hoods like the eyes of wolf-spooked sheep.

"We're going on," Holmes informed the men. The man on the left — Ryan — hugged himself in an unconscious gesture of self-preservation. "We're close now," Holmes continued, "maybe a few hours behind, and these savages are in no hurry."

"But our orders sir..." the man on the right — Culloden — began.

"You will follow them. Make camp close by. We've two good hours of sunlight left. Let us make use of them. Keep a close watch. These bodies will attract company sooner rather than later."

"You should'na go just the two of you sir," Culloden said.

Holmes smiled almost parentally. "You're good lads, and fine policemen, but you are not up to this. Make camp; get some food together. We'll be wanting dinner when we return."

Watson turned from the men, did his own calculations. Going back to Dawson and mustering a force was out of the question. The seal hunting season was drawing to a close and ice would be breaking up soon. Holmes was right: the chance was now, or never.

Two thoughts occurred to Dr. Watson: *There is nothing here to indicate that anyone has survived this massacre, or been taken from the scene* and *Holmes doesn't want witnesses where we are going.*

Anernerk stared at the chains which bound her to the sled, her manacled hands heavy in her lap, and thought: *These are too big for me.* The iron was old, rusted, foreign. She sat with her legs tucked up underneath her, staying quiet, staying still, as dogs pulled, and a man pushed at the handles just behind her. They need not have bound her. Their precautions were ridiculous. Where would she run? To whom would she go, now that her family had been extinguished?

She tried not to see the details. The moonlight punching through the roof of the igloo as the men bludgeoned their way in. The screams; the dull squish and thud of the killing strokes. She had screamed too, but had been stopped short by a gonging voice in her head — a voice not her own — and images that crowded out her own shrill thoughts of terror.

Stars. The voice had shown her stars, made her see a particular pattern, made her focus upon it. At first, the voice had spoken gibberish to her, but had changed in tone and articulation, almost as though sifting through sounds to find her language, and when it did, it said: "It is time. It is near equinox. You will come to me. You will come to me now."

She had closed her eyes then, listening to the distant screams, knowing there was nothing she could do. She had kicked out in reflex, fighting in futility as she was bundled out through the shattered ceiling of the igloo by strong, silent attackers. They had made no sound throughout the massacre — no war cries, no exultant shouts of triumph. They had killed with cold ferocity, like an Arctic blizzard unleashed. She was theirs now; she belonged to them even as they belonged to the voice. She did not weep, or wail, or bargain, for that was not the Nunamiut way.

Now, in an effort to repress the memories of slaughter, she recalled her father's voice singing a traditional lament in his husky, warbling tone:

Hard times, dearth times
Plague us every one
Stomachs are shrunken
Dishes are empty

Over and over she recited the words to herself and stared without expression at her lap. No tears fell, for a hard life had shaped her early for the acceptance of things. Sometimes, the caribou did not come in the spring. Sometimes, the seal holes could not be found. Her only hope was that it would be quick and painless, whatever they had in mind for her.

The sun had crept up on its low trajectory, and the sled had come to a stop at the crest of a shallow rise. Anernerk looked up then, and her mouth gaped open in astonishment for two reasons. The first was for the structure in the distance, immense and dark and utterly beyond her ability to comprehend.

The second was because one of the men had put back his hood to reveal his face. She knew him, had once shed the tears for him that she had yet to shed for her slain kinfolk. It was her grandfather, who had been left to die three winters ago on pack ice, unable at the last to walk on used up legs. He stood strong and straight now, though his hair blew whale-bone white in the slight northerly breeze.

He turned his face to look upon her without recognition, without pity.

His eyes were the washed out blue of a pack dog's, strange and horrifying and cold.

The jagged majesty of the ice filled Watson with primordial awe. He'd seen a fair piece of the world — been to every corner of the empire either with or without Holmes — but he had never quite seen anything to rival the vast bleak Canadian north. Walls of ivory jutting into the clear blue sky, and drifting, susurrant serpents of windblown snow. Cool pools of blue shadow in the lees of icy rises. Water so clear and clean it looked like glass. And treachery amidst the breathtaking beauty, lying in wait to pounce upon the slightest mistake.

"I quite honestly don't know what to make of it," Lieutenant-Colonel Gerald Reed had said back at camp in Dawson. He was a priggish man, but resolute enough, with a back straight as a mainmast, and a neck thick as a kilderkin. Before him, on his desk, lay the papers from Whitehall, complete with parliamentary seal, outlining the terms of Holmes' special service. "They are... well, that is to say... attacks, of some kind, as it were."

"Attacks." Holmes repeated. "Implying the imposition of main force? Warfare, I am given to believe, does not exist here, in the sense that we employ it."

"Whole settlements destroyed, Holmes. Systematically. Casualties exacted to the last man. Pursuit. That is not the tribal, vendetta way, no. It is rather more... European in nature. As it were."

"And you suspect..."

Reed swallowed, mustering his confidence. "The Russians."

"The Russians," Holmes repeated, this time failing to disguise his skepticism. "Hoping to secure control of the strategic seal-skin and blubber markets?"

"Well, damn it all, Holmes... that's what you are here to determine! All along the seal hunting grounds — entire settlements wiped out, and bloodthirsty work it is too. Not our business by and large, but if it is some Russian gambit..."

"Ah yes: a feint away from Afghanistan. A grand encirclement via the north pole."

"The Russians, Holmes," Reed's voice had frosted over, even as his cheeks warmed scarlet, "are always a potential regional threat; consequently we have an obligation to investigate. You are the pre-eminent investigator in her majesty's service; ergo you will put the theory to the test. We've men and supplies at your disposal, but I have it from The Chamber itself that you are not to engage. Find out what the devil is going on. Find out the why, and the who, but take no chances. London wants you on the case, but they don't want you harmed, or I shall answer for it."

"Indeed. So it is the great game of nations that brings me to your wasteland. I should have suspected no less."

Watson scowled at the memory. It was always difficult to interpret Holmes' motives, or even accept the initial premise of any case at face value. Was it the government asking for Holmes' assistance in this instance, or had he somehow engineered the invitation? Was Holmes truly acting in his capacity as special investigator for the empire, or did he have his own private reasons for pursuing the matter? Watson couldn't say, but the mere fact of his speculation told him how far their friendship had evolved over the years.

Watson's back ached, and the occasional step was announced by a loud, sclerotic popping of his right knee. The air was not so frigid as it would have been in high winter, but it still clawed at his tobacco-coated lungs. And his shoulder of course — the one that had taken that Jezail bullet at Maiwand — that throbbed in echo to his laboured heartbeats. *Shoulder*, he chided himself ruefully. *Be honest with yourself. Be as honest with yourself as you are suspicious of Holmes. That bullet took more than shoulder, and you know it.*

Holmes set a tireless pace, his long-shanked stride crunching rhythmically against hard-packed snow. Here and there, tracks were visible even to Watson, but Holmes did not trust to them alone. Now, out of sight of the constabulary, Holmes freely referred to the fourteen inch, cruel-looking Zulu blade with its elephant-tusk pommel and strange glyphs upon the steel. The metal glowed with an eerie incandescence, gently guiding Holmes towards his quarry with more surety than any tracker.

Watson suppressed a shudder. Again the Zulu knife was leading them on; the knife that Murray had laid upon him after defeat at Maiwand; the knife that had stopped the bleeding of his open and failing heart, and made him whole again. The knife that had kept them hidden all during that nightmare retreat to Kandahar, with Afghan warriors harassing and killing at every step of those 314 infernal miles.

"I dreamed of you," Murray had said, on the night that Watson had cheated death through Zulu sorcery. "I brought this damned thing out of Africa... for you. I want no part of it, John."

Murray had given him the knife, and soon thereafter, Watson had begun dreaming of Holmes — seeing him clearly before even knowing his face or name.

The injury, the long retreat, his honourable discharge ... all in the service of delivering an arcane artifact to a total stranger who would one day become closer than family.

Closer perhaps, but not nearly as familiar.

"You're brooding," Holmes said, without looking at his friend.

"I knew it was magic, Holmes, back at the settlement. Blast! Why the charade?"

"Leadership, my good doctor, the men were terrified. Brandishing a sorcerous artifact might well have routed them. Nothing holds the line like the imposition of true reason. They heard me make order out of chaos, and were becalmed."

Watson snorted.

"You're in a mood," Holmes observed.

"It's the forced march, I'm afraid. I'm feeling my age. We could at least have taken the sled."

Holmes smiled. "That's not entirely precise, is it?"

Watson scowled. "Damn it Holmes, I just... I do not understand why I can't simply tell the truth in my accounts. Every time I recount how you glean facts from observing minutiae, or deduce conclusions from seemingly unconnected events, I feel a charlatan. It weighs on me, you know? You have a singular talent — a gift beyond all science — yet you insist on these elaborate, outrageous tales of deduction."

"Are they not popular?"

"Yes! Yes damn it, they ARE popular, but that makes the lie all the heavier."

"Watson. There is no point in telling a truth to people who will not credit it. Look at Challenger's nonsense: tales to amuse old ladies and young boys, or so they are perceived. By couching my exploits in the language of science, you do more good than you know. I daresay you are pivotal to the entire enterprise, Watson. Trust me. You serve a higher purpose."

Watson glared. It was not the first time Holmes had deflected him from this topic.

"Could all this possibly be the Russians?"

Holmes barked laughter. "It may well turn out to be Cossacks, though I wouldn't lay odds on it. No Watson, there *is* a great game being played here, but I do not think the players are kings and earthly governments. I have never felt the pull of the blade as strongly as I do now. Something massive lurks in the distance Watson, I feel it!"

Holmes' eyes shone, catching the dagger's light, and Watson swallowed. The dagger had used them both — Watson as a messenger, and conveyance from Africa to England via Afghanistan; Holmes as an agent — but for what design, the Doctor had never been able to conceive. Were the horrors all connected in some way — all the stories he had retold as logical puzzles — could they be sewn together into a larger tapestry if the real details were laid out plain?

Watson simply didn't know. He was complicit in an elaborate ruse, the truth of which made no sense, and the lies of which proved best-sellers. In the end, he had to do what he had always done: trust Holmes. A hard thing to do, made harder with each passing adventure.

They soldiered on, passing from ridge to ridge at a steady pace. A gloom had descended upon Watson: too much mention of Afghanistan with its horrors both human and supernatural. Holmes for his part hummed as he strode, drifting from classical passages to music hall refrains as his mood dictated. With the dagger feeding him, drawing him on, he seemed to pulse in sympathy with its hellish glow. Cocaine had always seemed to Watson an appropriate metaphor for what the dagger did to Holmes.

With the sun sliding inexorably into the ice, and the indigo shadows growing longer around them, Holmes and Watson topped a gentle slope and dropped immediately to prone positions.

Holmes grinned too hard and too wide, his eyes dancing. Watson sucked in his breath, squinting his eyes against the cold. His vision was not what it once was, but it wasn't the clarity of what he saw that made him doubt his senses — only the sheer improbability of the hulk in the distance.

It was a galleon — shattered and ragged and black against the ice — which listed a quarter turn on its starboard side. She was three-masted, Spanish hulled, and a gigantic gash split her side, half filled in with blown snow. She was an old ship, probably three, four hundred years out of date — one of the great Atlantic deep-sea traders the Dons had used to empty Mexico of its gold.

Men moved upon the derelict's frozen and desolate decks, shuffling and battening down against the coming night. They had built and added onto the existing structure of the ship, ramshackle constructs, like webs stretched between rotted tree trunks. Canvas lean-tos and wooden sheds broke up the nautical lines of the once-proud vessel; hanging lanterns illuminated the scene in a hard yellow light.

"Our quarry, Watson," Holmes breathed.

The doctor shifted his position, wincing in discomfort. "They have the advantage of us, Holmes."

"We shall see. You're a fine hand with the service revolver, but how are you with the rifle?"

"Respectable, I daresay. But Holmes..."

"They are vermin, doctor. We shall show no mercy."

Watson thought of the hunting camp they had left behind; saw red-coated bodies slumped in their lines at Maiwand. He swallowed, and his throat was dry.

"Do we offer battle, or attempt a skulk?" Watson asked.

"There is a captive in the game," Holmes replied. "Perhaps dead already, though likely not. These reavers will fight to keep what they've shed so much blood to take. And if they fight, I would rather meet them out here, than in there."

Watson grunted, rising to one knee. The resulting pop was so loud, it almost sounded like the first gunshot. He slung the Enfield off his shoulder, and withdrew ammunition boxes from the cavernous pockets of his parka. He tilted the rifle up and let loose a shattering salvo into the twilight, the frozen air lending a sharpness to the retort that hastened its shriek across the ice.

Instantly, pack-dogs yelped and howled; men on the ship whirled and stood motionless, astonished at the presence of intruders. The amazement passed, and Watson saw the figures vanish into the ship's hold like a swarm of cockroaches to stream out onto the snow from the jagged tear in the ship's hull. Eight dark-cloaked figures fluttered in the distance, running full-tilt towards the duo like great rushing bats just skimming the surface of a great frozen lake.

Watson nestled himself soundly on one knee, slowing his breathing.

They had a good two hundred yards or more to clear to his position, up a gentle, but long incline. *Not a rifle amongst 'em,* Watson thought. *Not even a bow.*

They were all as good as dead, every man jack of them.

KRAK! The Enfield slammed against Watson's shoulder and he saw a figure jerk and drop backwards as though clothes-lined by an unseen wire. His accomplices rushed on, plunging forward as Watson ejected the cartridge and calmly reset the bolt. He had been modest in his self-assessment: he was a dead shot over the killing range of the Enfield. He'd proven it many times over the years, though his skill rarely made the written accounts. "It must be brains over brawn; science over force that forms the thrust of these tales," Holmes would frequently emphasize. It would never do to mention the blood Dr. Watson had been obliged to spill, on top of everything else.

KRAK! Watson recalled the ragged line at Maiwand: volley fire shredding howling ghazis on the approach.

KRAK! The tips of his fingers singed by the scorching heat of the chamber as comrades fell, and ragtag squares formed in doomed isolation.

KRAK! He'd killed men at Maiwand with this same lethal precision, and none of them, he knew, so deserving as the ones he claimed today.

KRAK!
KRAK!
KRAK!

He'd missed once and two men kept up their headlong pace, now less than a hundred yards from him. Blinking to refocus, operating in strict military cadence, he ejected and reloaded, brought butt to shoulder ... and froze, momentarily stunned by what he was seeing.

One of the downed had risen, was shaking off the shot, and was *staggering forward once again!* Another man Watson had sworn he'd hit square to the left side of the chest got to his knees, and reeled to his feet to renew his lurching advance. They were slowed, but those who had gone down now rose again, forcing the doctor to hasten his tempo.

He put another round into the first man he had downed, and another into the second. He shot the third man's thigh and dropped him again, only to watch him writhe, roll, rise and now *walk* forward. The hackles on Watson's burly neck rose, and he knew it wasn't from the cold. "Good Lord," he whispered, awe-struck.

"Indeed," Holmes countered.

The reavers had closed to within twenty yards.

Holmes grinned, and lunged forward, a canine snarl rippling his thin lips.

Watson had seen Sherlock Holmes close for hand-to-hand on many occasions, knew that his friend had made no little study of the combative arts, but the chilling efficiency and balance of the man routinely amazed nonetheless. He was wiry-strong, and naturally agile, but these components amplified by the dagger's eldritch energy made Holmes a thing of slashing lethality. And even without Zulu magic, no man alive was better at obtaining and keeping initiative. Holmes' judgment of distance and timing were exquisite.

Holmes bent low, put his shoulder into the first man's hip, using his own momentum to hoist him up and over in a tumble of seal skin cloak and hide-bound legs. The second man rushed in with a thrusting harpoon in both hands, but his angle was bad, and Holmes had position. He swept the point aside with his left forearm, and walked his man onto the point of the Zulu knife — the broad, killing blade sighing into the man's ribcage as though pushing through dense, wet clay.

The tribesman's hood fell back, and Watson felt a thrill of fear pulse down his spine at the sight. The man was native, distant kin to those butchered some leagues to the south, but his face was a feral, twisted parody of theirs, and his eyes shone an impossible robin's-egg blue. He clutched at his wound and slid off the blade, falling back onto his shoulders, his knees bent beneath him. Though he bled from a bullet wound in his chest, it had taken an African dagger to end the unspeakable life of this hellbound slayer.

Holmes whirled as the first man closed again, the tribesman's face grotesque with hate. The man had produced a rust-encrusted rapier, of all things, holding it as one might hold a simple club. Holmes sidestepped awkwardly, stumbling as snow bit at his calves, but he recovered nicely, drawing the keen edge of his blade across the man's jugular from an oblique angle. The native pitched face-first into the snow, hands clawing at his throat as his eerie life bled out crimson against the crisp, pristine white.

From there, Holmes pressed his attack to the others, but found that Watson's bullets had done most of the work after all. Incredibly, the wounded had dragged themselves up that sweeping ice hill, lungs collapsed or thighs belching blood from throbbing arteries. They clung grimly to savage life, and their faces bespoke the same dark, malicious energy upon which the first two had drawn.

The dagger took each in turn: one touch of it, so long as it drank of their blood, was all it took to still them. In moments, Holmes stood alone, chest heaving, breath condensing fog-white in the Arctic air. Watson closed from a respectful distance, eyeing his friend warily, noting the barely contained bloodlust in those usually reserved eyes.

"Holmes?" Watson said from fifteen feet away, not pointing the rifle at his friend directly, but holding it at the ready nonetheless.

Holmes nodded, panting. "Fear not, doctor. I am in complete control of my faculties."

"Grand," said Watson, not comforted by the fact that he needed to be told.

Holmes smiled. "Shall we?"

They stepped their way to the galleon, Watson noting eight fallen foes en route. *Poor devils*, he thought. He could not help but feel that ending them had saved them somehow, from something darker than death.

And then a thought unbidden: *would Holmes not also be saved thus?*

Watson clenched his teeth so hard, he heard them squeak in his head.

At the gaping maw of the hull breach, Holmes stopped, resting a foot against the lowered shards of shattered planks like so many broken teeth. Watson crept close, peering in around Holmes' shoulder, sensing large crates just out of sight in the gloom, and smelling a peculiar, vaguely familiar reek. Shouldering the Enfield, Watson prepared his service revolver, and whispered: "Ready."

Holmes eased himself into the ship with a lithe, silent cat's step, and Watson followed with the scrabbling grace of a bulldog charging a hedge.

The ship creaked and groaned under its own shifting weight, making Watson flinch at the erratic noises. Dim arctic light spilled in between gaps in the ancient planks, or through the massive puncture, turning absolute darkness into a frigid murk. Snow ground beneath their boots for a ways, then wood alone sounded out. Wooden crates lay in haphazard piles, worrying Watson with their proximity. Anything could be lying in the shadows, hidden from sight — just waiting for them to pass.

Inching forward, Holmes made the bulkhead door, sheathing the knife to work the portal with his gloved hands. "Heat," he murmured, glancing back at Watson, and gesturing at the sliding bolt that held the door fast. Slipping the latch back, Holmes shouldered the door open, and both men were instantly met by a fetid, sweltering breeze drenched with the odor of rotted vegetation, dank soil, and endless rain. It was downright tropical, that wind. Watson placed the smells, the temperature, and the humidity as something more Caribbean than Arctic in derivation.

A small access corridor cut longitudinally across the length of the ship, leading to darkened stairwells at both ends. Before the intruders, and slightly to the right, another bulkhead door led into what Watson supposed would be the cargo-hold proper. He grunted, and lifted the pistol off his hip, edging in front of Holmes to take the lead. With the clear view, he could see a pale, feeble light shining around the edges of the door. "Shoot to kill," Holmes whispered from very close behind. "This will be hot work at close quarters."

Watson heard the oily rasp of the knife being drawn from its sheath, and the sound made him think of Indian cobras.

Watson approached the portal, braced his legs wide as if in a scrum. He tried the knob and found it sticky, but unlocked. Turning it, he shouldered the door in and crouched down, blinking as a gust of air hit him in the face as though he'd just opened a baking oven.

Hanging seal-oil lamps cast even, gentle light around a large room, and Watson's mind reeled at the sight. Chests of doubloons and small ingots of gold lay open, or in smashed piles of wood and metal. Light caromed off emeralds and rubies set in rings and bracelets; turquoise and silver belts and bangles lay in casual heaps. It was all the wealth Watson could have imagined in three lifetimes of adventure, but he barely registered the opulence, so thunderstruck was he by the room's other contents.

The floor was overgrown with moss and a thick, spongy loam. A great tree trunk pushed up out of the floor and thrust up through the roof, presumably spreading out amongst the upper decks. And at the base of the tree lay an altar of human skulls, bracketed and reinforced with golden framing. A large gong stood off to one side, its face engraved in the style of the Aztecs to reveal a circular procession of creatures real and imagined. As Watson's eyes scanned the room, Aztec fixtures and carvings, furniture and treasure littered the scene: looted, and herein preserved before they could have been melted down and recast in Spanish forms.

A Nunamiut girl lay upon the altar, her arms and legs outstretched and quivering as though restrained by some unseen force. Her eyes stared and rolled in their sockets, reminding Watson of the horses at Maiwand as they bolted in panic. She was dressed head to toe in ornate woven feathers and reeds: a great head-dress; a sort of corset; a skirt and loincloth. Her pale limbs trembled, her northern pallor utterly alien to the clothing and the scene around her. Upon her breast, a cruel silver dagger lay flat, its edge curved like the undulating path of a winding serpent.

Watson moved into the room, throwing back his hood against the heat. Sweat poured from his brow, and he wiped his face with the sleeve of his left arm to clear his vision. Stepping towards the girl, he felt a thrill of shock shoot through him, like a tremendous charge of static electricity, and all at once he found himself transported...

From a great height, as though he were a gull on the wing, he looked down and watched as members of the Netsilik tribe abandoned one of their elderly to die alone on pack ice. In his fear and isolation, the man called out, and many leagues to the west, the altar answered. "I am Tezcatlipoca," a voice crooned in the tribesman's head. "Come to me and live."

The man came. On foot and alone, he should have perished, but he came. He and other outcasts, over the span of centuries crossed the ice at the altar's will, and were preserved by it in perpetuity. Hunting settlements with shamans and spells of protection could not hear the voice, would not heed it: when such settlements came close enough to the wrecked ship, they died. Watson saw it happen, heard it explained in a language not of words, knew it to be true even as all sense of distance and time drifted away from him.

A jungle rose up before John Watson, and great flat-topped pyramids of stone appeared. An endless parade of human sacrifices came and went, screaming and wriggling in unheeded agony. The sun blazed hot in a cloudless sky, its trajectory assured by the constant killing, and in the minds of the priests a voice was heard: "I am Tezcatlipoca. Kill for me and live!"

Arctic winds blew as huddled proto-Siberians crossed into North America for the first time, bringing with them the voice; naming it; speaking it. They spread down through the continent over the course of millennia, eventually becoming the Inca, the Maya and the Aztec, but they never forgot the ice deep and sub-merged in their hearts. "I am Tezcatlipoca, who was Tezkul-oc," the voice said, and the hot, moist, Aztec voice was tinged with ancient frost.

A storm raged at sea; a Spanish captain, eyes wild with hyste-ria, fought the elements as he lashed himself to his wheel. "I am Tezcatlipoca," the voice boomed in his head. "I will go home." That which had been plundered now took command; the altar with a hellish will of its own sped the ship ever northward to its icy doom.

"I am Tezcatlipoca," the voice now thrummed in Watson's head, roaring the way a pounding sea crashes against the surf. "Kill for me and live!"

Somehow, Watson had traversed the room, was standing next to the altar. He couldn't remember dropping his gun, but there it was at the roots of the tree behind him. In his hand, he held the serpentine dagger and had hoisted it high above his head. The girl on the altar squirmed in terror, her neck straining to release a scream that would not come. Watson gasped at the effort of resistance it took to stay his hand — the dagger poised to plunge down and into the chest plate of the trembling sacrifice.

And then: Sherlock Holmes.

The Zulu knife met the serpentine with a ringing clang, and lightning-blue light blasted forth from the contact. The girl unleashed her scream at last, a distant echo to the screams of long lost sisters who had died generations ago and continents away. The girl screamed, and Watson screamed with her as dark magicks surged through his body like a completed cir-cuit. Arcane war was fought out in his cells; his limbic system became a bubbling battleground. And all around, the room was drenched in the sudden white hot light of African and Mexican suns in collision.

The dogs were restless, tails twitching, ears twisting with every new sound. Sacks of golden treasure, jewels, ornaments, trinkets and artifacts weighed down the sled: everything needed for the trip back had been available on the ship. The girl, whose name might have been Anerkernek, although Watson couldn't be certain, sat atop a mound of treasure, bundled in caribou skins twice too large for her. She looked in the direction Holmes and Watson looked, and all three faces glowed with firelight.

The ship crackled and blazed, bathing the onlookers in brazen orange hues, and seething warmth. Lights arced into the sky from the burning hold — green and violet and pink — like an Aurora Borealis as the shattered altar within gave up its accursed energies. Watson felt the heat upon his face, smelled the smoke, thought of burning villages and endless campfires while on march with the 66th foot Regiment. *I was a pawn then, and am still,* he reflected. *What on Earth happened here? And what of Holmes? Does he still wield the dagger, or does the dagger wield him?*

"I don't envy you this one," Holmes chuckled, his voice straining for a jaunty tone, but failing under the weight of extreme fatigue. Watson winced at the sight of his friend: the eyes bloodshot and receding into their sockets; the cheeks sunken — that thin face turned gaunt by the exercise of the Zulu knife. If wielding the blade brought to mind the surging pleasures of cocaine, the aftermath recalled the physical cost of heroin. *Whatever game you're playing at, Holmes,* Watson thought, *the price is too bloody high.*

"Envy?" Watson said. "The devil do you mean?"

"The story. You've got your work cut out, I'd say."

"The story? You mean retelling this as one of your observational fantasies? Insanity! Cannot be done! Where on Earth would I start?"

"I would have thought that was obvious," Holmes managed a wan, secretive smile. "Start with the Russians."

KEVIN COCKLE lives in Calgary, Alberta and often incorporates Calgary-style boom-town themes in his work. A frequent contributor to *On Spec* magazine, Kevin has dabbled in screen writing, sports journalism and technical writing to fill out what would otherwise be a purely finance-centric resume.

SHERLOCK HOLMES
AND THE DIVING BELL

by Simon Clark

WATSON. COME AT ONCE. THAT WHICH CANNOT BE. IS.

That astonishing summons brought me to the Cornish harbour town of Fowey. There, as directed by further information within the telegram, I joined my friend, Mr. Sherlock Holmes, on a tugboat, which immediately steamed toward the open sea. The rapid pounding of the engine made for an urgent drumbeat. One that reinforced the notion that once more we'd embarked upon a headlong dash to adventure.

By the time I'd regained my breath, after a somewhat hurried embarkation, I saw that Holmes had taken up a position in the tugboat's bow. There he stood, straight-backed, thin as a pikestaff, hatless, and dressed severely in black. Every inch the eager seeker of truth. His deep-set eyes raked the turquoise ocean, hunting for what he knew must lie out here.

But what, exactly, was the nature of our case? He'd given no elaboration, other than that mystifying statement in the telegram. *That which cannot be. Is.*

I picked my way across the deck, over coils of rope, rusty chain and assorted winding gear that adorned this grubby little workhorse of the sea. The vessel moved at the limits of its speed. Steam hissed from pipes, smoke tumbled out of the funnel to stain an otherwise perfectly blue June sky. Gulls wheeled about our craft, for the moment mistaking us for a fishing boat. Either they finally understood that we didn't carry so much as a mackerel or, perhaps, they sensed danger ahead, for the birds suddenly departed on powerful wings, uttering such piercing shrieks that they could be plainly heard above the *whoosh!* and *shorr!* of the engine.

Likewise, I made it my business to be overheard above the machine, too. "Holmes. What's happened?"

That distinctive profile remained. He didn't even glance in my direction.

"Holmes, good God, man! The telegram! What does it mean?"

Still he did not turn. Instead, he rested his fingertip against his lips.

Hush.

My friend is not given to personal melodrama, or prone to questioning my loyalties by virtue of frivolous tests. Clearly, this was a matter of great importance. Just what that matter was I'd have to wait and see. However, a certain rigidity of his posture and grimness of expression sent a chill foreboding through my blood. Terrible events loomed — or so I divined. Therefore, I stood beside that black clad figure, said nothing, and waited for the tugboat to bear us to our destination.

Presently, I saw where we were headed. Sitting there, as a blot of darkness on the glittering sea, was a large vessel of iron. What I'd first surmised to be a stunted mast between the aft deck and the funnel was, in fact, a crane. A cable ran from the pulley at the tip of that formidable lifting arm to a grey object on the aft deck.

In the next half hour Holmes would speak but tersely. "Steel yourself, Watson." That was his sole item of conversation on the tugboat.

The dourness of countenance revealed that some immense problem weighed heavy on the man. His long fingers curled around the rail at the prow. Muscle tension produced a distinct whitening of the knuckles. His piercing eyes regarded the iron ship, which grew ever nearer. And he looked at that ship as a man might who'd seen a gravestone on which his own name is etched with the days of his mortal arrival and, more disconcertingly, his departure.

The tugboat captain fired off two short blasts of the steam whistle. The leviathan at anchor gave an answering call on its horn. A mournful sound to be sure.

Soon the tugboat drew alongside. A grim-faced Holmes took my elbow in order to help me safely pass from the heaving tugboat to the rope ladder that had been cast down for us.

My heart, and I readily confess the fact, pounded nearly as hard as the pistons of the tugboat. For, as I climbed up toward the guardrail fifteen feet above me, I saw an assembly of faces. They regarded me with such melancholy that I fully expected to be marched to a gallows where my noose awaited.

Panting, I clambered over the rail onto the aft deck. There, something resembling the boiler of a locomotive, lying horizontally, dominated the area. A pair of hawsers ran from this giant cylinder to a linking ring; from that stout ring a single hawser of great thickness rose to the crane's tip.

Holmes followed me on deck.

Immediately, a man of around sixty, or so, strode forward. His face had been reddened by ocean gales and the sun. A tracery of purple veins emerged from a pair of mutton-chop side-whiskers that were as large as they were perfectly white. Those dark veins appeared as distinct as contour lines on a map. Such a weather-beaten visage could have been on loan from the Ancient Mariner himself. His wide, grey eyes examined my face, as if attempting to discern whether I was a fellow who'd stand firm in the face of danger, or take flight. That assessment appeared to be of great importance to him.

Holmes introduced me to this venerable seaman. "Captain Smeaton. Doctor Watson." We shook hands. His grasp was steel. Holmes closed with the terse request: "Captain Smeaton, please explain."

The captain shared the same funereal expression as the rest of his crew. Not smiling once. Nevertheless, he did speak.

"Doctor Watson," he began in a voice long since made permanently hoarse from having to make himself heard above ocean storms, "I don't know what Mr. Holmes has revealed to you about our plight."

"Nothing." To avoid my friend's silence on this matter as being altogether too strange I added, 'I arrived from London in something of a rush.'

Captain Smeaton didn't appear concerned by my ignorance and continued swiftly. "You're on board the *Fitzwilliam*, a salvage vessel. Mr. Holmes spent the day with us yesterday, because... well... I'll come to that later, sir. I'll tell the story in plain-speak. There's no requirement for me to embellish with colorful or dramatic phrases, because what you'll witness is going to strike at the heart of you anyway."

Holmes stood beside me, listening carefully.

The Captain did as he promised, rendering his account in deep, whispery tones that were plain and very much to the point. "Five years ago, Doctor Watson, we were engaged by the admiralty to recover silver bullion from the *SS Runswick*, which lies ninety fathoms beneath our keel. The depth is too great for divers using Siebe Gorman suits. They can operate to depths nearing thirty fathoms or so — to go any deeper is certain death. So we use Submarine Chambers, such as this." He indicated the iron cylinder that occupied the deck. Moisture dripped from its massive flanks. Bulbous rivets held that hulking beast together in such a formidable way the thing appeared downright indestructible to my eyes.

"A diving bell?" I asked.

"As they are commonly known. Diving bells have been used since the time of the ancient Greeks, sir. Back then they'd simply invert a cauldron, trapping the air inside. This they'd submerge into the ocean. A diver would then visit the air pocket in order to breathe. That arrangement allowed sponge divers, and the like, much greater duration on the seabed."

"Remarkable," I commented, eying the huge vessel squatting there on the deck. "And this is the twentieth century descendent of the cauldron?"

"That it is, sir." Captain Smeaton's gaze strayed toward Holmes as if seeking permission to continue. Holmes gave a slight nod. "To get to the meat of the matter, sir, back in 1899 we used a diving bell to retrieve silver bullion from the sunken ship. One particular morning I ordered that the *Pollux*, which is the name of the bell, be lowered to the ocean floor. On board was a man by the name of George Barstow. The diving bell was delivered to the wreck by crane, as you see here, sir. It is both lowered, and raised to the surface by means of a steel hawser. Fresh air is pumped down to the craft via a tube. Contact is maintained between the ship and the diving bell by telephone. I tell you, gentlemen, I curse the hour that I ordered Barstow to man the craft. Not a day goes by without me reliving those terrible events." He took a deep breath, his grey eyes glistened. "Initially, the dive went well. Barstow descended to the wreck without incident. His function was to act as observer and to send directions, via telephone apparatus, to my men on the ship to lower a grappling hook in order to retrieve the cargo. We successfully hooked five cases of silver and brought them to the surface. Then I noticed a swell had begun to run. This poses a risk to diving bells as it puts excessive strain on the hawser. I gave the order to winch the craft back to the surface." He paused for moment. "That's when Barstow spoke to me by telephone. He reported that the diving bell had become caught on the superstructure of the wreck. The thing had jammed fast. We tried every which way to free the bell. Meanwhile, waves had started to break against the sides of the ship. So I told the winch-man to use brute force and haul the diving bell free." He paused again. Trying to avoid melodrama, he said simply. "The hawser snapped. As did the telephone line and air pipe. That was five years ago. The *Pollux* became George Barstow's coffin. He's been down there ever since."

"And now you are trying to recover the *Pollux* and the man's body?"

"Indeed we are, Doctor Watson." He nodded to where a hawser ran along a steel channel to a fixing point on deck. Barnacles and brown kelp sheathed the hawser. "That's from the *Pollux*. We recovered it three days ago."

"It's still attached to the diving bell?"

The captain nodded his grey head. "The *Pollux* is held down there on the seabed. Probably the old wreck's doing. Even so, we made fast the cable on deck here. I'm going to do my damndest to haul that diving bell out of Davy Jones's locker and bring the blasted thing back to dry land, so help me." His hands shook as a powerful emotion took charge. "Or it'll be the death of me in trying."

I looked to Holmes for some explanation. After all, a salvage operation? Surely that's a matter that doesn't require the intervention of the world's greatest consulting detective.

"Yesterday," Holmes said, "The diving bell's twin went in search of its sibling."

I turned to the vessel that so much resembled the boiler of a locomotive. On the side of that great iron cylinder was painted, in white, the name *Castor*. "And did it find its twin?"

"It did. The diving bell returned without apparent incident. However, the crew of two were, on the opening of the hatch, found to be quite dead."

"Quite dead!" thundered the Captain. "They died of fright. Just take one look at their faces!"

"What I require of my friend, Doctor Watson, is to examine the deceased. If you will kindly take us to the bodies."

"Holmes?" I regarded him with surprise. "A post mortem?"

"The simple cause of death will be sufficient, Watson."

"I can't Holmes."

"You must, and quickly."

"Not unless I am authorised by the local constabulary, or the coroner."

"You must tell me how they died, Watson."

"Holmes, I protest. I shall be breaking the law."

"Oh, but you must, Watson. Because I am to be—" he struck the side of the diving bell, "—this vessel's next passenger!"

Before I could stutter a reply a sailor approached. "Captain! It's started again! The sounds are coming up the line!" His eyes were round with fear. "And it's trying to make words!"

That expression of dread on the man's face communicated a thrill of fear to my very veins. 'What's happening, Holmes? What sounds?"

"We're in receipt of another telephone call." His deep-set eyes locked onto mine. "It hails from ninety fathoms down. And it's coming from the *Pollux*!"

Upon passing through a door marked *Control Room*, we were greeted by a remarkable sight.

Three men in officer's uniforms gathered before telephony apparatus on a table. Fixed to the wall, immediately in front of them, was a horn of the type that amplifies the music from a gramophone. Nearby, two young women stood with their arms round each other, like children frightened of a thunderstorm. Both were dressed in black muslin. Both had lustrous, dark eyes set into bone-white faces. And both faces were identical.

Twins. That much was evident.

The occupants of the room stared at the horn on the wall. Their eyes were open wide, their expressions radiated absolute horror. Faces quivered. They hardly dared breathe, lest a quick intake of breath would invite sudden, and brutal, destruction.

Holmes strode toward the gathering. "Are the sounds the same as before?"

An officer with a clipped red beard answered, but he couldn't take his bulging eyes from the speaker horn. "They began the same... in the last few minutes; however, they've begun to change."

A second officer added, "As if it's trying to form words."

The third cried, "Sir! What if it really is him? After all this time!"

"Keep your nerve, Jessup. Remember that ladies are present." Captain Smeaton tilted his head in the direction of the two women. Then he said, "Doctor Watson. Allow me to introduce

you to Mrs. Katrina Barstow, widow of George Barstow, and her
sister, Miss Claudine Millwood."

"Evidently," murmured Holmes, "this isn't the occasion for
formal introductions."

For the women in black disregarded me; they hugged each
other tight, desperate for some degree of comfort amid the
horror.

"A series of clicks." Holmes tilted his head to one side as
he listened. "Almost like the sound produced on a telephone
speaker when a thunderstorm is approaching."

Jessup cried, "Or the sound of his bones. They've begun
moving about the *Pollux*!"

Captain Smeaton spoke calmly. "Go below to your cabin,
Jessup."

Jessup fled from his post, and fled gratefully it seemed to me.

More clicks issued from the horn. The women moaned with
dismay. Mrs. Barstow pressed a handkerchief against her mouth
as if to stifle a scream.

Captain Smeaton explained, "After the hawser was recovered
from the seabed, my crew secured it to a deck bollard. One of
the ship's apprentices did what he was routinely supposed to do.
He attached the *Pollux*'s telephone wire to this telephone apparatus."

Holmes turned to the Captain. "And that's when you began
to hear unusual sounds?"

"Unusual?" exclaimed the red-bearded officer. "Terrible sounds,
sir. They come back to you in your dreams."

I listened to the leaden clicking. Very much the sound of old
bone striking against yet more bone. "Forgive me, if I ask the
obvious. But do you maintain that the telephone line connects
this apparatus with that in the diving bell, which has lain on the
seabed for five years?"

"Yes, Doctor Watson. I fear I do." Captain Smeaton shuddered. "And I wish circumstances did not require me to make
such a claim."

"And those clicks are transmitted up the wire from..." I
refrained from adding *"Barstow's tomb."*

Sherlock Holmes turned to me quickly. "Ha! There you have
it, Watson. *That which cannot be. Is.*"

"Then it is a fault with the mechanism. Surely?"

"Would I have come aboard this ship, Watson, to attend to an
electrical fault? They did not mistake me for a telephony engineer."

"But dash it all, Holmes—"

Then it issued from the horn. A deep voice. Wordless. Full of pain, regret, and an unquestionable longing.

"*Urrr... hmm... ahhh...*"

Ice dashed through my veins. Freezing me into absolute still-ness. "That sound..."

"Human?" asked Holmes.

"Decidedly. At least, it appears so."

"*Fffmm... arrnurr... Mmm-ursss...*" The deep, shimmering voice from the horn tailed away into a sigh comprised of ghost-ing esses. "*Ssss...*"

The pent-up scream discharged at last. Mrs. Barstow cried, "That's my husband! He's alive. Please bring him back to me. Please!"

Her sister murmured to her, reassuring her, comforting her.

"No, Holmes," I whispered to my friend. "That's impossible. No mortal man could survive five years underwater without air."

"Survive? Or evolve? As environment demands? Remember Darwin."

"Holmes, surely you're not suggesting—"

"I'm suggesting we keep our minds open. As well as our eyes."

The voice came ghosting from the horn again. That longing — yet it appeared to come from the lips of a man who had wit-nessed the unimaginable. His widow wept.

Captain Smeaton said, "Perhaps the ladies should leave."

"No!" Holmes held up his hand. "Now is the time to unravel this particular mystery!"

The syllables rising from the *Pollux* became a long, wordless groan.

"Mrs. Barstow." Holmes spoke briskly. "Forgive what will be difficult questions at this vexing time. What did you call your husband?"

The widow's eyes, which were surely as dark as the coal that fired water into steam in this very ship, regarded Holmes with surprise.

"Madam, how did you address your husband?"

She responded with amazement. "His name? Are you quite mad?"

"Madam, indulge me. Please."

"My husband's name is Mr. George Barstow."

His manner became severe. "You were husband and wife. Surely, you gave him a familiar name? A private name?"

"Mr. Holmes, I protest—"

"A nickname."

Miss Millwood stood with her arm around Mrs. Barstow, glaring with the utmost ferocity at my friend.

"If I am to unravel this mystery, then you must answer my questions."

The groaning from the horn suddenly faded. An expectant silence followed. An impression of someone listening hard. A *someone* not in that room.

Still Mrs. Barstow prevaricated. "I don't understand what you would have me say, Mr. Holmes."

"Tell me the private name with which you addressed the man whom you loved so dearly. The name you spoke when you and he were alone."

A storm of rage erupted. Not from any living mouth there. It came from the speaker horn that was connected by some hundred fathoms of cable to the diving bell at the bottom of the ocean. The roar came back double, then again many-fold. It seemed as if demons by the legion bellowed their fury, their outrage and their jealous anger from the device. The pair of ship's officers at the desk covered their ears and fled through the doorway.

At last the awful expulsion of wrath faded. The speaker horn fell silent. Everyone in the room had been struck silent, too. All, that is, except for Sherlock Holmes.

"Mrs. Barstow. A moment ago you said these words to me: 'My husband's name *is* Mr. George Barstow.'"

"Indeed." Recovering her composure, she stood straighter.

"*Is*, Madam, not *was*?"

"*Is!*"

"Therefore in the present tense. As if he is still alive?"

"Of course." She pointed a trembling finger at the speaker horn. "Because he lives. That's his voice."

"Then perhaps you will tell me your private name for Mr. Barstow? The one you use when the servants are gone, and all the lamps are extinguished."

The blast of sound from the instrument almost swept us off our feet. A glass of water on the desk shattered. At that moment, the widow's sister stiffened, her eyes rolled back, and she fell into a dead faint. Holmes caught the woman to prevent her striking the floor.

Nevertheless, he fixed Mrs. Barstow with a penetrating gaze. "Madam. I am still waiting for you to reveal the name — that secret name only you and he knew."

"*Katrina. Stay silent. Do not say it!*"

All heads turned to the speaker. That voice! Waves of such uncanny power radiated from every syllable.

"George," she cried.

"Do not speak with Sherlock Holmes. He is evil. The man is our enemy!"

"You heard with your own ears!" she shouted, her fist pressed to her breast. "My husband is alive!" She turned to Captain Smeaton. "Send the machine down to save him."

Captain Smeaton's weather-beaten face assumed a deeper shade of purple. "I will not. Whatever's down there can no longer be George Barstow. Not after five years."

"He's immortal," she cried. "Just as my sister promised."

My friend's eyes narrowed as the widow voiced this statement. Quickly, he settled the unconscious form of Miss Claudine Millwood into a chair at the desk. I checked the pulse in her neck.

"Strong... very strong. She's fainted, that's all."

"Thank you, Watson," said Holmes. "And I rather think the pieces of our jigsaw are falling into place." He picked up the handset part of the phone and spoke into the mouthpiece. "Whom do I have the honour of addressing?"

"Barstow."

"For a man dead these last five years you sound remarkably vigorous."

"So shall I be when you are dust, sir."

Holmes turned to Captain Smeaton. "You knew Barstow well. Is that his voice?"

"God help us. Indeed it is."

Mrs. Barstow clawed at Smeaton's arm. "Send the machine. Bring him to me!"

"No!" Captain Smeaton's voice rang out with fear, rather than anger.

"I agree with Mrs. Barstow." Holmes pulled on his black leather gloves. "Prepare the diving bell. I will visit the *Pollux* myself."

"Impossible."

"I insist. For I must see for myself who — or what — is the tenant of your lost machine."

Not many men thwart my friend, Sherlock Holmes. Ten minutes later, the crew had the *Castor* ready for descent. Holmes quickly returned to the control room. The twin sister still lay unconscious; the horror had overwhelmed her senses. The widow stood perfectly straight: her dark eyes regarded Holmes from a bone-white face.

"Mrs. Barstow," he intoned. "You do know that what you crave is an impossibility? Your husband cannot still be a living, breathing man after five years in that iron canister."

"I have faith."

"I see."

"Mr. Holmes, do you wish to hear that private name I gave my husband?"

Holmes spoke kindly, "That will no longer be necessary."

I couldn't remain silent. "Good God, man, surely you will not descend in that machine?"

"I have no choice, Watson."

"Please, Holmes, I beg—"

"Wait for me here, won't you, old friend?" He gave a wry smile. "Fates willing, this won't be a lengthy journey." He picked up the telephone's handset. "But first, one more question. Barstow?"

A sound of respiration gusted from the speaker.

"Barstow. Tell me what you see from your lair?"

"All is green. All is green. And yet..."

"And yet what?"

"The funnel of this wreck towers above the diving bell. Always I see the funnel standing there. A black monolith. A grave-marker. Do not come here..."

"It is my duty, sir. You are a mystery. I must investigate."

"No."

"My nature compels me."

"No! If you should dare to approach my vessel I will destroy you!"

"Sir, I shall be with you presently."

Holmes briskly left the room. The voice still screamed from the speaker: *"You will die! You will die!"*

We crossed the aft deck to the *Castor*.

With utter conviction I announced, "Holmes. I'm coming with you."

He gave a grim smile. "Watson. I was rather hoping you would."

Moments later, we clambered through a hatch into the huge iron cylinder. In shape and in size, it resembled, as I've previously described, the boiler of a locomotive. Within: a bench in padded red plush ran along one wall. In the wall opposite the seat, a pair of portholes cast from enormously thick glass. They were set side by side, and prompted one to envisage the bulging eyes of some primordial creature. Above us, the blue sky remained in view through the open hatch. Captain Smeaton appeared.

"Gentlemen. You will receive fresh air through the tube. If you wish to speak to me, use the telephone mounted on the wall there beside you. God speed!"

"One moment, Captain," said Holmes. "When Watson and I are despatched to the seabed, ensure that Mrs. Barstow and her sister remain in the control room with you. Is that understood?"

"Aye-aye, Mr. Holmes."

"Upon your word?"

"Absolutely."

"Good. Because their proximity to you might very well be a matter of life and death."

Then the hatch was sealed tight. A series of clanks, a jerking sensation, the crane lifted the *Castor* off the deck. A swaying movement, and I spied through the thick portholes that we were swung over the guardrail and dangled over the ocean; such a searing blue at that moment.

"*Castor* and *Pollux*," I whispered, every fibre tensing. "The heavenly twins."

"Not only that. In most classical legends *Pollux* is immortal. Whereas—" he patted the curving iron wall in front of him. "—*Castor* is a mere mortal. And capable of death."

The shudders transmitted along the hawser to the diving bell were disconcertingly fierce. The sounds of the crane motors were very loud. In truth, louder than I deemed possible. Until, that is, the diving bell reached the sea. With a flurry of bubbles it sank beneath the surface. White froth gave way to clear turquoise.

Swiftly, the vessel descended. Silent now. An iron calf slipping free of its hulking mother on the surface.

"Don't neglect to breathe, Watson."

I realized I was holding my breath. "Thank you, Holmes."

"Fresh air is pumped through the inlet hose above our heads."

"Hardly fresh." I managed a grim smile. "It reeks of coal smoke and tickles the back of the throat so."

"At least it is wholesome… if decidedly pungent."

The light began to fade as we sank deeper. I took stock of my surroundings. The interior of the cylinder offered little more room than the interior of a hansom cab. Indeed, we sat side by side. Between us hung the cable of the telephone. The handset had been clipped to the wall within easy reach.

And down we went. Darker… darker… darker…. The vessel swayed slightly. My stomach lightened a little, as when descending by elevator. I clenched my fists upon my lap until the knuckles turned white.

"Don't be alarmed," Holmes said. "The barometric pressure of the interior remains the same as that of sea-level."

"Then we will be spared the bends and nitrogen narcosis. The former is agonizing. The latter intoxicates and induces hallucination."

"Ah! You know about the medical perils of deep-sea diving."

"When a former army doctor sits beside a naval doctor at his club you can imagine the topics of conversation over the glasses of port." I clicked my tongue "And now I tell you this so as to distract myself from the knowledge that we are descending over five hundred feet to the ocean floor. In a blessed tin can!"

Holmes leaned forward, eager to witness what lay beyond the glass. The water had dulled from bright turquoise to blue. To deep blue. A pink jelly-fish floated by. A globular sac from which delicate filaments descended. Altogether a beautiful creature. Totally unlike the viscous remains of jelly-fish one finds washed ashore.

Holmes read a dial set between the portholes. "Sixty fathoms. Two thirds of the way there, Watson."

"Dear Lord."

"Soon we should see the shipwreck. And shortly, thereafter, this vessel's twin."

"Twin?" I echoed. "Which reminds me. I thought the twin sisters we encountered today were decidedly odd."

"Ah-ha. So we are two minds with a single thought."

"And no doubt you deduced far more than I could from their dress, speech and retinue of subtle clues."

"Supposition at the moment, Watson, rather than deduction. Before I make any pronouncement on the sisters, or the singular voice emerging from the telephone, I need to see just who is in residence in the *Pollux*. Which, if I'm not mistaken, is coming into view below."

He'd no sooner uttered the words when a shadow raced from the darkness beyond the porthole glass. Silently, it rushed by.

"What the devil was that?" I asked in surprise.

"Possibly a dolphin or a shark..." He pressed his fingertips together as he considered. "Although I doubt it very much."

The mystifying remark didn't ease my trepidation. And that trepidation turned into one of overt alarm when a clang sounded against the side of the diving bell. The entire structure lurched, forcing us to hold tight to a brass rail in front of us.

"Some denizen of the deep doesn't want us here," observed Holmes.

"Here it comes again."

The dark shape torpedoed from the gloom surrounding the diving bell. Once more it struck the iron cylinder.

"We should inform Captain Smeaton," I ventured.

"In which case he'll winch us back up forthwith. No, we must see the occupant of the *Pollux*. That is vital, if we are to explain what is happening here."

Darkly, I murmured, "Barstow didn't want us to call on him. He promised our destruction if we tried."

"Yes, he did, didn't he?" Holmes watched the cylinder resolve itself in the gloom beneath us. "So why does he — or what he has become — desire to remain hidden away on the seabed?"

"Hypothetically speaking, Holmes?"

"While we are in a speculative frame of mind: Barstow described his surroundings for us via the telephone. Be so good as to repeat his description."

"Let me see: Green. Yes, his words were 'all is green'."

"Continue, pray."

"And he made much of the wreck's funnel. How it loomed over him. A grave-marker as he put it."

"What color is the seawater down here. Green?"

"No, it's black."

"Indeed, Watson. And as for the ship's funnel? A great monolith of a structure?"

"Where is the funnel? I don't see one."

"Because there is no funnel. At least there isn't one fixed to the wreck. It must have become detached as the ship foundered years ago."

"So why did Barstow describe the wreck in such a way?"

"Evidently, Barstow cannot see the wreck as it really is, *sans* funnel. Nor can he see that the water at this depth is black — not green."

"So who did the voice belong to that we heard coming from the speaker?"

"It belongs to whoever is responsible for the deaths of those two men yesterday. And who will be responsible for our deaths today, if our wits aren't sharp enough." He clapped his hands together. "Pah! See the wreck. It's a jumble of scrap metal covered in weed. Barstow's description belonged to someone who has never seen a wreck on the ocean bed before. Instead, they based their description on pictures of ships that they see on sitting room walls."

"To repeat myself, Holmes, who did the voice actually belong to?"

"Ah, that can wait, Watson. Our descent is slowing. Soon we will look into Barstow's lair." He shot me a glance. "His tomb?"

The crane operator stopped paying out the hawser as we bumped against the bottom. Just a yard or so away lay the diving bell — the twin of the one we now sat in. Though confoundedly gloomy down here I could make out some detail. Kelp grew from the iron cylinder. The rounded shape was suggestive of some monstrous skull covered with flowing hair. Spars from the wreck had enclosed the diving bell like the bars of a cage, trapping it that fateful day five years ago. A grip so tight that the haulage gear had snapped the hawser as it strove to raise the doomed submersible to the surface.

Those black waters would reveal little. Not until Holmes closed a switch. The moment he did so, a light sprang from the lamp fixed to our craft.

"Now we can see who resides inside the *Pollux*." Holmes took a deep breath as his keen eyes made an assessment. "Are we of the same opinion of the occupant?"

Likewise, I took a steadying breath. I peered through our porthole and into the porthole of the craft trapped by the stricken bullion carrier, *Fitzwilliam*. "Now I see. But I don't understand how he speaks to us."

"Confirm what you observe, Watson."

"A cadaver. Partly mummified as a result of being confined in an airtight compartment. Inert. Lying on the bench at the rear of the vessel."

"The man would have been dead within a few hours of being marooned without an air supply. Is that not so?"

"Agreed."

"Notice that the hawser has been retrieved and snakes up to the surface. But notice, equally, that the telephone cable has been snapped at the point it should enter the *Pollux*. Barstow, alive or dead, never made so much as a single call once that cable had parted from the apparatus within his diving bell."

"So, who is responsible?"

"A creature of flesh and blood!" If it weren't for the confines of the diving bell an excited Sherlock Holmes would have sprung to his feet. "Miss Claudine Millwood! Twin sister of that man's widow." He inhaled deeply, his nostrils twitching in the manner of a predator catching scent of its prey. "You see, Watson, I shall one day write a monograph on an especially rarefied subject. Yet one which will be invaluable to police when interrogating suspects or, more importantly, discussing certain matters, within the hearing of a suspect. I have observed, during my career as a consulting detective, that the eyes of a human being move in such a prescribed way that they hint at what they are thinking. Strongly hint at that! With practice, one can become quite adept at reading the eye-line of a man or woman."

"Therefore, you studied Miss Claudine Millwood when you questioned Mrs. Barstow?"

"That I did, sir. In this case, as I spoke to the widow, I also took careful note of the direction of Miss Millwood's eye-line. When I mentioned Mr. Barstow by name the woman's gaze became unfocussed, yet directed slightly downward and some degrees off centre to her left. Trust me, Watson, how we arrange our limbs and direct our gaze reveals volumes to the competent observer."

"Therefore you could glean her unspoken thoughts?"

"To a degree. The direction of her gaze and the unfocussed eyes told me that Miss Millwood was in the process of recalling a memory that is not only secret to her, but one she knew would shock or revolt right-minded individuals. That was enough to arouse my suspicions."

"And you divined this by reading the eye-line? Remarkable!"

"Just as you, a medical man, can diagnose an illness from subtle symptoms. Moreover! The woman couldn't bear to hear her own sister reveal that private, intimate name, which, once upon a time, she murmured into her husband's ear. A name that Claudine Millwood, did not know."

"Millwood was in love with her sister's husband?"

"Without a shadow of doubt. Whether that love was reciprocated or not we don't know."

"And during the years Barstow lay in that iron tomb the love grew."

"Indeed! The love grew — and it grew malignantly. That obsessive love took on a life of its own. Millwood projected thoughts from her own mind into the telephone apparatus. She imitated the late Mr. Barstow."

"Why didn't she want us to venture down here?"

"That would have destroyed the fantasy. We would have returned to the surface, but not, however, with an account of finding a handsome young man full of miraculous life, still trapped within the diving bell. No! We would have returned with the grim fact that we gazed upon a shrivelled corpse." Holmes snapped his fingers. "We would have ruptured the fantasy. The woman has incredible mental powers, certainly — yet she is quite mad."

"So she killed the crew of the *Castor* yesterday?"

"In order to prevent them describing what we, ourselves, now see."

"Holmes, Captain Smeaton claimed they were frightened to death."

"Miss Millwood will have conjured some terrible chimera, no doubt."

"And the shadow that attacked us as we descended?"

"Millwood."

"Then she won't allow us to return to the surface?"

"No, Watson. She will not."

"Therefore, she won't stop at yet more slayings to keep her fantasy alive — that Barstow is immortal?"

"Indubitably. However, we do have recourse to the telephone." He picked up the handset.

"But the woman fell in a dead faint. I checked her myself; she's deeply unconscious."

"My good doctor, I don't doubt your assessment. However, recall the essays of Freud and Jung. Aren't the leviathans of deep waters nothing in comparison to those leviathans of our own subconscious?'

Holmes turned the handle of the telephone apparatus. At that precise instant, a dark shape sped through the field of electric light. This time the walls didn't impede its progress. A monstrous shadow flowed through the iron casing of the diving bell. Instantly it engulfed us. We could barely breathe as tendrils of darkness slipped into our bodies, seeking to occupy every nerve and sinew.

"Watson, I am mistaken! The woman's attacks are far more visceral than I anticipated."

"She's invading the heart. Those men died of heart failure. Ah…" A weight appeared to settle onto my ribs. Breathing became harder. My heart thudded, labouring under the influence of that malign spirit. "Holmes, you must tell the… the captain to distract her. Her flow of unconscious thought must be disrupted."

Holmes grimaced as he struggled to breathe. "A shock… how best to administer a shock?"

"Electricity."

With a huge effort Holmes spoke into the telephone. "Captain Smeaton. Ah... I..."

"Mr. Holmes?"

"Listen. We will soon be dead. Do as I say... uh... don't question... do you understand?"

"I understand." The man's voice was assured. He would obey.

"Is Millwood there?"

"Yes, she's still unconscious."

"Then rip the power cables from an electrical appliance. Apply the live wire to her temple."

"Mr. Holmes?"

"Do it, man... otherwise you haul up two more corpses!"

Then came a wait of many moments. Indeed, a long time seemed to pass. I could no longer move. The shadowy presence coiled about the interior of the diving bell as if it were black smoke. We sagged on the bench, our heartbeats slowing all the time. Another moment passed, another nudge toward death. That shadow was also inside of us, impressing itself on the nerves of the heart.

All of a sudden, a woman's piercing scream erupted from the earpiece of the telephone.

Immediately, thereafter, Captain Smeaton thundered: *"Damn you man, I've done as you asked. But you've made me into a torturer!"*

Instantly, the oppression of my cardiac system lifted. I breathed easily again.

Holmes was once more his vigorous self. "No, Captain. You are no torturer. You are our saviour."

I leaned toward the telephone in order to ask, "Is she alive?"

"Yes, Doctor Watson. In fact, the electrical shock has roused her."

The black shadow in the cabin dissipated. I heaved a sigh of relief as I sensed that entity dispel its atoms into the surrounding waters. The diving bell gave a lurch. And it began to rise from the sea bed. The ocean turned lighter. Black gave way to purple, then to blue.

Holmes, however, appeared to suddenly descend into an abyss of melancholy.

"We're safe, Holmes. And the mystery is solved."

He nodded.

"Then why, pray, are you so downcast?"

"Watson. I didn't reveal the purpose of my trip to Cornwall. I came here to visit an old friend. You see, his six year old daughter is grievously ill. No, I am disingenuous to even myself. The truth of the matter is this: she is dying."

"I am very sorry to hear that, Holmes. But how did that sad state of affairs bring you to investigate this case of the diving bell?"

"An act of desperation on my part." He rested his fingertips together; his eyes became distant. "When I heard the seemingly miraculous story that a man had been rendered somehow immortal I raced here. It occurred to me that Barstow in his diving bell had stumbled upon a remarkable place on the ocean bed that had the power to keep death at bay."

"And you came here for the sake of the little girl?"

"Yes, Watson, but what did I find? A woman that has the power to project a sick fantasy from her mind and cause murder. For a few short hours I had truly believed I might have a distinct chance of saving little Edith's life. However..." He gave a long, grave sigh. "Alas, Watson. Alas..."

SIMON CLARK lives in Doncaster, England with his family. When his first novel, *Nailed by the Heart*, made it through the slush-pile in 1994 he banked the advance and embarked upon his dream of becoming a full-time writer. Many dreams and nightmares later he wrote the cult zombie classic *Blood Crazy*. Other titles include *Darkness Demands*, *Vengeance Child* and *The Night of the Triffids*, which continues the story of Wyndham's Sci-Fi classic.

Simon's latest novel is *Whitby Vampyrrhic*, a decidedly gruesome and ultra-violent horror-thriller set in World War Two.

THE GREATEST MYSTERY

by Paul Kane

My dear and faithful reader. It is only now that I am able to recount the truly shocking events of what I firmly believe to be my dearest friend and colleague Sherlock Holmes' greatest ever mystery. Upon first reading these words, you may feel my claim is somewhat of an exaggeration. What about the case of the Baskerville Hound, you might ask, quite possibly his most famous adventure to date? What about his entanglements with the evil Professor Moriarty (the merest mention of which will later have great significance, I can assure you)? But I have faithfully chronicled the master detective's cases over the years and I can categorically attest to the validity of my statement. I alone was witness to its eventual outcome and, once you have finished this offering, I feel certain that you too will agree about the choice of title. I can also promise that while I have been taken to task in the past for what Holmes called my embellishment of these accounts — the addition of, to quote the man himself, 'color and … life' (the latter an irony, as you will soon see) — there is not a word of this that is not the whole truth. Whether you believe me or not is, in the end, your choice — all I can do is report the facts of this most singular case as I experienced them, no matter how strange they might seem.

The matter in question began with a simple case — although you might recall the air of strangeness and tension against which it was set, in the months approaching the turn of the century. Indeed, these very events were thought by some to be interlinked, though you will soon realize that this was not in fact so. The real explanation goes beyond that, beyond anything you might have thought possible. But I am getting ahead of myself once more.... The case in hand was an apparently straightforward crime, yet as Holmes is often at great pains to teach me, things are seldom what they appear at first glance.

And so, to the details. A lady by the name of Miss Georgia Cartwright called upon us one afternoon in late September, begging that we pay a visit to her cousin Simon.

"In jail," Holmes said, motioning for Miss Cartwright to sit down. When he noticed her look of confusion, he waved a hand and explained: "The faint marks on your dress and your arms, a distinctive pattern showing you have recently been pressed up against a set of iron bars.... Pray tell us of what your cousin is accused, Miss Cartwright?"

"I am sad to say Simon stands accused of... of... murdering his fiancée, and *my* best friend, Miss Judith Hatten," she told us, gratefully accepting a seat as well as a handkerchief; the latter to dry her eyes. "But he couldn't have... he simply could not."

Holmes sat down opposite her, steepling his fingers. "If you would furnish me with the facts, Miss Cartwright, and please do not leave anything out. Even the smallest detail might be of significance."

Sadly, it soon became clear, as she related what she knew, that the culprit could be *none other* than her relation. The night before last, Simon had visited Judith to discuss their forthcoming wedding. Upon hearing a disturbance in the living room, where Simon had been escorted only minutes beforehand, the girl's only living parent — her father — discovered the young man standing over the body of Judith. The young lady had suffered a tremendous head wound. In Simon's hand was a poker, dripping with blood. Mr. Hatten flew into a fury and had to be held back by his staff from attacking Simon himself, while Miss Cartwright's cousin was held down until the authorities arrived.

Holmes frowned, obviously reaching the same conclusion as I.

"He swears it was not him... says that he cannot remember what happened, Mr. Holmes. And I believe him. Simon is the gentlest man in the world and he did so love Judith. I know he did. He would never have raised a finger to hurt her."

Holmes raised an eyebrow. "It is so often the case, however, that we do not *truly* know our friends and loved ones Miss Cartwright."

"We grew up together and were as close as brother and sister. I *do* know him, Mr. Holmes. Please, I implore you," she said, clasping her hands together. "Visit him yourself."

Holmes glanced sideways, attempting not to let this sway his judgement, but in spite of his somewhat cool exterior, my friend has never been able to turn away anyone in such distress. Yet I have seen him reject far more intriguing investigations, so something about this particular case must have piqued his interest. I wish to God now, looking back, that he'd had the courage to simply inform Miss Cartwright he could not help. If that sounds harsh, believe me, it will not by the time I have finished this tale.

So it was that we found ourselves in a coach on our way to see her cousin at Scotland Yard's 'charming' prison. The journey at least afforded me some time to glean Holmes' thoughts about the case.

"Surely it would be wrong to get the young woman's hopes up," I told him. "The man's destined for the noose. There might not have been witnesses to the actual deed, but being caught with the murder weapon in one's possession implies just as much guilt."

Holmes steadfastly refused to be drawn on the matter until we'd seen the prisoner for ourselves. When we arrived and asked to see the man, Inspector Lestrade similarly conveyed the opinion that my friend was wasting his time.

"I can not understand why Miss Cartwright has brought you into such an affair," said the sly-looking policeman. "There was nothing untoward in the investigation, I can assure you, Mr. Holmes." His tone was defensive, as if he thought we were criticising his procedure. Nevertheless, he granted us full access to the man, in part because of all the help Holmes has been to the police in his career — often without due credit — but I think also because he was confident enough that nothing we discovered would make him look inferior to his men. "The father is baying for the man's blood," Lestrade called after us, as if he thought that might change our minds.

The young prisoner had a haunted look about him. He was staring at the stone wall opposite, and from time to time just shook his head as if he could not comprehend how he had arrived in this dark, dank place.

"Your cousin Georgia has asked that we speak with you," Holmes said, after making our introductions, but could elicit no response.

"She tells us that you deny any wrongdoing in the murder of Miss Judith Hatten," said I, at which I did notice a twitch of his eye. Then, suddenly, he was holding his head in his hands, tearing at his hair.

"I did not murder her," he whispered, almost inaudibly, then screamed: "I did not murder her!" Simon looked across at us, eyes as tearful as his cousin's were but an hour earlier. "P-Please... Please, you have to believe me..."

Holmes stepped closer to the bars. "Then tell us who did."

Simon shook his head again, but it wasn't a refusal; it was simply that he had no idea what to say. What *could* he say, when all the evidence pointed towards him? He would say nothing more, even when pressed, and we left not long afterwards — Holmes informing the guard on duty that he should be watched.

"I believe he may try to take his own life," Holmes told him.

The guard snorted. "It'd save us the trouble."

My friend flashed the guard a look of distaste. "Watson, let us take our leave of this place..."

As we walked out of the prison, and as I was attempting to match Holmes' stride, I commented, "You cannot blame the guard. Miss Cartwright's cousin offers no defence."

"Watson," Holmes said, suddenly rounding on me, "did you not see it in the man's eyes? That man is an innocent."

"But how can he be?" I argued. "You've heard all the—"

He held up a finger. "And yet he is still innocent. I cannot explain it, but I do believe it. He has no recollection of committing these acts, but I am certain he *saw* them being committed."

I rubbed my chin. "He's definitely a troubled man, but guilt can block out memories. Or are you perhaps suggesting a split personality?"

Holmes pursed his lips. "You have the medical knowledge, Watson..."

"Well, I'd need to study him more to—" I was interrupted this second time by the blowing of whistles and policemen running past us. There was something afoot, a crime in progress, and even though we were already committed to this first investigation Holmes is never one to let an opportunity for observation — or to lend assistance — pass him by.

We followed the police to a house but a few streets away. Holmes completely ignored Lestrade's warnings to stay back until they could ascertain what had happened and, dashing after my friend, I too witnessed the tail end of what occurred.

Later, we would learn that the house belonged to a Mr. and Mrs. William Thorndyke. An ordinary couple in every single way — Mr. Thorndyke being a retired schoolteacher.

Screams had been heard bursting from their home; a woman's screams. As we entered the dining room, Lestrade still trying to keep us back, we saw that these screams had indeed come from Mrs. Thorndyke, but not because she was being assaulted in any way. No, these were the screams of a woman holding a dinner-knife in her hand, standing, staring at the body of her husband, sprawled across the dining table. From what I could see, confirmed by later examination, I can tell you that he had been stabbed repeatedly by the instrument clutched in his wife's hand. It had been a frenzied attack; gore covered the table and dripped from the tablecloth. It would not be the final such scene we would witness in the course of this investigation.

As the police moved in closer, Mrs. Thorndyke stopped screaming and looked over in our direction. She wore that same lost expression that had so recently adorned the face of Miss Cartwright's cousin.

One of sheer and utter disbelief.

"Lestrade!" cried Holmes, but his warning came too late. Mrs. Thorndyke looked at the body of her husband, looked down at the bloodied knife in her hand, then before anyone could move to stop her she swiftly drew the blade across her own throat. A thick jet of blood sprayed across the room.

The police let me through then, but there was nothing that could be done for the poor woman. She had made a very thorough job of cutting through both the jugular vein and carotid arteries. My attempts to stem the tide of blood were in vain. As Holmes joined me we both heard her final gurgling gasp. "I… I didn't…"

Though we were fresh to the scene of this incident — able to examine it before, as Holmes would say, Lestrade and his men could contaminate it — we found nothing amiss … save for the brutal murder of Mr. Thorndyke.

As you know, I have long been a student of Holmes and his methods, so it was with a heavy heart that I watched him pace the room, sniffing the air, taking out his glass to pay close scrutiny to a piece of carpet here, the edge of a table there, only for him to concede that — as she must have done — Mrs. Thorndyke had plunged the knife into her husband during the meal. Holmes pressed a gloved finger to his lips. "Ah, but it is the way it happened that is the most curious, Watson," said he. "Note the way the plates are scattered on the table. The look of shock and surprise on Mr. Thorndyke's face. This happened quickly. As if something unimaginable came over the woman. One moment they sat eating dinner together, the next..." His sentence trailed off.

I nodded. "But what *could* have come over her?"

"Once again, you are the physician, Watson. I would suggest that you examine the body of not only Mr. Thorndyke," he encouraged, "but his wife as well. We shall also be needing access to the body of Miss Judith Hatten." Holmes looked over at Lestrade as he said this.

"I beg your pardon? What has the one to do with the other?" the policeman asked.

"Oh, come now, Inspector. Surely you can see the connection here?" The man could not, but I could. Two people murdered by their partners, both surviving halves — though Mrs. Thorndyke did not survive for long, I grant you — claiming that they did not commit the crime, in spite of all evidence to the contrary.

Lestrade allowed us to examine the body of Miss Hatten anyway, along with the others. But even as Holmes watched my explorations from a distance down in the icy morgue I could offer him no new leads.

"The causes of death are accurate," said I, "a head injury in the case of Miss Hatten and repeated stab wounds in the case of Mr. Thorndyke."

Holmes looked past me to the grey bodies on the tables, breathing in deeply — something I would not readily advise in such a situation. "But what of *Mrs.* Thorndyke?"

I shook my head. "Nothing that I could see, at any rate. Perhaps an examination of her blood..."

However not even that afforded us an explanation; no abnormalities that would have accounted for sudden changes in personality. Nor did Holmes' trip to the Hatten residence uncover a thing, largely because Judith's father would not grant us permission to view the crime scene once he learned who had enlisted our help.

"No matter," Holmes said as we climbed back into the cab, heading towards Baker Street once more. "After so long, I doubt whether it would have yielded anything of interest."

While Holmes attempted to make some kind of sense of the incidents thus far — littering his room with everything from articles on insanity to reports alleging bodily possession by demons ("You cannot seriously be considering that?" I said to him when I discovered his notes, but he just waved me away with his hand), playing his violin into the small hours of the morning — more incidents occurred.

In Kentish Town an antiques dealer named Falconbridge used an ornamental sword to disembowel his housekeeper then turned the weapon on himself. At Westminster Hospital a middle-aged builder's merchant called Robertson took it upon himself to secrete a hypodermic needle about his person and inject his elderly mother with an overdose of morphine ... a mercy killing, you might assume, but the woman was actually recovering from her malaise and was expected to be discharged within a matter of days. Colleagues of mine who were present informed me that the son, in a state of confusion and remorse, ran away. His body was later found in the Thames. Finally, passengers on a train bound for Waterloo described hearing piercing screams, only to witness a woman backing out of a carriage covered in blood and holding a fire axe. According to the ticket inspector her hands were trembling, as she looked left and right, then she dropped the axe and fled, eventually flinging herself from the moving vehicle. Inside the carriage were found the dismembered bodies of her husband and their twelve year old daughter.

It was the latter, I fear, that had the most telling effect upon Holmes. As we stepped onto that train, Lestrade now very glad of any assistance, my friend wavered, almost turning back. But he forced himself to look upon those remains. And I swear to you now, that in all my years and service in Afghanistan I had never seen the likes of it before — nor would I care to again.

"I should have been able to prevent this," Holmes said, under his breath, his gaze fixed upon the contents of that carriage.

"How?" I asked him, my own mouth dry as sandpaper.

"There *is* a pattern to these events... I simply cannot see it yet."

When we returned to Baker Street that evening, silence prevailing in the cab along the way, Miss Cartwright was waiting for us. She said nothing as Holmes stepped into the room, but merely strode towards him and slapped his face; before departing without a word.

We discovered not long afterwards that Simon had committed suicide in his cell by swallowing his own tongue. Lestrade said that there was nothing that could have been done, but I knew Holmes disagreed.

I did not see him for some time after that. On the single occasion I did knock and enter his chambers, I found the room empty apart from the usual detritus of the case. However, on the table I spied the means by which he was administering his seven percent solution; a habit from which I never did manage to free him.

Holmes staggered from his bedroom then, unkempt and wearing a dressing gown. He looked drawn and pale, a ghost of his former self.

"Holmes, I really must—" but before I could get out another word, he flew at me, enraged. I thought for a moment he might attack me in a murderous rage, but instead he simply shouted:

"Get out! Get out! *Get out!*"

I did as instructed, retreating and allowing him to slam the door behind me. I heard a lock being drawn on the other side and considered it was for the best that I should leave him alone, despite my grave concern.

An equally concerned Lestrade contacted me several times over the course of those next few weeks, informing me of yet more murders — drownings, beatings, stranglings — as well as suicides, asking if Holmes would be continuing his investigations. I lied and told him that the great detective was looking into several quite promising leads.

In reality, I feared that he had finally met his match. It is a conviction that I still hold to this day.

When I heard Holmes leave 221b Baker Street, it was the middle of the night. He told neither Mrs. Hudson nor myself where he was going, but after his tirade I was not at all surprised. When Lestrade called at the house, protesting that he was no longer able to prevent the papers from reporting this insanity that seemed to have gripped London, I had to admit that Holmes was not present.

"Then where is he, Doctor? And why aren't *you* with him?"

I said again that he was chasing a line of enquiry, but the Inspector's words struck a nerve with me. It wasn't the first time Holmes had retreated into himself, nor the first occasion he had vanished without warning — and Heaven knows he had justification this time — but Lestrade was right; I should be with him. I was deeply distressed about his condition, and if there was a connection between all of these bizarre events then I should be working with Holmes to uncover it.

I set out to look for my friend, searching all the places I could think he would go. Sadly I even tried some of the opium dens that he had been known to frequent from time to time. In Limehouse, I discovered that he had been spotted enjoying some of the more questionable vices it had to offer, but had departed some considerable time ago.

It was not until I had exhausted every single possibility that it struck me where I might find him. My years observing Holmes' methods have left me with some degree of aptitude for deduction myself.

When I arrived at my destination, he was indeed present. Standing, staring out into the middle distance just as the 'victims', those left behind after the murders, were wont to do. He looked no better for his absence; worse in fact, than he had in his chambers. I approached cautiously, after my last encounter with him — not knowing what kind of reception I would receive.

"Ah, Watson," said he in a quiet voice. "My faithful friend and companion... I knew that you would find me here eventually." Holmes looked down at the grave by which he stood, the one containing the bodies of the family who had died on the Waterloo train. "I am so sorry for my behavior when last we saw each other. I was... not myself." He gave a slight laugh, perhaps realizing the significance of his words, but there was no humour in it.

Not far away, I knew, were the final resting places of others who had perished during these past troubling weeks.

"What occurred was not your fault."

He shook his head and turned to me. "I could not see it until now, but we have been facing my greatest enemy."

"Not... the Professor," I said, struggling to hide the alarm from my voice.

"I *have* seen Moriarty, Watson, I will not deny it. My own punishment, perhaps... But no... my efforts at the falls were entirely successful. He remains among the deceased. Although through this experience, I have discovered why the murderers — if one can refer to them as such — are so quick to throw away their lives. I know now what they see... afterwards."

I frowned, conceding that I had no idea what he was talking about. If Moriarty had not returned from the grave — and the dark humour of my own musings was not lost on me, in light of where we were standing — then who exactly was it that we were up against? I ventured the question aloud.

"I've been a fool, Watson. It has been before my nose all along. Literally! The stench is so distinctive. But, you see, I've seen *Him* before as well, if only briefly. You recall the case of the Devil's Foot, which you so expertly set down?"

Good Lord, I thought to myself, *is Holmes making some kind of veiled reference?* Surely we were not facing the Fallen One himself; such a thing would have been even more preposterous than Holmes' theory about demonic possession. As it transpired, our foe was much more terrifying. I nodded, remembering the case well.

"It happened when I subjected us to the burning powder that was used to induce both madness and... death."

"Are you saying a similar poison has been employed here to drive people to such acts?"

He shook his head. "No, no, Watson. The *Radix pedis diaboli* has nothing to do with this affair, save for the fact that the one we must stop was present during that investigation also."

"I do not follow you."

"I have never spoken about what I witnessed under the influence of that powder, nor have I asked you what you saw."

"My dose appeared to be notably smaller than yours," I told him, remembering how I shook Holmes out of his hallucinogenic trance.

"Indeed..." He looked again at the headstone before him, then cast his eye over the entire graveyard. "Consequently, I saw our enemy, Watson. A brief... suggestion, you might call it. But nevertheless it was *Him*, of that I am certain." Was my friend speaking of prophecy now? "It was a state I have been attempting to recreate during my absence from Baker Street."

"And were you successful in your endeavours?" asked I, when all I really wanted to do was voice my concern; the state Holmes was talking about almost cost him his sanity, if not his life.

"I was indeed. I saw that which I was seeking, and more besides. I finally know what I must do... actually what *you* must do, Watson." I still wasn't following his line of reasoning and I told him so. He placed a hand on my shoulder. "At this moment I have more need of your skills as a physician than a detective. Do you trust me, old friend?"

"Of course, Holmes."

"Then I would ask you to visit your surgery, with the express intention of collecting the items we shall require for our task, and meet me back here tomorrow at sundown."

"Task, Holmes?" said I, still puzzled.

"Yes." He fixed me with a stare that I have never forgotten and then he said, more serious than I have ever heard him, "Watson, tomorrow evening I would ask that you kill me."

The logistics of Holmes' plan will soon become apparent, but you can appreciate my asking him to elaborate on his statement. However, he would not, merely indicating that the following night he would require me to end his life by stopping his heart.

"I simply refuse," I told him.

"Then more innocent people will die before this is all over," Holmes said to me. "The killer has a taste for this now. From what I can ascertain he is using more and more direct and personal methods. He is taking pleasure in the tactile aspect of ending lives. If you will not do this for me, Watson, then do it for the victims yet to be claimed."

Reluctantly, I agreed, returning to my surgery to gather what I would require. The safest way I could think of to stop Holmes' heart temporarily was by way of administering an injection; a lethal concoction of my own devising, for which I also had the antidote. Holmes had explained that he only required me to impede the beating of his heart muscle for a short amount of time. "Just long enough to lure our prey out into the open," Holmes informed me.

Quite how 'killing' my friend would achieve this, I did not know, apart from the obvious parallel it had with friends and loved ones suddenly doing the same thing across our city. Did he wish to recreate the madness of extinguishing a life in such a way? If so, he could scarcely have chosen a more apt person to perform this action; Holmes has always been and will forever remain, my best friend...

The wait of a day passed slowly, as I contemplated what I was about to do. In a few hours I would achieve what every single one of Holmes' adversaries had failed to do. Even Moriarty. I would murder the great detective, and he had asked me to do the very deed! The thought of it boggles the mind.

Nevertheless, at the appointed time, I found myself once more travelling back to that cemetery as another thick fog descended upon London. The sky was darkening and the overall effect chilled me to the bone. As I walked through that graveyard, knowing full well that the people contained therein could not harm me, I still found myself shivering. When Holmes stepped out from the depths of a bank of fog and tapped me on the shoulder, it was very nearly I who found my heart stopping that night.

"You gave me an awful fright, Holmes," I told him.

"My dear Watson, please forgive me…" In spite of the circumstances, and by the light of the lamp he was holding, I detected the hint of a smile playing on his lips. "Did you bring the required items?"

I nodded, showing him my medical bag.

"Splendid, then we shall begin." Holmes took me over to a flat slab of stone, a place for him to rest as I carried out his request. He placed the lamp beside him so that I could see.

"Holmes, are you quite sure about this…? I still do not understand why—"

He silenced me with a raised finger. "Please proceed. I know that I am in the most capable hands."

Sighing, I took out a hypodermic and a vial, siphoning off a massive dose of my concoction. Holmes, for his part, rolled up his sleeve. I saw the cost of his experimentations; red welts on his arm, dotting the lines of his veins. I frowned, but said nothing, instead taking up his arm to give him the injection: quite possibly the last I might ever administer to him.

As the needle sank into his flesh, Holmes reached over and patted my hand gently. Neither of us said a thing as he shut his eyes and waited for the drug to take effect. I sat there and noted the look of complete peace on Holmes' face; it was the first and only time I have seen him look so content.

I took his wrist and felt for a pulse. It was still there, but faint.

"I never got the chance to tell you this before, Holmes…" I whispered, still keeping hold of his wrist as the beats slowed. "But thank you. Thank you for everything…"

And, suddenly, the beating ended.

I bowed my head, choking back the wave of emotion I felt at seeing my companion as dead as those corpses I had examined after the murders. Then I felt it, a sudden jolt — so fierce I almost let go of Holmes' wrist. I wonder now if I would have seen what followed had I done so, for I firmly believe it was the physical connection to Holmes, at the moment his spirit departed his body, that allowed me to bear witness to what transpired. Yes, that is correct — you did not read wrongly. I can finally unburden myself of the knowledge of what happened in those ensuing seconds. It is an unspoken memory I have carried with me now for so very long…

A shape began to coalesce beside the slab, indistinct at first and shimmering — but as I blinked, refocusing on it, a familiarity began to reveal itself. A head, then shoulders, arms, legs ... it was a body, transparent but glowing white. Eventually it took its true form. It turned to look at me, and it was then that I saw the unmistakable visage of none other than Holmes himself. He mouthed something upon seeing me, but I could not hear him at that point and was too much in shock to reply anyway. I wondered whether Holmes had somehow infected me with his madness, for this must surely be what it felt like to experience insanity.

The fog parted, close by, and began swirling round, taking on a form itself. It was difficult to separate the darkness beyond our lamp and the glow of Holmes' spirit from that which was bending the mist to its will. I soon realized my mistake, however, because again this was not a thing of our world. It was nebulous in appearance, mist-like though not *of* the mist enveloping us. The only reason I could see it at all was because of my physical connection to Holmes.

It too settled on a form eventually: tall and black, wearing what looked like robes but not from any material known to man; rather fashioned from the same miasma as the rest of it. Its hands, when it reached out, were in contrast white and thin, almost bone-like but lacking substance. A finger shot out from the robe, pointing at my companion's shade.

And its voice, when it spoke, sounded like thousands of voices speaking at once in my mind. "*Sherlock Holmes,*" it stated simply. "*I have come for you.*"

All the times he had cheated Death, in particular that celebrated occasion at the Reichenbach Falls, and now I feared that it had sought Holmes out — all because I had ended his life. And Holmes was right, there was a distinctive smell; it was one I recognized all too readily from my time serving abroad, and my career as a doctor on these shores.

"No," I heard my friend say then, in a voice that was his, but not his. "I have come for *you.*"

There was silence then, as if the creature in front of Holmes did not quite know how to reply. That silence was filled eventually by an explanation of sorts.

"It wasn't quite enough for you, was it?" Holmes continued abruptly. "Taking lives like this. It wasn't... satisfying." He uttered the last word with all the contempt it deserved. "You have watched for so long as we have found new ways to kill one another. Watched and come for us when needed. All the while wondering what it might be like to actually kill, to tighten a cord until the last gasp of air emerged from a mouth, to plunge a knife through someone's heart until it beat no longer, to hack a child to..." Holmes paused. "I saw your pattern, you see. This isn't the first time you have slipped inside; you've worked your way through battlefields, have you not, choosing those who would not readily be missed. The poor, the destitute. I have seen them all... They told me what you have done. Yet that was not enough for you. The sweetest sensation, the longest and strongest high of all, comes from the murder of a loved one. To feel the connection severed at your hands. *Your very hands!*"

Listening to Holmes' explanation, something I have done on many occasions at the conclusion of a case, everything fell into place. The reason why Miss Cartwright's cousin, Simon, had done what he did — the reason those others did the same. It was a disturbing revelation to say the least.

"*You dare to pass judgment on me?*" came the voice that was a thousand voices, almost screeching the reply. It was filled with indignation that Holmes was even talking to it.

"When your actions result in..." Holmes' spirit looked over again at where the family from the train had their plot. "Yes. Yes, I do."

There was a snarl from the black mist-like shape, and it flung itself forward, just as Holmes had done back in Baker Street after wallowing in depression and indulging too much in his seven percent solution. The intent was different here, however, and we could both see it.

The shape raised both hands, in an effort to grab Holmes, to take him back with it, to drag him away and undo his very existence. I wished there was something I could do... But there was! I could bring Holmes back as he had instructed. We knew the identity of the killer, we just could not do anything about it — and never would be able to, I suspected.

It was time to administer the antidote and restart Holmes' heart.

He looked sideways and could see what I was about to do. "Not yet, Watson," he cried, then those hands grabbed him and Holmes was grappling with Death.

"You... have been... with me... every step of the way..." Holmes grunted as he struggled with his fearsome foe. "But even... you should know... there are consequences... to one's actions..."

Something was happening behind me. I took my eyes off the spectral pair, to glance around. More shapes in the mist, breaking through in fact: one after the other. It did not take them as long as Holmes or Death to form; they had been waiting for this moment and they were eager to strike. Here were there the victims of Death's atrocious crimes, Judith Hatten, Mr. Thorndyke, the husband and child murdered on the Waterloo Train, but also there were those who had been so tormented by their involuntary actions that they had taken their own lives — and, I had to wonder, given a helpful push by Death? So there followed Simon, Mrs. Thorndyke, the mother who'd turned that fire axe on her beloved husband and child, and more besides. I watched as those Holmes had spoken about, the earlier victims, both the murderers and the suicides gone unnoticed, unreported — the ones who had told Holmes their tales — all came marching through the mist. These were also joined by those who'd been lost during the last few weeks, while Holmes had been attempting to get to the bottom of the mystery: the ones Lestrade had not been able to keep from the morning editions. They marched through that graveyard as one, a spectral army converging on Death, all craving revenge.

The black figure — whose face was still unclear to me, and I would imagine to Holmes — turned towards them, letting go of my friend. The horde encircled Death, crowding in and raining down blows that I did not think would have any effect, but evidently did. They were backed by the power of those trapped between life and ... and whatever was on the other side. It suddenly dawned on me then exactly why Holmes had wanted to wait a day. It was October 31st, All Hallows' Eve — the time of year when these spirits would be at their most powerful.

"Now, Watson!" shouted Holmes, limping away from the scene. "Bring me back now!"

I snapped out of my daze, not wanting to let go of Holmes' hand because I wished to witness the last of this, wanted to see Death's end. But, of course, I should have known that Death is never, ever truly gone. How could it be? It is the other side to the coin of life. I saw the dark figure being smothered by the ghosts, then let go and watched as the vision faded. As I worked — injecting Holmes with the antidote, then pounding on his chest to get his heart beating again, I heard a faint voice. A voice made up of so many more. "*We* will *meet again*," Death promised Holmes, "*and not even your friend will be able to save you then*." The words filled me with dread.

I couldn't see the 'spirit Holmes' any more, couldn't see any evidence of the battle that had taken place, but that did not matter to me at that time. I beat on Holmes' chest one final time, and he sat bolt upright, taking in a lungful of night air. He began to cough, though whether it was the result of coming back or the fog still surrounding us, I had no clue. I held on to him anyway, until he was strong enough to sit up on his own. "Rest a little, Holmes," I warned him.

"I'm... I'm fine," he told me. "Thank you, Watson." And he clasped my arm.

I nevertheless had to half carry my friend through the graveyard and through the fog, into a more public place where we could hail a cab to return us to the relative safety, and sanity, of Baker Street.

Holmes spent the next few days recuperating, enjoying the ministrations of both myself and Mrs. Hudson. When Lestrade called on us once more, I was able to inform him of the conclusion of the case. "You should not see any more deaths like those," I assured him. I could not promise him the madness of the population would not continue, as indeed it did in the final days of the 19th century until everyone was certain the world would not end. Of the murders committed by loved ones and subsequent suicides, there were no more. Due note had obviously been taken of the repercussions. As I already mentioned, the matter was put down to the singular time of the year and our calendar. I would not be pressed further on what had been amiss with those people, in spite of Lestrade demanding answers from both myself and later from Holmes. For one thing, I did not know where to start; for another I was positive he would have us both committed if we spoke of what we'd uncovered. Nor did Holmes and I talk about what had happened and what we had seen that day. To do so seemed somehow to invite the premature return of the culprit.

So you see, it is only now, with my friend passed on and myself nearing the end of my years, that I am committing this to paper. Even now, I doubt very much whether it shall see the light of day. Instead it will probably be dismissed, I fancy, as a work of fiction less credible even than those by Mr. Stoker or Mr. Verne. The final ramblings of an aged adventurer.

But I know the truth.

Holmes once spoke about his greatest foe without realizing it, long before he ever encountered the thing, during a case a long time ago. *The Adventure of the Six Napoleons* I believe it was, though my memory is waning, I must confess. He was in the mortuary then, not the graveyard, but he mused: "I am just contemplating the one mystery I cannot solve. Death itself." How prophetic those words would turn out to be.

Because although he may have prevented more innocents from going the way of Judith Hatten and the others, spared future 'murderers' from the blame and guilt of something they had not done, Holmes had far from solved the mystery of exactly what Death was — nor what happens when we take our final breath.

The spectre had been right, of course. It *had* seen Holmes again, and to my everlasting regret I had not been able to save him. But that is a story for another time...

PAUL KANE is the award-winning author of the novels *The Gemini Factor* and *Of Darkness and Light*, plus the post-apocalyptic Robin Hood trilogy *Arrowhead, Broken Arrow* and *Arrowland*. His non-fiction books are *The Hellraiser Films and Their Legacy* and *Voices in the Dark*, and he is the co-editor of anthologies like *Hellbound Hearts* and *Terror Tales*. His work has been optioned for film and in 2008 his story 'Dead Time' was turned into an episode of the NBC/LionsGate TV series *Fear Itself*, adapted by Steve *(30 Days of Night)* Niles, directed by Darren *(SAW II-IV)* Lynn Bousman. Paul also scripted a film version of his story 'The Opportunity', which premiered at the Cannes Film Festival.

THE HOUSE OF BLOOD

by Tony Richards

He knew the man was real, but Lieutenant Vince Capaldi could scarcely believe it. That famous narrow face, framed against the background of a hotel window, with its hooked nose and very watchful eyes.

"My God," he breathed. "You can't have aged a day since Victorian times."

Holmes nodded.

"So you really are immortal?"

"I found it out after the Reichenbach Falls, when I suddenly returned to life with no sensible explanation. A definite case in point, Lieutenant—" and the great detective favoured him with a quirky half-smile— "of the last remaining solution to a puzzle, however improbable, being the correct one. I never thought that *I* would turn out to be the most striking example of that adage."

"And now," he went on quickly, "what is this murder you have come to me about?"

Capaldi's eyes widened. "I never said anything about any…"

"You have been wearing tight latex gloves recently," Holmes pointed out. "I doubt that you would do that for a mugging. There is a smear of luminol on the edge of your left shoe, a substance for detecting blood. And the gravity of your expression speaks of no lesser a crime than murder most foul."

"In fact," he continued before the policeman could break in, "I would hazard you have come to me about a fourth in the series of killings that began last week. I've, naturally, been following them on the TV news and in the press. And let me hazard at something else. Something you have contrived to keep from the newshounds and the general public. All the victims so far have been completely drained of their vital essence."

The color disappeared from the lieutenant's features, his mouth falling open.

"Luminol, my good fellow, is used to find mere trace elements of blood. So why would you use it around a freshly murdered human corpse except to discern if there was any blood at all?"

When he saw that he had rendered the man speechless, Holmes allowed himself another little smile.

"You're as bad as Lestrade," he commented. "You mean well, but you do not really think."

Then he encouraged his visitor to bring him up to date on the whole situation.

Stammering, Capaldi tried to get his thoughts together. He went over what had happened to the first victim. A certain Harriet Ellison, of Boise, Idaho, who was still fresh in his memory. She had won a massive jackpot from a slot machine ten days ago, been photographed with her reward, and then become surrounded by well-wishers and hangers-on with whom she had been partying. Halfway through the evening, she had headed off to the restrooms, only to mysteriously vanish. Her corpse, clad merely in its underwear, had been found in the desert on the edge of town next morning.

Lawrence Mark of Trenton, New Jersey, had been the next one. His case followed the same pattern. After a huge run of luck, at the craps tables, he had disappeared, only for it to be proved that he had suffered the same fate.

Daniel Besset of Oxford, Maryland, had been the third. He had recently won sixty thousand dollars, by means of his skill at Texas Hold'em.

This much, Sherlock Holmes already knew.

"And the last?" he prompted.

"Just this morning. Hasn't even made the papers yet. Kyle Monoghan from Boston, Mass."

"And he had won at?"

"Blackjack. According to the witnesses, it was a pretty amazing run of luck."

"Do you have a picture of the fellow?" Holmes enquired calmly.

Capaldi was aware of the detective's reputation, and had come prepared. He took a glossy photo from the inside pocket of his coat and handed it over, then watched with quiet awe as

Holmes studied the thing. It had been taken at the crime scene, Monoghan sprawled out in the desert dirt.

One of Holmes' narrow eyebrows lifted just a touch, but that was all.

"Let me make sure that I have got this straight. Nothing whatsoever connects the victims, not in terms of gender, age, hometown, occupation, or ethnicity. They were not even kidnapped from the same casino. The single thing that *does* connect them is that Lady Luck smiled on them beneficently shortly before they met their fate."

"That's right."

"And were their winnings taken?"

The lieutenant nodded. "Every time."

"Which would mark these cases as a simple string of murder-robberies. Except that..."

Each of the victims had been stripped practically naked and drained completely of their blood, by means of punctures at the throat and wrists. They'd already established that.

"My guys are calling them 'The Vampire Killings,'" Capaldi let slip.

"There are no such creatures," Holmes assured him. "Reports that have tried to pit me against Mr. Stoker's Transylvanian Count are much exaggerated."

He paused for a few moments, lost in thought.

"Very well. I shall take the case. But I'll require a fee."

"My chief has already okayed it."

Holmes grunted approvingly before turning his attention from Capaldi to the scene beyond his window. The flashing lights, the dreamlike outlines of the different hotels, the churning throng on the sidewalks below.

"Just out of interest, Mr. Holmes," he heard Capaldi venture, "what exactly do you think of Vegas?"

"Even by the standards of modern day America..." and the great detective lowered his tone, aware that honesty required being rude, "it is utterly preposterous."

Holmes weaved through the dense crowds on the Strip. The heat and noise seemed to lash at him like whips. People in this modern age moved so quickly and with such noisy bustle, even when they were taking their leisure. He missed London. He missed his flat over Baker Street. And most of all, he missed Watson, although that final emotion was tinged, as ever, with a faint coloring of guilt. The poor old fellow had finally succumbed to a pulmonary canker. Had voluminous doses of secondary pipe-smoke been the cause of that?

It was the worst thing about immortality, seeing those that you'd been close to disappear behind you on the river of implacable time. Lestrade himself. Mrs. Hudson. Even those urchins called the Baker Street Irregulars had grown up, then greyed and met their final hour before his very eyes. Perhaps that was why he had left England. He kept constantly on the move these days, as if he were trying to avoid growing attached too much to anything. Currently, he was travelling the length and breadth of the United States. But after those were done with, where might he wind up?

There was no point, he told himself, either in being maudlin or in wondering too deeply what the future might hold. His longevity was a fact that he had little choice but to accept. Focussing his thoughts on something that could not be changed was an absurd waste of his talents. It was better to stay in the realms of the possible and direct his mind to more constructive ends.

Like solving this terrible case, for instance. That would keep him busy for a while.

Holmes was in disguise, realizing his normal garb would draw too much attention to himself. He needed to blend in, so he had on a gaudy Hawaiian shirt, canvas shoes, a beige baseball cap and a pair of chinos. It was the best compromise that he could manage. He would rather die a hundred deaths than resort to jeans or shorts.

He had come here for two reasons only: First, to see the place with his own eyes, and secondly, to visit *Star Trek: the Experience.* He had become a devotee of the original show and its movie spin-offs, since he felt a great affinity with the character called Mr. Spock.

He'd intended to spend two or three days here at the very most. Then the murders had begun — he had immediately suspected his assistance might be called upon. In fact, he had already been making some enquiries of his own.

Most of the people around him were tourists, here for the shows, the restaurants and bars, the dolphins and white tigers and only a little flutter on the side. They interested him not a jot. At the heart of this case lay gambling in the serious sense and the caprices of fortune; he was utterly certain of it. That commodity could be found in any place here, any time of day and night. This was a town where the game was *constantly* afoot.

He headed for the Paris, the setting of Kyle Monoghan's triumph and the last place that he had been seen. There was one
thing Holmes was convinced of, whoever was behind this, there
were more than one of them. Harriet Ellison could have been
abducted by a single individual, and Daniel Besset had been
elderly and slightly built, but Monoghan and Lawrence Mark
were both robust and burly. No drugs had been found in the
toxicology, so there were at least two murderers involved.

He went through the lobby and into the labyrinthine depths
of the casino, his attention gliding watchfully from side to side.
Nothing that he saw surprised him after more than a week in
this place. Lights flashed everywhere, and there were constant,
repetitive clangs and hums and clatters. But that summed up
this ultra-modern age, now didn't it? For all of the advances that
mankind had made, most of it wound up as pointless sound and
fury.

The majority of the visitors in here were, as out on the sidewalk, merely tourists. They *were* gambling, but only with a sense
of merriment. These were the kind of folk who set a fifty dollar
limit, or smaller, for the entire evening. The kind who gambled
at all merely because they could not do the same back home.

Scattered among them were other individuals whose presence Holmes found considerably more ominous. Older women
wearing gloves, so that they'd not callous their fingers with their
constant tugging at the one-armed bandits. Pale, intense men
hunched as though in prayer over the blackjack tables. People
standing near the roulette wheels with starved-looking gleams
in their dull, tired eyes. There was nothing merry about these
sorts. Gambling fever had them in its grip as tightly — nay,
savagely — as any opiate. They had become slaves to the habit,
and poorly treated slaves, at that.

Mostly, they were cheaply dressed. There was evidence
that they had pawned watches and rings in some cases — all it
needed was a swift glance at their lower finger joints and wrists.
But it was their expressions that struck most at the great detective. Hope would flare up as the card was dealt, the wheel set
spinning, but it would give way, almost invariably, to horrible
disappointment, made all the more profound by the fact that it
was a familiar sensation.

He headed for the bar area, glad to leave the poor wretches
behind. It was not a busy hour of the day, and there was just one
man working behind the counter.

"What's your poison, buddy?"

Holmes ordered a piña colada, a drink for which he had acquired a taste. They'd not had much in the way of pineapples in Victorian London, and he relished the flavour.

"That unfortunate fellow they found this morning. He was in here yesterday, wasn't he?"

"You bet," the barman frowned. "Had an incredible run at the tables."

"Did he celebrate here afterwards?"

"Where else would he go?"

"And he attracted a big crowd?"

The barman grinned sardonically. "Pal, when you're on a winning streak in Vegas, hell, you've *always* got a load of friends. The dames especially... that is, till your luck runs out."

"Does anyone in particular linger in your memory?"

The man thought about it. "There was this chick dressed in black. Chinese or Japanese or something. She didn't kind of pounce on the guy. She just moved in on him slowly, till finally she had her arm around him."

Holmes felt his pulse quicken. In all the enquiries he had made so far, there had been mention of an Oriental woman.

"And did Monoghan leave with her?"

"Friend, I was too busy mixing drinks to even know."

Holmes thanked him and then headed back towards the gaming area. He already had a plan. In fact, he'd come to see that what he needed to attract these villains was a winner. Someone on a lucky streak. That was the kind of person who they targeted.

There was nobody he could make out who answered that description at the moment, so he would have to engineer it.

It would be childishly simple to join one of the high stakes blackjack games and start to win a fortune by the trick of counting cards, but establishments like this one were accustomed to such practices — the security goons would descend on him before the killers could. So Holmes turned to the roulette area instead.

The first three wheels that he looked at were functioning perfectly, but the fourth? There appeared to be some very slight wear to the bearings. Patterns — too small for a lesser intellect to notice — were being repeated in the places that the ball fell. Holmes stood back for fifteen minutes, taking mental notes. Finally, he felt confident a goodly amount of lucre could be made here.

By which time, he had decided that he ought not be the actual beneficiary. When these murderous fiends arrived, it would be

better to observe them from a slight remove at first. Once they'd
shown their true intentions, he would apprehend them. He had
his trusty revolver tucked away beneath his shirt.

So, who should be the lucky man? Holmes' gaze was immediately drawn to a short, middle-aged gentleman at the far end of
the table. They were similarly dressed, except the fellow wore no
cap, but that was where the resemblance ended. This hapless soul
was overweight, with thinning red hair, and his pores practically
oozed frustration. He had been doing badly at the wheel the whole
time the detective had been standing there. He was, in fact, down
to his last few chips.

Holmes wandered over to his elbow.

"Things have to look up some time," he murmured, apropos
of nothing.

The fellow turned and glanced at him with a look of surprise.

"You really think so?"

"Yes, I do."

"That accent? You a Limey?"

A fevered gleam had appeared in his eyes. Holmes understood
immediately what was happening.

People who were addicted to gambling all had one peculiar
quirk. They took anything different in the environment about
them, anything unexpected or new, as an omen that their luck
was due to change. This individual seemed to be in that exact state
of mind. He perceived the presence of an Englishman beside him
as some kind of talisman.

"Fred Bonner," the man announced, grasping Holmes firmly
by the hand.

"George Smith."

"Pleased to meet you, George. You stand right there and tell
me which number I ought to put these chips on."

Holmes gazed at the wheel.

"You should try number 12."

And when 12 came up, Fred crowed.

Over the course of the next half hour, he won repeatedly. Not
with every single turn, naturally. There were too many variables
for even Holmes to foresee every bounce and clatter of the little
silver ball, but enough times that the pile of chips in front of the
man grew impressively large. Predictably, a crowd began to gather.

Holmes kept his head tucked slightly down and his eyes
hooded, pretending to be absorbed in the game when he was actually not. Most of the folk around him appeared to be normal. A
couple were streetwalkers, and one chap near the back was almost

certainly a pickpocket, but the great detective had no time for such trivia on this occasion. When would the killers turn up?

An Oriental woman's face appeared in the throng across from him. He had to struggle not to look straight at her.

She was slender, very beautiful. It was hard to be certain with those who heralded from the East, but she was probably in her early thirties. Her hair was tied back in a bun. Her irises were jet black.

The woman was clad in some kind of silken trouser suit. The blouse had a high, stiff collar. Holmes' suspicions were immediately aroused. Why would anyone wear something so constricting in the kind of heat that reigned outside this gaming palace?

There were several other things he began to notice after a short while. Although her face looked fresh and natural at first glance, it was actually layered with foundation and make-up, so artfully applied as not to be obvious. Great care seemed to have been taken to make her eyes appear more slanted than they really were; her features flatter, and she was rather tall for a female from the Orient, which piqued his suspicions even more.

She had disguised her true appearance, in other words, but there'd be time to find the reason for that later. Urgency pressed at his heart. He had successfully dangled his bait. Now, it was time to let the villain try and take it.

"Whad'ya think?" Fred was asking him. "12 again?"

"I really think you ought to quit."

"You serious? I'm on a roll!"

"And all rolls come to an end. Cash your winnings, Mr. Bonner."

Holmes became afraid that he would not succeed in stopping this. The gleam in his new friend's eyes sharpened, the fellow's expression growing angry. He was in the grip of his addiction more firmly than he had ever been. Left to his own devices, he would stay at the wheel, frittering away every penny he had won.

Years ago, Holmes had spent a fortnight at a temple deep in the Laotian jungle, and had learnt some techniques from the monks there. He met Fred's gaze and kept his voice low, employing a mild form of hypnosis.

"That's me done. Drinks for everyone," he whispered to the man.

"That's me done! Drinks for everyone!" Fred bellowed, to the cheers and applause of the crowd.

Holmes allowed a distance of several yards to grow between himself and Fred as they headed for the bar. He was still an observer to this milieu, and would only become an active participant once he was certain that he had his felons. Drinks were mixed and passed around. The great detective found himself engaged in conversation with a claims adjuster from Birmingham, Alabama, but kept most of his attention fixed on what was going on around him.

The barkeeper had been absolutely right. The Oriental-looking woman did not close in immediately on her target. Rather, she hung about the edges of the man's personal space, casting sideways glances in his direction. There seemed to be some large item of jewelry underneath her black blouse; Holmes could see the bulge it made. Why did she not have it on display, like all the other women present?

And one time, when she dipped her head, her collar shifted and Holmes thought he caught a glimpse of a scar. He had no idea what that signified.

It was too much of a coincidence that she had happened to be in the Paris at the same time Fred began his winning streak. Which told Holmes that his notion about multiple miscreants had been absolutely right. There had to be eyes everywhere, spies in most of the casinos, looking out for situations such as this. In which case, how large a criminal conspiracy was this? But the detective could make out nobody who might be a confederate.

The woman reached across and lightly touched Fred's arm. Holmes excused himself politely, wandering away to a spot in the bar where he could continue to observe without himself being noticed.

She engaged Fred in conversation. Holmes could see immediately that she had the talents of a clever, subtle courtesan. She made a little joke, at which Fred smiled. And then, when he made one himself, she burst into uproarious laughter, pretending she needed to hold onto his forearm to support herself.

Her hand had moved to his shoulder a minute after that. And a while later, she was no longer addressing Fred's face, but murmuring in his ear.

Holmes saw him nod.

The curious thing was, the man had been forgotten by the others, by this time. He had been the centre of attention when he had been winning, but the fickle interest of this crowd had already moved on to other subjects. He had become all but invisible. *That* was how the victims had been spirited away from such busy venues. The mental inexactness of the common herd, its ability to be distracted so easily, never ceased to amaze Holmes, or appall him.

Fred and the woman started ambling towards the exit. The detective followed, taking great care not to close the gap.

This turned out to be one of the worst mistakes that he had ever made. Just as the couple reached the Strip, some coaches out front began disgorging their passengers. They were elderly to the last. The sidewalk became immediately snarled up with arthritic doddering and Zimmer frames. Trying to get past without bowling over some frail octogenarian became an almost impossible challenge. Holmes watched desperately as the two figures dwindled away from him. As soon as he found a passage through, he ran in their direction.

He was just in time to see the couple reach a corner and a van pull up. The rear doors were flung open, and — as though on some invisible cue — a group of people, maybe eight of them, detached themselves from the passers-by and surrounded Bonner, shielding him from view.

He was bundled into the van. The others followed him inside. The doors slammed shut. The Oriental-looking woman climbed in by the driver, shouting something. The vehicle roared away.

Holmes, who had his revolver half-drawn, watched it disappear. The only thing he could do now was call Lieutenant Capaldi and instigate a search.

Except he *still* had not got used to the maintenance of cell phones, and the battery in his was flat.

"It's my fault," he was murmuring at dawn the next morning. "Poor, poor Fred."

The desert sprawled around them, the temperature of its air already rising. Fred Bonner was lying in his boxers near the foot of a massive saguaro cactus, his skin so robbed of color that it might be alabaster.

"No use blaming yourself," said Vince Capaldi. "Wasn't you killed him."

"Wasn't it?" the great detective barked back angrily. "I should never have used an unwitting man as an instrument of such deception. No, I should have played the role myself!"

"In which case, you'd be lying here, and we'd be no closer to solving this. You say, apart from the woman, all the rest were normal-looking?"

That was not exactly what he'd said. Holmes recalled his brief glimpse of the people who'd abducted Bonner. There'd been nothing outstanding about them, certainly, but they all shared a quality that he had previously perceived in the casino.

They'd been cheaply dressed, their faces drawn. Their brows had been furrowed, their eyes squinting, like they were unaccustomed to the natural outdoor light. Some of them had been sporting pale bands of skin at their wrists where watches had once snuggled. They were, in short, the same kind of gambling addicts Holmes had mentally remarked on in the Paris.

Guilt gnawed at him on the ride back into town. Did Bonner have a family? He did not even know, but finally, a fresh sense of resolve gripped the detective. This terrible death would *not* be in vain. He would solve the case for Fred's sake!

Capaldi dropped him off at his hotel. Holmes, as soon as he was in his room, pulled on a new disguise: an old shirt, which he rumpled up before slipping on, a pair of grey nylon trousers and some old brown shoes. He took his wristwatch off and put it in a drawer, and mussed his hair up in the mirror before taking a wad of cash from the safe and going out.

At the Luxor, he converted the entire sum into chips. Then he went across to the blackjack tables and sat down; deliberately losing every single hand over the next two hours.

Were there eyes on him? He thought *yes*. Holmes could feel his neck prickling as the cards were dealt, but did not look around.

When practically all his chips were gone, he stood up with a defeated sigh, wandered over to the bar area and ordered a straight scotch.

He was careful to sit round-shouldered, and feigned a melancholy air. A shabby, grey-haired, rather dumpy figure eased herself onto the barstool next to his.

"Down on your luck, huh?"

Her tones revealed her as a Brooklynite. Holmes affected not merely an American accent but a convincing Deep South drawl when he answered her.

"Ma savings are all gone. Ma daughter's college fund. Cain't even afford a ticket home. What in the Lord's name am I gonna do?"

A look of understanding filled the woman's red-rimmed eyes.

"Try this place."

She handed him a card which read, *The House of Good Fortune* and gave an address, but nothing more.

Holmes frowned. "Another casino?"

"Nah, not a gaming house. A house of worship."

He squinted at her. "How's that gonna help?"

"If you join in…" and the woman's lips pursed deviously, "it might just change your luck a little. Don't take my word for it, son. Come and see for yourself. Directly after sundown, tonight."

She was gone from the stool the next instant, with a nimbleness that belied her age.

Holmes was left with hours to kill. Ought he call in the police? If, as he had already decided, this city was laced with underground informants, then the sudden emergence of conventional law officers might give the game away. Forewarned, the perpetrators might escape. No, he had got this far by himself; so he would have to carry it the rest of the way.

Holmes trudged along the Strip for a while, the bizarre sights around him melting to a tepid blur, the urgent sounds reduced to a static-like hissing in his ears. In his numerous decades on this Earth, he had seen society give up its quiet dignity in favour of spectacle, indulgence and excess, and it irritated him greatly sometimes.

This was precisely one of those occasions when a seven percent solution of cocaine would give his mind the few hours of sharpened perspicacity and tightened focus that it needed. Unfortunately the laws had changed and his conscience would not let him break them while he was still taking the LVPD's shilling.

He finally wound up back in his room, sprawled out on the bed watching old reruns of *Star Trek*, one of the few genuinely good, worthwhile developments of this modern age.

"It goes beyond the bounds of logic, Jim."

That was so beautifully succinct it almost made a tear well up.

Sleep practically overtook him, and he emerged from it with a jerk. Through his hotel window, he could see the sky had darkened. The colored lighting on the street below glowed with a lurid brilliance.

The entire town was being swallowed up in shadow. Holmes felt his heartbeat speeding up again. He was close to getting to the bottom of this whole affair — of that, he was certain. The same frisson which had to overcome a hunter had him in its clutches.

He reminded himself that adrenalin was also a drug, just as potent and confounding as the gambling addiction he had seen so often in this city. So he forced himself to slow down and think clearly. He was just one man, and headed into possible grave danger. He could not be killed, certainly, but he could be overpowered, imprisoned, even hurt. He could still remember, with agonising clarity, every bone-crunching knock he'd taken on his descent down the Reichenbach Falls, and had no wish to suffer anything like that again if it could be avoided.

How many congregants might be gathered at this 'house of worship'? His gaze drifted towards his trusty revolver on the nightstand.

Then it turned away, because he might need more than just five shots. In his time here in America, Holmes had purchased several brand-new items of equipment. So he vaulted off the bed to where his bags were stored.

To blazes with his trusty revolver. Where the devil were his trusty Glocks?

Holmes re-studied the small card that he'd been given on the way out. House of Good Fortune. The name described nothing, and was perfectly anonymous in its own way. In a city of this kind, it could be a small casino or a Chinese restaurant. It was in this manner that the people he was on the search for stayed below the radar.

By this time, he was quite convinced that he was dealing with a cult. He had encountered them before. They were more dangerous than any purely criminal organization, since their members were fanatical and hell-bent on their goals.

A hot breeze skirled on the evening air around him. Holmes was dressed as he had been earlier, but had put on a light rain-coat. Not that he expected rain, but the garment served to cover up the pair of sidearms, both which had extended clips.

The address he was headed to was several blocks behind the old part of the Strip. The clientele at these casinos were hardier than their uptown counterparts. There were vagrants in evidence, even on the main drag. The avenues further back had an ugly reputation, but Holmes had known streets of this kind in Victorian London, and he pressed on, undeterred.

He came, finally, to the building in question. His brow creased with mild shock. It was derelict, as he had already supposed, but he had not expected to find any place of worship in a closed-down porno theatre.

So far as he could make out, there was nobody guarding the exterior of the place. The front doorways were covered up with rusty corrugated iron. Holmes noticed immediately that one of them was badly bent. He went over to it. Sure enough, it pulled back easily, sufficient to allow him through.

He went cautiously into the theatre. The lobby was empty and perfectly dark, its air stagnant with the odor of decay, but from the double doors that led into the cinema, he could hear low chanting. There were chinks of colored light.

Feigning the manner of a man lost and bewildered, he ventured through ... to be confronted by a very deeply curious sight.

Up at the front of the auditorium, fires were blazing in large earthenware pots. The flames being cast out were not yellow. They were a startling crimson, giving the whole place a haematic aspect. The smoke from them rolled towards the ceiling, forming a miasma which let out a sickly stench.

There were perhaps a hundred congregants in here, far more than Holmes had expected. They stood between the rows of rotting seats, and did not even notice him enter. All were of the same kind he had remarked on earlier, blighted, shabby souls enthralled by the failed promise of the gaming tables. Men and women, young and old. Holmes went gently down the aisle, and found a place beside the same grey-haired individual who'd invited him this afternoon.

She realized he'd arrived. Greeted him with a tight smile and a brief nod, and then returned her attention to the front of the theatre, and did not look away again.

None of these folk did. The Oriental-looking woman had their complete attention.

She was standing at the centre of the open space out front, shaking a pair of large, crude rattles. Her face was tipped forwards and her eyes were closed. She was yelling out some kind of chant, a fevered caterwauling in a language that Holmes did not recognise.

To one side of her stood some sort of altar, hewn from a large block of stone. How it had been brought in here was anyone's guess. On top of it was ranked a row of goblets of dully-gleaming metal. It sickened one to think of their use.

The woman was dressed as before, except that now, the collar of the blouse had been fully unbuttoned. Her neck and throat and the top portion of her breastbone were revealed.

Holmes squinted in the sickly light. Was it just a trick of shadow, or were those narrow scars on the side of her neck, cut in deliberate patterns? He'd thought that he had caught the briefest glimpse of scar tissue before, but hadn't guessed at anything like this display.

Despite his parlous circumstances, Holmes allowed himself a knowing smile. He was beginning to understand.

From the darkened theatre wings, a gurney was wheeled out by four assistants, and his smile disappeared.

The man strapped to it was perfectly healthy. All that he had suffered so far was the indignity of being stripped down to his underwear. His mouth was gagged. He was struggling mightily, but to no avail. He might have been a taller, rather more muscular version of Fred Bonner.

This was without any shade of a doubt somebody else who had done well at some game of chance. It struck Holmes how badly all these congregants would like the opportunity to do the same.

But what was taking place here? How could capturing and killing such a man achieve...?

The woman's chanting stopped. Her face came up. The heat from the fires had caused some of her make-up to be sluiced away, and the true nature of her features was becoming apparent. Her cheekbones were more angular, and her eyes looked wider than they'd done when he had first encountered her. Yes, he had *thought* that was the case!

She laid the rattles to one side, then stooped over her victim, grinning hideously. Save for the crackling of the flames, the room had fallen silent.

"Be still now. You have what we want," Holmes thought he heard her mutter.

And she had to have some kind of mastery of hypnosis herself. Either that or what she had said served to freeze the unfortunate man with incomprehension and terror. He became completely motionless, his widened eyeballs following her when she moved away.

She stepped over to the altar, picked up one of the goblets and something else that Holmes could not make out, and then returned to her prey. Set the cup beside him on the gurney, and then turned her attention to the fellow's wrist. He gave a muffled gasp of pain. Holmes realized what she had been carrying in her other hand. It was a thick, crude needle with a length of rubber tubing running from it.

She pierced one of the man's veins. The tube was dangled into the goblet. Blood began to fill it. It looked black in this strange light.

Holmes knew the time for action was almost at hand, but his limbs felt very stiff. His mind was whirring. He ought to have been expecting something like this after all the evidence he'd been presented with — he knew that. What this woman and her followers hoped to gain by actions of this nature was impossible to fathom.

Next moment, though, he got an awful demonstration of it. The woman suddenly pinched off the tube, stopping the flow of gore. She picked up the goblet with both hands, raised it into the air in some form of supplication.

And then — to the detective's horror — put it to her lips and drank.

Even worse was to follow. The cup was passed on to the assistants who'd wheeled the man out. They each took a sip. Then the goblet was handed over to the people standing in the rows of seats, who began to follow suit.

It was as repulsive a sight as Holmes had ever witnessed. Behavior so degraded it was barely human. Were these the depths to which this miserable rabble had been reduced? Did they genuinely believe that if they drank the fluids of a victor at the tables they would become winners too?

It defied credulity, but equally, it made no sense.

They might try this one time, out of utter desperation, but it surely would make not the slightest difference to their fortunes, except that the grey-haired lady beside him was obviously a regular here. So were many others — it was beyond question. What on earth made them keep coming back?

It was of no real importance, he decided. There was no accounting for the demented behavior to which addicts stooped. The woman up front was preparing to drain her victim a second time. Holmes knew he had to put a stop to this.

He stepped back out into the aisle, drawing both his weapons, aiming one at the crowd, and the other at the black-clad figure.

And then shouted, in his sternest voice, "You are *not* what you would appear to be; are you, madam? I would suggest that you adopt an Oriental disguise to make yourself seem unremarkable and harmless. Who would be suspicious of a female hailing from the Buddhist lands, or even remember much about her save that single detail? If that is your reasoning then you're a true student of human nature, and for that I give you credit."

All movement stopped. Every eye turned towards him. Only the flickering red light of the flames continued as it had before.

"On closer inspection," Holmes went on, "you're a Native American. Had you gone to the casinos unmade-up, people would have noticed right away, recalled you instantly and in close detail. By the ritualistic scarring on your neck, you are some kind of shaman, and by your very behavior, not a benign sort, no. You are a practitioner of the dark arts!"

The woman's face screwed up with fury, and she jabbed a pointed fingernail at him.

"Get him!" she screamed to the others. "Rip the unbeliever limb from limb!"

Some of those nearest him began to shuffle forward, but it was hardly a determined effort. These were people in the throes of a devouring mental sickness, after all. Two swift shots above their heads and they drew back.

The detective allowed a smile to tug at the corners of his mouth, swinging his attention back towards the gurney.

"I would not rely on ravaged souls like these to fetch my morning paper, much less save my hide. If this is your best defence, madam, then Death Row awaits you."

The witch woman, however, seemed uncowed.

"You think that you are very clever, yes? You think you have this all worked out?"

A touch of recognition sprang into her dark eyes, her head tipping slightly to one side.

"I know who you are. That so-smart Englishman, who relies on logic and who laughs at death." Her own lips curled, more fiercely than his. "Well laugh at this! Where is your logic now?"

She pointed again, but this time above her. Suspecting some kind of trick, Holmes refused to raise his head at first, but then he realized the quality of light in the whole room was changing. From the direction of the ceiling, he could hear some kind of rumbling noise.

When his gaze lifted towards it, he was rendered utterly numb. His heart seemed to freeze up in his chest. His limbs became like marble. He could scarcely breathe. He had lived by deduction and science his whole life. So... how could this *be*?

The heavy smoke had formed a loosely rolling ball over the altar. As Holmes watched, it began to change shape. A massive face appeared within its contours. It had pointed ears. Its mouth had fangs. Its eyes, each as large as a man's fist, had slitted pupils and they glowed a baleful shade of carmine. Its expression was a twisted one of absolute malevolence.

At first, Holmes' mind simply could not accept it. His thoughts darted around like some agitated hive of instincts. He was trying to explain this in a logical, sane fashion, and could not. This was not some trick of the light. Nor could he make out any hint of a special gadget or projector.

He had to accept it, finally. At least it explained why the congregants kept coming back.

"An evil spirit," he concluded out loud, "called in these parts, so I believe, a Manitou. I should imagine it has wandered into Vegas from the bleak, surrounding desert, finding new believers here, and sustenance."

He hated being forced to descend to this level of intellect, but had little choice. His eyesight was not lying to him. The *true* solution to this case was paranormal, not material. The creature had set up home in this abandoned building. The woman was either its servant or familiar. The congregants gathered here, there was a sacrifice, and human blood was consumed. By means of their Master's otherworldly influence, these people would return to the casinos and finally win at the tables. Not an awful lot, Holmes supposed, or else they'd leave this city, but just enough to keep them solvent. Just enough to keep them hooked on this abominable practice.

Their needs were being partially fulfilled, and so were the monster's. It had an audience of supplicants, and there were fear and pain and blood and dying, which had to be like meat and drink to the foul thing.

All of this the great detective realized in a flash, but there was no triumph accompanying the knowledge, rather, it filled him with a terrible dread.

The witch woman was grinning at him openly.

"Those are pretty impressive guns you've got there, but they do not impress him. Go on, try your hand! He laughs at bullets!"

He was being mocked. Holmes knew it, but common sense told him that he at least ought to try. He pointed both Glocks at the creature and let loose a fusillade of shots.

The rounds passed through, doing no damage. The thing began to grow larger, swelling against the background of the mildewed ceiling.

"You've had your chance!" the woman was chuckling. "Now, it's his turn to strike back!"

Holmes did not know what she meant at first, but then he saw that it was not merely the head expanding. A neck and shoulders appeared. Then muscular arms, ending in broad hands tipped with savage claws.

In another few seconds, this monstrous entity would reach down and shred him like a sheet of tissue paper. It would not be a normal physical assault. It would be on a paranormal level. Could even he survive something like that?

Holmes wavered, uncertain what to do. He knew no spells. He had no knowledge of the magic arts. So how could he defeat this beast?

There was a humming noise as the air parted. The Manitou had lashed out. Holmes was forced to jump away; just in time. If he'd still been standing on the spot, he would have been ripped in two.

The beast continued growing. At this rate, it would become so large there would be no escaping it.

Desperately, Holmes glanced back at the woman. She was braying with laughter, quite unable to control herself. The insistent pressure on her lungs had doubled her forward; she was clutching at her belly. Then he noticed something else.

At the Paris casino yesterday, he had believed there was some item of jewelry hidden underneath her blouse. Now it had fallen clear, and he could see it. It was a pendant, a large, tulip-shaped gemstone on a silver chain and setting.

The translucent stone was the exact same color as the Manitou's eyes, and had the same unearthly lustre. Were they somehow linked?

If he discharged a weapon at it, though, he'd kill the woman too. Even under such dire circumstances, he rebelled at the idea of shooting a member of the fairer sex.

The creature took another swipe at him. Again, he narrowly avoided it. Half a row of seating was disintegrated by the blow. Holmes stumbled back.

Then, he noticed a change come across the witch woman that altered his original frame of mind. The beast's swelling shadow had spread across her, and in that vile penumbra, the true nature of her appearance was revealed.

All beauty fled, her face becoming leathery and wizened. Her eyes were sunken deep. Her open lips framed desolate gums, only a few rotted stumps of teeth remaining. Her body was hunched over and her fingers horribly gnarled.

She had to be hundreds of years old, a filthy hag, who had only kept herself alive by means of her dark conjurations. Holmes felt his resolve return. There was no further time to waste. His arm straightened. He took his shot.

His aim was true. The pendant burst into a thousand gleaming carmine shards and the woman was struck instantaneously dead, crashing to the floor.

The effect was immediate. An obscene wailing, followed by a sucking noise, made Holmes look up again. The Manitou was shrinking, disappearing, being siphoned away, almost certainly, into some other plane of existence in which only spirits dwelt.

As for the congregants, they took in what was happening and then — true to their debased natures — turned tale and fled, leaving the room by any exit they could find, in the same manner as a swarm of rats confronted in their nest.

It was over, thank God. Holmes used the sleeve of his raincoat to wipe perspiration from his brow. He remained where he was for half a minute, letting his breathing steady, and then he hurried down to help the kidnapped man.

A couple of hours later, Holmes and Capaldi found themselves sitting in front of the theatre. There was much activity around them, since the forensics boffins were still processing the scene. Two slim, attractive women, one auburn-haired, the other dark and slightly shorter, went past them into the building.

"We'll get the others. They'll be charged with being accessories," the lieutenant assured him.

"I'm pleased to hear it."

"Witch women?" Capaldi grunted. "Evil spirits? Man, that has to top even Moriarty."

Holmes just became stiff-lipped. "Believe me, Lieutenant. Nothing, however inhuman or vile, ever quite manages that."

"But he's long gone, ain't he?" the policeman smiled.

He was freshly surprised when Holmes responded with a brisk shake of his narrow head.

"Proposition one: I am immortal. Proposition two: Moriarty is my constant and unflinching Nemesis, as I am his. It therefore stands to reason that if I am still alive, then so…"

He let the final pair of syllables die unspoken on the hot night air. The two men gazed up at the purple sky, a depthless silence falling over them.

Which was finally broken when Capaldi asked, "Any idea where he might be?"

"Not a clue," Holmes muttered.

TONY RICHARDS is the author of such novels as *The Harvest Bride, Postcards from Terri* and more recently *Night of the Demons*. His collection *Going Back* was nominated for the British Fantasy Award.

THE ADVENTURE OF THE SIX MALEDICTIONS

by Kim Newman

Professor Moriarty did not readily admit his mistakes. Oh, he made 'em. Some real startlers. You were well-advised not to bring up the Tay Bridge Insurance Fiasco in his gloomy presence. Or the Manchester and Provincial Bank Robbery (six months' brain-work to set up, a thousand pounds seed money to pull off: seven shillings and sixpence profit). The Professor was touchy about failures. Indeed, he retained me — Sebastian 'Dead-Eye' Moran, Eton (interminably) and Oxford (briefly), decorated veteran of a dozen death-to-the-darkies campaigns, finest shot in our the Eastern Empire, et cetera et cetera — to keep 'em quiet.

However, one howler he would own to.

He was ruminating upon it that morning, just as the sensational events I've decided to call 'The Adventure of the Six Maledictions' got going. Jolly good title, eh what? Makes you want to skip ahead to the horrors, but don't … you won't fully appreciate the gut-slitting, dynamiting, neck-breaking, rawhead-and-bloody-bones business without understanding how we got neck-deep in it.

In our Conduit Street rooms, we were doing the books, perhaps the least glamorous aspect of running a criminal empire. Once a mathematics tutor, Moriarty enjoyed balancing ledgers — as much as he could enjoy anything, the sad old sausage — more than robbing an orphanage trust fund or bankrupting a philanthropic society. He opened a leather-bound book, and did that side-to-side snakehead thing which I've had cause to mention before. Everyone else who has met him remarks on it too.

"I should not have taken Mr. Baldwin as a client," he declared, tapping a column of red figures. "His problem was of minimal interest, yet has caused no little inconvenience."

The uninteresting, inconvenient Ted Baldwin was a union 'organiser' in Pennsylvania coal country. As ever in America, you can't tell who were the worst crooks: the mine-owning robber barons or the fee-gouging workers' brotherhood. In our Empire, natives dig dirt, plant tea and fetch and carry for the white man. Red Indians don't take to the lash and the Yanks fought one of the century's sillier wars over whether imported Africans should act like proper natives. Now, America employs — which is to say, enslaves — the Irish for such low purposes. A sammy takes only so much field-slog before up and cutting your throat and heading into the bush. Your bog-trotter, on the other hand, grumbles for seven hundred years, holds rowdy meetings, then decides to get very, very drunk instead of doing anything about it. On the whole, I prefer natives. They might roast you on a spit, but won't bore the teats off you by blaming it on Cromwell and William the Third. Yes, I know Moran is an Irish name. So is Moriarty. That comes into it later, too.

Baldwin's union — the Vermissa Valley Scowrers (don't ask me what that means or if it's spelled properly) —were undone by a Pinkerton operative who, when not calling himself John McMurdo, went by the unbelievable name of Birdy Edwards. The Pinkerton Detective Agency is a disgrace to the profession of Murder for Hire. If you operate in a country where captains of industry and hogs of politics make murder *legal* so long as it's a union organiser being murdered, what's the point, eh? Moriarty never lobbied for laws to make it all right for him to thieve and murder and extort.

Posing as a radical, Edwards infiltrated the Scowrers. Most of the reds wound up shot in their beds or hanged from mine-works, but Baldwin was left in the wind at the end of the blood-letting, with a carpet-bag full of union funds. In his situation, I'd blow the loot on women and cards, but Baldwin was of the genus *bastardii vindice*. Just to rub it in, this Birdy flew off to England with Baldwin's sweetheart. Hot on the trail, and under the collar, Baldwin came to London and called on the Firm of Moriarty and Moran. A wedge of greenback dollars hired us to locate the Pink, which we did sharpish. Sporting the more plausible incognito of John Douglas, Edwards was sunning himself at Birlstone, a moated manor.

An easy lay! Shin up a tree in the grounds and professionally pot the blighter through the leaded library window as he sits at his desk, perusing *La Vie Parisienne*. Aim, pull, bang ... brains on the wall, Scotland Yard Baffled, notice in *The Times*, full fee remitted, thank you very much, pleasure to do business with you! But, *no*, the idiot client got all het up and charged off to Birlstone to do the deed himself. Upshot: one fool face blown through the back of one fool head. Yes, sometimes *they* have guns too. A careful murderer is mindful of the risk inherent in turning up at a prospective murderee's front door with a red face and a recital of grievances.

With the client dead, you might think we'd close the account and proceed to the next *profitable* item of deviltry. Not how the racket works. We'd accepted a commission to kill Edwards-McMurdo-Douglas. Darkly humorous remarks about persons not being dead when Professor Moriarty has been paid to polish them off were heard. Talk gets started, you lose face. Blackguards with inconvenient relatives take their business elsewhere. The Assassination Bureau, Ltd. or that Limehouse chink with the marmoset would be delighted to accommodate them.

So, *at our own expense*, we pursue Edwards, who has booked passage to Africa. This is where you might remember the bounder. He — ahem — *fell overboard* and washed up on the desolate shore of St. Helena. We *could* have shoved Birdy off the dock at Southampton and been home for tea and — ahem, encore — crumpet in Mrs. Halifax's establishment for licentious ladies. Not obtrusive enough, though. Nothing would do for the Prof but that the corpse be aimed at the isle of Napoleon's exile, and he spent hours with charts and tide-tables and a sextant to make sure of it. Moriarty was thinking, as usual, two or three steps ahead. There was only one place on Edwards' escape route anyone — specifically, anyone who scribbles for the London rags — has ever heard of. A mysterious corpse on St. Helena gets a paragraph above the racing results. A careless passenger drowned before embarkation doesn't rate a sentence under the corset endorsements. Advertising, you see. Moriarty strikes! All your killing needs satisfied!

Still, it was Manchester and Provincial all over again. Baldwin's dollars ran out. On St. Helena, the Professor insisted we take the sixpenny tour and poke around the eagle's cage. He acquired a unique, if ghastly, souvenir which figures later in the tale — this is another ominous intimation of excitements to come! The jaunt entailed five different passports apiece and seventeen changes of mode of transport across two continents. Expenses mounted. The account was carried in debit.

"Politics will be the ruination of the fine art of crime," Moriarty continued. "Politics and religion..."

This is the moral, Oh My Best Beloved — never kill anyone for a Cause.

For why not, Uncle Basher?

Because Causes don't pay, Little Friend of all the World. Adherents expect you to kill just for the righteousness of it. They don't want to pay you! They don't understand why you want paying!

Not ten minutes after our return, malcontents were hammering at our door, soliciting aid for the downtrodden working man. Kill one Pinkerton and everyone thinks you're a bloody Socialist! Happy to risk your precious neck on the promise of a medal in some 20th Century anarchist utopia. I wearied of kicking sponging gits downstairs and chucking their penny-stall editions of *Das Kapital* into the street.

Reds fracture into a confusion of squabbling factions. The straggle-bearded oiks didn't even want us to strike at the adders of capital. That would at least offer an angle: rich people are usually worth killing for what they have about their persons or in their safes. No, these firebrands invariably wanted one or other of their comrades assassinated over hair's-breadth differences of principal. Some thought a Board of Railway Directors should be strung up by their gouty ankles on the Glorious Day of Revolution; others felt plutocrats should be strung up by their fat necks. Only mass slaughter would settle the question. If the G. D. of R. has not yet dawned, it's because Socialists are too busy exterminating each other to lead the rising masses to victory.

I think this circumstance gave the Prof a notion about Mad Carew's quandary. Which is where the blessed maledictions I mentioned earlier — you were paying attention, weren't you? — come in, and not before time.

II

Just after the Prof let loose his deep think about 'politics and religion', the shadow of a man slithered into the room. Civvy coat and army boots. Colonially tanned, except for chinstrap-lines showing malarial pallor. Bad case of the shakes.

I knew him straight off. Last I'd seen him was in Nepal. He'd been plumper, smugger and, without shot nerves, attached to the British Resident. Attached to the fundament of the British Resident, as it happens. Never was a one for sucking up like Mad Carew. Everyone said he'd go far if he didn't fall off a Himalaya first.

Fellah calls himself 'Mad' and you know what you're getting. Apart from someone fed up of being stuck with 'Archibald' and dissatisfied with 'Archie'.

There's a bloody awful poem about him…
He was known as 'Mad Carew' by the subs at Khatmandu,
He was hotter than they felt inclined to tell;
But for all his foolish pranks, he was worshipped in the ranks,
And the Colonel's daughter smiled on him as well.

Reading between the lines — a lot more edifying than reading the actual lines — you can tell Carew knew how to strut for the juniors, coddle the men, sniff about the ladies of the regiment (bless 'em) and toady to the higher-ups. Officers like that are generally popular until the native uprising, when they're found blubbing in cupboards dressed as washer-women. Not Carew, though. He had what they call a *streak*. Raring off and getting into 'scrapes' and collecting medals and shooting beasts and bandits in the name of jolly good fun. I wore the colors — not the sort of Colonel with a daughter, but the sort not to be trusted with other Colonels' daughters — long enough to know the type. Know the type, I *was* the type! I'm older now, and see what a dunce I was in my prime. For a start, I used to do all this for army pay!

'Mad' sounds dashing, daring and admirable when you hold the tattered flag in the midst of battle and expired turbanheads lie all over the carpet with holes in 'em that you put there. 'Mad' is less impressive written on a form by a Commissioner for Lunacy as you're turned over to the hospitallers of St. Mary of Bedlam to be dunked in ice-water because your latest 'scrape' was running starkers down Oxford Street while gibbering like a baboon.

Major Archibald Carew was both kinds of Mad. He had been one; now, he was close to the other.

"Beelzebub's Sunday toasting-fork, it's Carew!" I exclaimed. "How did you get in here?"

The bounder had the temerity to shake his lumpy fist at me.

After a dozen time-wasting Socialist johnnies required heaving out, Moriarty issued strict instructions to Mrs. Halifax. No one was admitted to the consulting room unless she judged them solvent. Women in her profession can glim a swell you'd swear had five thou per annum and enough family silver to plate the HMS *Inflexible* and know straight off he's putting up a front and hasn't a bent sou in his pockets. So, Carew must have shown her *capital*.

Moriarty craned to examine our visitor.

Carew kept his fist stuck out. He was begging for one on the chin.

Mrs. Halifax crowded the doorway with a couple of her more impressionable girls and the lad who emptied the piss-pots. None were immune to the general sensation which followed Carew about in his high adventures. Indeed, they seemed more excited than the occasion merited.

Slowly, Carew opened his fist.

In his palm lay an emerald the size of a tangerine. When it caught the light, everyone on the landing went green in the face. Avaricious eyes glinted verdant.

Ah, a gem! So much more *direct* than notes or coins. It's just a rock, but so pretty. So precious. So *negotiable*.

Soiled doves cooed. The piss-pot boy let out a heartfelt 'cor lumme'. Mrs. Halifax simpered, which would terrify a color-sergeant.

Moriarty's face betrayed little, as per usual.

"Beryllium aluminium cyclosilicate," he lectured, as if diagnosing an illness, "colored by chromium or perhaps vanadium. A hardness of 7.5 on the Mohs Scale. That is: a gem of the highest water, having consistent color and a high degree of transparency. The cut is indifferent, but could be improved. I should put its worth at..."

He was about to name a high figure.

"Here," said Mad Carew, "have it, and be done...."

He flung the emerald at the professor. I reached across and caught it with a cry of 'owzat' which would not have shamed W. G. Grace, the old cheat. The weight settled in my palm.

For a moment, I heard the wailing of heathen worshippers from a rugged mountain clime across the roof of the world. The emerald sang like a green siren. The *urge* to keep hold of the thing was nigh irresistible.

Our visitor's glamour was transferred to me. Mrs. Halifax's *filles de joie* regarded my manly qualities with even more admiration than usual. If my piss-pot needed emptying, I wouldn't have had to ask twice.

The stone's spell was potent, but I am — as plenty would be happy to tell you if they weren't dead — not half the fool I sometimes seem.

I crossed the room, dropped the jewel in Carew's top pocket, and patted it.

"Keep it safe for the moment, old fellow."

He looked as if I'd just shot him. Which is to say: he looked like some of the people I've shot looked after I'd shot them. Shocked, not surprised; resentful, but too tired to make a fuss. Others take it differently, but this is no place for digressions. Without being asked, Carew sank into the chair set aside for clients — spikes in the back-rest could extrude at the touch of a button on Moriarty's desk, and doesn't that make the eyes water! —and shoved his face into his hands.

"Privacy, please," Moriarty decreed. Mrs. Halifax pulled superfluous spectators away, not forgetting to tug the piss-pot boy's collar, and closed the door. Listeners at the key-hole used to be a problem, but a bullet hole two inches to the left indicated Moriarty's un-gentle solution to unwanted eavesdroppers.

Carew was a man at the end of his tether and possessed of a fortune. An ideal client for the Old Firm. So why did I have that prickle up my spine? The sensation usually meant a leopard prowling between the tents or a lady of brief acquaintance loosening her garter to take hold of a poignard.

Before he said any more, I knew how the story would start.

"There's a one-eyed yellow idol to the North of Khatmandu," began Mad Carew...

Lord, I thought. Here we go again.

III

Some stories you've heard so often you know how they'll come out. "I was a good girl once, a clergyman's daughter, but fell in with bad men...", "I fully intended to pay back the rhino I owed you, but I had this hot tip straight from the jockey's brother...", "I thought there was no harm in popping in to the Rat and Raven for a quick gin...", "I must have put on the wrong coat at the club and walked off wearing a garment identical to — but *not* — my own, which happens to have these counterfeit bonds sewn into the lining...". And, yes, "There's a one-eyed yellow idol to the North of Khatmandu...".

I've a rule about one-eyed yellow idols — and, indeed, idols of other precious hues with any number of eyes, arms, heads or arses. Simply put: hands off!

I don't have the patience to be a professional cracksman, which involves fiddling with locks and safes and precision explosives. As a trade, it's on a level with being a plumber or glazier, with a better chance of being blown to bits or rotting on Dartmoor — not that most plumbers and glaziers wouldn't deserve it, the rooking bastards! Oh, I have done more than my fair share of thieving. I've robbed, burgled, rifled, raided, waylaid, heisted, abducted, abstracted, plundered, pilfered and pinched across five continents and seven seas. I've lifted anything that wasn't nailed down — and, indeed, have prized up the nails of a few items which were.

So, I admit it — I'm a thief. I take things which are not mine. Mostly, money. Or stuff easily turned into money. I may be the sort of thief who, an alienist will tell you, can't help himself. Often, I steal (or cheat, which is the same thing) just for a lark when I don't especially need the readies. If a fellow owns something and doesn't take steps to keep hold of it, that's his look-out. But *even I* know better than to pluck an emerald from the eye-socket of a heathen idol ... whether it be North, South, East or West of Kathmandu.

Ever heard of the Moonstone? The Eye of Klesh? The Emeralds of Suliman? The All-Seeing Eye of the Goddess of Light? The Crimson Gem of Cyttorak? The Pink Diamond of Lugash? All sparklers jimmied off black men's idols by white fools who, as they say, Suffered the Consequences. Any cult which can afford to use priceless ornaments in church decoration can extend limitless travel allowance to assassins. They have on permanent call the sort of determined, ruthless little sods who'll cross the whole world to retrieve their bauble and behead the infidel who snaffled it. That goes for the worshippers of ugly chunks of African wood you wouldn't get sixpence for in Portobello Market. Pop Chuku or Lukundoo or a Zuni Fetish into your Gladstone as a souvenir of the safari, and you wake up six months later with a naked porroh man squatting at your bed-end in Wandsworth and coverlets drenched with your own blood. Come to that, common-or-garden, non-sacred jewels like the Barlow rubies and the Mirror of Portugal are usually pretty poison to the crooks who waste their lives trying to get hold of 'em. Remember the fabled Agra treasure which ended up at the bottom of the Thames? Best place for it.

Imagine stealing something you can't actually *spend*? Oversize gems are famous, thus instantly recognizable. They have histories ('provenance' in the trade, don't you know? —a list of people they've been stolen from) and permanent addresses under lock and key in the coffers of a dusky potentate or the Tower of London where Queen Vicky (long may she reign!) can play with them when she has a mind to. Even cutting a prize into smaller stones doesn't cover the trail. Clots who loot temples are too bedazzled by the booty to take elementary precautions. Changing the name on your passport doesn't help. If you're the bloke with the Fang of Azathoth on your watch chain or the Tears of Tabanga decorating your tart's *décolletage*, you can expect fanatics with strangling cords to show up sooner or later. Want to steal from a church? Have the lead off the roof of St. Custard's down the road. I can more or less guarantee the Archbishop of Canterbury won't send implacable curates after you with scimitars clenched between their teeth.

Since the tale has been set down by another (one J. Milton Hayes — ever heard of anything else by him?), I'll copy it long-hand. Hell, that's too much trouble. I'll shoplift a *Big Book of Dramatic and Comic Recitations for All Occasions* from W. H. Smith & Sons and paste in a torn-out page. I'll be careful not to use 'Christmas Day in the Workhouse', 'The Face on the Bar-Room Floor' or 'The Boy Stood on the Burning Deck (His Name Was Albert Trollocks)' by mistake. Among the set who stay away from the music halls and pride themselves on 'making their own entertainment', every fool and his cousin gets up at the drop of a hat — who really drops hats, by the way? —to launch into 'The Ballad of Mad Carew'. You've probably suffered Mr. Hayes' effulgence many times on long, agonising evenings, but bear with me. I'll append footnotes to sweeten the deal.

There's a one-eyed yellow idol to the North of Khatmandu,
There's a little marble cross below the town;
There's a broken-hearted woman tends the grave of Mad Carew,
And the Yellow God forever gazes down.

He was known as 'Mad Carew' by the subs at Khatmandu,
He was hotter than they felt inclined to tell;
But for all his foolish pranks*, he was worshipped in the ranks,
And the Colonel's daughter§ smiled on him as well.

* eg: setting light to the *bhisti's* turban, putting firecrackers in the padre's thunderbox … oh how we all laughed! —S. M.
§ Amaryllis Framington, by name. Fat and squinty, but white

women are in short supply in Nepal and you land the fish you can get —S. M.

> He had loved her all along, with a passion of the strong,
> The fact that she loved him was plain to all.
> She was nearly twenty-one* and arrangements had begun
> To celebrate her birthday with a ball.

* forty if she was a day —S. M.

> He wrote* to ask what present she would like from Mad Carew;
> They met next day as he dismissed a squad;
> And jestingly she told him then that nothing else would do
> But the green eye of the little Yellow God§.

* since they were at the same hill station, why didn't he just *ask* her? Even sherpas have better things to do than be forever carrying letters between folks who live practically next door to each other —S. M.
§ that's Colonel's daughters for you, covetous *and* stupid, God bless 'em —S. M.

> On the night before the dance, Mad Carew seemed in a trance*.
> And they chaffed him as they puffed at their cigars;
> But for once he failed to smile, and he sat alone awhile,
> Then went out into the night beneath the stars.

* *kif*, probably. It's not just the natives who smoke it. Bloody boring, a posting in Nepal —S. M.

> He returned before the dawn, with his shirt and tunic torn,
> And a gash across his temple dripping red;
> He was patched up right away, and he slept through all the
>   day*,
> And the Colonel's daughter watched beside his bed.

* lazy malingering tosser —S. M.

> He woke at last and asked if they could send his tunic
>   through;
> She brought it, and he thanked her with a nod;
> He bade her search the pocket saying 'That's from Mad Carew',
> And she found the little green eye of the god*.

* if you saw this coming, you are not alone —S. M.

She upbraided poor Carew in the way that women do*,
Though both her eyes were strangely hot and wet;
But she wouldn't take the stone§ and Mad Carew was left
     alone
With the jewel that he'd chanced his life to get.

* here's gratitude for you: the flaming cretin gets himself half-killed to fetch her a birthday present and she throws a sulk —S. M.
§ which shows she wasn't *entirely* addle-witted, old Amaryllis —S. M.

She thought of him* and hurried to his room;
As she crossed the barrack square she could hear the dreamy
     air of a waltz tune softly stealing thro' the gloom.§

* the least she could do, all things considered. Note that M. C. being stabbed didn't stop her having her bally party —S. M.
§ poetic license at its most mendacious. You imagine an orchestra conducted by Strauss himself and lilting, melodic strains wafting across the parade-ground. The musical capabilities of the average hill station run to a corporal with a heat-warped fiddle, a boy with a jew's harp and a Welshman cashiered from his colliery choir for gross indecency (and singing flat). The repertoire runs to ditties like 'Come Into the Garden, Maud (and Get the Poking You've Been Asking For All Evening)' and 'I Dreamt I Dwelled in Marble Halls (and Found Myself Fondling Prince Albert's Balls)'.

His door was open wide*, with silver moonlight shining
     through;
The place was wet and slipp'ry where she trod;
An ugly knife lay buried in the heart of Mad Carew§,
'Twas the 'Vengeance of the Little Yellow God'.

* where were the guards? I'd bloody have 'em up on a charge for letting yak-bothering clod-stabbers through the lines —S. M.
§ how much worse than being stabbed with a pretty knife, eh? —S. M.

There's a one-eyed yellow idol to the north of Khatmandu,*
There's a little marble cross below the town;
There's a broken-hearted woman tends the grave of Mad Carew,
And the Yellow God forever gazes down§.

* yes, J. Milton skimps on his poetical efforts by putting the first
verse back in again. When Uncle Bertie or the Bank Manager's
Sister read it aloud, they tend to do it jocular the first time, emphasizing that rumty-tumty-tum metre, then pour on the drama for
the reprise, drawing it out with exaggerated face-pulling to convey
the broken-heartedness and a crack-of-doom hollow rumble for
that final, ominous line. I blame Rudyard Kipling.
§ Have you noticed the ambiguity about the idol? Is it only one-
eyed because M. C. has filched the other, or regularly configured
like Polyphemus and now has its single eye back? Well, Mr. Hayes
was fudging because he plain didn't know. To set the record
straight, this was always a cyclopean idol. And the poet didn't
hear the end of the story.

Oh, I know what you're thinking — if Mad Carew's emerald-
pinching escapade led to a twit-tended grave North of Khatmandu,
how did he fetch up unstabbed in our London consulting room,
presenting a sickly countenance? Ah-hah, then read on…

IV

"I took the eye from the idol," Carew admitted. "I don't care
what you've heard about why I did it. That doesn't matter. I took
it. And I didn't give it away. I *can't* give it away, because it comes
back. I've tried. It's mine, by right of… well, conquest. Do you
understand, Professor?"

Moriarty nodded. If he understood, that was more than I did.

"I had to fight — to kill — to get it. I've had to do worse to keep
alive since. They've not let up. They came for me at the hill station.
Nearly had me, too. If letting them have the stone'd save my hide,
I'd wish it good riddance. But it's not the gem they want, really.
It's the *vengeance*. Blighters with knives have my number. Heathen
priests. That's an end to it — they think, at any rate. Some say they
did get me, and I'm a ghost…"

I'd not thought of that. He didn't look like any ghost I'd run
across, but — then again — *they* don't, do they. Ghosts? Look like
what you're expecting, that is.

"I didn't just take this thing. I copped a fortune in other stones and gold doodads, too. Not as sacred, apparently. Though most folk who bought from me — chiselled at a penny in the pound, if that — are dead now. Even with miserly rates of fencing, I netted enough to buy out and set myself up for life. Thought I could do a lot better than Fat Amy Framington, I tell you. Resigned my commission, and left for India... with the little brown men after me. More of 'em than I can count. Some odd ones, too — brown in the face, but hairy all over. *White*-hairy, more brute than man. There are a few of 'em left in mountain country. *Mi-go* or *yeti* or Abominable Snowballs. They're the trackers, when the priests let them off their leashes. They dogged me over India, into China... across the Pacific and through the States and the Northern Territories. Up to the Arctic with them after me on sledges... they have *yeti* in Canada too, *sasquatch* and *windigo*. I heard the damned beasts hooting to each other like owls. Close scrape in New York. Had to pay off the coppers to dodge a murder charge. Steam-packet to blighty. They nearly got me again in a hotel in Liverpool, but I left six of 'em dead. Six howling brown bastards who won't make further obeisance to their bloody little yellow God. Now I'm here, in London. The white man's Kathmandu. I've still got this green lump. Worth a kingdom, and worth nothing..."

"This narrative is very picturesque," said Moriarty, "though I would quibble about your strict veracity on one or two points. You could place it in the illustrated press. What I fail to perceive, Major Carew, is what exactly you want *us* to do?"

Carew's eyes became hooded, shifty. For the first time, he almost smiled.

"I heard of you in a bazaar in Peking, Professor. From a ruined Englishman who was once called Giles Conover..."

Him, I remembered. Cracksman, and a toff with it. Also enthusiastic about precious stones, though pearls were his line. Why anyone decided to set a high price on clams' gallstones is beyond me. Conover went for whole strings. Lifted the Ingestre necklace from Scotland Yard's Black Museum to celebrate the centenary of the burning-down of Mrs. Lovat's Fleet Street pie shop. I'll wager you know *that* story.

The Firm had done business with Conover. Before his spine got crushed.

"You are... what was Conover's expression... a consultant? Like a doctor or a lawyer?"

Moriarty nodded.

"A consulting *criminal*?"

"A simple way of stating my business, but it will suffice. Professionals — not only doctors and lawyers, but architects and detectives and military strategists — are available to any who meet their fees. Individuals or organizations have problems they have not the wits to solve, and call on those with expertise and experience to do so. Criminal individuals or organizations have problems too. If sufficiently *interesting*, I apply myself to the solution of such."

"Conover said you helped him...

"*Advised* him.

"...with a robbery. You — what? —drew up plans he followed? Like an engineer?"

"Like a playwright, Major Carew. A dramatist. Conover's problem required a certain flamboyance. Parties needed to be distracted while work was being done. I suggested a means of distraction."

"For a cut?"

"A fee was paid."

The Prof was being cagey about details. We arranged for a runaway cab to collide with a crowded omnibus at the corner of Leather Lane and St. Cross Street. This convenient calamity drew away night-guards at Tucker & Tarbert's Gemstone Exchange long enough for Conover to nip in and abstract a cluster known as 'the Bunch of Grapes' or, more vulgarly, 'the Duchess of Borset's White Piles'. Nobody died except a drunken Yorkshireman, but seven passengers were handily crippled — including a Member of Parliament who couldn't explain why he was in the hansom with two tight-trousered post office boys and had to resign his seat. A fine night's work, all round.

Carew thought about it for a moment.

"They are in London. The brown priests. The *yeti*. They mean to kill me and take back their green eye."

"So you have said."

"They nearly had me in Paddington two nights ago."

The Professor said nothing.

"Consider this an after-the-fact consultation, Moriarty," said Carew, taking a plunge. "I don't need help in planning a crime. The crime's done with, months ago and on the other side of the world. I need your help in *getting away with it*."

It became clear. The Professor ruminated. His head oscillated. Carew hadn't seen that before and was startled.

"You *will* be killed," said the Professor. "There's no doubt about it. In all parallel cases — you have heard of the Herncastle heirloom, I trust — the, as you call them, "little brown men" have prevailed. Unless some other ironic fate overtakes him first, the despoiler is routinely done to death by the cult. Did Conover tell you of the Black Pearl of the Borgias?"

"He said he'd lost the use of his legs and been driven from England because of the thing, and he didn't have it in his hands for more than a minute or two."

"That is so," Moriarty confirmed. "There are differences between your circumstances, between your Green Eye and his Black Pearl, but similarities also. With the Borgia pearl, the attendant problem was not presented by brown men, but by a white man, if man he can truthfully be called. The Hoxton Creeper. He has haunted the pearl through its unhappy chain of ownership, breaking the backs of all who try to keep hold of it. He crushed Conover's bones to powder, though the prize was already fenced. I dare say the Creeper, a London-born Neanderthal atavism, is as abominable as any Himalayan Snowman."

Some in dire situations are gloomily happy to know others have been in the same boat. Not Carew.

"Hang the Creeper," he exclaimed. "There's only one of him. I've a whole congregation of Creepers, Crawlers and Crushers after me!"

"So, you must die and that's all there is to it."

The last remaining puff went out of Mad Carew. He might as well change his daredevil nickname to Dead Carew and be done with it.

"...and *yet*..."

Now the Prof's eyes glowed, as other eyes glowed when the emerald was in view. His blood was up. Profit didn't really stir Moriarty. He loved the *numbers*, not the spoils they tallied. It was the *problem*. The challenge. Doing that which no one else had done, which no one else *could* do.

"All indications are that you must die, Carew. The raider of the sacred gem is doomed, irrevocably. Yet, *why* must that be? Are we not greater than any fate or superstition? I, Moriarty, am not content to let little brown men or a big white man or whatever size man of whatever color decree what must be. I refuse to accept any so-called inevitability. We shall take your case, Major Carew. Give Colonel Moran a hundred pounds as a retainer."

Surprised and suspicious, Carew blurted out 'gladly' and produced a cheque-book.

"Cash, old fellow," I said.

"Of course," he nodded glumly, and undid a money-belt. He had the sum about him in gold sovereigns.

I piled them up and clinked them a bit. Sound. Coin, I can appreciate!

"You are to take lodgings in our basement. There is a serviceable room, which has been used for the purpose before. Meals are provided at eight shillings daily. Breakfast, dinner, supper. Should you wish high tea or other luxuries, make private arrangements with Mrs. Halifax. I need not tell you only to eat and drink what comes to you from our kitchen. We must preserve your health. I prescribe scotch broth."

Now, he was talking like a doctor. The Moriarty Cure, suitable for maiden ladies and gentlemen of a certain age.

"One other thing…"

"What? Anything?"

"The Green Eye. Sell it to me for a penny down and a penny to pay at the end of the week, with the stone returned to you and the first penny forfeit if I fail to make the second payment. I shall have a legal bill of sale drawn up."

"You know what that would mean?"

"I know what *everything* would mean. It is my business."

"I've sold it before. It comes back, and the buyers… well, the buyers are in no position to come back, ever."

The Professor showed his teeth and wrote out a legible receipt.

"Moran, give me a penny," he said.

Without thinking, I fished a copper from my watch-pocket and handed it over. Seconds later, it struck me! I'd roped myself in along with Moriarty on the receiving end of the curse. Don't think the Prof hadn't thought of that, because — as he said — he thought of bloody everything.

Moriarty exchanged the coin for the emerald.

It lay on his desk like a malign paperweight.

So, we were all for the high jump now.

V

Our client was snug in the concealed apartment beneath the store-rooms — a cupboard with a cot, where we stashed tenants best-advised not to show their faces at street-level. Mrs. Halifax, alert to the clink of a money-belt, supplied tender distractions and gin at champagne prices. When Swedish Suzette (who was

Polish) went downstairs, Mrs. H called it a 'house call' and charged extra. If Mad Carew wasn't dead by the end of the week, he'd be dead broke.

Professor Moriarty disappeared into the windowless room where he kept his records. We were up to date on the *Newgate Calendar*, the *Police Gazette* and *Famous Murder Trials*. The Professor knew more about every pick-pocket and high-rip mobster than their mothers or the arresting officers. The more arcane material was in code or foreign languages, or translated into mathematics and written down as page after page of numbers. He said he needed to look into precedents and parallels before deciding on a plan. I had an intimation that would be bad news for some — probably including me.

While the Prof was blowing the dust off press cuttings and jotting down cipher notes, I had the afternoon to myself. Best to get out of the flat and beetle about.

I decided to scratch an itch. On constitutionals through Soho, I had twice had my trousers-cuffs assaulted by a pup in Berwick Street market. The tiny creature's excessively loud yapping was well-known. It was past time to skewer the beast. You could consider it a public service, but the truth is — and I don't mind if it shocks more delicate readers — killing an animal always perks me up. I'd prefer to stalk big game in the bush, but there's none of that in London except at the zoological gardens. Even I think it unsporting to aim between the bars and ventilate Rajah the Lion or Jumbo the Elephant, though old, frustrated guns have tried to swell their bags this way when gout or angry colonial officials prevent them from returning to the veldt.

A small, annoying dog should take the edge off this hunter's blood-lust. The prey would be all the sweeter because it was the pet of a small, annoying boy. I've a trick cane which slips out six inches of honed Sheffield steel at a twist of the knob. The perfect tool for the task. The trick was to stroll by casually and perform a *coup de grâce* in the busy street market without anyone noticing. In Spain, where they appreciate such artistry, I'd be awarded both ears and the tail. In London, there'd be less outrage if I killed the boy.

I swanned into the market and made a play of considering cauliflowers and cabbages — though drat me if I know the difference — while idly twirling the old cane, using it to point at plump veggies at the back of the stalls, then waving it airily to indicate said items didn't come up to snuff under closer scrutiny. The pup was there, nipping at passing skirts and swallowing tidbits fed it by patrons with a high tolerance for noisome canines. The boy, who kept a tomato stall, was doting and vigilant, his practiced eye out for pilferers. A challenge! Much more than the fat, complacent PC on duty.

For twenty minutes, I stalked the pup. I became as sensible of the cries and bustle of the market as of the jungle.

Which is how I knew *they* were there.

Little brown men. Not tanned hop-pickers from Kent. Natives of far shores.

I didn't exactly *see* them. But you don't. Oh, maybe you glimpse a stretch of brown wrist between cuff and glove, then turn to see only white faces. You think you catch a few words in Himalayan dialect amid costermongers' cries.

At some point in any tiger hunt, you wonder if the tiger is hunting you — and you're usually right.

I approached the doggie, *en fin*. I raised the stick to the level where its tip would brush over the pup's skull. My grip shifted to allow the one-handed twist which would send steel through canine brain.

From a heap of tomatoes, red eyes glared. I looked again, blinking, and they were gone. But there were altogether too many tomatoes. Too ripe, with a redness approaching that of blood.

The moment had passed. The pup was alive.

I rued that penny. Though not strictly the present possessor of the Green Eye of the Yellow God, I had financed the transfer from Carew to Moriarty. I was implicated in its purchase.

The curse extended to me.

I hurried towards Oxford Street.

The pup knew not how narrow its escape had been. I only left the market — where it would have been easy for someone to get close and slip his own blade through my waistcoat — because I was allowed to. The bill wasn't yet due.

Eyes were on me.

I used the cane, but only to skewer an apple from a stall and walk off without paying. Not one of my more impressive crimes.

Hastening back to our rooms by a roundabout route, I forced myself not to break into a run. I didn't see a *yeti* in every shadow, but that's not how it works. They let you know there is a *yeti* in *a* shadow, and you have to waste worry on *every* shadow. Invariably, you can't keep up the vigilance. Then, the first shadow you *don't* treat as if it had a *yeti* in it is the one the *yeti* comes out of. Damn strain on the nerves, even mine — which, as many will attest, are constituted of steel cable suitable for suspension bridges.

Only when I turned into Conduit Street, and spotted the familiar figure of Runty Reg — the beggar who kept look-out, and would signal on his penny whistle if anyone official or hostile approached our door — did I stop sweating. I flicked him a copper, which he made disappear.

I returned to our consulting room, calm as you like and pooh-poohing earlier imaginings. Professor Moriarty was addressing a small congregation of all-too-familiar villains. The Green Eye shone in plain sight on the sideboard. Had he summoned the most light-fingered bleeders in London on the assumption one would half-inch the thing and take the consequences?

"Kind of you to join us, Moran," he said, coldly. "I have decided we shall follow the example of the Tower of London, and display a *collection* of Crown Jewels. This emerald is but the first item. You might call this gem *matchless*, but I believe I can match it."

He reached into his coat-pocket and pulled out something the size of a rifle-ball, which he held up between thumb and forefinger. It glistened, darkly. He laid it down beside the Green Eye.

The Black Pearl of the Borgias.

VI

Before Moriarty, the last person unwise enough to own the Black Pearl was Nicholas Savvides, an East End dealer in dubious valuables. Well-known among collectors of such trinkets, he was as crooked as they come — even before the Hoxton Creeper twisted him about at the waist. When the police found Savvy Nick, his belly-button and his arse-crack made an exclamation mark. His eyes were popped too, but he was dead enough not to mind being blind and about-face.

The peculiar thing was that the Creeper didn't want the pearl for himself. He was the rummest of customers, a criminal lunatic who suffered from a glandular gigantism. Its chief symptoms were gorilla shoulders and a face like a pulled toffee. He lumbered about in a vile porkpie hat and an old overcoat which strained at the seams, killing people who possessed the Borgia pearl, only to bestow the hard-luck piece on a succession of 'French' actresses. These delights could be counted on to dispose of the thing to a mug pawnbroker, and set their disappointed beau to spine-twisting again. He'd been through most of the *can-can* chorus at the Tivoli, but — as they say — who hasn't? The Creeper had been caught, tried and hanged by whatever neck he possessed, and walked away from the gallows whistling Offenbach. To my knowledge, he'd been shot by the police, several jewel thieves and a well-known fence. Bullets didn't take. Once, he'd been blown up with gelignite. No joy there. Something to do with thick bones.

I had no idea Moriarty had the Black Pearl. Since his arse was still in its proper place, I supposed the Creeper hadn't either. Until now. If the prize were openly displayed, the Creeper would find out. He lived rough, down by the docks. Eating rats and — worse — drinking Thames-water. Some said he was psychically attuned to his favoured bauble. Even if that was rot, he had his sources. He would follow the trail to Conduit Street. As if we didn't have enough to worry about with the Vengeance of the Little Yellow God.

Moriarty's audience consisted of an even dozen of the continent's premier thieves. Not the ones you've heard of — the cricketing ponce or the frog popinjays. Not the gents who steal for a laugh and to thumb their noses at titled aunties, but the serious, unambitious drudges who get the job done. Low, cunning types we'd dealt with before, who would do their bit for a share of the purse and not peach if they got nobbled. When we wanted things stolen, these were the men — and two women — we called in.

"I have made 'a shopping list'," announced the Professor. "Four more choice items to add lustre to the collection. It is my intention that these valuables be secured within the next two days."

A covered blackboard — relic of his pedagogical days — stood by his desk. Like a magician, Moriarty pulled away the cloth. He had written his list clearly, in chalk.

1:   ~~The Green Eye of the Yellow God~~
2:   ~~The Black Pearl of the Borgias~~
3:   The Falcon of the Knights of St. John.
4:   The Jewels of the Madonna of Naples
5:   The Jewel of Seven Stars
6:   The Eye of Balor

I whistled at Item Five — an Egyptian ruby with sparkling flaws in the pattern of the constellation of the plough, set in a golden scarab ring, dug out of a Witch Queen's Tomb. Most of the archaeologists involved had died of Nile fever or Cairo clap. The sensation press wrote these ailments up as 'the curse of the Pharaohs'. I knew the bauble to be in London, property of one Margaret Trelawny — daughter of a deceased tomb-robber.

Simon Carne, a cracksman and swindler who insisted on wearing a fake humpback, put up his hand like a schoolboy.

"You have permission to speak," said the Professor. It's a wonder he didn't fetch his mortar board, black gown and cane. They had been passed on to Mistress Strict, one of Mrs. Halifax's young ladies; she took in overage pupils with a yen for the *discipline* of their school days.

"Item Three, sir," said Carne. "The Falcon. Is that the *Templar Falcon?*"

"Indeed. A jewelled gold statuette, fashioned in 1530 by Turkish slaves in the Castle of St. Angelo on Malta. The Order of the Hospital of St. John of Jerusalem intended it to be bestowed on Carlos V of Spain. It was, as I'm sure you know, lost to pirates before it could be delivered."

"Well, I've never heard of it," said Fat Kaspar, a promising youth. His appetite for buns was as great as his appetite for crime, but he'd a smart mind and a beady eye for the fast profit.

"It has been sought by a long line of obsessed adventurers," explained Carne. "And hasn't been seen in fifty years."

"So some say."

"And you want it here *within two days?*"

Moriarty was unflapped by the objection.

"If there's no fog in the Channel, the Templar Falcon should join the collection by tomorrow morning. I have cabled our associate in Paris, the Grand Vampire, with details of the current location of this *rara avis*. It has been in hiding. A soulless brigand enamelled it like a common blackbird to conceal its value."

"The Grand Vampire is stealing this prize, and *giving* it to you?"

I didn't believe that either.

"Of course not. In point of fact, he won't have to steal it. The Falcon lies neglected in Pére Duroc's curiosity shop. The proprietor has little idea of the dusty treasure nestling in his unsaleable stock. We have a tight schedule, else I would send someone to purchase it for its asking price of fifteen francs. If any of you could be trusted with fifteen francs."

A smattering of nervous laughter.

"I have offered the Grand Vampire fair exchange. I am giving him something he wants, as valuable to him as the Falcon is to us. I do not intend to tell you what that is."

But — never fear — I'll release the feline from the reticule. On our St. Helena excursion, Moriarty took the trouble to validate a rumor. As you know, Napoleon's imperial bones were exhumed in 1840 and returned to France and — after twenty years of lying in a cardboard box as the frogs argued and raised subscriptions — interred in a hideous porphyry sarcophagus under the dome at Les Invalides. You can buy a ticket and gawp at it. However, as you *don't* know, Napoleon isn't inside. For a joke, the British gave France the remains of an anonymous, pox-ridden, undersized sailor. The Duke of Wellington didn't stop laughing for a month. On the island, the Prof found the original unmarked grave, dug up what was left of the Corsican Crapper and stole Boney's bonce. That relic was now on its way to Paris by special messenger, fated to become a drinking cup for the leader of France's premier criminal gang. A bit of a conversation piece, I expect. Les Vamps run to that line of the dramatic the Frenchies call *Grand-Guignol*. It's supposed to make their foes shiver in their beds, but is hard to take seriously. Grand Vampires don't last long. There's a whole cupboard full of drinking cups made out of their skulls.

"Moran, you're *au fait* with the Jewel of Seven Stars, I believe?"

I admitted it. Just for a jolly, while idly considering the locations of the most valuable prizes in London, I'd cased Trelawny House in Kensington Palace Gardens and thought it fair-to-middling difficult. But, see above, my remarks on Famous Gems: Thorny Problem of Converting Same Into Anonymous Cash. Also, the place had a sour air. I'm not prey to superstition, but I know a likely ambush from a mile off. Trelawny House was one of those iffy locations — best kept away from. Might I now have to take the plunge and regret the fancy of planning capers one didn't really wish to commit?

"The jewels of the Madonna are of less intrinsic interest," continued Moriarty. "These gems — mediocre stones, poorly set, but valuable enough — bedecked a statue hoisted and paraded about Naples during religious festivals. I see I have your interest. A notion got put about that they were too sacred to steal. No one would dare inflict such insult on Mary — who, as a carpenter's wife in Judea, was unlikely to have sported such ornament in her lifetime. As it happens, the *real reason* no one tried for the jewels was that the Camorra, the Neapolitan criminal fraternity, decreed they not be touched. Italian *banditti* who would sell their own mothers retain a superstitious regard for Mother Mary. They wash the blood off their hands and go to mass on Sunday to present pious countenances. However, as ever, someone would not listen. Gennaro, a blacksmith, stole the jewels to impress his girlfriend. They have been 'in play' ever since. Foolish Gennaro is long dead, but the Camorra haven't got the booty back. At this moment, after a trans-European game of pass-the-parcel-with-corpses, the gems are hidden after the fashion of Poe's purloined letter. One Giovanni Lombardo, a carpenter whose death notice appears in this morning's papers, substituted them for the paste jewels in the prop store of the Royal Opera House in Covent Garden. Signorina Bianca Castafiore, 'the Milenese Nightingale', rattles them nightly, with matinees Wednesday and Saturday, in the "jewel scene" from Gounod's *Faust*. It is of scientific interest that the diva's high notes are said to set off sympathetic vibrations which burst bottles and kill rats. I should be interested in observing such a phenomenon, which might have applications in our line of endeavour."

"What about the eye-tyes?" asked Alf Bassick, a reliable fetch-and-carry man. "They've been a headache lately."

"Ah, yes, the Neapolitans," said the Professor. "The London address of the Camorra, as you know, is Beppo's Ice Cream parlour in Old Compton Street. They present the aspect of comical buffoons but, by my estimation, the activities of their Soho Merchants' Protective Society have cut into our income by seven and a half per cent."

The S. M. P. S. was a band of Moustache Petes selling insurance policies to pub-keepers and restauranteurs. Don't agree to cough up the weekly payments and your place of business has trouble with rowdy, window-breaking customers. Stop paying and you start smiling the Italian smile. That's a deep cut in your throat, from ear to ear. It really does look like a red clown's grin.

"Hitherto, the London Camorra have merely been an inconvenience. Now they know their blessed jewels are in the city, they will be more troublesome. It is a cardinal error to classify the Camorra as a criminal organization, an Italian equivalent to *Les Vampires…*"

Or us, he didn't say. He liked to think of our firm as an academic exercise. Abstruse economics. Sub rosa mathematics.

"…at bottom, the Camorra — and their Sicilian and Calabrian equivalents, the Mafia and the 'Ndrangheta — are a romantic, fanatic religious-nationalist movement, as remorseless and unreasonable as the priests of the Yellow God. They care not about dying, as individuals. This makes them exceedingly dangerous."

He let that sink in.

"Don Rafaele Lupo-Ferrari, Chief of Chiefs of the Camorra, has vowed to return the jewels to the Madonna. He has taken an oath on the life of his own mother. He has personally followed the jewels across Europe and is presently in London. He paid a call on the late Signor Lombardo at his place of business yesterday. Measures must be taken to pluck the fruit before he can get his hands on it."

To scare each other, criminals told stories about Don Rafaele. You can imagine how they run. It is said that when a devoted lieutenant thoughtlessly spit out a cigar-end in church on a saint's day, the pious Don had him strangled with his only son's entrails. He took his culture seriously, too, and had a sense of humour. When a critic ridiculed the performance of Don Rafaele's current inamorata as the Duchess Hélène in *I Vespri Siciliani*, the man wound up with his ears cut off and a donkey's nailed onto his head in their place. I was surprised to learn this monster had a mama. If it were a matter of keeping his word, Don Rafaele would personally sink the old biddy in the Bay of Naples.

"What about Item Six?" chipped Carne.

"The Eye of Balor," said Moriarty. "A gold coin, named for a giant of Irish mythology, reputed to have been taken from a leprechaun's pot... lately the 'lucky piece' of 'Dynamite' Desmond Mountmain, General-in-Chief of the Irish Republican Invincibles. Which brought him only poor luck, since last week an infernal device of his own manufacture went off in his face when he thumped the table too hard at a meeting of his Inner Council of Immortals."

I told you Ireland would come into it.

"The Eye of Balor is currently among Mountmain's effects, in the possession of the Special Irish Branch of Scotland Yard. Half a dozen sons and cousins and brothers would like to obtain the coin. It's said that, if 'the Wee Folk' approve, the owner will ascend to the office of Mage-King of Ireland. Whatever that means. The chief contestant for the position is Desmond's son, Tyrone."

That was foul news. Another 'romantic, fanatic religious-nationalist movement'. Your paddy bomber is a mite more concerned with his own individual skin than your wog throttler or guido knifeman, though too hot-headed as a rule to preserve it. Dynamite Des wasn't the first Fenian to blow himself up with his own blasting powder.

Tyrone Mountmain, the heir-apparent, figured high on my list of people I hoped never to meet again.

So, now we had to worry about brown priests and marauding Mi-Go, the Hoxton Creeper, Mysteries of Ancient Egypt, the Knights Templar, the Naples Mob, the little people and the bloody Fenians! It was a wonder Malvoisin's Mirror, the Monkey's Paw, Cap'n Flint's treasure and Sir Michael Sinclair's Door were off the 'shopping list'.

How cursed did Professor Moriarty want to be by the end of the week?

VII

Recall my remarks, in re: nuisance value attendant on one little murder carried out in the service of a trade union?

Ask anyone who knows us (and is still in a position to talk) and you'll be told we are a mercenary concern. We kill anyone, of whatever political stripe or social standing. For a price. It's not true that money is all that interests us. The thrill of the chase is involved. If nothing else is on, I'd cheerfully pot someone or steal something just to keep my hand in. Moriarty claims pure intellectual interest in the problem at hand and can be inveigled into an enterprise if it strikes him as out of the ordinary. I believe he feels pepper in the blood too, in the planning, if not the execution. The moment of clear thrill which burns cold — as a perfect shot brings down a tiger or an Archduke — is the closest I can get to the fireworks which whoosh off in the Prof's brain when his reptile head stops oscillating ... and he suddenly *knows* how an impossible trick can be brought off.

We have no Cause but ourselves. We have no politics. We have no religion. I believe in Sensation. Moriarty believes in Sums. That's about as deep as it needs run.

It was an irritant when the misconception set in that we were in sympathy with the working man. That inconvenience was *as nothing* beside the notion that fellows with names like Moriarty or Moran *must* support Irish Independence.

From time to time — usually when an American millionaire who'd never set foot on the isle of his ancestors for fear of being robbed by long-lost cousins decided to fund the Struggle — one or other of the many branches of Fenianism secured our temporary services. If Desmond Mountmain weren't so all-fired certain he could handle his own bomb-making, he might have been buried in one piece. It takes a more precise touch to blow the door off a strong-room than the medals off a Chief Constable. Dynamiters on our books have names like 'Steady Hands' Crenshaw, not 'Shaky' Brannigan.

As a rule, Irish petitioners were much more trouble than they were worth.

Over the years, half-a-dozen proud rebels had tried to enlist us on the never-never in fantastic schemes of insurrection. You could separate the confidence men from the real patriots because simple crooks venture sensible-sounding endeavours like stealing cases of rifles from the Woolwich Arsenal. Genuine Irish revolutionaries run to crackpottery like deploying an especially-made submarine warship (the *Fenian Ram*) to overthrow British rule in Canada. We decided against throwing in with that and you can look up how well it turned out. Canada is still in the Empire, last I paid attention, though I've no idea why. The place has nothing worth shooting (unless you count Inuit and *sasquatch* which, at that, I might) and boasts fifty thousand trees to every woman.

When a bold Fenian's proposal of an alliance — with our end of it providing the funds — is rejected, he acts exactly like a music hall mick refused credit for drink. Hearty, exploitative friendliness curdles into wheedling desperation then turns into dark threats of dire vengeance. Always, there's an appeal to us as 'fellow Irishmen'. If the Prof or I have family connections in John Bull's Other Island, we'd rather not hear from them. We've sufficient unpleasant English relatives to be getting on with. I thought *pater* and the unmarriageable sisters a shabby lot till I ran into Moriarty's intolerable brothers, which is a story for another day.

It is possible the Professor is a distant cousin of Bishop Moriarty of Kerry, though rebels know better than to raise that connection. The Bishop — in one of the rare sensible utterances of a churchman I can recall — declared 'when we look down into the fathomless depth of this infamy of the heads of the Fenian conspiracy, we must acknowledge that eternity is not long enough, nor hell hot enough to punish such miscreants'. Far be it from me to agree with anything said in a pulpit, but the Bish was not far wrong.

So: Tyrone Mountmain.

Here's why he wasn't at the meeting of the Inner Council of Immortals of the Irish Republican Invincibles which ended with a bang ... he was the only man in living memory to devote himself with equal passion to the causes of Irish Home Rule and Temperance. A paddy intolerant of strong drink is as common as a politician averse to robbing the public purse or a goose looking forward to Christmas. An Irishman who goes around smashing up bottles and barrels has few comrades and fewer friends. If he weren't a six-foot rugby forward and bare-knuckle boxer, I dare say Tyrone wouldn't have lasted beyond his first crusade, but he was and he had. His dear old Da, whose favoured tipple was scarcely less potent than the dynamite which did for him, could not abide a tee-totaller in his home and exiled his own son from the Invincibles. They had a three-day donnybrook about it, cuffing each other's hard heads up and down Aungier Street while onlookers placed bets on the outcome.

After the fight, Tyrone quit the Irish Republican Invincibles and founded the Irish Invincible Republicans. He attracted no followers except for his demented aunt Sophonisiba, who advocated the health-giving properties of drinking from her own chamber-pot, the tithing of two pennies in every shilling to establish an Irish Expedition to the Planet Mercury and (most ridiculous of all) votes for women. Tyrone promulgated a plan for bringing Britain to its knees by dynamiting public houses. The Fenian Brigades would never countenance such a sacrilegiously un-Irish notion. With Desmond dead, Tyrone rallied the unexploded remnants of the I. R. I. and folded them into the I. I. R. Claiming Aunt Soph was in touch with his Da on the ethereal plane, Tyrone relayed the story that if Dynamite Des hadn't been so annoyed at a wave of recent arrests made by the Special Irish Branch he wouldn't have hit the table so hard. That made Desmond a martyr to the Cause. Tyrone declared war on the S. I. B. As has been said about any number of conflicts, including the Franco-Prussian War and the Gladstone-Disraeli feud, it's a shame they can't *both* lose.

Somehow, Tyrone got a bee in his bonnet about the Eye of Balor.

Soph put it into his head that he must have the coin to rise to his true position. Desmond, who never explained how he got the thing in the first place, thought it an amusing relic to show off to his drinking cronies. Tyrone, who had no drinking cronies, believed it possessed of supernatural powers. The only reason he hadn't yet tried to steal it back from Scotland Yard was that

Soph said she knew from 'a vision' that if the Eye of Balor were not in the hands of its rightful owner, 'the little people' would bring about the ruination of anyone who had the temerity to hang onto it. So, the Irish Invincible Republicans were waiting for the Special Irish Branch to be undermined by leprechauns. I assumed they were all down the pub, against Tyrone's orders, leaving him home with only a vial of his own piddle, as recommended by potty aunts everywhere, to warm his insides.

Ireland! I ask you, was ever there such a country of bastards, priests and lunatics?

VIII

As promised, another Item for our collection arrived first thing the next morning. Hand-delivered by an *apache* from Paris, who took one sniff at an English breakfast, muttered '*merde alors*', and hopped back on the boat train. Can't say I blamed her.

1:   ~~The Green Eye of the Yellow God~~
2:   ~~The Black Pearl of the Borgias~~
3:   ~~The Falcon of the Knights of St. John.~~
4:   The Jewels of the Madonna of Naples
5:   The Jewel of Seven Stars
6:   The Eye of Balor

The fabulous gold, jewel-encrusted Templar Falcon didn't look like much. A dull black bird-shaped paperweight. A label attached by string to one claw indicated decreasingly ambitious prices. Generations of Parisian tat connoisseurs had not nibbled. On principle, the Grand Vampire had stolen the bird — murdering three people, and burning the curiosity shop to the ground — rather than meet the fifteen francs asking price (which, I'm sure, Pére Duroc would have lowered yet again, if pressed). I trusted our esteemed colleague was enjoying his afternoon *anis* from the skull of the Emperor Napoleon.

"Are you sure there are *jewels* in that?" asked Fat Kaspar, who was trusted with dusting the sideboard.

Moriarty nodded, holding the thing up like Yorick's skull.

"What was the point of it again?" I enquired.

"After the Knights of St. John were driven off Rhodes by Suleiman the Magnificent, the Emperor Carlos let the order make stronghold on Malta and demanded a single falcon as annual rent. He expected a live bird, but the Knights decided to impress him by manufacturing this fantastically valuable statue … which was then stolen."

Fat Kaspar prepared a spot for the bird, and Moriarty set it down.

"What happened afterwards?" the youth asked.

"What usually happens when rent isn't paid. Eviction. The Templars were booted out of Malta. In shame. Later, they were excommunicated or disavowed by the Pope. In Spain and Portugal, they practiced 'unholy' rites. The usual orgiastic behavior such as you'd find in any brothel when the fleet's in, but with incense and chanting and vestments. Other orders made war on them, hunted them down. It is said the last of them were hung up on cartwheels and left for the crows to peck out their eyes. But the Knights of St. John still exist. I am sure they wish the return of their property. I doubt the present Grand Master feels any obligation to deliver it to the Spanish Crown."

"Who's this Grand Master wallah?" I asked.

"Marshall Alaric Molina de Marnac."

"Never heard of him."

"That would be why it's called a *secret* society, Moran. The Knights of St. John have many other names in the many territories where they operate. In England, they are a sect of Freemasons, and have conjoined with several occult groups and societies for Psychic Research. Their Grand Lodge, in the catacombs under Guildhall, is abuzz with preparations for a visit from the Grand Master. The call has gone out and the Holy Knights will answer. De Marnac heard that the falcon had surfaced in Paris…"

"What little bird whispered that in his ear?"

Moriarty's thin lips approximated a sly smile. "He set out by special train from the Templar fastness in Cadiz, but arrived too late… as the embers of the Duroc establishment were settling. A troop of men-at-arms, in full armor, clashed with *Les Vampires* in Montmartre. Lives were lost. I calculate our French colleagues delayed the arrival of de Marnac on these shores by eighteen hours. The Grand Vampire will be less inclined to do us favours in the future. I had taken that into account. We shall have to do something about France, when this present business is concluded."

I did not think to remind him that our purpose was simply to save one rotten Englishman's hide. Moriarty had not forgotten Mad Carew. He was playing a much larger game, but the original commission remained.

Fat Kaspar looked at the falcon. He brushed its jet wings with his feather duster, and the thing's dead eye seemed to glint.

Something was going on between boy and blackbird.

Moriarty had already assigned the day's errands. Simon Carne was off in Kensington 'investigating a gas leak'. Alf Bassick was in Rotherhithe picking up items Moriarty had ordered from a cabinet-maker whose specialty was making new furniture look old enough to pass for Chippendale. Now, it was my turn for marching orders.

"Moran, I have taken the liberty of filling in your appointment book. You have a busy day. You are expected at Scotland Yard for luncheon, the Royal Opera for the matinee and Trelawny House for late supper. I trust you can secure the items needed to complete our collection. Take who you need from our reserves. I shall be in my study until midnight. Calculations must be made."

"Fair enough, Prof. You know what you're doing."

"Yes, Moran. I do."

IX

So, how does one steal a coin from a locked desk in Scotland Yard? A castle on the Victoria Embankment, full to bursting with policemen, detectives, gaolers and ruthless agents of the British State. An address — strictly, it's New Scotland Yard — law-breakers would be well-advised to stay away from.

Simple answer.

You don't. You can't. And if you could, you wouldn't.

For why?

If such a coup — a theft of evidence from the Head-Quarters of Her Majesty's Police — could be achieved, word would quickly circulate. The name of the master cracksman would be toasted in every pub in the East End. Policemen drink in those pubs too. Even if you left no clue, thanks to the brilliance of your fore-planning and the cunning of the execution, your signature would be on the deed.

Rozzers don't take kindly to having their noses tweaked. If they can't have you up for a given crime, they take you in on a drunk and disorderly charge, then tell anyone foolish enough to ask that you fell down the stairs. Once inside the holding cells, any number of nasty fates can befall the unwary. When the Hoxton Creeper was in custody, the peelers got shot of seven or eight on their most-hated felons list by making them share his lodgings.

No, you don't just breeze into a den of police with larcenous intent and a set of lock-picks. Unless you've a yen for martyrdom. You walk up honestly and openly, without trace of an Irish accent. You ask for Inspector Harvey Lukens of the Special Irish Branch and *buy* whatever you want. Not with money. That's too easy. As with the Grand Vampire, you find something the other fellow wants more than the item they possess which you desire. Usually, you can cadge a favour by giving Lukens the current addresses of any one of a dozen Fenian trouble-makers on the 'wanted' books. The Branch was constituted solely to deal with a rise in Fenian activity, specifically a bombing campaign in the '80s which got under their silly helmets — especially when the *pissoir* outside their office was dynamited on the same night some mad micks tried to topple Nelson's column with gunpowder.

Here's the thing about the Special *Irish* Branch: unlike their colleagues in the Criminal Investigation Department, they didn't give a farthing's fart about *English* criminals. As far as Inspector Lukens was concerned, you could rob as many post offices as you like — abduct the post-mistresses and sell 'em to oriental potentates if you could get threepence for the baggages — just so long as you didn't use the stolen money in the cause of Home Rule. When it came to Surrey stranglers, Glasgow gougers, Welsh wallet-lifters, Birmingham burglars or cockney coshers, the S. I. B. were remarkably tolerant. However, any Irishman who struck a match on a public monument or sold a cough-drop on Sunday was liable to be deemed 'a person of interest', and appear — if he survived that far — at his arraignment with blacked eyes and missing teeth.

Shortly after luncheon — a reasonable repast at Scotland Yard, with cold meats and beer and tinned peaches in syrup — I left the building, frowning, and made rendezvous with a small band of fellows. Thieves, of course. Not of the finest water, but experienced. *All* persons of special interest.

Michaél Murphy Magooly O'Connor, jemmy-man.

Martin Aloysius McHugh, locksmith.

Seamus 'Shiv' Shaughnessy, knife-thrower.

Pádraig 'Pork' Ó Méalóid, hooligan.

Patrick 'Paddy Red' Regan, second-storey bandit.

Leopold MacLiammóir, smooth-talker.

They did not think to wonder what special attributes qualified them for this particular caper. The Professor was in it, so there'd likely be a pay-out at the end of the day.

"It's no go the bribery," I told them. "Lukens won't play that game. So, it's the contingency plan, lads. The coin's in the desk, the desk's in the basement office. I've left a window on the latch. When the smoke bomb goes off and the bluebottles run out of the building, slip in and rifle the place. Take anything else you want, but bring the Professor his Item and you'll remember this day well."

Half a dozen nods.

"Ye'll not be regrettin' this at all at all, Colonel, me darlin'," said Leopold — who laid on the brogue so thick the others couldn't make out what he was saying. He was an Austrian who liked to pretend he was an Irishman — after all, whoever heard of a Dubliner called Leopold? It's possible he'd never even been to the ould sod at all at all.

Ó Méalóid pulled out a foot-long knotty club from a place of concealment and Regan slipped out his favorite stabbing knife. McHugh's long fingers twitched. Shaughnessy handed around a flask of something distilled from stinging nettles. The little band of merry raiders wrapped checked scarves around the lower halves of their faces and pulled down their cap-brims.

I left them and strolled back across the road. Pausing by the front door, I took out a silver case and extracted a cylinder approximately the size and shape of a cigar. I asked a uniformed police constable if he might have a lucifer about him, and a flame was kindly proffered. I lit the fuse of the cylinder and dropped it in the gutter. It fizzed alarmingly. Smoke was produced. Whistles shrilled.

My thieves charged across the road and poured through the open window.

And were immediately pounced on by the S. I. B. Head-Knocking Society.

The smoke dispelled within a minute. I offered the helpful constable a real cigar he was happy to accept.

From offstage came the sounds of a severe kicking and battering, punctuated by cries and oaths. Eventually, this died down a little.

Inspector Lukens came out of the building and, without further word, dropped a tied handkerchief into my hand. He went back indoors, to fill in forms.

Six easy arrests. That was a currency the S. I. B. dealt in. Six Irish crooks caught in the process of committing a stupid crime. As red-handed as they were red-headed.

This might shake your belief in honour among thieves, but I should mention that the micks were hand-picked for more than their criminal specialties and stated place of birth. All were of that breed of crook who don't know when to lay off the mendacity ... the sort who agree to steal on commission but think for themselves and withhold prizes they've been paid to secure. Dirty little birds who feather their own nests. Said nests would be on Dartmoor for the next few years. And serve 'em right.

It didn't hurt that they were of the Irish persuasion. I doubt if any one of them took an interest in politics, but the S. I. B. would be happy to have six more heads to bounce off the walls or dunk in the ordure buckets.

You might say that I had done my patriotic duty in enabling such a swoop against enemies of the Queen. Only that wouldn't wash. I've a trunkful of medals awarded on the same basis. Mostly, I was murdering heathens for my own enjoyment.

I unwrapped the handkerchief, and considered the Eye of Balor. It didn't look much like an eye, or even a coin — just a lump of greenish metal I couldn't tell was gold. In legend, Balor had a baleful, petrifying glance. On the battlefield, his comrades would peel back his mighty eyelids to turn his medusan stare against the foe. Stories were confused as to whether this treasure was that eye or just named after it. Desmond Mountmain claimed it had been given to him during a faerie revel by King Brian of the Leprechauns. I suspected that the brand of pee-drinking lunacy practiced by his sister ran in the family. It was said — mostly by the late Dynamite Des — that any who dared withhold the coin from a true Irish rebel would hear the howl of the banshee and suffer the wrath of the little people.

At that moment, an unearthly wail sounded out across the river. I bit through my cigar.

A passing excursion boat was overloaded with small, raucous creatures in sailor suits, flapping ribbons in the wind. The wail was a ship's whistle. Not a banshee. The creatures were schoolgirls on an outing, pulling each other's braids. Not followers of King Brian.

Ever since the tomato stall, I'd had my whiskers up. I was unused to that. This business was a test for even my nerves.

After a few moments, I carefully wrapped the coin again and passed it on to a small messenger — a street urchin, not a bloody leprechaun — with orders to fetch it back to Conduit Street. Any temptation to run off with the precious item would be balanced by the vivid example of the six Irishmen. The lad took off as if he had salt on his tail.

I summoned the not-for-hire cab I had arrived in.

"The Royal Opera House," I told Craigin, the Firm's best driver. "And a shilling on top of the fare if we miss the first act."

X

Some scorn opera as unrealistic. Large licentious ladies, posturing villains, concealed weapons, loud noises, suicides, thefts, betrayals, elongated ululations, explosions, goblets of poison and the curtain falling on a pile of corpses. Well, throw in a bag of tigers, and that's my life. If I want treachery, bloodshed and screaming women, I can get enough at home, thank you very much. I dislike opera because it's *Italian*. The eye-tyes are the lowest breed of white man, a bargain-priced imitation of the French. All hair-oil and smiling and back-stabbing and cowardice, left out in the sun too long.

This brouhaha of the Jewels of the Madonna of Naples was deeply Italian, and thoroughly operatic. The recitative was too convoluted to follow without music.

The gist: a succession of mugs across Europe got hold of the loot first lifted by Gennaro the Blacksmith, also known as Gennaro the Damned and Gennaro the Dead. A merciless, implacable brotherhood was sworn to kill anyone who dared acquire the treasure, but no fool thought to return the loot and apologize. They all tried for a quick sale and a getaway, or thought to hide the valuables until 'the heat died down'. Under the jewels' spell, they forgot about the only institution ever to combine the adjectives 'efficient' and 'Italian'. The Camorra carry feuds at least to the fifth generation; there's little to no likelihood of anyone or their great-grandchildren profiting from Gennaro's impetuous theft.

As mentioned, the latest idiot was Giovanni Lombardo, a prop-maker for the Royal Opera. He'd received the package from an equally addled cousin who expired from strychnine poisoning at a Drury Lane pie stall a few hours later. Lombardo had been victim of a singular, fatal assault in his Islington carpenter's shop. His head chanced to be trapped in a vice. Several holes were drilled in his brain-pan. A bloodied brace and bit was found in the nearby sawdust.

An editorial in the Harmsworth press cited this crime as sorry proof of the deleterious effects of gory sensationalism paraded nightly in Italian on the stage, instead of daily, in English, in the newspapers, as was right and proper. That *Faust* was sung in French didn't trouble the commentator. Generally, the French are to be condemned for license and libertinism and the Italians for violence and cowardice. When foreigners copy each other's vices, it confuses the English reader, so it's best to ignore the facts and print the prejudice. The Harmsworth theory, which Scotland Yard was supposedly 'taking seriously', painted the culprit as a demented habitué of the opera, sensibilities eroded by addiction to tales of multiple murder and outrageous horror. No longer satisfied with the bladders of pig's blood burst when a tenor was stabbed or the papier maché heads which rolled when an ingénue was guillotined, this notional fiend had become entirely deranged. He doubtless intended to recreate gruesome moments from favorite operas with passing innocents cast in the roles of corpses-to-be. No one was safe!

This afternoon, a gaggle of ladies of a certain age loitered outside the Royal Opera House with banners. One pinned a 'suppress this nasty foreign filth' badge on my lapel. I assured the harridan I'd sooner send my children up chimneys than expose their tender ears to the corrupting wailing of the so-called entertainment perpetrated inside this very building. If there were still profit in selling brats as sweeps, I'd be up for it. Only the mothers of my numberless darling babes, mostly dark-skinned and resident in far corners of the Empire, would insist on their cut of the purse and render such child-vendage scarcely worth the effort.

While chatting with the anti-opera protester, I cast a casual eye about Covent Garden. No more suspicious, olive-skinned loiterers than usual. Which is to say that anyone in sight could — and perhaps would — turn out to be a Camorra assassin. One or two of the protesting ladies wore suspicious veils.

Lombardo's wounds consisted of two medium-size holes, one small (almost tentative) hole and one large (ultimately fatal) hole. He had kept the secret of the jewels until that third hole was started. Then, the final hole was made to shut him up. All very Italian.

Lombardo had asked around London fences for prices on individual stones, so the spider in the centre of his web heard of it. Moriarty also knew the carpenter had been commissioned to provide props for the current production, and saw at once where the loot was hidden. In Act Three of *Faust*, Marguerite, the stupid bint who passes for a leading lady, piles on a collection of tat gifted her by the demon Mephistopheles and regards herself in a mirror. She gives vent to 'the Jewel Song' ('*Ah! Je ris de me voir si belle en ce miroir!*'), an aria which sets my teeth on edge even when sung in tune (which is seldom). It's about how much lovelier she looks when plastered with priceless gems.

Thanks to Moriarty's learned insight, we knew about the jewels. Thanks to strategic cranial drilling, Don Rafaele knew about the jewels. The Camorra could have saved some elbow-work if they'd read their Edgar Allan Poe. The only person in the case — I dismiss Scotland Yard, of course — who *didn't* know about the jewels was Bianca Castafiore, the young, substantial *diva* presently enjoying a triumphant run in the role of Marguerite. When the Milanese Nightingale performs 'the Jewel Song', the unkind have been known to venture she would look lovelier still with a potato sack over her head. However, la Castafiore had a devoted *clique* of ferocious admirers. I knew the type: several of Mrs. Halifax's regulars couldn't get enough of the Welsh trollop known as Tessie the Two-Ton Taff.

As I entered the foyer of the Opera House, I thought the banshee associated with the Eye of Balor had pursued me. A wailing resounded throughout the building.

Then I recognized the racket as that bloody 'Jewel Song'.

A commissionaire was worried about a chandelier, which was vibrating and clinking. A small, crying boy was led out of the auditorium by an angry mama and a frankly relieved papa. I swear they were all bleeding at the ears. In the Garden, dogs howled in sympathy. The silver plugs in my teeth hurt.

Vokins, the Professor's useful man at the opera, awaited me. Not an especially inspiring specimen: all pockmarks, bowler hat, and whining wheedle. His duties, mostly, were to fuss around the petticoats of chorus girls who no longer believed they'd be whisked off and married by a baronet — usually, being whisked off and something elsed by a baronet put paid to that illusion — or could rise to leading roles by virtue of their voices. Alternative methods of employment were always available to such. A modicum of acting ability came in handy when seeming to be delighted at the prospect of an evening — or ten expensive minutes — with Mrs. Halifax's more peculiar customers. Vokins, officially an usher, also scouted out the nobs in the boxes and passed on gossip ... all part of the great mosaic of life in the capital, Moriarty was wont to say.

First off, I asked if there'd been any break-ins or petty thefts lately.

"No more'n usual, Colonel," he said. "None who didn't tithe to the Firm, at any rate."

"Seen any remarkable Italians?"

"Don't see nothing else. The diva has a platoon of 'em. Dressers and puffers and the like."

"Anyone very recently?"

"We've a 'ole new set o' scene-shifters today. The usual lot, 'oo come with the company, didn't turn up this morning. Took sick at an ice cream parlour, after hours. All of 'em, to a man, 'ad cousins ready to step in. Seventeen of 'em. Now you mentions it, they are a *remarkable* bunch, for eye-talians. Oh, you can't mistake 'em for anythin' else, Colonel. To look at 'em, they're eye-tye through and through. Waxy 'taches, brown complexions, glittery eyes, tight trews, black 'air. But there's a funny thing, a *singular* thing — they don't squabble. Never met an eye-tye 'oo didn't spend all the hours o' the day shoutin' at any other eye-tye within ear-shot. Most productions, scene-shifters come to blows five or six times a performance. Someone storms out or back in. Elbow in the eye, knee in the crotch, a lot o' monkey-jabber with spitting and hand-gestures 'oose meanin' can't be mistook. There's been woundin'. Cripplin', even. All over 'oo gets to pick up which old helmet. This lot, the substitute shifters, work like clockwork. Don't say anythin' much. Just get the job done. No arguments. Management's in 'eaven. They wants to sack the no-shows, and keep this mob on permanent."

So, the Camorra were already in the house.

They couldn't have the jewels yet, because the song was still going on. It would last a while longer. The Castafiore *clique* would call at least two *encores*. The rest of the house might be impatient to get on with the story — especially the bit in Act Five where Marguerite is hanged — but the diva would milk her signature tune for all it was worth.

I peeped through the main doors. Marguerite's jewels sparkled in the limelight and her mirror kept flashing.

"When she goes offstage, what happens to her props?" I asked Vokins.

"A dresser takes the jewels and the mirror off her. 'Attie 'Awkins. She's took ill, too. Must be somethin' goin' round. But 'er sister turned up with the others. Not what you'd expect, either. Funny that a yellow-'aired Stepney bit called 'Awkins 'as a sister called Malilella who's dark as a gypsy. I made 'umble introductions and proffered my card, enquiring as to whether she'd be interested in a fresh line of work. This Malilella whipped out one o' them stiletters and near stuck me adam's apple. You can still see the mark where she pricked. She's in the wings, waiting for the jewels."

I saw where the snatch would be made. There was no time to be lost.

"Vokins, round up whoever you can bribe, and get them in the hall. I need you to reinforce the Castafiore *clique*. I need as many reprises as you can get out of her. Keep the "Jewel Song" going."

"You want to 'ear it *again*!"

"It's my favorite ditty," I lied. "I want to hear it for twenty minutes or more."

Enough time to get round to the wings, minding out for the girl with the stiletto and her seventeen swarthy comrades.

"No accountin' for taste," said Vokins. I gave him a handful of sovereigns and he rushed about recruiting. Confectionary stalls went unmanned and mop-buckets unattended as Vokins lured their proprietors into an augmented *clique*.

Bianca Castafiore, up to her ankles in flowers tossed by admirers, paused to take a bow after concluding her aria for the third time. Even she looked startled when the crowd swelled with cries of *'encore encore'*. Never one to disappoint her public, she took a deep breath and launched into it.

"Ah! Je ris de me voir si belle en ce miroir..."

Groans from less partisan members of the audience were drowned out, though more than a few programs were shredded or opera glasses snapped in two.

This is where the Moran quick-thinking came into it.

The situation was simple: upon her exit, the diva would surrender the Jewels of the Madonna without knowing they were real. The valued new staff of the Royal Opera House would quit en masse.

So, why hadn't the jewels been lifted *before* the performance? Well, if Don Rafaele Lupo-Ferrari held one thing almost as sacred as the Virgin Mary, it was opera. A once-in-a-lifetime opportunity to see the Jewel Scene performed with real jewels was an overwhelming temptation. He would be in one of the boxes, enjoying the show before fulfilling his obligation to avenge the indignity perpetrated by Gennaro. I hoped his brains had been boiled by la Castafiore's sustained high notes, for I needed him distracted.

Once the jewels were offstage, they were lost to me.

So, what to do?

Simple. I would have to seize them before they made their exit.

By a side door, I went backstage. In a hurry, I picked up items as I found them on racks in dressing rooms. When I told the story later, I claimed to have donned complete costume and make-up for the role of Mephistopheles. Actually, I made do with a red cloak, a cowl with horns and a half-face mask with a Cyrano nose.

I noticed several of the new scene-shifters, paying attention to the noise and the stage and therefore not much interested in me. I found myself in the wings just as la Castafiore, whose prodigious throat must be in danger of cracking, was chivvied into an unwise, record-setting seventh encore. A little man with spikes of hair banged his fists against the wall and rent his shirt in red-faced fury, screeching 'get that sow off my stage' in Italian. Carlo Jonsi, the producer, had little hope his pleas would, like Henry II's offhand thoughts about a troublesome priest, be acted on by skilled assassins. Though, as it happens, the house was packed with skilled assassins.

The dresser's supposed sister Malilella — she of the stiletto — was waiting patiently for her moment. I wouldn't have put it past her to fling her blade with the next jetsam of floral tributes and accidentally stick the star through one prodigious lung.

"Can't someone end this?" shouted Maestro Jonsi, in despair.

"I'll give it a try," I volunteered, and made my entrance.

To give her credit, the *camorrista* sister was swift to catch on. And her knife was accurately thrown, only to stick into a scenery flat I happened to jostle in passing. I boomed out the barrack room lyrics to 'Abdul Abulbul Amir', lowering my voice to deep bass and drawing out phrases so no one could possibly make out the words or even the language.

Marguerite was astonished at this demonic apparition.

Most of the audience, who knew the opera by heart, were surprised at the sudden reappearance of Mephistopheles but — after eight renditions of 'the Jewel Song' — were happy to accept whatever came next just so long as it wasn't a ninth.

"Those joooo-oooo-wels you muuuuu-ust give baaaa-ack," I demanded. "Your beau-uuuuu-ty needs no suuuu-ch adorn-meeee-ent!"

I picked up the prop casket in which the jewels had been presented and pointed into it.

With encouragement from Vokins' clique, who chanted 'take them off' in time to the desperately vamping orchestra, Bianca

Castafiore removed the necklaces and bracelets and dropped them into the casket. I was aware of commotion offstage. A couple of scene-shifters tried to rush the stage but were held back by non-Italians.

As the last bright jewel clinked into the casket, I looked at the woman in the wings. Malilella drew her thumb across her throat and pointed at me. I had added to my store of curses. Again.

There were Camorra in the wings. Both sides.

So I made my exit across the orchestra pit, striding on the backs of chairs, displacing musicians, knocking over instruments. I didn't realize until I was among the audience that I had trailed my cloak across the limelights and was on fire.

I paused and the whole audience stood to give me a round of applause.

Clapping thundered throughout the auditorium. Which is why I didn't hear the shots. When I saw holes appear in a double bass, I knew Don Rafaele was displeased with this diversion from the libretto.

I shucked my burning cloak and dashed straight up the centre aisle, out through the foyer — barging past a couple of scene-shifters on sheer momentum — and out into Covent Garden, where Craigin awaited with the cab.

I tossed my mask and cowl out of the carriage as it rattled away.

Cradling the jewel-casket in my lap, I began to laugh. The sort of laugh you give out because otherwise you'd have to scream and scream.

That is how I made my debut at the Royal Opera.

XI

After such a day, with two coups to the credit, many a crook would feel entitled to a roistering celebration. It's usually how they get nabbed. Your proud bandit swaggers into his local and buys everyone drinks. Asked how he comes to be suddenly in funds, he taps the side of his hooter and airily mentions a win on the dogs. No track in London pays out in crisp, freshly-stolen bank-notes. Every copper's nark in the pub recalls a sick relative and dashes off into the fog to tap the plods 'for a consideration'. So, in my case, no rest for the wicked.

However, before proceeding to the evening's amusement, I had Craigin drive back to Conduit Street. I chalked off the latest item myself.

1:   ~~The Green Eye of the Yellow God~~
2:   ~~The Black Pearl of the Borgias~~
3:   ~~The Falcon of the Knights of St. John.~~
4:   ~~The Jewels of the Madonna of Naples~~
5:   The Jewel of Seven Stars
6:   ~~The Eye of Balor~~

Moriarty emerged from his thinking room with sheets of paper covered in diagrams. Finding the celebrated circles and clown-smile squiggles named for the mathematician John Venn inadequate to the task, he had invented what he said — and I've no reason to doubt him — was an entirely new system for visually representing complex processes. He was delighted with his incomprehensible arrays of little ovals with symbols in them, stuck together by flowing lines interrupted by arrows. Indeed, the diagrams excited him more than his latest acquisition. He waved aside the casket of jewels in his eagerness to show off a form of cleverness I was incapable of making head or tail of. If he hadn't been distracted, he might have taken steps to introduce his system to the wider world. Schoolboys destined for the dunce cap could curse him as the inventor of Moriarty Charts. As it is, Mr. Venn rests on his inky laurels.

Mrs. Halifax reported that Mad Carew was given to noisy spasms of terror. He was losing faith in the Professor's ability to save his hide. She'd sent Lotus Lei to the basement with a six-penny opium pipe which would cost the client seven shillings, in the hope that a puff might calm his nerves. However, at the sight of the celestial poppet, the loon took to gibbering. The brown-skin monks of Nepal have slant eyes. In the gloom of the basement, Lotus reminded him of the sect sworn to avenge the stolen eye.

"Funny thing is." I remarked. "The chinks are about the only fanatic race we *haven't* offended this week."

"I considered adding the Sword of Genghis Khan to our shopping list," said the Professor. "The hordes of Asia will rally to any who wield it. I know where it can be found. The Si-Fan would certainly view it falling into Western hands as sacrilege. But the tomb in Mongolia would take months to reach. For the moment, it can stay where it is."

That was a relief. I've reasons for not wanting to go back to Mongolia. Under any circumstances. It's a worse hole than Bognor Regis.

Discarded on the desk were the *cartes de visite* of Marshall Alaric Molina de Marnac, Don Rafaele Lupo-Ferrari and Tyrone Mountmain, Bart. A wavy Nepalese dagger lay beside them, gift of the priests of the Little Yellow God. The Creeper didn't run to cards, but the broken-backed corpse left on our doorstep in a laundry basket probably served the same function. Runty Reg wouldn't be at his post from now on. So, I gathered the interested parties all knew their most precious preciouses were arrayed on our sideboard.

"I trust we've reinforcements coming," I said.

The Professor arched an eyebrow.

"This little lot don't play tiddlywinks," I continued. "Runty's liable to be just the first casualty. Consider that stand which has just set up across the road. Feller who's bawling 'get-a ya tutsi-frutsi ice-a cream-a' could be a certain opera lover dressed up in a white hat and apron. The monks soliciting alms for the poor on the corner *creak* under their robes. Steel jerkins and chain mail long-johns. The friends and relations of the Irishmen we handed over to the peelers this lunchtime are drunker and rowdier than usual in the Pillars of Hercules. It'll be the Battle of Maiwand out there soon. I doubt that Mrs. Halifax standing on our doorstep looking stern will keep the blighters out long."

Moriarty mused, making more calculations.

"Not quite yet, I think, Moran. Not quite yet. The constituent elements are volatile, but one more is required for combustion. Now, off with you to Kensington to fetch the Jewel of Seven Stars."

He patted me warmly on the chest — a unique gesture from him, with which I was not entirely comfortable — and disappeared into his den.

As few men, I had his trust. Which was terrifying.

Outside, I found Craigin by his cab, just about to stick his tongue into an ice cornet freshly-purchased from the furious Don Rafaele.

"Don't eat that," I warned, dashing the cornet into the gutter. It fizzed surprisingly.

More than the usual amount of rubbish and rags were in the street. Some of the piles were shifting. I saw glittering eyes in the trash-heaps. Our original Nepalese admirers remained foremost among the array of annoyed maniacs which came along with our Crown Jewels.

I climbed into the cab, ignoring the gypsy death signs chalked on the doors, and we were away — for more larceny.

XII

The street-lamps were on, burning blue. Autumn fog gathered, swirling yellow. Craigin's cab rattled down Kensington Palace Road, and drew up at a workman's hut erected beside a grave-sized hole in the gutter. Signs warned of a gas-leak.

Simon Carne had watched Trelawny House all day from inside the hut. He wore another of his disguises, an old Irishman he called 'Klimo'. Dialect humour was superfluous to the simple look-out job, but Carne was committed.

Other residences on the street had roaring stone lions flanking their driveways. Trelawny House favoured an Egyptian motif: sphinxes stood guard at the gate, the columns beside the front door were covered in hieroglyphs, and a pyramid topped the porch.

Carne gave a brief report. This evening, Margaret Trelawny was entertaining. Many carriages had come and gone, depositing well-dressed people who took care about not letting their faces be seen. Their coaches were of quality, many with black paper gummed over coats of arms on the sides. Vaguely musical sounds and rum, spicy smells emanated from the house.

"I have managed to secure an invitation," Carne said.

He led me into the hut, where two of our associates sat on a large, purple-faced fellow who was securely bound and gagged.

"Isn't that Henry Wilcox? The colossus of finance?"

At mention of his name, Wilcox writhed and purpled further, about to burst blood-vessels. Known for sailing close to the wind in his business and personal life, he had just capsized. I kicked him in the middle. When an opportunity to boot the goolies of capital presents itself, only a fool misses it. Karl Marx said that, and it is the only Socialist slogan which makes sense to me.

From their captive, Carne's men had taken a gilt-edged card bearing the sign of the ram. Wilcox's bag contained a long white robe and a golden mask with curly horns and a sheepish snout.

Obviously, this was my day for fancy-dress.

I got into the ridiculous outfit and took the card.

Wilcox protested into his gag. Another kick quieted him.

I climbed back into the cab and Craigin made great show of delivering me to the front door of Trelawny House.

The knocker was in the shape of a green-eyed serpent. At a single rap, the door was opened by a gigantic negro prize-fighter wearing harem pantaloons. His face and chest were painted gold. I handed over the ram card, which he dropped into a brazier. He stood aside.

I followed the noise and the — slightly intoxicating — smell. Through the reception hall, which boasted the usual clutter of elephant's foot umbrella stands and potted aspidistras gone to seed. Down a set of stone steps into a cellar, where scented oil-lamps cast odd shadows. People dressed like silly buggers gyrated to the plinkings of musical instruments I couldn't put names to. A proper knees-up.

The large cellar was decorated like an Egyptian tomb. I should say, it was decorated *with* an Egyptian tomb. All around were artefacts looted from the burial place of Queen Tera in the Valley of the Sorcerers. Each item was cursed seven ways to sunset.

The guests were all of a type with Wilcox. Robes and masks didn't conceal thick middles, bald pates and liver-spotted, well-manicured hands. Well-to-do and well-connected, I judged. Members of Parliament and the Stock Exchange, commanders of manufacturing empires and shipping lines, high officers of the law and the armed forces, princes of the church and our ancient institutions of learning. More money than sense, more power than they knew what to do with. So, the hostess was working a high-class racket. With marks like these on her lists, Miss Trelawny was very well set-up.

Mixed among the robed, masked guests were professional houris of both sexes, immodestly clad in gold paint and little else. They sported Egyptian fripperies: hawk head-dresses, golden snake circlets, ankhs and scarabs, that eye-in-the-squiggle design. Some might have been imported from Eastern climes, but I recognized a body or two from the city's less exotic vice establishments. Mrs. Halifax had mentioned a few of her younger, prettier earners had gone missing lately; that mystery was now solved.

At the far end of the cellar was an altar, where two little black boys waved golden palm fronds at the high priestess of this congregation.

Margaret Trelawny dressed to show off her person, though she would frankly have stopped traffic in a nun's habit. Already a tall girl, she towered well over six and a half feet with the famous crown of Queen Tera set on her masses of jet black hair. The head-dress consisted of seven intertwined, jewel-eyed serpents with onyx-inlaid cheek-guards. As a connoisseur, I would venture her frontage — judged by size, firmness and 'wobble factor' — finer than Lily Langtry's ... and, after a couple of gins, Lily could crack walnuts between her knockers. To display the goods, Miss Trelawny wore an intricate yet minimal *bustier* composed of interlinked gold beetles. A transparent skirt gathered in a knot under her bare belly. If tautness of tummy were your prime requirement in womanly form, she'd pass the bounce-a-sixpence-off-it test with flying colors. A big sparkling ruby was set in a ring on her forefinger. The Jewel of Seven Stars looked like a congealed gobbet of blood. Her eyes had a mad, green-and-red lustre. Her face had a commanding — indeed *demanding* — beauty uncommon among the milk-and-water ladies of Kensington.

Miss Trelawny danced, which is to say *undulated*, in a shimmy which drew further attention — as if attention were required — to her broad hips, serpentine stomach and generous bosom. Beneath an exotic arrangement, I recognized the tune her three-piece slave band was playing. 'The Streets of Cairo, or the Poor Little Country Maid'. You probably don't know the title — I had to ask a cocaine-injecting trumpet-player from the Alhambra to tell me — but it's sung the world over by dirty-minded little boys of all ages. You can hear many, many variations on the rhyme 'oh, the girls in France/do the hoochy-koochy dance ... and the men play druu-u-ums/on the naked ladies' buu-u-ums', et cetera, et cetera.

For the moment, I was willing to entertain the possibility that Margaret Trelawny was — as she claimed — wicked Queen Tera reborn. She possessed at least one demonstrable supernatural power. Thanks to her presence, I suffered a prominent inconvenience in the trousers. I believe this condition was shared by not a few of the other gentlemen present.

I was drawn through the crowd, as if by magnetic attraction ... or an invisible thread knotted about my gentlemen's parts. I was gripped by tantalizing, almost painful desire. I had to concentrate on the real object of my visit — the ruby. Its redness grew large, tinting my whole view. I suspected there was something funny in the incense.

All about, houris were groped by guests and responded with a fair simulation of wild abandon. Divans were set aside for continuance of these activities, several already in use by knots of two or three — or, in one rather dangerous-looking conjunction, five — dedicated, conscience-free revellers. Some masks had slipped. A prominent social reformer and a tiresomely staunch advocate of female emancipation were sandwiching a slave-boy; the maiden ladies who signed their petitions and wore their banners would probably disapprove. A magistrate known for harsh sentences was bent over a wooden horse, taking a spirited whipping from two Cleopatra-wigged girls. Jamjars of sweet, sticky cordial were passed around, suitable for drinking or smearing. I forgot myself and took a swallow of the stuff, which seemed laced with gunpowder.

I had a notion that Margaret Trelawny wouldn't give up her prize as easily as Bianca Castafiore.

The music rose in a frenzied crescendo. The dancing — and other activity — in the room became faster and faster. Someone indeed played drums on the posteriors of unclad maidservants, slapping with more enthusiasm than skill. I was near the altar-dais now, and the crowd was thicker. A girl with bared teeth and wide eyes tore at my robe, but I discreetly kneed her in the middle and threw her aside to be pounced on by the Mayor of a provincial city who had kept on his chain of office but nothing else.

Miss Trelawny's exertions were extraordinary.

My inconvenience throbbed like a hammered thumb.

Then, a gong was struck — resounding throughout the cellar — and everything stopped.

Masks came off, en masse. I made no move to doff mine, but it was gone anyway.

Margaret Trelawny took a scimitar from her alter and lashed, precisely, at my head. I was unharmed, but unmasked. No, not quite unharmed. A line across my forehead dribbled blood. I clamped a hand to the wound.

My imperious hostess held a blade to my throat.

"Balls," I said, with feeling.

XII

I woke in darkness, wearing clothes not my own. Not even clothes, I realized as my senses crawled back. Tight wrappings which smelled of moth-balls. I wriggled and found my legs teth-ered together and my arms bound to my chest. I was bandaged all over! I shifted my shoulders and banged against confining walls.

With a grinding sound, darkness went away. Something heavy shifted and I found myself looking up at Margaret Trelawny. A fork-bearded lesser cove I didn't immediately recog-nise stood next to her, wearing a steel balaclava. I was lying in an Egyptian sarcophagus, trussed like a mummy.

"Apologies for the 'rush job', Colonel Moran," said my hostess. "Before wrapping, you should have had your heart, lights and liver removed to be placed in canoptic jars and your brains pulled out through your nostrils. Revival of the arts of Egypt proceeds slower than I would like."

Why had they wrapped and entombed me, then taken the trouble to re-open the sarcophagus? Miss Trelawny must want something from me before I was buried for the archaeologists of three thousand years' hence to exhume and put on display. I swear, the maledictions upon Moriarty's Crown Jewels are a Sunday stroll compared to the curses I'll lay on those fellows. Beware the wrath of Basher Moran, you unborn tomb-looters!

The party had broken up. I hoped not on my account.

I couldn't get that da-da-*daaaah*-da-da 'Streets of Cairo' whine out of my head. *Oh, the girls in France...*

"I'll be humming it for days," I said. "Don't you hate it when that happens?"

Margaret sneered, magnificently. She still wore her queenly vestments. This angle afforded me a fine view of those excellent tits. With every breath, those metal scarabs seemed to crawl over all that pink *poitrine*. My bandages stirred, which was all I needed. My hostess was less likely to be flattered by the response than swat the swelling with her handy scimitar.

She dangled a hand in front of my face. My eyes and mouth were free of bandages.

That bloody jewel loomed like the sun and the moon and — most particularly — the stars. I saw the sparkling flaws, in the shape of the constellation of Ursa Major. I've never been able to see the Plough or a Bear in it, just seven dots which look more like a saucepan with a too-long handle. Now I had cause to wish myself upon some far star, rather than in a Kensington basement at the mercy of this monumental (if decorative) cuckoo. Maniac Marge took the Queen of Ancient Egypt business seriously. To her, it wasn't a racket, but a *religion*. Another lunatic, albeit more tempting... I've no idea why anyone would be willing to blow themselves up for Irish Home Rule or get their throat cut for the honour of a tatty Neapolitan statue, but a tumble with the fleshly incarnation of wicked Queen Tera might well be worth small discomfort. At this point, that was a distant prospect.

I tried to sit up, but had no joy. You think of mummy wrappings as rotten old things, but new linen bandages are stout stuff.

Then rough hands grabbed handfuls of bandage where my lapels would have been and hauled me half out of the coffin. The angry man beside Miss Trelawny had lost patience. He snarled in my face. He wore iron gauntlets and a tabard with a crusader cross.

"Calm down, Marshall Alaric," said our hostess, soothing and commanding.

"He must be put to the Question! The Falcon must be recovered!"

I thumped back into my coffin, bumping my head on a stone pillow.

Margaret patted me on my chest. If the ring had a smell, it would have been in my nostrils.

I realized I'd just met Marshall Alaric Molina de Marnac, Grand Master of the Knights of St. John. I supposed it should have come as no surprise these people all knew each other. There were occult, Masonic ties between the Templars and Queen Tera's orgiastic cult. Rivalries, too, but a lot in common. They would have friendly competitions, like the Oxford-Cambridge boat race or the Army-Navy rugby match but with more sacrificed virgins and obscene oblations. Though — even after an evening in the basement of Trelawny House — it was hard to credit that Margaret could preside over *anything* more chaotically perverted than the piss-up which follows the Army-Navy brawl.

De Marnac, a foreigner, spat.

"I won't tell you where the Falcon is," I swore — knowing that, realistically, I'd tell him before he got to the fingers of my right hand. I can stick more pain than most but I've tortured enough to know everyone talks in the end.

"It's on your Professor's sideboard, silly," said Miss Trelawny. "All London knows. Among other trinkets, you also have the Green Eye of the Little Yellow God and the Jewels of the Madonna of Naples. Once Moriarty took to collecting, word got round."

Again, I should have known that would happen.

My hostess made a fist and pressed her ring to my forehead.

"I can't think what goes on in that head of yours, Colonel," she said. "Did you really believe you could wander in here and take the Jewel of Seven Stars. It's the focus of aetheric forces which have enabled me to endure centuries in darkness and enter this shell to live anew. I was hardly likely to give it up."

"You all *say* that..."

She slapped me, lightly.

"So, you are asking yourself why we're having this conversation. Why are you not screaming in a tomb, using up precious air?"

I did my best to shrug.

"While we were going through your clothes, an odd item came to light..."

I had French postcards in my wallet, but nothing likely to shock Queen Tera Redivivus. The derringer holstered in my sock, perhaps?

"Why was this in your waistcoat lining?"

She held up a shiny black oval. The Borgia pearl. I remembered Moriarty patting me, and thinking it an odd gesture — now, I knew he had slipped me one of his crown jewels. However, I had no idea why...

"Swapsies?" I suggested.

Would she have the thing set in another ring? Wearing the Jewel of Seven Stars *and* the Black Pearl of the Borgias would be asking for trouble... I'd been collecting asking-for-trouble items for the past two days, and what had I got for it? Mummification and the prospect of burial alive.

The Marshall made an iron fist and aimed at my face.

"Steady on, old man," I said, "try not to lose your rag."

Of course, that was calculated to inflame him further. I'd the measure of the Grand Master. Wrath was his presiding sin. He launched a punch. I shifted my head to the side of the sarcophagus. Metalled knuckles rammed the stone pillow. He swore in French and Spanish and bit his bluish beard.

"You mustn't let things get on top of you, chummy. Try whistling."

This time, he put his hand flat on my chest and pressed down. That hurt. Quite a bit. I didn't consider whistling.

"You are a puzzle, Colonel," said Margaret. "I don't suppose you would consider... an arrangement?"

She pouted, prettily. The snakes set off her face.

In disgust, de Marnac left me alone. He had disarranged my bandages and, as I'd hoped, torn through a few. If you loosen one, you loosen 'em all. My sister Augusta knitted me a cardigan for my twelfth birthday which suffered from the same flaw. A tiny dropped stitch and the whole thing unravelled. I made a play of breathing heavily, expanding and contracting my chest inside the bandages. I fancied I'd be able to get my arms loose.

"Employment with me offers 'benefits' I doubt you get from that dried-up old stick of a maths tutor," Margaret said, trailing fingers over my face. "A desirable package is offered."

Leaving Moriarty's employ wasn't as simple as she suggested. And, when working with him, I wasn't likely to be transformed into an ass simply by a wink and a shimmy. I knew myself well enough to know this would not be the case if I became an attendant to Queen Tera. When there's a woman in the crime, you always think you'll get 'benefits' but get dirked in the arras. I speak from sorry experience, witness: Irene 'that Bitch' Adler, Sylvia 'Worm Woman' Marsh, Hagar 'Thieving Pikey' Wilde, et cetera, et cetera.

"The Falcon, the Falcon," muttered the Marshall, obsessively. There was something about these *objects*. You set out to own them, and they end up owning you. Tera Trelawny was a ring wearing a woman.

Above, outside, there was a crashing noise, and a drawn-out scream.

I hoped for Simon Carne leading an army of Moriarty's hand-picked roughs in a well-armed, brilliantly-conceived frontal assault, intent on my rescue. The quality of the screams suggested otherwise. No matter what disguise Carne wore, he wasn't as terrifying as whoever was attacking Trelawny House.

Margaret and de Marnac exchanged anxious looks. I managed to sit up, arms free under the bandages, and wasn't instantly slapped down.

"What is that?" said the Grand Master.

A huge shape blocked the cellar door. A huge shape topped with a porkpie hat. A knocked-over lamp underlit a jowly, pig-eyed face which seemed to have melted. Big fists opened and closed.

De Marnac drew a sword.

The Hoxton Creeper tottered into the room, eyes fixed on Margaret, but not for the reason most blokes stared at her. In her open palm glistened the black pearl.

"Who are you?" demanded de Marnac.

The Creeper whistled the 'Barcarolle' from *Tales of Hoffman*. He had a tune in his head, too. As he advanced he loomed bigger. His shadow grew.

"Here," said Miss Trelawny, "Grand Master, you'd better have this."

She popped the pearl into the back of his tunic and it disappeared. He reached awkwardly for the back of his neck, but couldn't trap it. He wriggled, as if a bug were burrowing under his armor.

The Creeper wheeled about and stared at the Knight of St. John. He raised his arms.

Margaret's blackamoor prize-fighter, blood streaming from his broken face, came into the room and laid hold of the Creeper's shoulder, only to be shrugged off and thrown against the wall.

All the while, I was unpicking my bandages. I rose from the coffin. Bereft of jewels, I was of no interest to anyone.

De Marnac slashed at the Creeper, who blocked with his arm. The blade bit into the giant's knotted sinew like an axe in wood, then wouldn't come free. The Creeper got a hold of the Grand Master and twisted him round. The crack of his spine snapping was louder than the squeak of scream he managed before the angry lamps went out in his eyes.

Something small, like a marble, rolled from his armor onto the floor.

Miss Trelawny looked at the dropped pearl. It fascinated her as she fascinated me — a nigh-irresistible urge to *seize*. The Creeper, too, sighted the object he was fixated on.

I saw where this was going. And rooted around for the scimitar, which I found lying on the altar. I doubted it'd be any more use against the Creeper than the sword he was prising out of his arm.

The Creeper bent down and tried to take the Borgia pearl.

It had not occurred to me, but fingers thick as bananas were a handicap when it came to picking up something the size of a boiled sweet. The Creeper scrabbled, rolling the pearl this way and that, unable to get a grasp.

I had a good two-handed grip on the scimitar. I judged the distance to the door.

The hostess took pity on the monster. She plucked the pearl in her delicate fingers and dropped it into the Creeper's cupped palm. He peered at it, content for the moment — but also perplexed. He didn't know what to do now. Then he *saw* Queen Tera. She stood up, magnificent. Her fluence struck the brute man like a bucketful of ice-water. The Creeper's eyes glowed too, with fresh adoration. Could Margaret *can-can*? With her long legs and that outfit, high kicks would be worth seeing.

Like a queen, Miss Trelawny extended her hand. She snapped her fingers.

Shyly, the Creeper gave away his precious. And stood back, in worship. Would the transference take? I'd not be surprised if from now on, the giant's heart beat to follow Queen Tera. If so, I was about to land myself in his bad books.

Margaret Trelawny again made a fist around the Borgia pearl.

I ran towards her and scythed my blade down on her wrist, neatly lopping off her hand. She shrieked and blood gouted into the Creeper's face. I snatched up the hand — still shockingly warm — before its grip could relax, and bolted for the door.

The giant was temporarily blinded. Miss Trelawny was temporarily distracted. The Grand Master was permanently dead.

I ran through the hallway, naked but for a bandage loincloth, streaking past dazed houris — the gilt had mostly rubbed off — and a sticky Law Lord. I nearly tripped over a spine-snapped corpse or two. Why didn't people just get out of the Creeper's way when they had the chance? Miss Trelawny's cringing staff would have to clear up more mess than usual. Mr. Pears' soap is recommended for getting blood out of your Egyptian altar hangings, by the way. Still clutching my gruesome prize, I bounded out of Trelawny House. My cab was still waiting. The Creeper hadn't done away with Craigin on his way in.

"Conduit Street," I ordered. "Chop chop!"

I laughed. Chop chop! I'd only needed one chop. In my lap, Margaret Trelawny's hand opened like a flower. I took the pearl and the ring, and tossed the thing into the gutter for the dogs to fight over. If Queen Tera had all the powers she claimed, her hand might take to crawling after me like a lopsided, strangling spider. I could do without that.

It had been an interesting, eventful day.

XIII

I had a teeth-gnasher of a rage on. Often in the course of our association, I felt an overwhelming urge to box Professor Moriarty's ears. Or worse. He had taken me into the Firm because — not to put too fine a point on it — I had proven myself more than willing to gamble my skin on any number of occasions, just to feel the iron rise in my blood and cock a snook at Death. So, by his lights, I had volunteered to be put repeatedly in harm's way, and shouldn't even complain about it.

However, that little trick with the Borgia pearl — slipped into my supposedly undetectable secret pocket — was typical of his high-handedness. Admittedly, things had sorted themselves out in our favour. Equally admittedly, if the Prof *had* troubled to inform me of this stratagem, I'd have refused to go along with it. All for risk, disinclined to suicide: that's me.

Deep down, despite what I knew of his genius, I couldn't help but think Moriarty threw the pieces up in the air and hoped for the best, then claimed it had come out exactly to plan. It'd have been the same to him if the Creeper had crushed my spine or Maniac Marge had mummified me or the Grand Master had done whatever it is Grand Masters do to those who annoy them. He wasn't notably upset by the fate of Runty Reg, and the look-out had been with the Firm longer than I.

Still, with a balloon of brandy and a fresh set of clothes, I calmed down and could even feel a pride of achievement. Every item on the shopping list was scored through.

1:    ~~The Green Eye of the Yellow God~~
2:    ~~The Black Pearl of the Borgias~~
3:    ~~The Falcon of the Knights of St. John.~~
4:    ~~The Jewels of the Madonna of Naples~~
5:    ~~The Jewel of Seven Stars~~
6:    ~~The Eye of Balor~~

Any one of these keepsakes would have been a premier haul, but six within forty-eight hours was a miracle.

The Professor stood in front of the glittering sideboard, hands out as if feeling the warmth of a fire. His head oscillated. Then, he clapped his hands.

"Nothing," he said. "No detectable *supernatural* power. These objects effect no change in temperature or barometric pressure. Miracles or malign mischances do not occur in their vicinity. They are simply *trouvées* men have arbitrarily decided to value."

"I don't know, Moriarty," I said. "I've been feeling rum all day. I don't say it's the curses, but your crown jewels have *something*. If enough people pray to the things, maybe they pick up juju the way a blanket gets wet if you empty a bucket of water on it?"

The Professor's lip curled.

"Whatever you or I think, plenty have invested so much belief in those prizes they'd kill or die to get them back," I said. "If that's not supernatural, I don't know what is."

"Foolishness, and a distraction," he said.

I conceded, with a shrug, that he might be right. All the wal-lahs who were after these pretties grew stupider as they neared their objects of desire. Even the Creeper, who was already an imbecile. At a glimpse of the sparklers, they lost habits of self-preservation. A fanatic flame burned in the lot of 'em. You could see it in their eyes.

"One thing puzzles me yet," I admitted.

Moriarty raised a hawkish eyebrow, inviting the question.

"What has this collection got to do with saving Mad Carew's worthless hide? The heathen priests are still after him. After us, too, since we've got their Green Eye. Now, we've also to worry about the Creeper, the Templars, the Fenians, the Camorra and the Ancient Egyptian Mob. We're more cursed now than when we started and Carew's no better off."

Using a secret spy-glass — which meant not presenting a tempting silhouette in the front window — Moriarty had kept up with the comings and goings outside. Mostly comings.

We were besieged.

The *gelato* stand was still open, well after the usual hours and in contravention of street trading laws. Don Rafaele Lupo-Ferrari was at his post, though he'd dropped the tutsi-frutsi call. A gang of scene-shifters were gathered around, with dark-eyed Malilella of the Stiletto. They all stared up at the building, licking non-poisonous ice cream cornets.

The Pillars of Hercules had fallen ominously silent, but stout sons of Erin loitered outside, whittling on cudgels. Among them, I distinguished a tall, better-dressed goon with a bright green bowler hat and a temperance ribbon. Tyrone Mountmain, with a pocketful of dynamite. Aunt Sophonisiba was there too. No one quaffed from the flask she offered round, disproving the old saw that an Irishman will drink anything if it's free.

The armored monks held their corner. Bereft of a Grand Master, they still had vows to uphold. Moriarty said a new Grand Master would be elected within hours. The Knights of St. John openly held swords and crossbows. We'd already had a bolt through the window and stuck in the ceiling.

A dark carriage was parked across the street. In it, a veiled woman — with an alabaster hand — sat alongside a grim giant. Margaret Trelawny and the Creeper remained, at least for the moment, an unlikely item. How had she got the hand made so quickly? A few of her cult-followers stood about, fancy dress under their coats. Slaves, I suppose.

As for our original persecutors, the priests of the Little Yellow God … some of the rubbish heaps stood up on brown legs. A troupe of Nepalese street jugglers put on a poor show. Did they feel crowded by the presence of so many other groups of our enemies?

A pair of constables, on their regular beat, took one look at the assembled factions, turned about-face and strolled away rapidly.

"I suppose we can only die once," I said. "I'll fetch out the rifle with telescopic sights. I can put half a dozen of the bastards down before they take cover. Starting with Temperance Ty, I think..."

"You will do no such thing, Moran."

The Professor had something up his sleeve.

The doorbell rang. I adjusted the spy-glass to see which fanatic was calling. It was only Alf Bassick, with a large carpet-bag, back from Rotherhithe.

I pulled a lever which — by a system of pulleys and electric currents — unlocked our front door. Moriarty had designed the system himself. Wood panelling over sheet steel, our entrance was more impregnable than most bank vaults. Even the dynamite boyos would have trouble shifting it.

Bassick didn't immediately come upstairs.

Moriarty told me to go down and determine the cause of the delay. Bassick was stretched out on our mat in the hallway, with a Nepalese dagger stuck between his shoulders. If we'd sent Carne on Bassick's errand, he might have come through it — that fake hump at least protected his back. After midnight, the besieging forces were bolder.

I turned Bassick over and ignored his gasped last words — blather about his mother or money or the moon — to get the bag. Whatever Moriarty sent him for, death was no excuse for failure.

Returning upstairs, I didn't need to tell the Prof what had happened. I assumed he'd taken it into account in his squiggle charts.

Moriarty opened Bassick's bag and took out six identical caskets. He lined the boxes on his desk and flipped their lids open. Each was different inside to contain a different treasure, with apertures ranging from a bird-shaped hole for the Templar Falcon to a tiny recess for the Borgia Pearl. Every Jewel of the Madonna had a nook. The Professor fit his acquisitions into their boxes and shut the lids.

"There should be keys," he said.

I rooted about in the carpet bag and found a ring of six keys. Moriarty took a single key and locked all the boxes with it.

He shuffled the boxes around on the table.

"Moran, pick any two of these up."

They weighed the same.

"Shake them."

They rattled the same.

"In addition to their respective jewels, each box has a cavity holding loose weights," the Professor explained. "Any would balance a scale exactly with any other. They sound alike. They look alike. Tell me, Moran, could an object-worshipper differentiate between them?"

"If they can, they're sharper pencils than me."

"Is it possible some may be *supernaturally* attuned to the contents? They'll be able to pick out their own hearts' desires through *magic*?"

"If you say so."

"I say not, Moran. I say *not.*"

I tapped a knuckle on a box. It was not just wood.

"A steel core, like our front door, Moran," Moriarty explained. "The boxes will take considerable breaking."

I still didn't know what he was up to. Later, when I did, I still didn't see what he thought it would accomplish.

He put the boxes back in the carpet bag. And pulled on his ulster and tall hat. He regarded himself slyly in the mirror, checking his appearance but also catching his own clever eye. Odd that someone so unprepossessing should be a monster of vanity, but life is full of surprises.

"We shall go outside... and surrender our collection. But, remember, only one box to a customer."

"What's to stop us being killed six ways as soon as we open the door?"

"Confidence, Moran. Confidence."

Terrifyingly, that made sense to me. I stiffened, distributed three or four pistols about my person, and prepared to put on an almighty front.

XIV

Professor Moriarty opened wide our front door and held up his right hand.

Everyone was too astonished to kill him.

He walked down our front steps, casual if a little too pleased with himself. I followed, a thumb-cocked six-shot Colt Peacemaker in one hand, a Holland & Holland fowling piece tucked under my other arm. If this was where I died, I'd take a bag of the heathen down with me.

Moriarty signalled for the interested parties to advance. When they moved *en masse*, he shook his head and held up his forefinger. Only one of each faction was to come forward. There was snarling and spitting, but terms were accepted.

Tyrone Mountmain, chewing a lit cigar. That meant he had dynamite sticks about him, with short fuses.

Don Rafaele Lupo-Ferrari held back, and sent my old girlfriend Malilella. She spat at my boots and I noticed inappropriately that she was damned attractive. Shame she was a bloody Catholic.

A Templar Knight unknown to me crossed himself and advanced.

Margaret Trelawny let the Hoxton Creeper help her down from her carriage. She was more modestly dressed than on the occasion of our last meeting, but her veil was pinned to the snaky head-dress. She looked no fonder of me than the stiletto sister.

They stood on the pavement, wary of each other, warier of us.

"One more, I think."

A heap of rags by the rubbish bins stirred. A brown, lean beggar crept forth. He had a shaved head and a green dot in the centre of his forehead. The High Priest of the Little Yellow God.

"You each wish something which is in our possession," said Moriarty.

Mountmain swore and his cigar-end glowed. Malilella flicked out her favorite blade. Margaret Trelawny flipped back her veil with her alabaster hand — she must have been practicing — and glared hatred.

"I intend to make full restitution…"

"Ye'll still die ye turncoat bastard," said Mountmain.

"That may be. I do not ask any payment for the items you believe you have a right to. Nothing but a few moments' truce, so Moran and I might return to our rooms and set our affairs in order. After that, we shall be at your disposal."

I held up the sack like Father Christmas. The boxes rattled.

Six sets of eyes lit up. I wondered if the fanatics could sense which box held which desired, accursed object.

Don Rafaele gave the nod, accepting terms, binding the others to his decision. That made him the biggest crook in the assembled masses, if only the second biggest on the street.

"Moran, do the honours of restitution."

I was at sea. How was I to know which box went to which customer?

"Do you await a telegram from the Queen, perchance?" said Moriarty.

He was enjoying himself immensely. I wanted to kill him as badly as anyone else.

Without fuss, I took out a box.

"Ladies first," I said, and shoved it at Margaret Trelawny. She tried to take it with the hand whose fingers wouldn't close and it nearly fell, but then caught it with her remaining hand and clutched it to her ample chest.

"And you, big fellah," I said, delivering a box to the Creeper. He considered it as an ape might consider a carriage clock.

"Malilella, *grazie*," giving her a prize.

"The gentleman from Nepal," to the little brown priest.

"Worthy Knight," to the Templar.

"And you, Tyrone. Fresh from the pot at the end of the rainbow."

Mountmain took his box.

Recipients examined their gifts and thought about trying to get into them. Suspecting trickery, not unreasonably, Tyrone handed his box to a follower and told him to open it with a cudgel.

Moriarty took a step backwards. I did too.

Eyes were on us again. I shot out a street-lamp, as a diversion, and we whipped inside. The door slammed shut. A Templar sword thudded against it, splitting wood and scratching steel.

From the hall, we heard the commotion outside.

We went back upstairs and took turns with the spy-glass. The Creeper had the wood off his box, but it was still shut. A long-fingered Camorra man worked with a set of picklocks. Tyrone's cudgel man gave his box a good hammering.

"Let's make it a little easier," said the Professor.

He opened our front window a crack, sure to stay out of the line of fire, and tossed six loose keys into the street.

The brown priest was first to pick one up. And first to be disappointed. He was the new owner of the Black Pearl of the Borgias.

The Creeper, sensing this, threw his own box into the gutter and strode towards the little man, arms outstretched. Nepalese jugglers got in the giant's way, but were tossed aside, twisted into shapes fatal even to a full-fledged fakir. Before the giant could get a grip on the pearl-clutching priest, another — larger — bundle of rags stirred. Something the acromegalic Neanderthal's own size, red-eyed and white-furred where skin showed, barrelled across the road to protect its master. The Creeper and the *mi-go* locked arms in a wrestler's grip, then rolled out of sight.

Other keys were found. Other discoveries made.

The knight was rewarded. He opened his box and actually found what he wanted. The Templar Falcon was at last restored to the Order of St. John! He was shot by a blind-drunk Irishman anyway, setting off a Fenian-Templar scrap. Cudgels against swords wasn't an equal match, but when dynamite came into it, armor didn't hold up. Tyrone tossed fizzing sticks at the monks, who were hampered by heavy armor and confining robes.

The Camorra pitched in with knives and garrottes. Mountmain and Don Rafaele tried to throttle each other over a prize neither of them wanted, the Jewel of Seven Stars. Malilella and Margaret Trelawny circled each other, stiletto against scimitar. Maniac Marge had surprising left-handed dexterity with the blade, but shocked the *camorrista* by lashing her across the face with her new, unyielding hand. Malilella responded with unkind words in Italian and a series of stabs which struck sparks off Tera's serpent crown.

Blood ran in the gutters. It did my heart good. My nerves were back. We settled in to enjoy the show.

There were alarms and a great deal of smoke. A few fires started. Even the police would have to show up soon.

The Templars, who initially got the worst of it, threw over the hand-cart from which they had been soliciting alms to reveal one of Mr. Gatling's mechanical guns. Evidently, the mediaeval order kept up with the times. Fire raked the pavement, throwing up chips of London stone. Irishmen, faux Egyptians, Neapolitans and Nepalese scattered. Dead bodies jittered back into a semblance of life as bullets tore into them.

Half of me wanted to be out in the street, stabbing and shooting and scything with the rest. A more cautious urge, carefully cultivated, was that I should stay well out of this. Still, it was a jolly show!

The barrel organ of death chattered for a long minute, until an asp-venom dart from an Egyptian blowpipe paralysed the gunner. Then, things quieted a little.

The fight wasn't out of everyone, but few were in a condition to continue.

Moriarty took the speaking tube and ordered Mrs. Halifax to bring him his nightly cocoa.

I was not surprised he could sleep.

This time, he really had thrown all the pieces up in the air just to see where they'd come down.

XV

Most of the rest of it was in the newspapers. I can't give you a thrilling first-hand account because I wasn't there. However, here's a run-down of the outrages.

In the next two days, fifty-seven people were murdered. Micks, wops, knights, innocent parties, Nepalese itinerants, well-regarded members of society with Masonic connections, scene-shifters, fences, fortune-hunters, policemen, a retired white hunter who set out to bag the *mi-go* for the Horniman Museum, and so on. Two members of the Castafiore clique fought a duel with antique pistols, and blew each other's chests out — tricky shooting with unreliable weapons, considered a draw. A great many smiled the Italian smile. Not a few displayed the Killarney Cudgel Cavity in their skulls. Most expired from wounds unassociated with any particular region.

The ice cream parlour on Old Compton Street was destroyed by a supposed act of God. Don Rafaele returned to Naples an invalid, accompanied by Malilella — they came out of the wars with the best loot, though they didn't get back the Jewels of the Madonna. These days, the virgin of Naples is paraded about with the Jewel of Seven Stars and the Eye of Balor. An influx of Irish and Anglo-Egyptian tourists might not let that situation continue.

The Hoxton Creeper had vitriol dashed at his chest. He was seen falling into the Thames, clutching the Templar Falcon. I knew better than to think him dead.

With the Falcon lost, reputedly in the mud with the Agra treasure, the party of the late Grand Master Alaric Molina de Marnac had to gouge out their own eyes and flagellate for six days and six nights to atone. Rumors persist that the black bird has turned up in Russia or China and the search goes on. There may be more than one flapping out on the market. The Templars aren't the only interested party. Fat Kaspar, who had never heard of the *rara avis* before the Professor mentioned it, was struck queer by the curse of obsession and took off after the statue. He didn't believe it was in the river. Another promising career ruined.

Margaret Trelawny's house was blown up, supposedly due to a gas leak. Found barely alive in the ruins, she's in hospital now, mummified in bandages and speaking a tongue not heard on the Earthly plane in thousands of years. The membership lists of Queen Tera's Circle happened to be delivered to the *Pall Mall Gazette* with scandalous photographs. Resignations, retirements, suicides and scandal ensued.

Tyrone Mountmain expired from drinking poisoned ginger beer. His Auntie was hanged for it. There are more Mountmains, though — so the Struggle goes on. Eternally.

XVI

Early the next morning, the Professor had me roused from Lotus Lei's bed — all that killing naturally had my blood up; and there was but one handy treatment for that — and insisted we take a promenade across the battlefield.

Conduit Street was strewn with debris. Bullet-pocks scarred walls and pavements. All the windows were broken. Don Rafaele's stand smouldered. Other residents were appalled, and complaining. Not all the corpses had been carted off. A Templar was crucified across the doors of the Pillars of Hercules. A pile of rags lay on our front step, brown hands outstretched and empty. A policeman — one of 'ours' — shooed away busybodies.

The street was full of trash.

Margaret Trelawny's white hand, all but two fingers broken off, lay in a pool of congealed, melted ice-cream.

A few of the jewels of the Madonna were about too, amid the crushed ruin of one of Moriarty's trick boxes. Their settings were bent and broken.

Moriarty spotted the Green Eye of the Little Yellow God and the Black Pearl of the Borgias, rolling together in a gutter like peas in a pod. Someone's real eye, red tangle of string still attached, lay with them.

"Pick those up, would you, Moran? We've still a client to service."

"Just the Green Eye?"

"We'll have the Black Pearl, too."

"We'd better hope the Creeper drowned."

"I'm sure he didn't. Excessive lung capacity. An entirely natural, if freakish attribute, before you ask. For the moment, there's little risk."

Moriarty was pleased with his handiwork.

"This wasn't about Archie Carew, was it?"

"Not entirely, Moran. Very perspicacious of you to notice. I never get your limits. You have them, of course. No, the Green Eye was the least of our items of interest."

"A lot of trouble for an item of little interest."

"There is always a lot of trouble in situations like these. I can't abide a fanatic, Moran. They are variables. They do not fit into calculations. The mumbo-jumbo is infinitely annoying. Consider the Camorra — a perfectly sound criminal enterprise, poisoned by infantile Marianism. Really, why should a bandit care about a statue's finery? Likewise, the Fenians and their hopeless Cause.

They may free themselves from British rule, but for what? The Irish will still have priests to rob and rape them and bleat that it's for their own good, and they never think to shrug off the yoke of Rome. The Templars — who knows what they are for? They've forgotten themselves. At bottom, none are any better than the Creeper. Baby-brains fixated on shiny things. It is best for us, for the interests of the Firm, that these cretins be taken off the board. The Italians and Irish and pseudo-Egyptians shall trouble us no longer. The Soho Merchants' Protective Society is smashed. Our tithes will be paid without complaint. Navvies and poets who might have been tempted to sink monies in the Irish Invincible Republicans will gamble and drink and whore in establishments we have an interest in. The wealthy and powerful who need to be blackmailed will not have to dress up as pharaohs to do it."

For the only time I can remember, Moriarty smiled without showing teeth.

This morning, as on few others, he was content. His sums added up.

"What about the little brown priests?" I ventured. "They'll still come for us. We have the emerald."

"If I do not pay the remainder of the purchase price today, ownership reverts to Major Carew. Moran, do you have a penny about you?"

"Why, yes, I…" I began, fishing in my watch-pocket. I caught Moriarty's eye, and my fingers froze. "No, Moriarty," I said, "I'm short of funds."

"Pity. We shall have to return Carew's property, with apologies."

The man himself was in the street, blinking in the daylight. He took in the carnage and destruction.

"Is it over? Am I safe?"

"That's for you to decide. I can guarantee that you will not be murdered by the priests of the Little Yellow God."

Carew laughed, still mad — but happy, too.

He walked down to the dead priest and kicked him. The Nepalese rolled over. He had been shot neatly through the dot in his forehead. Serve him right for painting on a target.

"That's what I think of your blasted yellow dog of a God," he said.

Moriarty gave Carew back his emerald, and he waved it in the dead priest's face. A laughing daredevil again, he cast around for ladies to impress with his flash.

"I'll have this green carbuncle cut up in Amsterdam, and sold to the corners of the Earth. Then I'll have the last laugh! Hah!"

"My bill will be sent to your club," said Moriarty. "I suggest you settle it promptly."

"Yes, yes, whatever... but, hang it, I'm alive and this brown blighter's dead. All the brown blighters are dead. You're a miracle worker."

I knew — with an instinct that the Professor wouldn't call supernatural — Mad Carew would gyp us. He was that sort. Couldn't help himself. One implacable foe was off his back — for the moment, at least — yet he was thoughtlessly on the point of making another.

Carew pumped my hand and pumped Moriarty's hand. The Professor gave our client's shoulder a friendly squeeze and pushed him away. Carew walked off with a bounce in his stride, whistling a barrack-room ballad.

We watched him leave.

"One thing, Moriarty," I said.

"Yes, Moran."

"You promised Carew he wouldn't be murdered by priests of the Little Yellow God. Even if the London nest is wiped out and their hairy pet is on the run, there are others back home in the mountains. An army of them, just like this fanatic. Sworn to get back the emerald. They'll know of this mess soon enough, and they'll send other priests across the globe for Carew and the Eye."

"True."

"So you lied to him?"

"No. I seldom lie. It spoils the equations. When I clapped his shoulder, I gave him a present..."

He opened his hand. The Black Pearl of the Borgias wasn't in it.

"It will take the next assassins months to get here from Nepal, Moran. It will take but hours for the Hoxton Creeper to get out of the river."

XVII

So, now you know how it came out. According to Carew's will, he was to be buried at his last posting. They fit him in a coffin, face up but toes down, and some obliging Nepalese who happened to be visiting London transported him all the way there. The emerald went with him and was stolen from his body before burial. So, the poet had the truth of it, after all — with the exception that Amaryllis Framington married a tea-trader and retired to Margate.

> There's a one-eyed yellow idol to the north of Khatmandu,
> There's a little marble cross below the town;
> There's a broken-hearted woman tends the grave of Mad Carew,
> And the Yellow God forever gazes down.

KIM NEWMAN is a novelist, critic and broadcaster. His fiction includes *Anno Dracula, Life's Lottery* and *The Man From The Diogenes Club*. His non-fiction includes *Nightmare Movies, Horror: 100 Best Books* and *BFI Classic Studies of Cat People* and *Doctor Who*. He is a contributing editor to *Sight and Sound* and *Empire*. His Moriarty and Moran story 'The Red Planet League' appeared in *Gaslight Grimoire: Fantastic tales of Sherlock Holmes*.

Our titles are available at major book stores and local independent resellers who support Science Fiction and Fantasy readers like you.

Alphanauts by J. Brian Clarke (tp) - ISBN: 978-1-894063-14-2
Apparition Trail, The by Lisa Smedman (tp) - ISBN: 978-1-894063-22-7
As Fate Decrees by Denysé Bridger (tp) - ISBN: 978-1-894063-41-8
Avim's Oath (Part Six of the Okal Rel Saga) by Lynda Williams (pb)
   - ISBN: 978-1-894063-35-7

Black Chalice, The by Marie Jakober (hb) - ISBN: 978-1-894063-00-7
Blue Apes by Phyllis Gotlieb (pb) - ISBN: 978-1-895836-13-4
Blue Apes by Phyllis Gotlieb (hb) - ISBN: 978-1-895836-14-1

Captives by Barbara Galler-Smith and Josh Langston (pb)
   - ISBN: 978-1-894063-53-1
Children of Atwar, The by Heather Spears (pb) - ISBN: 978-0-88878-335-6
Chilling Tales: Evil Did I Dwell; Lewd I Did Live edited by Michael Kelly (pb)
   - ISBN: 978-1-894063-52-4
Cinco de Mayo by Michael J. Martineck (pb) - ISBN: 978-1-894063-39-5
Cinkarion - The Heart of Fire (Part Two of The Chronicles of the Karionin)
   by J. A. Cullum - (tp) - ISBN: 978-1-894063-21-0
Circle Tide by Rebecca K. Rowe (pb) - ISBN: 978-1-894063-59-3
Clan of the Dung-Sniffers by Lee Danielle Hubbard (pb) - ISBN: 978-1-894063-05-0
Claus Effect, The by David Nickle & Karl Schroeder (pb) - ISBN: 978-1-895836-34-9
Claus Effect, The by David Nickle & Karl Schroeder (hb) - ISBN: 978-1-895836-35-6
Courtesan Prince, The (Part One of the Okal Rel Saga) by Lynda Williams (tp)
   - ISBN: 978-1-894063-28-9

Dark Earth Dreams by Candas Dorsey & Roger Deegan (comes with a CD)
   - ISBN: 978-1-895836-05-9
Darkness of the God (Children of the Panther Part Two)
   by Amber Hayward (tp) - ISBN: 978-1-894063-44-9
Demon Left Behind, The by Marie Jakober (pb) - ISBN: 978-1-894063-49-4
Distant Signals by Andrew Weiner (tp) - ISBN: 978-0-88878-284-7
Dreams of an Unseen Planet by Teresa Plowright (tp) - ISBN: 978-0-88878-282-3
Dreams of the Sea (Part 1 of Tyranaël) by Élisabeth Vonarburg (tp)
   - ISBN: 978-1-895836-96-7
Dreams of the Sea (Part 1 of Tyranaël) by Élisabeth Vonarburg (hb)
   - ISBN: 978-1-895836-98-1
Druids by Barbara Galler-Smith and Josh Langston (tp)
   - ISBN: 978-1-894063-29-6

Eclipse by K. A. Bedford (tp) - ISBN: 978-1-894063-30-2
Even The Stones by Marie Jakober (tp) - ISBN: 978-1-894063-18-0
Evolve: Vampire Stories of the New Undead edited by Nancy Kilpatrick (tp)
   - ISBN: 978-1-894063-33-3
Evolve Two: Vampire Stories of the Future Undead edited by Nancy Kilpatrick (tp)
   - ISBN: 978-1-894063-62-3

Far Arena (Part Five of the Okal Rel Saga) by Lynda Williams (tp)
  - ISBN: 978-1-894063-45-6
Fires of the Kindred by Robin Skelton (tp) - ISBN: 978-0-88878-271-7
Forbidden Cargo by Rebecca Rowe (tp) - ISBN: 978-1-894063-16-6

Game of Perfection, A (Part 2 of Tyranaël) by Élisabeth Vonarburg (tp)
  - ISBN: 978-1-894063-32-6
Gaslight Arcanum: Uncanny Tales of Sherlock Holmes
  edited by Jeff Campbell & Charles Prepolec (pb)
  - ISBN: 978-1-8964063-60-9
Gaslight Grimoire: Fantastic Tales of Sherlock Holmes
  edited by Jeff Campbell & Charles Prepolec (pb)
  - ISBN: 978-1-8964063-17-3
Gaslight Grotesque: Nightmare Tales of Sherlock Holmes
  edited by Jeff Campbell & Charles Prepolec (pb)
  - ISBN: 978-1-8964063-31-9
Green Music by Ursula Pflug (tp) - ISBN: 978-1-895836-75-2
Green Music by Ursula Pflug (hb) - ISBN: 978-1-895836-77-6

Healer, The (Children of the Panther Part One) by Amber Hayward (tp)
  - ISBN: 978-1-895836-89-9
Healer, The (Children of the Panther Part One) by Amber Hayward (hb)
  - ISBN: 978-1-895836-91-2
Healer's Sword (Part Seven of the Okal Rel Saga) by Lynda Williams (pb)
  - ISBN: 978-1-894063-51-7

Hell Can Wait by Theodore Judson (tp) - ISBN: 978-1-978-1-894063-23-4
Hounds of Ash and other tales of Fool Wolf, The by Greg Keyes (pb)
  - ISBN: 978-1-894063-09-8
Hydrogen Steel by K. A. Bedford (tp) - ISBN: 978-1-894063-20-3

i-ROBOT Poetry by Jason Christie (tp) - ISBN: 978-1-894063-24-1
Immortal Quest by Alexandra MacKenzie (pb) - ISBN: 978-1-894063-46-3

Jackal Bird by Michael Barley (pb) - ISBN: 978-1-895836-07-3
Jackal Bird by Michael Barley (hb) - ISBN: 978-1-895836-11-0
JEMMA7729 by Phoebe Wray (tp) - ISBN: 978-1-894063-40-1

Keaen by Till Noever (tp) - ISBN: 978-1-894063-08-1
Keeper's Child by Leslie Davis (tp) - ISBN: 978-1-894063-01-2

Land/Space edited by Candas Jane Dorsey and Judy McCrosky (tp)
  - ISBN: 978-1-895836-90-5
Land/Space edited by Candas Jane Dorsey and Judy McCrosky (hb)
  - ISBN: 978-1-895836-92-9
Lyskarion: The Song of the Wind (Part One of The Chronicles of the Karionin)
  by J.A. Cullum (tp) - ISBN: 978-1-894063-02-9

Machine Sex and other stories by Candas Jane Dorsey (tp)
  - ISBN: 978-0-88878-278-6
Maërlande Chronicles, The by Élisabeth Vonarburg (pb)
  - ISBN: 978-0-88878-294-6
Moonfall by Heather Spears (pb) - ISBN: 978-0-88878-306-6

Of Wind and Sand by Sylvie Bérard (translated by Sheryl Curtis) (pb)
- ISBN: 978-1-894063-19-7
On Spec: The First Five Years edited by On Spec (pb)
- ISBN: 978-1-895836-08-0
On Spec: The First Five Years edited by On Spec (hb)
- ISBN: 978-1-895836-12-7
Orbital Burn by K. A. Bedford (tp) - ISBN: 978-1-894063-10-4
Orbital Burn by K. A. Bedford (hb) - ISBN: 978-1-894063-12-8

Pallahaxi Tide by Michael Coney (pb) - ISBN: 978-0-88878-293-9
Passion Play by Sean Stewart (pb) - ISBN: 978-0-88878-314-1
Petrified World (Determine Your Destiny #1) by Piotr Brynczka (pb)
- ISBN: 978-1-894063-11-1
Plague Saint by Rita Donovan, The (tp) - ISBN: 978-1-895836-28-8
Plague Saint by Rita Donovan, The (hb) - ISBN: 978-1-895836-29-5
Pock's World by Dave Duncan (tp) - ISBN: 978-1-894063-47-0
Pretenders (Part Three of the Okal Rel Saga) by Lynda Williams (pb)
- ISBN: 978-1-894063-13-5

Reluctant Voyagers by Élisabeth Vonarburg (pb) - ISBN: 978-1-895836-09-7
Reluctant Voyagers by Élisabeth Vonarburg (hb) - ISBN: 978-1-895836-15-8
Resisting Adonis by Timothy J. Anderson (tp) - ISBN: 978-1-895836-84-4
Resisting Adonis by Timothy J. Anderson (hb) - ISBN: 978-1-895836-83-7
Rigor Amortis edited by Jaym Gates and Erika Holt (pb)
- ISBN: 978-1-894063-63-0
Righteous Anger (Part Two of the Okal Rel Saga) by Lynda Williams (tp)
- ISBN: 897-1-894063-38-8

Silent City, The by Élisabeth Vonarburg (tp) - ISBN: 978-1-894063-07-4
Slow Engines of Time, The by Élisabeth Vonarburg (tp)
- ISBN: 978-1-895836-30-1
Slow Engines of Time, The by Élisabeth Vonarburg (hb)
- ISBN: 978-1-895836-31-8
Stealing Magic by Tanya Huff (tp) - ISBN: 978-1-894063-34-0
Strange Attractors by Tom Henighan (pb) - ISBN: 978-0-88878-312-7

Taming, The by Heather Spears (pb) - ISBN: 978-1-895836-23-3
Taming, The by Heather Spears (hb) - ISBN: 978-1-895836-24-0
Technicolor Ultra Mall by Ryan Oakley (tp) - ISBN: 978-1-894063-54-8
Ten Monkeys, Ten Minutes by Peter Watts (tp) - ISBN: 978-1-895836-74-5
Ten Monkeys, Ten Minutes by Peter Watts (hb) - ISBN: 978-1-895836-76-9
Tesseracts 1 edited by Judith Merril (pb) - ISBN: 978-0-88878-279-3
Tesseracts 2 edited by Phyllis Gotlieb & Douglas Barbour (pb)
- ISBN: 978-0-88878-270-0
Tesseracts 3 edited by Candas Jane Dorsey & Gerry Truscott (pb)
- ISBN: 978-0-88878-290-8
Tesseracts 4 edited by Lorna Toolis & Michael Skeet (pb)
- ISBN: 978-0-88878-322-6
Tesseracts 5 edited by Robert Runté & Yves Maynard (pb)
- ISBN: 978-1-895836-25-7
Tesseracts 5 edited by Robert Runté & Yves Maynard (hb)
- ISBN: 978-1-895836-26-4

Tesseracts 6 edited by Robert J. Sawyer & Carolyn Clink (pb)
   - ISBN: 978-1-895836-32-5
Tesseracts 6 edited by Robert J. Sawyer & Carolyn Clink (hb)
   - ISBN: 978-1-895836-33-2
Tesseracts 7 edited by Paula Johanson & Jean-Louis Trudel (tp)
   - ISBN: 978-1-895836-58-5
Tesseracts 7 edited by Paula Johanson & Jean-Louis Trudel (hb)
   - ISBN: 978-1-895836-59-2
Tesseracts 8 edited by John Clute & Candas Jane Dorsey (tp)
   - ISBN: 978-1-895836-61-5
Tesseracts 8 edited by John Clute & Candas Jane Dorsey (hb)
   - ISBN: 978-1-895836-62-2
Tesseracts Nine edited by Nalo Hopkinson and Geoff Ryman (tp)
   - ISBN: 978-1-894063-26-5
Tesseracts Ten: A Celebration of New Canadian Specuative Fiction
   edited by Robert Charles Wilson and Edo van Belkom (tp)
   - ISBN: 978-1-894063-36-4
Tesseracts Eleven: Amazing Canadian Speulative Fiction
   edited by Cory Doctorow and Holly Phillips (tp)
   - ISBN: 978-1-894063-03-6
Tesseracts Twelve: New Novellas of Canadian Fantastic Fiction
   edited by Claude Lalumière (pb)
   - ISBN: 978-1-894063-15-9
Tesseracts Thirteen: Chilling Tales from the Great White North
   edited by Nancy Kilpatrick and David Morrell (tp)
   - ISBN: 978-1-894063-25-8
Tesseracts 14: Strange Canadian Stories
   edited by John Robert Colombo and Brett Alexander Savory (tp)
   - ISBN: 978-1-894063-37-1
Tesseracts Fifteen: A Case of Quite Curious Tales
   edited by Julie Czerneda and Susan MacGregor (tp)
   - ISBN: 978-1-894063-58-6
Tesseracts Q edited by Élisabeth Vonarburg and Jane Brierley (pb)
   - ISBN: 978-1-895836-21-9
Tesseracts Q edited by Élisabeth Vonarburg and Jane Brierley (hb)
   - ISBN: 978-1-895836-22-6
Those Who Fight Monsters: Tales of Occult Detectives
   edited by Justin Gustainis (pb) - ISBN: 978-1-894063-48-7
Throne Price by Lynda Williams and Alison Sinclair (tp)
   - ISBN: 978-1-894063-06-7
Time Machines Repaired Whie-U-Wait by K. A. Bedford (tp)
   - ISBN: 978-1-894063-42-5